A LOVE THAT MELTED A CAPO'S COLD HEART

MISS JENESEQUA

CONTENTS

MISS JENESEQUA

Sex Ain't Better Than Love: A Complete Novel

Down For My Baller: A Complete Novel

Bad For My Thug 1 & 2 & 3

The Thug & The Kingpin's Daughter 1 & 2

Loving My Miami Boss 1 & 2 & 3

Giving All My Love To A Brooklyn Street King 1 & 2

He's A Savage But He Loves Me Like No Other 1 & 2 & 3

Bad For My Gangsta: A Complete Novel

The Purest Love for The Coldest Thug 1 & 2 & 3

The Purest Love for The Coldest Thug: A Christmas Novella

My Hood King Gave Me A Love Like No Other 1 & 2 & 3

My Bad Boy Gave Me A Love Like No Other: A Complete Novella

The Thug That Secured Her Heart 1 & 2 & 3

She Softened Up The Hood In Him 1 & 2 & 3 & 4

You're Mine: Chosen By A Miami King: A Complete Novel

A Love That Melted A Capo's Cold Heart: A Complete Novel

~ SYNOPSIS ~

After fleeing her hometown for ten months due to her broken heart, Danaë Westbrook is summoned home and forced to get her act together. No longer fond of her free-spirited nature, Danaë's father wants the apple of his eye to put her brains to use and makes her his newest employee. The weekend before starting her new job, or imprisonment as she calls it, Danaë takes a spontaneous night out with her best friend and the night leads to an innocent game of Truth or Dare. A game that soon lands Danaë in the path of a dangerous new attraction.

Cassian Acardi is a man of few words, but when he speaks, you sure as hell are going to listen. The tragic loss of his daughter made an icebox form where his heart once was. Leaving no room for him to care about seeking a genuine romantic connection. His family's empire is his number one priority in life. As a boss, he's used to being the one that sets everything in motion. So when Danaë approaches him first, placing him in the passenger seat, Cassian is intrigued. However, he tries to suppress his curiosity about the gorgeous stranger who boldly stepped to him, *until their paths cross again. This time, neither of them can run from fate's hypnotic pull determined to bring them together.*

Could Danaë be the one to melt the cold-hearted Cassian or will Cassian fall victim to his inner demons, convincing himself that he doesn't deserve love and ultimately pushing Danaë away for good?

"Now baby don't go playin' with my lovin'
Don't make me regret fallin' in love..."
—Lucky Daye x Joyce Wrice♫

CHAPTER 1

~ DANAË ~

ruth or dare?"

"Truth."

"You pussy."

My bottom lip dropped as I gave her a wide-eyed stare.

"What?" She let out a light chuckle. "I'm just calling it how I see it."

Laughter erupted out of me before I reached for my cocktail glass and downed the rest of my dirty martini. The cool liquor slid down my throat, creating a fiery sensation in my chest.

"Enough with the truths. I already know everything there is to know about you, Danaë. You know damn well you're overdue for a dare."

She was right. My time for a dare was long overdue and since I'd already given her a dare, it was only fair game that she got the chance to give me one too.

"Fine." I dropped my empty glass to the table. "Dare."

And just like that, Adina's dark brown eyes seemed to light up like diamonds and her heart shaped lips curved into a pleased smile. She scanned the room, looking for the poor soul who she could torment with my presence for the night. While she scanned, I admired everything about the delicate features my best friend owned.

From those innocent, brown eyes, to her flawless golden honey exterior, and those high cheekbones, Adina Lewis was an undeniable stunner. It was a damn shame that she didn't see her beauty the way I, and everyone else, saw it.

I knew Adina had found her victim from the second her eyes locked back on mine and she pressed her index finger to her lips. She was trying her hardest to keep her mischievous grin at bay but no matter how hard she tried, I could see that sneaky little look in her eyes.

See, I knew my best friend well. *Very* well. She was what one would call, *out of her rabbit ass* mind. Especially when it came to us playing truth or dare while drinking. Call it childish all you like but we were two twenty-five-year-olds who loved playing games. Hosting games nights used to be our regular pastime back in college and I think our joint love of UNO was one of the reasons why our friendship was so damn strong today.

I'd already dared Adina to stand up and randomly dance the Macarena. It didn't seem like a bad dare until she remembered where we were. In a packed-out bar, sitting in a center table where everyone could see us. Of course she did it like the champ she was while I wildly laughed at her. I knew deep down; she was gearing up her payback.

Payback had finally come.

"Lay it on me then," I voiced, my fear growing at her silence.

The dare couldn't have been that bad, right?

"I want you," she flashed her pearly whites at me as she grinned hard, "to go up to the bar and tell the man dressed in a burgundy suit that you want him to buy you a drink."

Oh, that's it?

And here I thought she was about to give me the worst dare she could think of.

Relief spread through my veins as I replied, "Okay, got i—"

"I'm not finisheddddd," she sang in a playful tone, making my relief vanish. "I want you to go up to him and tell him you want him to buy you a drink so..." her eyes grew large, "he can have his way with you all night."

And. There. *She*. Was. There was my best friend who was out of her rabbit ass mind.

"Adina, I'm not doin—"

"Aht, aht, aht!" Her brows squashed together as she frowned. "A dare's a dare, hoe."

I let out a light sigh. I hadn't even seen this man yet because Adina was facing the bar whereas I had my back to it. I was tempted to turn around and look but I fought against my desire.

"And after you've said it, you can tell him it was just a dare or better yet, sit down and let him buy you that drink."

"I know what you're doing, Dina, and it's not going to work."

She giggled and reached across the table for my hand, squeezing it tight. I stared into her brown pools, reading the excitement burning within her.

"It wouldn't kill you to get your back blown you know."

"Dina!"

"I'm just saying!" She lifted her hands up in protest, giggling some more. "You've been back in the city for what... two weeks now and you've been avoiding men like the plague. Daphne's kickback last week: you refused to come once you found out men were attending and you had me feeling like a lost puppy without you. Babe... I know he did you wrong but it's been a whole year. You need to let it go."

But I couldn't let it go. Even after all this time, it still fucking hurt so as far as I was concerned it was fuck men for all eternity.

Okay... maybe *fuck men for all eternity* was an unreasonable statement to make because every single man on this planet wasn't to blame for the vile transgressions of my ex. I guess my father was right about my late mother's dramatic streak passing down to me. But Adina was right, I needed to let it go. I'd had a whole year to let it go.

"It's just a dare, Nae," she continued talking, sidetracking away from the subject of my past. She knew it was a touchy subject for me. "If you fail... you gotta take three tequila shots back-to-back."

Another sigh seeped past my lips and just as she made a move to grab her Cosmopolitan, I beat her to the punch and lifted the long-stemmed glass to my lips.

"Hey!"

I took a swig of her remaining cocktail and placed the glass back down once it was empty.

"Just a dare," I repeated her previous statement, getting up from my seat.

After a gulp of Adina's cocktail, a wave of courage washed through me and all of a sudden, I was up to the challenge that this dare had to offer.

I turned around to lay eyes on my new sponsor for the night but when my eyes spotted Mr. Burgundy, his back was turned. My head whipped back around to Adina only to see the devilish grin she was now sporting. She lifted her hands and shooed me away, knowing full well what trouble she'd started in my head.

She hadn't seen Mr. Burgundy's face which meant there was a 50-percent chance that he could be so *not* my type. From what I could see at a distance, he had a low-cut fade indicating that he was a brotha.

Okay so he's Black. That's already a sign he could be your type. You've got this, girl. It's just a dare. You're good at dares.

The suit he was wearing was filled out quite well also indicating that he was a regular gym attendee.

And he's in good shape? This is sounding like a piece of cake to me, girl! You can easily tell this guy you want him to buy you a drink without feeling like you want to vomit.

I took a deep breath and released it as I started walking over to where Mr. Burgundy sat by the bar.

Despite the numerous faces scattered across the room, some I could sense looking in my direction as I pressed ahead, I paid them no mind. My attention was solely on Mr. Burgundy. I hadn't even seen his face or heard him speak yet, but there was something growing inside me, telling me to get as close to this stranger as quickly as I possibly could.

Once by him, I slid into the empty stool next to him and slowly faced him or should I say, faced the side of his face. A whiff of spicy sandalwood and saffron immediately caught my attention and I was taken aback by how good this man smelt.

God... How can a man smell like money?

"Hi."

He turned to look at me and one look from him was all it took to make my brains turn into mush. We were in a bar full of people but one look from him and everything around me became nonexistent. Suddenly, it was just him and I in a world of our own.

Sweet Lord Jesus.

Those russet brown eyes held me hostage but he didn't utter a single word in a response to my greeting. He didn't have to. Because as far as I was concerned, I was ready to get the hell out of here and go wherever he wanted to go. He could tell me to follow him right up to hell's gate and baby, I'd be the one looking for the key to get in.

He simply reached for his glass and took a sip from his brown liquor without breaking eye contact from me. While he sipped, I examined, unable to stop the warmth forming between my thighs as his Adam's apple bounced up and down.

Oh sweet, sweet, sweet Lord Jesus!

This man right here was a dangerously attractive man. Attractive to the point that it seemed too good to be true. My eyes dropped to his juicy pink lips that were perfectly lined by his neat moustache. His moustache extended into a well-groomed, low beard that coated his entire jawline. He had a large nose that suited his face well. On his left cheek, I noticed a tiny beauty spot sitting on his smooth light beige tone and I smiled internally at his cute feature.

He placed his glass back down, interrupting my examination session. I expected him to talk but he didn't. The coldness gleaming from his eyes had me feeling some type of way but nonetheless I had a dare to accomplish and I planned to win.

"Hi," I repeated again. This time in a much cheerier tone.

"Are you lost?"

His question made me blink repeatedly. Not only had his question caught me off guard but his voice... his voice was almost as dangerous as his face. Deep, husky and laced with a soothing remedy.

"N-No."

"You must be since you decided to leave your girl to come sit next to me."

What the... he knew I was with someone? This was a surprise to me because I was convinced he'd been minding his business by the bar, not concerned with looking behind him.

"I'm not lost."

"So what do you want?"

Damn, this nigga is kinda rude. Can't a girl say hi now?

"For you to buy me a drink," I told him before pausing as I braced myself to say my next bold words.

He's lucky he's fine as hell or I would have backed out of this dare due to his attitude.

"...And for you to have your way with me all night."

"Is that right?" He let out a low chuckle that had my insides stirring with heat. "You want me to have my way with you?"

"Yes." My heart skipped several beats as our stare down intensified. He refused to look away and that only encouraged me to keep giving into his intense gaze.

"You don't even know me," he replied. "What if I turn out to be your very worst nightmare?"

Lord, if this man's a nightmare then I never want to have a good dream ever again. Nightmares only from here on out. Please.

"That's a risk I'd be willing to take."

I had no idea where this bravado was coming from. Blame it on the liquor that was providing me with a confidence like no other or blame it on the fact that I was dangerously enticed by this complete stranger.

"It's a risk that you wouldn't be able to back away from. If I had my way with you, you wouldn't be able to walk up on strangers at bars, playing silly little dares on them. You'd belong to me and only me. If you were to forget that shit, I'd have to tie you up and punish you until you remember exactly who you belong to."

Wait... what?

His words seemed to steal all the oxygen pumping through me and I was left breathless for a few seconds. Still determined to win this dare, I breathed in and pushed on.

"P-Punish me?"

"You heard me."

Oh I'd definitely heard him but I wanted to hear him say it again.

"What if I don't want to be punished?"

"Believe me, you'll be begging to be punished and you'll enjoy every single second of it."

I believed his punishment had already begun because the dampness that had formed on my panties, was a sign of his cruel authority over my body that he hadn't even laid a finger on. We'd only just met and he already had me dripping like a faucet from his words.

He reached for his drink and studied the brown liquor, rolling around his glass as he swirled it. Silence formed between us but my thoughts were anything but silent. All I could hear were endless thoughts of me wanting to hear this man talk more. Talk more about him punishing me and me actually seeing him do it.

You don't even know this man, Danaë... this was only supposed to be a dare. Nothing more.

He slugged back the last of his drink and raised himself to his feet. Heat stained my cheeks as he towered over me. It was only now I realized just how tall this man was and not only was he very tall, but he was also a lot bigger in shape than I expected. His arms amply filled out his sleeves and his suit coated his physique in the most alluring way. Our eyes connected and my heart pounded away as he watched me carefully. I was tempted to say something but he beat me to the punch.

"A good girl like you wouldn't be able to handle a man like me." He leaned in close to whisper into my ear, "Cute little dare though. Next time, stick to following your friend and doing the Macarena rather than stepping to a man who you have no business stepping to."

Mr. Burgundy then left my side and headed out the bar. Leaving me frozen in my seat, unable to get up. My knees had turned to jelly and my mind was filled with conflicting notions about the handsome stranger who had left me completely speechless.

He'd known all along about my game with Adina. He must

have been watching us at a point in time, only I hadn't even known he existed until now. *Shit.* Now he's gone and I don't even know his name.

"Naë!"

The yell of my name moments later made me turn around and I spotted Adina a short distance away rushing towards me.

"Girl, what happened? Did Cassian buy you a dri... Oh." Laying eyes on the empty glass in Mr. Burgundy's spot made her realize that I'd failed. "Awww man, what happened? Don't tell me you scared his ass off."

I was too lost in my own thoughts to notice that Adina had mentioned a name. She took his empty seat and raised a hand out for the bartender to come our way. Once his attention had been caught, Adina looked back over at me with a concerned look.

"Naë... what happened?"

"Nothing," I replied in a low tone, staring down at my hands. "He wasn't interested."

"What the..." She sucked her teeth. "His loss anyway! Don't worry, boo. Take these three tequila shots as badges of honor for your good attempt."

"What can I get you ladies?"

"Three tequila shots for our pretty loser over here and two..."

As she rattled off our order to the caramel skinned bartender, I couldn't stop thinking about the man I'd encountered just moments ago.

He's gone now, Danaë. You're never going to see him again. Forget him.

And that was the problem. I was never going to see him again, didn't even know his name... *wait a damn minute.*

"Adina."

"Yes, love?" She broke her focus away from the bartender preparing our drinks to look over at me.

My hard stare on her strengthened and she looked at me like I was the crazy one here.

"What?"

This little heifer.

I said nothing and continued to look at her. It took her a few seconds to finally crack and when she did, she bit her lip before opening up to say, "Yes I know him."

"You snake," I called her. "You set me up."

"No, no, no!" She repeatedly shook her head 'no' and reached for my arm, pulling me close. "I didn't... Well, not intentionally. I saw him enter when I was doing the Macarena and at first I was going to tell you but then I thought, he'd be the perfect candidate for your first dare of the night."

"My *last* dare of the night," I corrected her, attempting to unlink my arm out of her grasp but she just held on tighter. "So all that pretending to scan the room... that was just for show."

She gave me a shy nod, a small smile creeping on her lips. Our bartender suddenly placed our drinks in front of us and Adina reached for the shots, placing each glass in front of me.

"How do you know him?"

"He's my boss... well one of them."

From what I knew of Adina's job, she was a social media manager of one of Chicago's hottest hotels, The Acardi Palazzo (Palace). From what she'd told me, her bosses were two half African American and half Italian brothers who owned The Palazzo. It wasn't a cheap place and because of how well she was doing handling the luxury hotel's social media presence, she was bringing in close to six figures after only being there for under a year.

"Adina!" Now I was even more mortified by this situation. "You let me go up to your boss and embarrass myself in front of him."

"Hey, hey, you didn't embarrass yourself..." She paused so she could survey me carefully. "Right?"

"...Not exactly but I feel like a total embarrassment since he didn't buy me a drink as you wanted."

"Okay and like I said, his loss."

"Wow." I let out a deep breath and pouted. "You cheated so you're the one that's really supposed to be taking these shots."

"Nice try loser but there's nothing in the rule book that says anything about me knowing the people you do dares on. I didn't even know he was coming to this bar tonight, that was pure coincidence."

I hated that she was right. There was nothing in the rule book that said anything about her knowing the people we did dares on because first and foremost, there was no rule book and secondly, we weren't wimps.

Adina gave me a puppy eyed look and reached for my cheek.

"Stop being a big baby and take these shots like the true champ you are."

I was unable to stop the lifting corners of my mouth. Even after all these years, she still knew how to melt into my tough exterior and make me smile.

"That's my girl."

She picked up my first tequila shot and moved it towards my mouth before announcing, "Bottoms up, baby."

Like a champ I took the first shot and Adina cheered me on as if she was my own personal cheerleader.

Adina said that Cassian was the one that had taken a loss tonight but deep down I knew that was a lie. Despite him being her boss, I still didn't know who he really was and he wasn't the friendliest being. That still didn't change the fact that I wanted to see him again and how could I forget the one thing on my mind currently...

I wanted to be punished by him.

CHAPTER 2

~ CASSIAN ~

"Nah but they're actually crazy. For starters, they bleed every single month and don't die from the blood loss. That shit don't sound crazy to you?"

I swear some of the things that came out this nigga's mouth really had me laughing up a storm. Today was different though. I was too focused on my own personal thoughts to laugh at my brother's battles with the opposite sex.

"That shit don't sound crazy to you, Cass?"

The elevator doors slid open and I stepped out first, ignoring his fixed gaze that I could feel on me.

"Cass?"

He trotted along behind me as I led the way down the wide corridor leading to our desired destination.

"Nah, not really," I simply replied. My eyes glued on the large oak doors ahead. "They can't die from something a part of their natural systems, something designed specifically for them."

"Hmmph," he said. "Still think they're crazy as hell."

Once in front of the door, I stopped and Christian stood beside me.

"I didn't realize you'd finally started yours too." I turned to him and the corners of my mouth hiked up. "How's the cramps, baby?"

"Fuck off," he playfully dismissed me, making me chuckle.

I lifted a hand to knock twice on the door and by the time my hand was back by my side, the door opened.

In we stepped and we were greeted to a gold-veined marble floored room. Cream paint covered the walls, providing the room with an elegant vibe. Two matching cream couches were positioned in the center of the space with a white marble coffee table dividing them.

"I miei bambini! *(My babies!)*"

A petite, tanned skin woman rushed over to us from her seat and I couldn't help but grin at how she broke protocol every time it came to us. We were the ones supposed to come to her first but here she went, being her extra out of the ordinary self.

She reached for Christian first and he bent low so she could plant kisses all over his face. Then she came over to me and I did the same, bending so her short statue could reach my six five frame. After she was done with her kisses, she grabbed each of our hands and pulled us deeper into her sanctuary.

"Ho creato tutti i tuoi preferiti! *(I've made all your favorites)*," she told us once we were seated opposite her. "I've been slaving away in the kitchen all morning."

"Zietta *(Auntie)*, you shouldn't have," Christian said in a fake concerned tone.

He knew damn well he wasn't concerned about her being in the kitchen all morning and to be completely honest, neither was I. She loved cooking and she was bomb at doing it so who was I to ever stop her?

"Nonsense! My boys need to eat," she voiced proudly. "And I'm always going to make sure they eat good."

Meet Francesca Acardi.

She was the only mother I'd ever known since my mother passed away after giving birth to Christian. Francesca was our Zietta (auntie) and had raised us when I was four and Christian not even a day old. She was the sister of my late father, Massimo Acardi.

"So how are my boys doing? What's new?"

Christian and I made small talk with Zietta, telling her how things were going businesswise. Owning the most popular hotel in the city was a title that my brother and I were truly proud of. We'd created a new empire off the Acardi name and became unstoppable. No other hotel in the city was doing as well as we currently were. Every night every single one of our rooms were booked with customers, not just from Chicago, but from all over the world. We'd created a luxury haven for all walks of life to temporarily inhabit while they enjoyed the city of Chicago. I knew that our Zietta was proud of the successful men we'd become today.

"And how did things go yesterday Cass with... la nostra piccola peste *(our little pest)*?"

My eyes darted to the right side of the room where Zietta's two bodyguards stood on each side of the door before I said, "He's handled."

I wanted to be the one to personally take care of the man who thought he could betray my Zietta and get away with it. Thankfully, he was a fan of one of Chicago's best bars and I'd followed him down here knowing exactly what time he came and left.

"A good girl like you wouldn't be able to handle a man like me." I leaned in closer to whisper into her ear, "Cute little dare though. Next time, stick to following your friend and doing the Macarena rather than stepping to a man who you have no business stepping to."

My time with this bold beauty was officially over once I spotted my target getting up from his seat and walking over to the exit. I reluctantly left her side and stalked after him.

Just before I left the bar, my eyes met Adina's and she sent an amused smile my way which made me send a simple nod her way. Then I was out the door and trailing behind the man that owed me his life.

He didn't see me coming. No one ever did because I knew how to keep myself hidden until I wanted to be found. He also hadn't spotted me in the bar because he'd never actually been graced with the privilege of meeting me. Not a lot of people had met me or Christian but they definitely knew we existed. My father had always placed an importance on keeping his children secluded away from members of the business because he didn't want our faces being known too well by just anyone. It was his way of protecting us and Zietta had decided to stick with it after his death. Only those who needed to see us saw us, and that was a very small bunch.

The traitor was casually walking towards his car on the next street and it wasn't until he crossed the road that I pulled out my strap from my waistband. I continued following him and his dumb ass hadn't even turned around yet to notice that he was being followed. I guess the liquor he'd been drinking had gotten to him after all, even though he appeared to be walking normally.

He brought out his key once getting by his car but he never got the chance to open his door because I'd sent my first bullet of the night right through his flesh.

"Ahhhhhhhhhhhhhhhhhhhhh!"

My silencer had done a pretty good job of keeping the shot quiet but this idiot started crying like a little girl and my annoyance heightened. No one was around so if he thought his cries would save him tonight, he thought wrong. He fell to his car and looked up from his bloodied hand to me.

"So you like being a sneaky little bitch, huh?" *A cold, hollow laugh fell out my mouth watching the color drain from his face. "How does it feel to be sneaked up on?"*

"P-Please! P-Please, don't... don't do this!" he yelled with ragged breathing and shaky hands. "Please... if it's money you want, I've got plenty!"

This disrespectful ass bitch.

I fired another shot into him, this time into his chest and he slumped to the floor. I crouched down to my knees in front of him and observed the blood now spluttering out of his mouth. I was actually disgusted that he thought I was here to rob him.

"Let this be a lesson for trying to backstab Frankie," I whispered. "You cross her, you owe me your life."

It was at that moment that his eureka moment finally happened. His cognac eyes bulged and his mouth widened, allowing a faster flow of blood to spout out of him.

"You're... you're an Acardi?" He coughed and tried to reach out for me. "Acardi, please. I'm s-sorry!"

I cocked my head to the side, studying him closely as he bled out. He was more Italian than me since I was only half but he didn't deserve to be one. He'd backstabbed Zietta by attempting to do a greedy side deal with a trusted associate. He didn't deserve to be a part of the Acardi family and now he wouldn't ever be part of my family again.

"Sorry just ain't going to cut it, traditore (traitor)."

I shot one final bullet through the middle of his forehead and the life in him instantly dissipated. Providing me with a satisfaction like no other.

I straightened up, pulled out my phone and headed to my contacts to call an important service. My call was picked up on the first ring, just how I loved it.

"Capo (Boss)?"

"Sweep needed at my location."

I heard fingers typing then a click.

"Evoni's?"

"The next street."

"Got it."

"That's my boy." Zietta sent a warm smile my way. "Okay, who's ready to eat?"

Without hesitating, Christian sprung up from his seat and his eagerness made Zietta giggle excitedly.

Hours later, Christian and I had spent quality time with Zietta and enjoyed a large home cooked meal. We said our goodbyes to her before heading home in our separate cars.

The house gate was opened for us by Zietta's uniformed gate guard and Christian's Rolls Royce Phantom led the way whereas I followed behind in my Lamborghini Urus. I gave an appreciative nod to the gate guard and he waved before turning away, allowing me to see the AK-47 mounted on his back.

I could always leave Zietta's knowing she was in safe hands. She had men in every corner she needed them to be, ready to lay their lives on the line for her. She was a true queen and I'm sure my father was smiling down proud of the boss she'd become today.

Christian's Phantom turned left and I turned right. Although we lived in the same building, Christian wasn't heading home. I didn't even have to hear him tell me he was going to see his newest *friend* of the week. He talked all that shit about women being crazy but he couldn't stop messing with them even if he tried. They'd forever be his kryptonite. His own special dose of cocaine that he wouldn't stop sniffing. In ways, I could relate to his addiction but I definitely knew my limits and when not to get carried away.

I headed home in my Lambo and a few minutes into driving, I felt the sudden urge to lay down. The itis was coming for my neck and I blamed Zietta and her bomb ass cooking. She'd made some of my favorite Italian dishes, gramigna pasta with Bolognese sauce and sausage, caprese salad with pesto sauce, lasagna, Fiorentina steak, ribollita soup and focaccia bread.

Future and Drake rapping all about how they really were the plugs filled my car as I drove through the streets of Chicago. Unable to help myself, my mind wandered to the events of yesterday and I remembered that soft yet sassy voice of hers.

"What if I don't want to be punished?"

She'd been real bold to step to me the way she did. I'd fought the urge to play her game but goddamn it, the curiosity to see how red rope would have looked around her flesh really grew in me last night. But I knew better.

It took me fifteen minutes to arrive home. I parked my car in the parking lot of my hotel and headed up the private elevator to my penthouse floor.

Being the owner of The Acardi Palazzo definitely had its perks. The perk I loved the most was the privilege of getting to my door without having anyone else in my way.

As soon as I stepped through my front door, I headed straight upstairs to my room on the second level. The motion sensor lights illuminated my surroundings and I began unbuttoning my shirt once a few seconds away from my bedroom.

Ten minutes later and I had stripped down to nothing but my silk pajama pants. I was stepping out my bathroom when vibrations suddenly caught my attention.

I strode over to the black rectangular ottoman positioned in front of my bed, grabbing my vibrating phone off it. Warmth filled my chest as I stared at the caller ID.

Coconut Head

"Look who finally remembered they have a brother," I announced once I'd picked up.

"Wait what? I have a brother? I'm pretty sure I'm adopted."

"Haha very funny, Coconut Head."

She tittered at my words before reminding me, "You know I've been super busy with my gaming tournaments."

"I know." I strolled over to my bedside with my phone glued to my ear. "Proud of you, Caia. You won just like I knew you would."

"Look who's been keeping tabs on me," she commented and I could picture the smug smile spreading across her lips right now. "Thank you, Cassi."

I took a seat on the edge of my bed, staring off into the magnificent night view of Chicago from my bedroom window.

"You lucky I love you 'cause I'd fuck you up for always insisting on calling me a girl's name."

Everyone who mattered to me nicknamed me 'Cass' but my sister had to be the odd one out and call me 'Cassi,' which was basically a girl's name in my eyes.

"You know you love it."

She was right, I did.

"When are you coming home, Caia?"

"Not anytime soon, Cassi," she admitted. "LA's just where it's at right now for me."

I frowned.

"But LA isn't home."

"It isn't... but it's everything I want right now." She sighed deeply. "I never wanted that life... you know I never did and there's no way I'd be able to live a normal life in Chicago. Zietta would never let me."

"Yes she would."

"No she wouldn't," she insisted. "She's the most powerful female capo in the city and she wanted that power continued through me. I just couldn't... I just couldn't do it, Cassi. I can't do it. I'm good with being plain old Caia in LA."

"Plain old Caia my back foot." I scoffed. "You're a professional gamer, Caia, bringing in five figures off every game tournament you win, not to mention you have over 1.5 million subs on YouTube and over 100k on IG. You are most definitely *not* plain old Caia. You're Caia mothafucking Acardi, the gamer, and you're killing it."

Her giggles filled the line before she queried, "Are you looking for a job? 'Cause I think I need to make you my professional hype man. What are your rates?"

My laughter couldn't be contained after her last statement. That was one of the things I loved about her. She never failed to make me laugh.

"I'm serious!" She laughed alongside me. "No but for real... thank you Cassi. Thank you for being such a great big brother. Thank you for understanding me."

"That's what I'm here for, Coconut Head."

Out of everyone in our family, Caia was the closest to me. She could confide in me about anything because she knew that I would never judge her. I was here to listen to her concerns, not add to them, and I'd been doing that for the past twenty-three years of Caia's life.

We were half siblings but that didn't change our love for one another. As far as I was concerned, she was my full sister and I'd take a bullet for her if I had to.

We talked for a few more minutes before Caia had to go to sleep. There was a two-hour time difference between Chicago and LA, LA being the city ahead and right now it was ten-thirty p.m. in LA. She had another game tournament tomorrow morning that she needed to be up bright and early for.

My sister was really out here making serious paper from being

a gamer and I loved that shit. She was dominating a male domi-
nated industry and putting these niggas to shame with her skills. I
was very proud of her and glad that she'd found the thing that
made her happy this early in her life. At only twenty-three she was
living her dreams and as her brother all I could do was be over the
moon for her.

Ding!

My phone chimed in my hand seconds after my call with Caia
ended and I read the new text that had flown in.

*So you thought you were just going to slide through to my bar
yesterday and not slide into me?*

I knew that one of her employees must have told her about my
presence at her bar, something that never went unnoticed, which
is why I rarely visited Evoni's.

Reading her text made me grow hot. Hot with the urge to wrap
my hand around her throat which is exactly what I knew she
wanted. But she wasn't about to get that satisfaction from me
tonight. Ignoring her message, I switched off my phone, placed it
down to my lamp stand and got up to pull back my silk sheets. I
climbed in and got reacquainted with my bed. Once tucked in, my
head met my pillow and I shut my eyes to fall into my slumber.

Images of yesterday flashed into my head and I was reminded
again of the woman who'd approached me.

Really nigga? Even after all this time she's still on your mind?

Indeed she was and despite me knowing I was never going to
see her again, I kept entertaining thoughts of her.

I'd spotted her and her girl in the center of the space when I'd
discreetly entered from the bar's back entrance. Knowing the bar's
owner definitely worked in my favor, allowing me to come and go
as I pleased without being detected by a soul.

She had her back to me so I hadn't seen her face yet but her
friend I knew quite well.

Adina Lewis was the social media manager of The Acardi Palazzo and had been doing a pretty amazing job so far. She hadn't even reached a full year of being our social media manager and had already gained an extra 1.5 million followers on all our social media accounts combined. Because of her, we'd been able to tap into the female influencer market and had some of the baddest IG models staying at The Acardi, promoting our establishment to their followers.

When Adina got up from her seat to perform the Macarena just before I took my seat, I clocked onto what they were doing and their childish antic had me shaking my head with a small smirk. I didn't think Adina had noticed me until I got up to leave and saw her smiling amusingly at me. It was then that I knew Adina had been toying around by getting her friend to come over to me as a dare. Something that I definitely hadn't expected. And I most definitely hadn't expected her friend to be so fucking pretty.

She had big dark brown eyes... so dark they almost looked black. They were seductive eyes that tempted me, making me want to hear the life story that this woman had. Tempted yes but actually wanting to know?

No.

I'd seen the empty cocktail and shot glasses scattered across their table. That was already a red flag. No woman of mine consumed that much alcohol. And no woman of mine stepped to me. I did the stepping and I made it clear that that ass belonged to me and only me.

I quickly shut down thoughts about her and decided to sleep. She wasn't important and quite frankly, we were never going to see each other again. There was no need for me to think about her.

I didn't want her.

CHAPTER 3

~ DANAË ~

A stranger.

He was a complete stranger and I couldn't get him out of my damn head. Twenty-four hours later and the only person who ruled my mind was him.

"I'm so excited for you to start tomorrow, Angel. I had Kamora decorate your office with all your favorite colors."

I didn't like that I was thinking about him. I had done a pretty good job staying away from men for the past few months and now that had ended. Adina's dare had awoken something in me and now I was stuck thinking about a mysterious man that I didn't truly know. A man that I was never going to see again and that's what pained me the most.

"Now just because you're my daughter that doesn't mean you're getting any extra benefits. You need to work of the same high standard as all my other employees. Be punctual and alert at all times."

He said he would tie me up... it didn't take a rocket scientist to figure out that he was into some real kinky shi—

"Are you listening to me, Danaë?"

"Yes, Daddy," I replied, shaking all thoughts of Cassian out my head and focusing intently on my father. "I'm listening."

"Good... how about lunch tomorrow at NoMI? My treat. We need to celebrate your first day, Angel."

I nodded at him through my bright screen and decided to throw in a large smile to show my enthusiasm. Enthusiasm was the last thing I felt when it came to this predicament though.

My father, Trenton Westbrook, was the owner and CEO of the biggest accountancy firm in Chicago, Morgan & Westbrook. He'd founded it thirty years ago at age twenty-five alongside my mother, Tanaya Morgan. Their love of numbers had brought them together at Stanford University and they became joined at the hip, never seen without each other.

From the way my father glowed every time he brought her up, I knew she was a phenomenal woman. It was just unfortunate that I didn't remember her because she died when I was four. Cancer was a real bitch and I'd forever hate it for taking my mother away from me too soon.

One thing I was certain about once I'd finished high school was that I wanted to be able to make my mother proud. I too pursued accountancy like my parents had and graduated top of my class at Stanford. Just like my parents, I loved all things numbers so I didn't struggle in school.

The most obvious choice after graduating was for me to work for my father's company and he was ecstatic for me to join the firm but honestly, my heart wasn't in it.

I wanted to branch off and do my own thing which I did. I worked for a few startup companies and took on a few private clients who I essentially told what to do with their money. When it came to investing and budgeting your finances, I was your woman.

My life and career were going great until my ex-boyfriend

crushed me in the worst way by revealing his whole other life back in Philly with a wife and two kids.

Two fucking kids.

How did I not see it coming? Well, let's just say that this particular ex of mine was a real charmer. He'd woo me with poisoned words and actions, knowing fully well that he was a taken man. He was only in Chicago temporarily but he'd fed me with lies about wanting to move down here for good with me. One thing I realized after the whole ordeal was that men were becoming better and better every single day at hiding their kids. He could have been a whole serial killer and my ass wouldn't have known a thing.

I'd fallen deep for Houston so his betrayal was enough to send me down a dark path. I couldn't eat, sleep or work for weeks. Even after cutting him off for good and trying to move on with my life, I was still a mess. I then realized how much of a trigger my hometown was for me since we'd spent so much time going out on dates around the city so I did what I needed to do.

I fled.

I jumped from flight to flight around the globe without having to worry about anyone but myself. It was fun. Especially because I was exploring the world on my father's dime.

Being his 'Angel' definitely had its advantages and I didn't have to touch my savings until six months into my adventures when my father hit me with the "I'm cutting you off" speech. That was his way of telling me I needed to come home but I wasn't ready to come.

Four months later and he got on a flight to Tokyo and personally came to get me. The stubborn mule in me was not planning on going anywhere until I got a text from Chase Bank that all three of my accounts were locked. My checking account, my business account and savings account. Even my Wells Fargo savings account was locked too.

My father held serious weight in the finance industry so he could make fucked up shit like that happen. It reminded me of how he could be nasty when he wanted to be. Though it killed him to have to hurt his Angel, if it meant that I came home, then he was hurting his Angel without a doubt in his mind.

So here I was. Forced to work for my father's company for a year to prove to him that I wasn't squandering my time away because of a boy. My father knew all about what had happened with Houston so he understood my reasons for wanting to get away for a month. But when a month turned into three months and then three into six, my father wasn't impressed with me anymore. He couldn't fathom why I was no longer putting my summa cum laude GPA to use. I'd not only quit my job, but I'd also taken a break from my financial consulting business and basically dropped the three clients I'd had onboard. The three *high paying* clients who loved working with me and I loved working with them too but work just wasn't on the cards for me after Houston broke my heart. Work was the last thing I cared about and the sudden ditching of my career was an abomination in my father's eyes. He wanted his only child prioritizing her career. Not her heart.

"Are you excited, Angel?"

Excited? Hell no but I wasn't about to disappoint my father with my words.

So I lied.

"Yeah, Dad. I'm excited."

His cheeks hiked and he lightly hummed, a habit he did when he was pleased with me.

"My first meeting of the day is at ten a.m. and I want you there."

"Uh-huh, got it." My eyes drifted to my MacBook that I had open on Google.

I'd been laying on my bed, about to do some personal research until my father called. The search *'being tied up'* was on my screen and I was just about to click on the first link titled *'8 women on what it's like being tied up in bed during sex'* until my father called.

"I'm serious, Danaë. It's with two of my very important clients and I want you to meet them. Don't be late."

"I won't be," I promised, taking in his serious expression. "I'll be on time, Daddy."

"That's my girl."

And just like that his seriousness faded from his face and I was back to talking to the gentle giant that my father truly was.

I looked nothing like him. I resembled only my mother and knew I was basically her twin from all the pictures I'd seen of her. The fact that I was her twin was the main reason why Trenton couldn't stay mad at me for too long. She'd been the love of his life, completely owning his heart, and 'til this day, he hadn't remarried anyone else.

"You should call Kamora and thank her for decorating your office."

I instantly rolled my eyes and looked away from him.

"Danaë."

A deep, unimpressed sigh escaped my lips.

"Danaë. Be nice."

"I'll be nice when she's nice to me," I retorted, looking back in the direction of my phone that was resting against my MacBook and spotting my father's pout.

My father refused to get remarried but there was one woman who was desperate to change his mind.

"She is being nice. She decorated your office."

Yeah and probably made it ugly as hell just to fuck with me.

"You need to say thank you and appreciate the effort she's trying to make with you."

I remained silent and this time it was his turn to sigh.

"My daughter clearly wants her father to be old and lonely forever."

My heart almost broke at his statement.

"You're not old, Daddy... well you sure as hell don't look it."

He smirked as I gassed him up. I wasn't lying about him not looking old. My father was fifty-five but still looked in his mid-thirties. Not even the gray sprinkled in his bushy beard could age him. His dark chocolate skin was wrinkle free and smooth as silk. To put it simply, my Daddy was a very good-looking man so I understood why women of all ages threw themselves at his old ass.

"And you're definitely not lonely when you have me."

The love he had for me shined in his eyes and he moved closer to the camera.

"I know that Angel but I also have Kamora. She's a part of my life... *our* lives and I really need you two to get along. You know you're my only family and Kamora wants to get to know you better. She doesn't have any family; her parents are both gone and her brother she doesn't speak to anymore. He's involved in a life that she wants no parts of so she really doesn't have anyone but me."

My shoulders slumped and my head fell, allowing me to avoid his face once again.

"Please, Danny... do it for me."

Kamora was my father's girlfriend and they'd been together for two years now. She was two years older than me, making her twenty-seven and she was chasing after my fifty-five-year-old father. I'd always thought that she was just another one of his play things and things between them weren't that serious until she moved into our family home last year.

She started making her presence known by redecorating the house and my father being a feen for her bossy ass allowed her too. It was all the confirmation I needed to move out and find my own apartment sooner than later. Something I'd put off for a long time because my father's home was massive and it was the only home I'd ever lived in. If we wanted to, we could go days without seeing each other in the ten thousand square feet space, something we never did anyway. I also didn't want to leave him all alone in that house with no one but our housekeepers. Staying in my childhood abode allowed me to save my coins instead of pouring money into an apartment every month.

However with Kamora now in the picture, my father was never alone.

I didn't want to admit it but my father had love for Kamora. Whether he was in love with her, I wasn't too sure about that but she made him happy. Surprisingly, she wasn't here for my father's coins because I'd seen her turn down numerous of his luxurious gifts with my very own eyes. She claimed there were more important things to spend money on. If it was an act she was putting on, she was doing a pretty good job at performing because even I couldn't turn down the Chanel bags my father bought for me.

I would have to put aside the personal issues I had with her... and believe me there were many. However for now I would leave them be. My father's happiness was important to me and I understood that as a fifty-five-year-old man he needed the presence of a woman in his life.

"Okay, Dad..." I took in a breath then released it as I fixed on his mahogany orbs. "I'll be nice."

"Thank you, Angel."

I'd play nice with Kamora for now but when she messed with me and believe me, she will, I'd mess with her too.

CHAPTER 4

~ CASSIAN ~

*M*onday morning finally arrived and I was up early at six a.m. for my morning jog along the lakefront trail and the Chicago Riverwalk five minutes away from The Palazzo. Nipsey Hussle motivated my run as I listened to him talk his shit about grinding all his life. Something I could greatly relate to. Despite coming from such a powerful family, I still felt the pressures of making a name for myself and I'd done that so far with my hotel. An hour later, I'd showered, dressed and was fixing my protein shake.

"She must be tweakin' if she thinks I'm not getting a test run of the BBL that I paid for..."

Now here I was. Sitting in the backseat of my brother's limo while his driver took us to our meeting.

I was being subjected to listen to my baby brother's newest battle with the opposite sex. Hearing him mention how he'd just paid for a shorty's BBL made me realize that he really did have a serious problem.

He loved women too damn much.

"She's talking about she gotta wear some damn farrah shit for two months."

I frowned as I pulled out my phone from my pocket.

"A farrah?" My fingers tapped away on my screen. "What the fuck is that?"

"Some shit she has to wear twenty-four-seven after having the BBL apparently," he replied. "I told her she can wear her farrah whatever shit as long as she likes, just as long as she knows I'm sliding up in there..."

While he talked, I searched. I was curious to know exactly what a 'farrah' was and from the way Christian had described it, I knew he didn't have a clue what it actually was. Moments later and I'd figured out that he'd been saying the wrong shit all along.

"It's actually called a *faja*, you idiot." I chuckled, staring down at my phone screen.

"What? Lemme see that..." I pushed my phone in his direction, allowing him to see what I'd googled. "Ohhhh my bad. Don't matter what it is anyways, I'm still tapping that ass. Faja or no faja."

"You make me sick." I grinned and shook my head, looking out the tinted windows until my attention was caught.

"Imperia called me." Christian's announcement made me press my head against the leather head rest and I stared out the windows once again while gripping my phone in my right palm.

"Oh did she now?"

"Yeah she did," he replied. "She's been struggling to get through to you and says she wants to talk."

No what she really wanted to do was fuck and that was one thing I couldn't do with her anymore. We hadn't fucked in over two months and I knew she was having withdrawals.

"Just call her, Cass." Him pleading her case was kinda cute. "She's still hurting and needs your support."

I was hurting too but you didn't see me hounding down her phone with calls every day. A part of me wanted to just block her but I couldn't do that. She'd been an important part of my life prior to her carrying my child. We'd been best friends which is why having a child with her was something that I welcomed. I couldn't cut Imperia off completely but what I could do was avoid her as much as possible. What she wanted from me I couldn't give. I couldn't give her love and affection as her man anymore because the day our baby girl died was the day our relationship died with her. We were never real lovers, just two close friends who got caught up in a moment. A very long moment.

"I'll call her soon," I muttered, just to get him off my chest.

It worked because the rest of our journey, he tapped away on his phone whereas I kept a fixed gaze out the window.

Three years ago, a tragedy struck and it was a tragedy that I'd done a decent job at keeping locked out of my mind over the years. It was only when Imperia came around that I became shattered inside, filled with anguish and agony like no other. That's why I kept myself at a distance from Imperia. Yeah we had great sex but that didn't change the reality of things. By being in her space all the time, she was the constant reminder of the biggest heartbreak I'd experienced and no matter how hard I tried to forget, I couldn't forget us being one happy family, decorating our daughter's nursery waiting for her arrival, picking out her name, clothes and toys, looking at her face via ultrasound, feeling her kicks in Imperia's stomach until three months before she was due that godforsaken day occurred.

"Sirs, we've arrived," I heard Christian's driver announce five minutes later and it was only now that I realized I hadn't actually been paying attention to our surroundings. Something I rarely ever did.

I looked out the window properly this time and saw the tall glass building we were parked in front of.

The Morgan & Westbrook Accountancy Firm.

This was the building that housed a man that Christian and I truly cherished. He was our accountant and a man that we could genuinely say we could depend on when it came to our hotel finances. Christian and I didn't depend on anybody but ourselves so saying that we could depend on someone who wasn't blood, was us saying a lot.

"Right this way, Mr. and Mr. Acardi."

Moments later, we were inside the firm, being led to the boss' office by an attractive brunette.

Of course, my eyes and Christian's too naturally wandered to the way her ass moved in her black skirt but while I looked for a moment and focused on our path ahead, Christian looked for a century. I had to nudge him to get back on task. We were here on business, not pleasure.

Our footsteps echoed on the travertine flooring as she took us down a walkway leading to a row of glass doors. Once she got close to them, two doors slid out the way, granting her entry. She walked ahead and we followed.

"Mr. Westbrook, the Acardis."

"Ahhh, there's my two favorite clients!"

Trenton Westbrook was a tall man, much like myself only he was shorter by a few inches and where my beard was cut low, his was thick and bushy. He was a dark-skinned man with mahogany eyes that sat on an oval shaped face.

He had others in his office with him. They were seated in the far left of the large office but upon our entry they stood up and moved closer to us.

Trenton made it to us first, shaking our hands and patting our backs. Then we shook the hands of his three male employees.

They were accountants that handled our business accounts along-side Trenton. With all the money we brought in each month, it wasn't a surprise that we had more than one accountant.

After we greeted one another, we all went over to the seating area where our beverages and snacks awaited us on a glass coffee table. There were fresh jugs of orange juice, apple juice and bottles of Fiji water including croissants, strawberries, bananas and muffins. I didn't indulge in sugary foods often so I stuck to a bottle of Fiji whereas Christian grabbed the biggest croissant and poured himself a glass of apple juice.

A flip chart stood a few meters away from the seating area with The Acardi Palazzo logo on the front page. Trenton was one hundred and ten percent prepared for this meeting and that's the number one thing that made him so damn good at his role. He was always ten steps ahead.

"Y'all want tea, coffee?"

I shook my head no.

"Nah I'm good," Christian voiced before biting into his croissant.

"So how have my best men been?" Trenton asked seconds later.

"I don't know, Trey, you tell me," Christian answered after swallowing, a firmness settling in his face.

"Well I'd say you've both been pretty damn good with all the benjis you've been making! I'm ready for y'all to adopt me now."

We all burst out into laughter and I fell into the velvet sofa I was sitting on, feeling right at home.

It was always a breath of fresh air seeing Trenton because not only was he our accountant, but he was also our good friend. He took care of our accounts, making sure we were straight with the tax man and we took care of him by paying his company a fat check every month.

"So tell me boys... what's on your mind? You said that you're ready to expand now?"

I nodded and lifted my back off my seat. I leaned forward as I held my hands together and placed my elbows on my knees.

"We are. That downtown branch needs a sister."

"I agree," Trenton said. "Have you any idea on where you want it to b—"

"Daddy! I'm so sorry I'm late, traffic got the best of... me."

We all turned around to see the intruder who had just stepped into the room. The shock that marred her face was the same shock that filled my body.

Shit... it's her.

"That's okay, Ange... Miss Westbrook." Her father's quick correction of her name almost made me crack a smile but I hid it well as my eyes stayed sealed on hers. "Come on in. I want you to meet my two best clients."

She didn't move though. All she did was remain in her stance with her mouth slightly parted, unblinking eyes and her hands now clutching the sides of her thighs.

Her work attire was graceful yet sexy. She wore a light gray tailored pant suit with black heels gracing her feet and a black medium sized Telfar bag over the shoulder. Those long legs of hers were elevated and I loved everything about the way her curves were accentuated by her pants. She wasn't on the super slim side nor the super thick side but baby girl had a gorgeous physique that suited her well.

"Danaë... come in."

Her father's order made her snap out of her frozen state and she nodded, inching her way towards where we all sat. I didn't stop looking at her as she came closer and even though she'd stopped looking at me, my hard gaze on her remained. Even when she took her seat across from me, I continued to ogle her.

Not giving a fuck about how intimidating I was coming across as.

"Danaë, this is Cassian and Christian Acardi. The owners of The Acardi Palazzo. Cassian, Christian, this is my daughter, Danaë. She'll be working at the company full time and helping me with a few clients. She's a qualified accountant and financial consultant so I'm sure she'll be of great help to the both of you."

I'm sure she will.

Her eyes fell from her father's to Christian and then to me.

"It's nice to meet you both."

"Nice to meet you too," Christian greeted her.

"Likewise," I said, watching her avoid my gaze once again.

My eyes swept up and down her sienna brown face, examining those seductive eyes that I hadn't been able to forget, those perfectly arched brows, those full glossy lips and that button nose of hers. Her jet-black hair was in a side parting, exactly how it'd been when I'd first seen her. Only this time instead of it being curled, it was straightened, giving her a professional appearance. I much preferred the curls though and what I'd prefer even more was me wrapping those curls around my hand before I pulled her head up and down my dic—

"So Cassian and Christian are expanding..."

While her father talked business, my focus was only on her. I'd told myself that I didn't want this woman but it had all been one big fat lie. I admit, the way she stepped to me at the bar was definitely something that caught me off guard because like I said before, I did the stepping. I'd also noted the fact that she drank so much alcohol with her girl that night but it'd just been something I'd used as one of the reasons to pretend that I didn't want her. From the way I was looking at her now, it was almost as if she belonged to nobody else but me.

Quit lying to yourself, nigga. You know you want her.

She was trying her hardest to not look my way and somewhat succeeding until moments later, Christian reached ahead for a strawberry and her instinct to look gave in and before she knew it, she was looking exactly where she needed to be looking. Right at me.

Yeah, take a good look, Danaë. Take a good look at the man who's going to punish you real good with this dick.

I was done pretending like I didn't want her. I'd take things slow, make her wait but best believe, I was going to give her what she'd wanted from the start...

For me to have my way with her all night.

CHAPTER 5

~ DANAË ~

9:40 a.m.

I stiffened in my seat as I glanced down at the gold face of my watch.

Shit... I'm gonna be late.

"I really don't believe this..."

What was supposed to be a fifteen-minute journey was now turning into a thirty minute one.

"Sorry, lady... we should be moving soon," my Uber driver gently said to me.

I looked up at the front view mirror to see a warm smile sitting on his tawny-colored face. I appreciated his optimism, but we were not moving anywhere anytime soon. I didn't even know why I had faith in my city when it came to driving around peacefully. Chicago was ranked second on the cities with worst traffic list but here I was, thinking I could get to work smoothly this morning.

We'd been stuck on lake shore drive for ten minutes because there was a lane closure due to an accident. All the days of the week for an accident to happen and it had to be this one.

Just great!

I crossed my arms and rested against my seat, letting out a huff. The only reason why I was mad was because I didn't want to break my promise to my father. I'd told him I'd be on time for his meeting, and I genuinely wanted to be.

I saw the way his eyes filled with glee when I told him I was excited to be working for his company and I know I said I'd lied but waking up this morning and getting ready for work felt good. I was excited to work for my father's firm and I felt that all those days of rejecting my father's request to work for him had been building up to this very day.

My first day at Morgan & Westbrook.

I hated disappointing him even when I did it intentionally by fleeing from Chicago ten months ago. And today on my first day of work, I hated disappointing him one hundred times more.

Eventually the traffic started moving and I looked down at my gold watch again, only to grimace at the time.

10:50 a.m.

Trenton's meeting started in ten minutes and I was still in the middle of the highway.

I shut my eyes and took calm breaths as my driver sped down the route. It must have been the heavenly grace of God above because somehow seven minutes later I was outside my father's building. My eyes popped open, and I felt light all of a sudden. I thanked my Uber driver, promised to give him a five-star rating and raced into the building.

My hopes of making my father's meeting just in time were crushed when I couldn't get past the security gates. I thought they'd slide out the way for me, but they didn't, resulting in my legs to bang into the metal barriers. Fiery slices of pain flared up my legs.

"Miss Westbrook?" the front receptionist's voice sounded, and

I turned around to see her waving a blank card at me with a friendly look. "Good morning, Miss Westbrook. It's good to have you here at Morgan & Westbrook. You just need to set up your key card and you'll be good to go."

I'd been too busy trying to rush past the gates to even notice the curved dark oak reception desk a few short yards away.

It took me about three minutes for me to get my key card set up with Deyjah who turned out to be a real sweetheart by the way. I was then racing up to the top floor where my father's office was and rushing along the corridor leading to glass doors. As soon as they slid out the way for me, I quickly stepped in and made my presence known verbally.

"Daddy!" My eyes landed on his hooded ones. "I'm so sorry I'm late, traffic got the best of... me."

Before my last word, I felt moved to look around the room and I did, only to suddenly wish I hadn't.

No. Way.

"That's okay, Ange... Miss Westbrook," he quickly corrected himself. "Come on in. I want you to meet my two best clients."

Hell no! That's not... Cassian.

He was sitting opposite my father and had no one in his sights but me. A heavy feeling formed in my chest and despite my father's instruction to "come on in" I did no such thing.

Lord please wake me up from this dream. This must be a dream... right?

This was no dream. Cassian was here. Right now. In this meeting.

My hands glued to my thighs and as much as I knew I needed to stop acting like a damn mannequin, I couldn't help it.

"Danaë... come in."

My father's deep voice was all it took to make me snap out my trance and slowly walk over to the seated men. Three of the men I recognized as my father's employees and I'd met them several times at my family home. Kyle, James, and Reggie each sent welcoming smiles my way and I returned one back.

I took the empty seat next to my father, placing my handbag to the floor and the second my butt hit the chair, an uncomfortable wave ran through me.

I knew that all these men were looking at me, but it was the stare of one man in particular that left me uncomfortable. I looked solely at my father who didn't seem upset with me. He looked neutral but I still prayed he wasn't too pissed about my tardiness.

"Danaë, this is Cassian and Christian Acardi. The owners of The Acardi Palazzo hotel. Cassian, Christian, this is my daughter, Danaë. She'll be working at the company full time and helping me with a few clients. She's a qualified accountant and financial consultant so I'm sure she'll be of great help to the both of you."

I looked over at Christian first then... *him.*

"Nice to meet you both."

"Nice to meet you too," Christian spoke up first.

Like his brother, Christian was very easy on the eyes. They shared the same light beige skin and large nose but that was about it. Christian's lips were slightly smaller than Cassian's and so were his eyes. His lips were bordered by a thin moustache and he had a light full-face beard. He also had light curls spiraling from his scalp. Nonetheless you could tell they were related.

"Likewise."

Cassian's baritone seemed to knock the wind out of me, and I looked back over at my father, quickly regaining my breath. He got up from his seat and walked over to the free-standing flip chart a short distance away from us all.

"So Cassian and Christian are expanding..."

Father talked but his daughter was sure as hell not listening to a word. I mean I paid attention here and there, but I found my thoughts being distracted. Not only could I feel Cassian's stare on me, but I could also feel myself being drawn to want to look right back at him.

Just one more look. That can't hurt, right?

I wasn't trying to give into staring at him like one creep but as soon as my body sensed motion, I looked in the direction of said motion only to realize that Christian was picking up a strawberry. My gaze fell on Cassian, thinking he was now looking away from me, but I was wrong. He was looking right at me with this look that evaded my soul. It was as if from this one look, Cassian had made it clear that I now belonged to him.

Our eyes never left one another, and I took the chance to admire him. Today he wore a black suit with a white shirt and matching black pants. No jewelry graced his neck and I remembered he hadn't been wearing any neck jewelry when I'd first met him. The only jewelry he had on was a silver diamond stud in each ear and a silver iced out watch secured around his wrist. He was a simple man but nothing on him looked *simple.*

"And Danaë, Cassian and Christian are big investors in the tech industry. They've got stocks in Tesla, Apple, Netflix..."

My father addressing me directly made me focus on him again. My focus only lasted for about a minute before my eyes were back on Cassian. And his back on mine.

We didn't seem to care that we were both in the middle of an important meeting because we refused to look away from each other.

Luckily no one had noticed us gazing into each other's eyes because Christian and my father's employees looked at my father. Whereas my father's eyes moved from his flip chart to around the room at everyone else. Whenever I felt him looking at me, I would look right at him to assure him I was paying attention to his presentation. But of course my eyes landed right back on Cassian when he got lost in his flip chart presentation again.

It was only minutes later when I felt Christian beginning to stare at me that I stopped looking at Cassian and decided to reach ahead for a glass of orange juice. The jug was over by Cassian's side of the table and I attempted to reach for it until Cassian beat me to the punch.

Our fingers touched and heat curled down my spine at the connection. My eyes rose to his. Without saying anything, he lifted the jug and poured a glass. Once it was full, he handed it over to me and I mouthed, "Thank you."

Moments later and the meeting came to a close. My father said his goodbyes to Cassian, Christian and his employees but not to me. Telling me all I needed to know about was what to come.

"Five minutes late, Angel. Really?"

"I'm sorry, Dad. There really was traffic. I left on time, but I got caught up on the highway because of an accident."

My father stood by his floor to ceiling glass window that showcased downtown Chicago. His back was to me, but his hands were tightly clasped behind his back, indicating his displeased mood.

"It won't happen again," I said, trying to convince myself more than him.

He finally turned around to face me and his face suddenly brightened up.

"Okay, Angel. No worries. Don't forget I'm taking you out for lunch later."

And there he was. There was the gentle giant my father truly was. We talked some more about what my job role entailed now that I was at Morgan & Westbrook. The first line of business my father wanted from me was to set up a private meeting with Cassian and Christian.

"Why?" I asked.

"Because they are my two important clients, Danaë, and as my two important clients, I always need them happy. They're looking to expand, and I want you to run point on this whole thing. Y'all young people connect better than us old folk. I need you to be my eyes and ears, Danny. My eyes and ears."

After our talk, I headed to my office on the third floor and my eyes bulged when I stepped into the space.

I came to stand in the center of the room and began to circle it. It was a medium sized office and it had been transformed to my very own oasis. The room had seamless windows showcasing the mesmerizing view of the city. White oak wood graced the floors below me and white walls coated only three walls. The fourth wall behind my desk was a teal accent wall to match my teal office chair with a large abstract painting hanging in the middle. There were two teal office chairs on the other side of my desk for my future clients. My desk was a white marble table with gold steel legs. Gold desk organizers sat ready on top with all the equipment I needed. I also noticed the potted palm plants standing in the two corners of the room behind my desk.

Wow.

And here I thought Kamora was about to decorate the office with a whole lot of pink and sparkly shit. Dad must have given her the heads up about me hating pink.

After marveling over my new office space, I got settled in my seat and pulled out my iPad Air from my bag. The only thing missing from my office was an iMac which Dad explained was being delivered in the late afternoon. By the time we were back from our lunch break, my iMac would be set up by the company's I.T. technician.

My father's assistant had already emailed me with all important contacts of the firm, and I scrolled down the list until I laid eyes on Cassian's name.

I chuckled at the previous reality of me being embarrassed to see Adina's boss, the same boss who rejected me. Now I could tell that my feeling embarrassment had all been for nothing. The way he looked at me was confirmation enough that the man wanted me.

I think I need some time away
I took a little time I prayed
We gon' be alright okay

Jorja Smith's melodic voice filled my ears and I reached across the table for my handbag, pulling out my phone. As soon as I clocked the caller ID, I sighed.

The Witch

"Hello?"

"Hello, Danaë. How are you?"

"Good and yourself?"

"I'm good. Just wanted to know how your first day at work is going and how you're finding your new office."

I tapped on my iPad, starting a new email addressed to both Cassian and Christian.

"I love it, Kamora. Thank you so much."

I briefly looked around the office again, admiring her work. I couldn't lie... she'd done her thing with the office. The least I could give her was a thank you.

"You're welcome, hun. I wanted to make sure it was to your taste entirely and..."

While she talked, I wedged my phone between my ear and shoulder and got to typing.

Dear Mr. and Mr. Acardi,
It was a pleasure meeting you both today. I wanted to book a meeting
with the two of you to discuss more about your hotel expansion. If you
could please let me know your availability for this week or the next that
would be great.
Kind Regards,
Danaë Westbrook

I sent the email and placed my iPad down to my desk.

"...I know we haven't always seen eye to eye, but I really do want us to have a relationship, Danaë."

"Okay," I simply said, not completely buying her act.

It was going to take a whole lot more than decorating my office for me to warm up completely to Kamora, but this was a start.

"I'm looking forward to getting to know you better," I told her, trying to be nice as I possibly could. She'd extended an olive branch and I needed to learn how to slowly latch on.

"So am I, Danaë," she replied, and I could hear the smile in her voice. "Well, let me not hold you up on your first day. Enjoy the rest of your day and I'll speak to you soon."

"Thank..."

My sentence halted when I noticed a new Gmail notification appear on my iPad.

"...Thank you, Kamora," I quickly finished my sentence. "Have a good day."

Our call ended and I picked up my iPad, swiping up once the face ID granted me entry. My heart skittered as I read his swift reply.

Dear Miss Westbrook,
It was much better meeting you in a more professional setting than our first encounter.

His reference to the first time we met made me smirk.

My only availability is tomorrow afternoon at two p.m. but Christian isn't available. The rest of my week is pretty booked up but we're both free next week. I don't mind seeing you alone. Let me know what works for you.
Cassian Acardi
CEO, Acardi Palazzo Inc.

My dad told me to see them both but seeing them separately wouldn't be a crime, right?

A part of me wanted to email Cassian back and tell him that I would just see him next week with Christian when they were both free. But another part of me wanted to email him that tomorrow was perfect, and I'd be seeing him then.

Cassian and I had never been alone together, and it was a fact that had heat warming my cheeks. He'd said I had no business stepping to a man like him. Well, clearly, I did have business stepping to a man like him since my father's company handled his business accounts.

Without wasting time, I typed, *'Tomorrow afternoon at two p.m. works fine. See you then'* and pressed send.

CHAPTER 6

~ CASSIAN ~

*L*ike clockwork, her email came flying in and I quickly opened it to read her response to my proposition.

Dear Mr. Acardi,
Tomorrow afternoon at two p.m. works fine. See you then.
Kind Regards,
Danaë Westbrook

"I knew it, I knew it, I knew it!"

My head turned to Christian who was sitting right next to me. We were in the backseat of his limo, being driven to our next destination after our meeting with Trenton, his employees and... *her.*

"At first, I thought... nah, maybe they're just staring at each other occasionally but y'all were literally eye fucking each other in that meeting. Took me a minute to actually notice but believe me, I noticed."

I fought the grin trying to crease my face and stayed silent. My head dropped back down to my iPhone and I read her email one last time.

"Now you got me ignoring her email about the meeting cause your ass wants to see her alone," he commented, chuckling lightly. "You must really want her, huh?"

Instead of granting my baby brother with a reply, I looked back down at my iPhone and began scrolling through other unopened emails.

"She's a baddie though," he continued talking. "Shit, if you weren't interested in her, I'd be tapping tha..."

Christian's words trailed off once I sent a threatening glare his way. He gave me this surprised look before amusement poured from his eyes.

"Oh yeah." He laughed once again. "Your ass definitely wants her."

My face eased up and I kept scrolling through my Gmail, trying to find any emails worth opening and sending a quick reply to.

"Looking at me like you about to kill me and shit, damn, nigga. Calm down. You don't even know her yet."

I don't know why I'd given my brother a threatening look over a woman that I didn't know but it was what it was. I had my mind set on having her and told myself that's what was happening but now that Christian was pointing out my defensive nature over her already, doubt tugged at my heart.

Fuck... maybe this ain't a good idea. She not only works for your accountant's company, but she's also your accountant's daughter. She's someone you're now in business with. Are you sure you want to go down that path with her, only to leave when you no longer have a use for her? 'Cause you know damn well a relationship is the last thing you'll ever be looking for, nigga.

"Shit, she's even badder on IG..."

It took me a few seconds to notice that Christian was now tapping away on his phone but when I heard him mention Instagram, I knew exactly what he'd done. I stared at him as he stared at his phone and I focused in on his bright screen. Times like these I was grateful as fuck for my twenty-twenty vision.

Photos of Danaë appeared and not just any type of photos... I'm talking thirst trap central type pictures.

"God damn..."

I don't know what pissed me off more. Hearing Christian lust over her or seeing from a distance the way her body looked so fucking good in each picture. She wasn't even naked in the ones Christian had browsed through so far, she was fully clothed, but each piece of clothing did wonders for her body. Whether it was a tight-fitting dress or figure-hugging jeans, Danaë Westbrook was no ugly sight. She knew her angles well and knew exactly how to bring a man weak to his knees. Then there was a picture of her in nothing but a beige bikini and seeing the way the thin fabric hugged her large mounds was enough to make me want to buss in my pants.

I tore my eyes away from Christian's screen and looked back down at my own.

"She really is one bad bitc—"

"Enough," I cut him off. "Quit with all the lustful comments."

I didn't even have to see his face to know that he was grinning.

"Someone a lil' jealous?"

The amusement dripping in his tone confirmed that he was indeed grinning. Refusing to look his way, I tapped away on my screen, no longer in the mood to be the butt of Christian's teasing. Minutes later, Christian had seen what I'd sent out.

"Damn I thought you wanted to see her alone?"

"Nah, I'm good," I simply said. "We'll see her together next week."

I was anything but good.

I'd locked off my phone and placed it on do not disturb so I couldn't see Danaë's response when it came through to my mailbox. I had no idea how she'd react to my sudden change of plans, but I was going to convince myself that I didn't care.

"Business is moving very well. I'm proud of you all and as you know Frankie is proud of you too..."

However, convincing myself that I didn't care was a complete failure even hours after I'd sent Danaë that email.

That stupid email.

Just thinking about it pissed me off.

Dear Miss Westbrook,
Please ignore my previous email about me being able to see you alone. Christian and I will see you next week together. The same time and day as today's meeting works for us both.

"Frankie much prefers being behind the scenes as you all know. She's aware of everything and is glad that The Family is perfectly functioning. As her second in command, I'm your first and only point of contact you need when it comes to any issues you may be facing."

Sending that email was the last thing I'd wanted to do but at the same time, I didn't want Christian teasing me for all eternity about the fact that I'd wanted to see her privately. I also didn't think pursuing her was a good idea anymore. One thing that my late father had instilled into me was to not mix business with pleasure and by indulging in my desires for Danaë Westbrook, I would be mixing business all the way with pleasure.

"Cassian."

A deep baritone broke me away from my private thoughts. I looked straight ahead at the olive-skinned man sitting in the head seat of the long rectangular shaped table.

"Yes, Capo *(Boss)*?"

"Everything's okay on your end, I'm sure. Guns moving in and out just how they should?"

I nodded before replying, "Yes, sir."

He studied me closely for a few seconds without saying another word. Then he nodded with understanding.

My last name never meant much to me until the day I turned thirteen and I saw my father shoot a man five times without blinking. That's when I recognized the type of family I was a part of.

The Acardi Family had settled in Chicago back in the seventies. My grandfather had made a name for himself by becoming a man that many respected, feared and also hated. Alongside his younger brother, they'd created a business that became unstoppable; what we all knew today as The Family. The Acardis did what they had to do in order to survive and exist in this cold world, enlisting the help of various capos and associates of various races and cultures to help them succeed.

My grandfather, Abramo Acardi, passed down his knowledge and power to his son, my father and also my auntie, his daughter. Acardi women weren't supposed to be part of the gritty world that The Acardi men were part of but my grandfather was a king amongst men. He knew that women couldn't be sheltered from a life that they lived in and he understood that enemies could come for not just the men he loved but the women he loved too. That's why he taught Massimo and Francesca Acardi everything there was to know about being an Acardi and by the time he'd passed, Massimo and Francesca were down for any and everything.

You could say my grandfather was somewhat of a feminist because he believed in women having equal rights to men and I respected that. Women deserved to have the same opportunities as men, be making the same money as men if not more and they deserved to express themselves freely and sexually as they wanted to.

Since my father, Massimo, was the oldest, he automatically stepped into place as the head capo once my grandfather died but instead of choosing one of his male cousins to be his underboss, he chose his sister, Francesca Acardi.

The underboss of a head capo was the second in command so after my father's fatal heart attack, there was no question about Frankie taking his place. She'd been trained for this moment since she'd turned eighteen and wasn't naïve to how The Acardi Family operated. As innocent and sweet as she looked, Frankie was far from it.

Right now, Christian and I were in a meeting with Julius Acardi, Frankie's cousin and her underboss. He'd become in charge of our monthly meetings and was Frankie's spokesperson. Frankie only appeared when she needed to and because of how solid The Family was, that was rare. She was getting older, so I understood her distance towards the business and wanting to ease into retirement. She wanted to ensure that things were smooth running ship without her because as she loved to remind me, she wasn't going to be here forever.

Julius was also our cousin, but we saw him more as an uncle. Julius had been my father's cousin, the son of my grandfather's only brother. Julius' sons, Santiago and Romero were in the meeting too. There were many more capos in the family but we were the top four, handling the four main businesses for The Family as we were direct relatives of the head capo. Romeo was an assassin with his own assassin organization, Santiago was a dope dealer, providing weight to the top gangs in Chicago, Christian was a counterfeit pusher who worked exclusively on the dark web and sold counterfeit to whoever needed them and trust me, a lot of mothafuckas out there were dying for high quality counterfeit dollar bills. I guess all those years of studying computers really paid off for my little brother and I was truly proud of him for doing something so out of the norm that brought in a lot of damn paper. I on the other hand, liked keeping shit simple and handled weapons, specifically guns. Those were my babies and selling guns was the next thing I loved after running my hotel.

"I know I asked about business earlier but how are you, son? It's been a minute since we caught up."

After the meeting, everyone began to say their goodbyes and I let everyone say their farewells to Julius first before I stepped to him. We'd just engaged in a loving hug and our hands were still joined in the center as we broke our embrace.

"I'm good, Ju."

He nodded and lifted his free hand to pat my back. He understood that I was a man of few words, but he also knew whenever something was bothering me. After my father passed, Julius automatically got into position as the new father figure for Christian and I. He'd always had a strong presence in our lives since he was our father's cousin but after his death, our bond tightened.

I knew Julius asking me if I was good was his way of prying and usually, I would have been all for voicing my troubles but only when it came to business. Since business was going amazingly well, there was nothing to voice. There wasn't something bothering me, it was *someone* but that wasn't something I was about to tell my older cousin. When it came to women, I was private as fuck which is one of the reasons why Christian teased me about my defensive nature toward Danaë.

Danaë.

God damn it... even her name was beautiful. I was intrigued to google what her name mea—

Focus, Cassian. She's not important.

I listened to the voice in my head and shook off thoughts about her.

After our family meeting, Christian and I headed home to The Palazzo. Since we owned the building, it was only right we lived in the best rooms of the hotel. We stayed on the top floor known as the presidential floor because the rooms on this floor were the best rooms money could buy. They were rooms fit for a president and no expense was spared when it came to constructing them.

"See you later, bro'."

"Later," I told him after we dapped each other.

Chris went down the corridor to his room whereas I walked ahead to mine. I pulled out my silver key card, and hovered it over my door's electric sensor and was given the green light to go in.

Chicago's afternoon daylight spilled through my penthouse's windows, brightening up my pathway as I made it to my bedroom to quickly shower and dress into something more comfortable. Half an hour later and I'd showered and dressed into black sweats and a black Fear of God Essentials t-shirt. I checked my phone one last time and went straight to Danaë's response to my email that I'd read earlier while in the car home with Christian.

See you both next week, she'd replied, and it was a response that left me burning.

Why?

Well, I guess a small part of me wanted her to question my abrupt decision to see her with Christian next week. But of course, that wasn't happening. She only cared about business and so did I.

I pocketed my key card, leaving my phone on the ottoman by my bed before stepping out my home in my D&G slides.

I had only one destination to go but still my thoughts were

determined to take me to the one destination that I didn't want to go to.

It took me a few minutes to get down to the sixth floor but by the time I was outside my desired destination, I'd successfully managed to eradicate all thoughts about Miss Danaë Westbrook.

I brought out my key card, hovered it over the door's sensor and entered once the green light appeared. Another great thing about owning the hotel – I had the master key card that could get into every single room in the building.

I stepped in, laying eyes on the empty living room space and sauntered through the space until I was on the other side where the bedroom resided.

I twisted the golden knob and pushed the door open to see her exactly how I wanted her to be. She was on all fours, laying on her arms with her large butt tooted in the air. Upon my entry, she looked over her tatted shoulder and her mouth began to curve.

"Who told you to turn around?"

Her smile faded and she turned back to face her front. I let the door shut behind me and raised my shirt off my body.

Stepping closer to the double bed, I recognized her antsy state because of the way she kept shifting her legs behind her. Instinctively, I lifted a hand to spank her ass and she whimpered at the impact.

"Acardi... I missed you."

I delivered another slap to her butt, this time harder and with my fingers more apart to create a stinging sensation. The sounds she emitted were a mixture of pain and pleasure which weren't enough for me. This time when I spanked her, I kept my hand positioned on the lower half of her soft flesh.

"Acardi!"

It was what I knew to be her sweet spot because not only was it the spot that sent vibrations straight to her pussy, but it was also the spot that had her screaming for me to never stop.

My spanks were continuous and so were her moans, begging for more. Eventually I stopped and let go of her to ditch my sweats. Before pulling them down, I reached for the Magnum XL in my pocket and slipped it between my lips as I undressed.

Once my sweats were down to the floor and I'd shielded my shaft, she turned around and that was the moment the beast inside me was done playing around. I grabbed her long ponytail, yanking her head back and rested my chin on her shoulder.

"Clearly you weren't listening the first time I said it," I spoke directly into her left ear. "Who the fuck told you to turn around?"

"N-No one."

"Exactly. No one," I repeated after her, letting go of her hair to wrap my hand around her throat. "Don't make me have to say that shit again."

"Y-Yes," she promised.

"Yes who?" I loosened my grip on her neck so she could answer my question clearly.

"Yes, Acardi."

My hold retightened and I pressed up harder against her small frame, feeling how warm she was. I knew all this waiting around was only starting to drive her crazy, but she knew I wasn't one to rush the build-up. She had to be dripping wet for me before I slid into her.

My free hand slid down her front, grazing her right breast and rubbing down her stomach until I was able to palm her pussy. I began massaging her wet passage with my whole hand, feeling her body slightly shake against mine. I nibbled at her ear lobe before giving it a slow lick. Her moans soon followed, and I stroked her bundle of nerves in a steady rhythm.

"Uhhhh..."

I'd been a fool to think I'd successfully eradicated all thoughts of Danaë out of my head because as I brought a different woman to her first orgasm of the night, my only desire was to be able to give Danaë this pleasure instead.

An image of Danaë in that beige bikini popped into my head and rage boiled inside me.

I released Evoni's pussy and neck, pushing her down to the mattress. Already knowing what time, it was, she reached for a pillow, but I grabbed it before she could, pushing it under her stomach.

"Acardi, aren't you..."

Her words halted when I pushed past the wet seal of her entrance. A soft moan suddenly left her lips.

"...aren't you going to tie me up?" She finished talking, clutching on the silk sheets below her.

She knew better than to ask me that shit. After the bullshit she'd pulled last week, being tied up was the last thing she deserved.

I hadn't moved out of her yet and that was enough to make her make the biggest mistake of turning around. She realized her mistake as soon as she did it and tried to act like she hadn't, but it was too late.

"Acardiiiiiii!"

"What the fuck... did I say, huh? What I tell your ass?"

"Not to... not to... ahhhhhh!"

Her cries filled the space, but they did nothing to stop my thrusts.

I had both her arms pinned to her back like she was about to be arrested for a crime. The only crime she'd committed was disobeying me when she knew how much I despised that shit. My drilling was relentless, and I showed no mercy. Each pound I gave her made her entire body shake and her deafening cries only heightened. Thank God I'd been smart enough to make each room in my hotel soundproof.

"What... did... I... tell... you?" I asked her between each hard pump that was quickening with each passing second.

"Not to... turn arounnahhhh!"

Harder and harder I fucked her, keeping her arms locked behind her back so she couldn't run.

"I'm... I'm sorry, Acardi. You know I am!"

I froze, keeping my shaft nested deep inside her tightness.

"And you know better than to disobey me, Evoni. You're asking me about being tied up when we both know you don't deserve that shit after what you did."

She went silent but I wasn't done.

"You forget what you did?"

She shook her head 'no' and my irritation mounted.

"Speak the fuck up."

"No," she said. "I didn't forget."

"Remind me what you did, Evoni."

"I was late last week."

"How late?"

"Two hours," she whispered.

"Two hours." I pulled out of her only to slam right back in. "Two *fucking* hours."

I began to move in and out of her again, quickly picking up the pace and providing her with deep thrusts that made her say things that I'm sure weren't from any language on this planet. Moments later, I forced her head up by pulling her ponytail until her head was resting against my chest.

Despite how attractive she was, with those mahogany eyes, plump lips and chiseled cheekbones, this wasn't the face I wanted to see under me right now. Once again I pushed away thoughts of the woman trying to take over my mind and focused on the one below me.

Beads of sweat had broken out on Evoni's forehead and quick pants left her lips. I yanked her hair harder, causing her head to jolt up and her eyes glued on mine.

"You're getting fucked in every hole tonight, Evoni."

She bit her lip.

"And you're not allowed to cum until I say so."

"Yes, Acardi."

"Then maybe... just maybe, I might consider giving you what you want."

Her caramel face now housed a small smile and she opened up her mouth for me like a good little girl.

I spat in her mouth a couple times before pressing my lips to hers and dipping my tongue to collide with hers. Seconds later, I pushed her back down to the bed and slipped back inside her warm cave.

Our session lasted for about two hours; breaks included. Once I'd finally let Evoni cum, she was knocked out and I took my leave.

The satisfaction I thought I'd get from fucking Evoni didn't come. Even when I arrived back in my penthouse, I expected to feel that familiar prideful rush, but it didn't come.

All that fucking and she's still the only one you want.

I couldn't help but titter at my predicament as I strolled to my bedroom. This was cruel. What Danaë had done to my head was too cruel.

I was about to head to my en-suite to take one last shower but my phone suddenly lighting up caught my attention. I looked over at it sitting on my ottoman and went to grab it.

My brows snapped together as I surveyed the four Gmail notifications that had come in from... *her.*

I unlocked my phone to read each one in detail.

The first one addressed only to me read:

Dear Mr. Acardi,
I don't appreciate your sudden change of plans. But it's all good. See you
next week.

The second one:

Actually, it's not all good. We had a plan and you decided to break it
because????????

Another one:

It's cool. I know a coward when I see one.

Then the final one:

I just realized I called you a coward when what I really meant to call
you was... a pussy. Yes you read correctly. You're a pussy. A big fat
PUSSY!!!

I did a double take, blinking rapidly to make sure my eyes were
not deceiving me.

There's no way, she just called me a pussy?

But indeed she had and my chest tightened at the fact that she
thought I was the type of nigga to let shit like that slide.

Wow.

I had a feeling she was intoxicated since it was ten p.m. right
now but that changed nothing. She had no idea of all the things I
was capable of but believe me, she was officially going to find out. I
had a busy day tomorrow but I was definitely going to move some
things around to see her.

I began typing out my reply.

Dear Miss Westbrook,
I'll be seeing you tomorrow in your office at two p.m. Alone. I want to
hear you tell me how much of a pussy I am to my face.
Enjoy the rest of your night, Danaë.

Send.

CHAPTER 7

~ DANAË ~

"*B*itch, you could have warned me that they work with my father."

"Ummm, FYI, I'm here for a check first and foremost. I don't keep up with all things Acardi.com."

She had a point. One thing about my girl that I couldn't deny even if I wanted to, was that she was about her coin and she worked really hard for it.

"I really had no idea your father was their accountant. Wow. Chicago really is small as hell."

I'd arrived back at my office after my lunch break with my father which turned out to be quite nice. NoMI wasn't cheap at all but when it came it to me, my father spared no expense. We were both fans of sushi, so we ended up getting almost everything on the menu.

Spending quality time with my father was something I always enjoyed because we had the best conversations. My father was an open book and spoke his truth regardless of anything. We'd spent the afternoon talking about taking risks in life. My father told me how starting a company with my mother had originally felt like the biggest risk in his life. He explained that at the time a lot of naysayers were in his ear, telling him that starting a company with his girl was a bad idea and it would flop. Well, he'd certainly proved them wrong because Morgan & Westbrook was one of the top accountancy firms in Chicago today.

"Risks are funny because people tend to assume that taking a risk means you're setting yourself up for failure. But they're wrong. Taking a risk means you're setting yourself up for the endless possibility of chances. Success comes with risk and if you're not bold enough to take risks then you're not bold enough to grow."

My father had raised me to be strong willed, courageous and most of all, ambitious. They were three qualities in him that he'd wanted in me, so I understood why he'd personally gotten on a flight to Tokyo three weeks ago to get me.

I was back in Chicago being the ambitious woman he wanted me to be but most importantly, I was back in Chicago being the ambitious woman *I* wanted to be. I was not only working for my father, but I was working for myself again and had restarted up my financial consulting company, Westbrook Wealth LLC. I'd called the three clients who I'd been working with previously and just like I'd imagined, they had missed me dearly and were all willing to work with me again. I booked separate meetings with the three of them from Wednesday to Friday to discuss all the updates with their businesses and finances that I'd missed over the last few months.

Now I had Adina's voice talking through my AirPods as I looked over a cosmetic company's account that my father wanted me to take the lead on. He'd wasted no time in laying me with work and honestly, I wasn't complaining. I liked staying busy, so it was refreshing to now be taking charge of three companies' finances. The first one being The Acardi Palazzo, the second being

RX Cosmetics and the third one being Cofield's Wine. They were all different businesses bringing in a large amount of revenue every month and I was excited to be able to keep up their accounts, advising them on all the financial decisions they should be making and making them look good for the tax man.

"But shit, you and Cassian..." I could sense the laugh dying to get out of her mouth. "This must really be fate."

"Adi, don't." My eyes scanned my screen as I looked at numbers on the QuickBooks software ahead.

"What?" She finally giggled. "I'm just saying. First you meet him at Evoni's last weekend and now you're meeting him on a business level at your father's company. Sounds like fate to me!"

"Well Miss Matchmaker for your information, we'll only be keeping things at a business level."

"Booooooo," she commented with disdain. "Boring!"

Now it was my turn to laugh. Another thing about Adina that I loved was that she wasn't afraid to voice her true thoughts about my decisions.

"I'm not going down that route, Adina. He's business and I never mix busin—"

"Business with pleasure," she finished my sentence for me. "Yeah, yeah, I know. Again... boring!"

"What's boring about me just wanting to keep things professional?"

"Sis, the moment you went up to him at Evoni's, that professional manner went out the window. I'm pretty sure once you two laid eyes on each other today, you couldn't stop ogling one another."

I hadn't even told her all the details of the meeting yet and she'd already caught onto what went down.

"...Maybe."

"I knew it!"

"Adina."

"I knew it, I knew it, I knew!" She exclaimed, clapping excitedly. "Mannnn, I already know he's gonna rock your worl—"

"Adi, no," I cut her off, turning in my seat to look over at my potted plant. "I'm keeping things professional between us. I already went through so much bull with Houston that I still haven't healed from fully yet and jumping into another situation isn't going to help. I just need to stay far away from men for a while."

She was quiet for a few seconds before she yelled out, "Booooooo!"

I frowned then sighed deeply.

"Okay, fine. I get it. You're still healing and that takes time."

"Yes it does."

"But shitttt, can't you tell your healer to hurry the hell up? I'm tryna see my bestie get her back blown in the best way."

"Adina!"

"Jokeeeee!"

I appreciated Adina's eagerness with trying to get me some action but that was the last thing I required right now. What I needed most of all was to stay focused on my coins and goals.

Adina and I were seeing each other again on Friday for another girl's night out that I was looking forward to very much. There was never a dull moment with my bestie and that's why we were inseparable. We also had a friend joining us, one of my good friends and a client of my consultation company.

"Imperia's tagging along on Friday," I told Adina. "Her and I have a business meeting on Friday which we'll leave together and meet you at the Hookah bar."

"Sounds like my type of party," Adina approved. "It's been a minute since we all caught up. I'm excited to see her."

"Same here."

I spent a few more minutes on the phone with Adina before focusing solely on work again. While checking my Gmail, I was reminded of the email Cassian had sent me a few hours ago.

Please ignore my previous email about me being able to see you alone. Christian and I will see you next week together. The same time and day as today's meeting works for us both.

It was unexpected to see his change of our meeting and also quite disappointing. A part of me was looking forward to seeing him in my office without anyone else watching over us. However, I wasn't about to dwell on it. I would be seeing him next week with Christian. End of story.

Hours later, closing time came and I said my goodbyes to my father who was working late. He insisted that I go home with his driver, Ethan, so I did and found myself in the comfort of my abode fifteen minutes later.

"Hey, Nala. How you doing, chica? How's my little baby doing?"

I beamed as I bent low to stare into the glassy, unblinking eyes of my goldfish Nala.

Since arriving back in Chicago and moving into a new place, I figured the next best thing for me to get was a pet.

I was more of a cat lover than a dog one, but I didn't think I could handle having a cat right now. I wanted something small and something that wouldn't accidentally poop all over my apartment. A goldfish was the perfect choice and after having her for ten days I could honestly say I loved Nala. She was cute and small and had a large tank filled with gravel stones and artificial plants. Sis was really living her best life in her tank. The only thing I feared was her being too lonely. I knew sooner than later I would need to get her a sister, brother or even a man. Although the thought of them making a bunch of babies made me nervous. I wasn't ready to be a grandmother yet.

"You've been eating real good today, boo," I commented, checking her automatic food feeder that was attached to the top of her tank. "Momma's tryna get like you."

After talking to Nala, I headed to my kitchen to fix my dinner. I settled on making spaghetti Bolognese, garlic bread and fresh salad coupled with a glass of Pinot Noir that I'd already been drinking while cooking.

Two hours later, my meal was ready, and I got comfy on my sofa with my plate in my hands and an episode of Girlfriends playing on my mounted plasma screen. I was done eating fifteen minutes later and topped up my glass of wine. I was already on my second bottle of the night.

Drinking red wine with a home cooked meal was one of my favorite things to do so tonight was no different. However, I didn't usually have more than one bottle which should have been a sign to me that tonight wasn't going to be an ordinary night. I should have just stuck to one bottle but instead I allowed the devil on my shoulder to coax me into devouring more red wine. The red wine was a dry yet smooth taste. It was everything I needed after my first day of work. I tried to focus on the Girlfriends episode as best as I could and was succeeding until the visage of Cassian Acardi popped into my brain an hour later.

While Joan gossiped to her girlfriends about the new man in her life, I was transported back to this afternoon, meeting Cassian for the second time. He hadn't uttered more than one word to me today and that one word was enough to move my soul in ways I didn't realize were possible.

"It's nice to meet you both."

"Nice to meet you too."

"Likewise."

I pressed my lips to the glass' rim, taking another sip of the wine that was beginning to make me grow feverish.

How dare he change our meeting to next week?

I'd pretended like the change of plans for our meeting hadn't affected me. I chuckled at the thought when I knew fully well that a tightness had formed in my jaw as I read his email.

Next fucking week.

I continued sipping on my liquor before jumping out my seat seconds later to rush over to my bedroom.

I need to see his response one last time. That's all. No big deal.

I grabbed my handbag where my iPad resided and once the small device was nested in my palms, I tapped on its screen while strolling back to the living room.

Christian and I will see you next week together.

I was seated again on my couch and staring down at his reply.

How dare he?

I chugged the rest of my red wine down my throat, dropped the empty glass to the coffee table and refilled my glass once again.

How dare he suddenly change our plans?

Once my glass was filled, I lifted it to my lips and chugged the entire glass down again. I was tempted to fill my glass one last time, but I decided against it. I'd drank enough and I knew having anymore would take me down a path I wasn't going to be able to come back from.

My eyes dropped to my bright screen and I read his email for what seemed like the fiftieth fucking time.

Get a grip, Danaë. What the hell has gotten into you tonight?

Cassian Acardi had gotten into me and there was no remedy in sight to help me get him out.

Unable to stop myself, I grabbed the bottle of Pinot Noir and pressed it to my lips. The alcohol flowed eagerly down my throat and I didn't stop sipping until the bottle was empty. I dropped the empty bottle to the couch space next to me once it was finished.

I shut my eyes, taking deep breaths to try and keep the fire burning within me tame.

You don't appreciate what he's done, and he deserves to hear about how much you don't appreciate it. Yeah! He deserves to hear you. So talk, girl. Tell him exactly how you feel.

The voice in my head had done a solid job at convincing me on what I needed to do next. I entered my iPad, spotted Cassian's email still open from when I'd been looking at it a few minutes ago and hit the reply button.

I don't appreciate your sudden change of plans. But it's all good. See you next week.

I clicked send and warmth spread through my body at the satisfaction of speaking my mind. By now the Pinot Noir had me feeling very nice so I also couldn't stop smiling. However, as quickly as my smile appeared on my lips, it disappeared as I realized that my response wasn't true.

It's not all good. He broke off our plans!

I clicked the reply button once again to type:

Actually, it's not all good. We had a plan and you decided to break it because????????

Send

Then before I knew it, I was sending him another email:

It's coooooooool! I know a coward when I see one.

And another one:

I just realized I called you a coward when what I really meant to call you was... a pussy. Yes you read correctly. You're a pussy. A big fat PUSSY!!!

It took me a minute to realize the error of my ways. I'd been too busy gazing down at my last email with a large grin only to suddenly snap out of lala land and realize I'd just emailed a major client at my father's firm and called him a... pussy.

Oh. My. God.

It was at that moment I knew that I'd fucked up. I'd fucked up majorly by insulting a top client.

Shit!

I flung my iPad away from me to the opposite end of my seat like it was some infectious disease that I wanted no parts of.

Shit, shit, shit!

My hands started to tremble, and I swallowed hard at the fact that Cassian was going to see every one of those emails.

What would he do? Would he spazz out on me? Would he... *shit.* Would he tell my Dad?

Now I was more mortified than when I'd been rejected by him at the bar. This was embarrassing. I was an embarrassment.

Would do I do now? Should I email him back? No, Danaë you've already made things worse by calling him a pus—

Ding!

My head instantly snapped to the direction of my iPad and I got a glimpse of the new Gmail notification.

Oh no.

My heart pounded and I slowly lifted my hands to reach the device, but they started shaking again. I clutched my hands to my chest, my heart now in my throat. I was no longer tipsy. I was certain that fear had flushed all the alcohol out of me.

You called him a pussy but look at what you're doing now? Being a pussy by not reading his reply. You called him it, so own your shit. Own it.

I drew in a long breath, released it seconds later and reached for my iPad. I opened it and Cassian's email popped up first on my list. My finger cautiously clicked on it.

Dear Miss Westbrook,
I'll be seeing you tomorrow in your office at two p.m. Alone. I want to hear you tell me how much of a pussy I am to my face.
Enjoy the rest of your night, Danaë.

My mouth fell open and a flush of adrenaline surged through my body. I had to read his email one last time to make sure I wasn't imagining things. After reading it again and realizing that Cassian had confirmed that he was seeing me tomorrow my heart wouldn't stop racing.

He's joking, right? Surely he must be joking.

I didn't waste time to send my response.

Dear Mr. Acardi,
Please, please, please, ignore my last few emails. I was wrong and I shouldn't have called you that. It was a BIG mistake and I'm really sorry.

Send

I nibbled on my bottom lip, awaiting his reply. I waited for five minutes. Then ten minutes. Ten minutes turned into twenty minutes. Forty minutes went by and before I knew it, an hour had gone by.

Not one response came in from Cassian.

Maybe he's gone to sleep?

I glanced at the digital clock at the top of my screen seeing that it was 11:11 p.m.

He must be sleeping.

I settled on sending him one last email before going to sleep. It was a miracle at how I could entertain going to sleep after what I'd done but the Pinot Noir was starting to catch up to me and my heavy lids were slowly starting to close as my tiredness roamed through me.

Dear Mr. Acardi,
Again I deeply apologize for my previous emails. Please ignore them. I've been drinking tonight, and I really shouldn't have sent all that to you.
Please forgive me.

I cringed internally at the fact that I was begging for his forgiveness because of my childish ways.

I hope to still see you next week with Christian to discuss the expansion of your hotel. However, if you no longer want me as your lead accountant then I'd completely understand, and I'll let my father know that someone else would be better suited for the job.
Kind Regards,
Danaë Westbrook.

All I could do was hope and pray that I hadn't completely fucked up my father's business relationship with the Acardis by deciding to call Cassian a pussy.

Man... why did I have to be such a childish idiot tonight?

One thing was certain, I was staying far away from Pinot Noir from now on. It was the devil's juice and had turned me into a completely different woman tonight. I needed to stay away from it for good.

When I arrived at work the next day, I was bright and early. Despite tossing and turning in my sleep all night, I'd made it to work without feeling like I wanted to die.

Cassian still hadn't responded to my emails and it had me feeling anxious knowing there was a possibility he was coming down here today to hear me tell him how much of a pussy he was.

I scrunched my face up at the thought. How could I ever tell a man like him to his face that he was a pussy? I didn't have the balls to do that at all but the liquor courage I'd received last night had tricked me into thinking I could when I sent him that email.

He's not coming. Just relax, Danaë. He's a busy man who hasn't got time to waste. Just relax.

So that's what I did. I relaxed and stayed busy with work. My iced chai tea latte from Starbucks kept me motivated to complete my tasks and by twelve-thirty p.m. eighty percent of my to-do-list for the day was done.

Knock! Knock!

"Hello, Miss Westbrook."

I looked up from my desk to see Deyjah standing in the doorway of my office. She didn't actually have to knock because today I'd decided to leave my door wide open so I could see anyone that wanted to enter. I appreciated her polite nature though.

Deyjah was an attractive woman. Her ebony brown face housed sharp, chocolate eyes, thin brows and a dainty nose. She rocked a black pixie cut and I somewhat envied the fact that she rocked short hair so well.

"Hey, Deyjah. You okay?"

"Yeah I'm okay." She nodded. "I just wanted to check in on you and ask if you've had your lunch yet?"

"I'm just about to," I told her. "Wanna eat together?"

"Yes, girl." Joy bubbled within me at her agreement. "I'd thought you'd never ask."

My father had a private catering company provide free lunches for all his employees every day. They never really had to spend money on food unless they really wanted to.

Deyjah and I headed to the staff cafeteria on the second floor and grabbed our lunch. This was the perfect opportunity for me to get to know the beauty that worked at the front desk and the perfect distraction from thinking about Cassian. The catering company was serving Mexican food today, so we had a variety of Mexican meals to choose from.

While we ate our chicken tacos and fries, Deyjah told me all about her time here at Morgan & Westbrook. She'd been working at the company for six months and absolutely loved it from the sound of things.

She loved my father and said he was the kindest boss she'd ever had. She loved the work culture at Morgan & Westbrook and how friendly most people were. She loved all the benefits she got such as free food, a free gym membership at one of the best gyms in Chicago, health insurance, paid vacations and sick leave, including a free MacBook to work on. One thing no one could deny about my father, he spoiled those who he loved.

I also learned that Deyjah was a year younger than me and a single mother. She showed me a picture of her son and his cuteness melted my heart. He was the spitting image of her.

We were done with our lunch an hour later and said our good-byes. She headed back down to the ground floor whereas I went to my office on the third floor.

While on the elevator, I checked my phone to see the time was one-thirty p.m.

He's not coming, Danaë. Don't trip.

By the time I was back in my office, sitting on my chair, I plugged my AirPods into my ears and got right back to work as Megan Thee Stallion's *Tina Snow* EP played in my ears.

I kept myself zoned in on work, too focused to check the time. However, twenty minutes later the time was made known to me when two firm knocks sounded through my music.

I took out an AirPod, looking over at my glass door that showed Deyjah's friendly face. I motioned for her to come in and she nodded before stepping in. I glanced over at my iMac's clock to see that it was *one-fifty p.m.*

"Hey, sorry to interrupt you once again, Miss Westbrook."

I shook my head at her to dismiss her weary look.

"No, no, it's fine, girl. You saved me in fact. I was getting lost in these facts and figures," I explained with a warm smile. "What's up?"

"Well..." She sauntered over to my desk and plopped down on the teal seat opposite me. I know you'll be looking for an assistant soon, Miss Westbrook and I kno—"

"Please, Deyjah, call me Danaë."

She enthusiastically nodded.

"Danaë... I know you'll be looking for an assistant and we're still getting to know each other but I'd loved to be consider—"

"You're hired," I told her.

"Wait... what?" Her eyes bulged.

"You're hired," I repeated. "You're my new assistant, Deyjah."

My father had told me yesterday that he wanted me to hire an assistant and I told him I'd already found the perfect woman for the job. He was shocked to find out I wanted his receptionist as my new assistant, but he was all for it.

Yesterday when she'd been so accommodating in helping me set up my key card to get past the security gates, I knew that this was a woman I'd love having around me every day. Her energy was vibrant and refreshing and having lunch with her today proved what I already knew.

She was my new assistant.

And my father knew that too because he'd already gotten her replacement ready to start whenever. He was just waiting on me to break the news to Deyjah about her new role and now that I'd done that, my father would go ahead and get her replacement in.

I'd been planning to tell Deyjah the news at the end of work as a surprise for her to go home with but since she'd brought up the topic of being interested in being promoted as my assistant, I knew the best time to tell her was now.

"Oh my God!" she exclaimed, clapping her hands together. "Oh my God. Thank you, Danaë. Thank you so much! I promise I won't let you down."

I observed her happy reaction with a smile before my eyes fell to my iMac's clock on the top left-hand corner.

2:04 p.m.

Told you he wasn't coming.

Reassurance poured through me and my smile strengthened. I had nothing to worry about because he wasn't coming.

"Okay, okay, let me leave you and get back to work downstairs. For the very last day!" She squealed and jumped out of her seat.

I giggled.

"Yes, beautiful. For the very last day."

"Ahhh!" She squealed once again. "Thank you! Thank you! Thank you! I swear I could just kiss you right now, but I won't, don't worry."

I laughed harder.

"Okay, okay, I'm gone. Promise!" She flashed me a toothy grin before she skipped all the way out my door, closing it behind her.

There was no greater feeling than being able to put a smile on someone's face and I was so grateful to have done that for Deyjah.

Five minutes later I was back in my zone and listening to Megan Thee Stallion telling me how much of a big ole freak she was until the telephone on my desk rang. I pulled out my left AirPod, resulting in my music to pause as I pressed the phone to my ear.

"Hello?"

"Hey, Miss Westbro... I mean, Danaë."

"Hey, Deyjah." The corners of my mouth lifted at her correcting herself. "What's up?"

"Just calling to let you know that Mr. Acardi is coming up to your office right now. The security guards let him through when I was away from my desk and I saw him just as I came out the elevator. He asked for your floor number and I told him."

I swear my soul left my body at the exact second she'd finished telling me what she'd done.

"W-What?"

"Mr. Acardi is here to see you and I told him your floor. He should be with you any second now."

Jesus.

"Miss Wes... Danaë, is there a problem? Did I do something wrong?"

"No, Deyjah, yo—"

Knock! Knock!

I couldn't bring myself to turn to look at my door straight away like I usually did whenever someone knocked.

"Thank you, Deyjah."

"You're welcome. Enjoy the rest of your day."

The line dropped and I carefully removed the phone from my ear to place it back to its holder.

I slowly turned to the door and that's when I saw him. Penetrating my soul with those sexy eyes of his. I took in how great he looked in all black. He was clad in a black blazer, a black turtleneck and matching black pants. Today he wore a gold Cuban link chain that complimented his outfit well and he had two diamond studs locked in each ear.

I quickly got up from my seat as he pushed open the door to enter. Once he stepped in, I immediately began talking.

"Good afternoon, Mr. Acardi," I greeted him in the politest tone I could muster as he took bold strides into the room. "It appears that you didn't see my email expressing my apologies about the stupid remark I made yesterday and explaining that seeing you next week as planned with Christian would be best, unless you wanted a new accountant."

The stoic expression he held as he walked deeper into my office did nothing to suppress my nerves. His silence was deafening too.

Seeing that he was almost to the front of my desk made me continue speaking.

"Mr. Acardi, once again I'm sorry for what I..." My words cut short when I saw him walk around my desk and like a deer caught in headlights, I froze. That was until I remembered he was coming closer to me and I tried to back away but ended up backing into my chair. My breath hitched as he caught up to me and left the tiniest gap between us. That heavenly saffron scent of his filled my nostrils and heat stirred inside me.

I was looking right up at him which I didn't have any choice but to do since this man was so damn tall. I was sure he was well over six foot three. Those alluring eyes and plump lips were the two main features I couldn't keep my eyes off.

Lord... this man is too fine. It has to be a sin at how fine his ass is.

He hadn't said a word yet and it was starting to drive me crazy. I needed to hear him speak because all this silence between us was only building the tension. The way he was staring down at me was intimidating. Intimidating and yet here I was, liking every second of his piercing gaze.

You can't just stand here in silence. Say something, Danaë.

"Mr. Acardi, you haven't responded to what I've said and now you're standing right in front of me, quite close I might add. Is everything okay?"

"No everything isn't okay," he finally spoke, still not taking his eyes off me. That baritone of his was a drug I knew I would never be able to get enough of. "I've heard everything you said but I haven't heard you say the one thing you emailed me last night."

My heart skipped a beat at his mention of last night.

"Mr. Acardi, I told yo—"

"Quit acting like you don't know my name," he cut me off, a tightness forming in his eyes.

"Cassian," I corrected myself after a quick breath. "I told you it was a mistake."

"No it wasn't. You meant exactly what you wrote, and I want to hear you call me it right now."

My heart skipped a few more beats and I decided that I needed to distance myself away from this man.

I gave him one last look before turning away from him and saying, "Cassian, I shouldn't hav..."

His hand grabbed my arm and I looked down at it. A tingling sensation formed on my skin, then my eyes landed up on his brown pools that oozed with seriousness.

I was pulled back in his direction and once facing him again, his grip loosened on my arm and this time, he lifted both hands to my waist. Like a flame to a candle, I'd been lit and the fire burning throughout my body I didn't see going out anytime soon.

He leaned towards my ear and said, "I want to hear you call me a pussy, Danaë."

I could do no such thing. I didn't have it in me, and I knew he knew that. The courage I'd received yesterday from my liquor had been a façade. One big fat façade.

Hearing him say the word pussy sounded too sexy and I wanted to hear him say it again. I *needed* to hear him say it again.

He moved away from my ear, standing in front of me once again and stared down at me.

"If I have to repeat myself, we're going to have a problem and you don't want a problem with me."

His grip on my waist tightened and feeling those large hands of his press deeper into my skin through my high waisted skirt was enough to make me want to risk it all with this man right here, right now. The affect this stranger had on me was truly insane.

"Cassian, I made a mistake," I admitted. "You're not a pussy. I was drunk and I said some shit that I didn't mean."

"Keep lying to me like I won't knock all this shit off your desk and lay you on it so I can spank you till you learn your lesson."

Oh. Shit.

"You meant what you said, Danaë. I changed the plans of our meeting and you got mad. Didn't you?"

I took a deep breath and as I exhaled, my head slowly moved up and down.

"I can't hear you."

"Yes," I revealed, feeling inclined to obey his every wish and command. "I was mad."

"And why were you mad?"

"Because I wanted to see you alone."

I really couldn't believe how easy and quick my responses were now flowing out my mouth. This man was dangerous. He'd been wearing burgundy the first day I'd ever set eyes on him, screaming his dangerous nature but today he wore black telling me that he could easily become the death of me if I didn't watch out.

"Now that wasn't so hard to admit, was it?"

His hands left my waist, and he lifted a hand to the side of my neck, gently caressing my skin with his fingers. Chills went up my spine at his simple yet impactful touch.

Silence filled the space again and as he stroked my flesh, our eyes never left each other.

This man was dangerous and yet I knew I wanted him. I'd wanted him from the very moment I'd set eyes on him and today, nothing had changed. My body ached for him in the worst way and most of all, my yoni was dying to feel him slide inside her.

I extended my neck, allowing him to get a better feel of it and I reached up to touch him but the moment I moved was the same moment he let go and stepped away from me. My spirits fell at his lack of touch and the new distance between us. I took a closer look at him, noticing how his lips were now pressed together and his posture stiff.

I decided to kill our silence by saying, "Clearly you wanted to see me alone too since you decided to show up today after all."

He broke into a small smile that eased the hardness settling into his face.

"I definitely wanted to see you alone, Danaë," he voiced coolly. "And I definitely want to do plenty more things to you. Things I want to do to you right now on this desk..." My breath caught in my throat at his words. "But that can wait until tonight."

I blinked a couple times, caught off guard by his last sentence.

"Tonight?"

"Yes, tonight," Cassian repeated, walking back over to me until the gap between us was gone.

His hand wrapped around my throat and my nipples hardened at his gentle yet firm grip. He pressed his lips to my flesh, kissing up my throat until he reached my ear. When I felt his tongue lick on my ear lobe, a moan was fighting to get out of me, but I kept it at bay. One slow lick was all he gave me before he whispered, "You're going to be my little slut tonight, Danaë."

My mouth parted slightly and the passage between my thighs was now leaking at an alarming rate.

With his lips still close to my ear he asked in a low tone, "You ready to become my pretty little slut, Miss Westbrook?"

I didn't hesitate to answer him.

"Yes."

"Address me properly, Danaë."

"Yes, Cassian," I corrected myself. "I'm ready."

"Good girl," he praised me before moving away from my ear and staring down at me. Holding me captive with one single look that made my pussy throb. "I suggest you take the rest of the day off. You're gonna need all the rest you can get because I'm not letting you out of my sight once I have you in my home tonight, Danaë. I haven't forgotten what you called me and don't think you won't be punished for it because you will. Be ready at eight. You'll be picked up outside your apartment then. Before you ask, yes, I have your address and no, you don't need to know how I got it. I'll be seeing you tonight."

After saying those last words, he released my neck, stepped away from me and headed to the exit. Leaving my office and me completely speechless.

Even seconds after his departure, I hadn't moved from my spot and my entire body felt numb. I wasn't even sure I was still on this planet anymore because I felt like I was having an out of body experience.

That definitely just happened, right?

Indeed, it had and the memory of Cassian's hands on my body, his tongue on my ear and his warm breath tickling my skin while he whispered the nastiest shit in my ear had my cheeks hiking.

That man screamed danger and me being the thrill seeker, wanted every part of his dangerous ways. I'd told myself that all I wanted to do was stay focused on my career and my coins and believe me, I had no intentions of breaking my focus. It's just that now... someone had been added to my list.

I was focused and ready to be anything he wanted me to be.

CHAPTER 8

~ CASSIAN ~

*A*ll I need was one night.

One night to have my way with her and I was sure that would be it. One night to explore the warm passage between her thighs, get a plentiful taste of her juices and that would be it. One night to have that gorgeous body of hers all to myself with no distractions and I would be good. I would no longer want her.

8:05 p.m.

I took a peek at my phone's clock only to lock its screen and place the device down to the counter.

The car I'd had pick her up was on its way to me now and with each passing moment the anticipation overwhelmed my soul. Just the thought of me being able to smell that heavenly scent of hers that I'd been thinking about all damn day, the thought of being able to touch her and place my lips in places I'd wanted to from the moment I first laid eyes on her was enough to make me brick hard.

I gripped my glass, chugging down the remaining brown liquor it housed. The liquid spilled eagerly down my throat and once I was done, I dropped the empty glass down with one hard slam. My face hardened as my throat burned from the aftertaste and the fire travelled to my chest.

Where is she already?

I knew damn well the drive from her apartment to mine was about ten minutes and here I was, letting impatience convince me that she could get to me in less than that time.

I thought back to this afternoon, in her office when I'd finally had the chance to see her alone. I knew my arrival had surprised her and she probably thought those cute little emails she sent me were enough to make me forget about what she'd called me last night. Well, she was dead wrong for thinking that. She'd awoken the beast in me, and he wasn't going anywhere until he'd got what he wanted.

Ding!

My eyes dropped to my phone to see a text from Pierro, one of my trusted soldiers and occasional driver.

Pierro: *Arrived, Capo.*

Pierro: *Heading up.*

I saw the time was *8:12 p.m.* and I smiled at the fact that she was here.

I left my kitchen, walked out of my house and headed to the doors of the private elevator a short distance away from my door. I watched as the elevator's number box above started going up and I swear, each time it increased onto the next level, it felt like a damn eternity was going by. I dug my hands into the pockets of my sweats, waiting for the elevator to arrive. Eventually, the top floor was reached, and the silver doors slid out the way to reveal Pierro.

"Capo," he greeted me with a firm head nod, and I sent him one back.

He moved out the way and it felt like time had suddenly stopped.

Why is she so fucking beautiful?

She had her hair lightly curled in that way that I loved the most, minimal make up which was a good call because by the time I was done with her tonight, it was about to look like Picasso had gone crazy all over her face. My eyes roamed down to the mocha brown jacket and Fendi scarf shielding her body and my hands flexed in my pockets at the image of me taking all that shit off. I looked up to gaze into those brown eyes of hers that had a mixture of excitement and nervousness.

"Appreciate you, P," I told him without taking my eyes off her. "You forget how to say hi?"

Seeing that I was finally addressing her, she blinked a couple times before a small smile graced her glossy lips.

"Hi," she said, stepping forward.

I grabbed her hand before she could utter another word and took her straight ahead to my ajar front door. I let her go inside first before I followed and kicked the door shut behind me.

"Cassian..."

Once we were inside, I pushed her up against my front door before taking a few steps back 'til there was a reasonable sized gap between us.

She'd said my name but that was the last thing I was thinking about right now. I needed to be able to look at her freely without anyone else's eyes on me. Now I finally had the chance to do so.

Those dark brown eyes looked right back at me, not backing down. The first time I'd met her, I'd been tempted by those eyes to know what story this woman had. Now that I'd caught a glimpse into her story when I'd met her again at her father's firm, I'd successfully been persuaded to have my way with Danaë Westbrook. It wasn't just her eyes that tempted me though, it was her whole aura. There was just something about her that radiated in ways that words could not describe. From the way she looked at me to the way she carried herself - that was enough to convince me that this is what I needed. Plus, the drunk emails that she'd sent had provided a great incentive in washing away any doubt I had about us fucking.

"You're checking me on not saying hi when you've clearly forgotten how to say hi too," she spoke up moments later, ending our silent stare down.

That sassy little mouth of hers.

I couldn't even lie, I loved it. I loved how she wasn't afraid to speak up, especially to me.

"When you deserve a hi, I'll let you know."

"Oh, so I don't deserve one right now?"

I shook my head 'no', watching her carefully. Initially, she'd been taken aback by my words but now amusement flowed from her eyes.

"Why not, Cassian?"

God, did I adore the way my name rolled off her tongue.

I opened my mouth to respond but she beat me to the punch.

"What exactly," her hands moved to her scarf, tugging at the fabric until it was off her body, "is it," she dropped it to the floor and went for the first button on her coat, "that I," then the second one, "deserve?"

And by the time she was finished talking, the third one had been unbuttoned and she pulled open her coat, sliding it off her shoulders until it dropped to the floor.

My heart started beating so fast that I was positive that the only stage for it to go into next was a heart attack.

Oh, she knows what she's doing.

I inhaled sharply as I took in every part of her.

She knew exactly what she was doing to me and that right there was a problem.

Danaë Westbrook wore a red mesh bra and a matching thong

with a garter belt attached to stockings. The color red, my favorite color I might add, never looked better and I had to remind myself to breathe, exhaling deeply as I couldn't stop watching her. More like ogling the fuck out of her.

That body I'd lusted over since seeing it on her IG, I had right in front of me. It was even more perfect in person. She had ample sized boobs that I badly wanted to squeeze, a soft looking stomach that I wanted to brush my lips across and long legs that I was anxious to see the flexibility of.

I'd thought that I'd be the one solely in charge tonight but Danaë coming dressed to see me like this? She'd officially got one up on me. I was the one supposed to be punishing her, but it was clear that I was the one being punished by the fact that I'd been deprived of this beauty for so mothafucking long.

"Like what you see... Capo?"

The little Italian that had slipped out of her was enough to make a small drop of pre-cum leak in my boxers.

"Get on your knees," I ordered. "Right now."

A coy smile grew on her lips. She started going low until her thighs touched the floor and she was on her knees in front of me.

"I'm the one supposed to be punishing you tonight, Danaë." I took a step forward, shortening the gap between us. "And here you come, looking sexy as fuck in lingerie in my favorite fucking color..."

By the time I paused talking, the gap between us was gone and she looked up at me while I towered over her.

"Calling me boss in Italian and looking at me like you're the innocent one here. You're asking for trouble; you know that shit, right?"

The smile on her lips only strengthened before she replied, "I know and that's exactly what I want."

I felt her dainty hands touch my calves through my sweats and a fire flickered inside me.

"I already told you I'm ready to become your pretty little slut tonight, Capo."

Her hands travelled up the back of my thighs before circling round to touch the front of them. She stroked upwards, aiming to land her palms on my crotch and that's when I stopped her by grabbing her wrists. She focused back on me with a confused look.

"You don't get to touch me until I say so."

Her confusion vanished and all that remained was a look that told me she knew exactly what time it was.

"Hands behind your back, Danaë."

She quickly obeyed.

"And don't you dare move them."

I lifted my shirt, removing it from my body and chucking it over my head before moving to my sweats. I noticed the way she admired my physique, staring hard until her eyes raised to mine again. Our eyes stayed locked as I pushed my sweats down my thighs and my manhood quickly sprang up to attention.

The mixture of admiration and apprehension that shined in her eyes was enough to make me smile but I fought against it. She was happy by what she could see but also fearful and I didn't blame her. I wasn't carrying an average weapon between my thighs, so I understood her reaction, but it changed nothing.

One night. That's all I wanted. Scratch that - it's what I *needed* to be clenched of the thirst I had for this woman.

Once my sweats were down to my ankles, I stepped out of them, kicking them to the side. I straightened up and reached forward for Danaë's face. I gently stroked her cheek, feeling into her smooth skin before moving my fingers towards her lips. Without even having to tell her, she opened up for me and I slid two fingers into her mouth which she slowly and eagerly sucked on.

"Mmmh, look at you..." I couldn't help but chuckle. I was truly pleased at her mood. She wasn't lying when she said she was ready to be my slut for the night. "I wanna see that same energy when the real thing goes in your pretty little mouth."

She nodded, still sucking both my fingers in a slow, steady rhythm that only made my hardness worse.

I pulled them out her mouth only to cup my base and position my shaft right in front of her lips. Her mouth opened but before she could swallow me whole, I pulled back and her face lifted.

"Don't you dare move those hands forward, Danaë," I warned before pushing ahead and she opened up wider, allowing me to send my dick down her throat as far as it would go.

From the way her mouth molded perfectly around my length, to the way she kept looking up at me, this was the feeling of pure bliss. I was controlling the speed and rhythm, but Danaë was controlling the connection and right now I never felt more controlled.

"Shit."

Back and forth I moved out of her mouth, feeling her saliva and my juices mix together to coat my shaft. As I moved I could see her head moving too, meeting my thrusts. So I decided to stop and let her do her thing. She worked her magic, going back and forth, gradually increasing her speed. I bit my bottom lip, marveling over the sight of her eating me up as best as she could. Her gag reflex started acting up a couple times, so I spoke up.

"Squeeze your left thumb in your palm behind your back," I instructed as I pulled out of her mouth.

She went quiet for a few seconds, but I sensed she was doing as I said.

"Done?"

She nodded.

"Good. Now keep it there and open up."

Again her lips opened for me and I slid right back into place for her to do her thing. It only took a few moments for her to realize what the tip I'd given her did. Now her gag reflex was almost non-existent, giving her a better chance to take more of me.

"There you go... suck that shit... all the way to the back of your fucking throat... that's a good girl."

Danaë did her thing and I mean she really did her thing. She still had her hands behind her back, but she didn't need them because baby girl was doing bad all on her own. Her mouth was relentless. Swallowing my shit up like a popsicle that she just couldn't get enough of. Then she started doing circular motions with her tongue just below the part where my tip ended, and I swore I almost lost it.

I wasn't a moaner. That was something I left to the women that I engaged with but tonight with Danaë's soft mouth wrapped around my dick, I felt the sudden urge to moan.

"Ughhh, fuck!"

And just like that I did, shocking the hell out of myself.

My hands suddenly went to the back of her head and just like I'd pictured having the pleasure of doing, I wrapped my fingers in her curls and began to control her head movement.

"You're trying to turn me into a little bitch tonight, huh?"

Up and down my rod she went, according to my control. The squishy noises of her mouth moving with my juices and her saliva sounded.

"Making me moan and shit."

I heard her moan while I kept pumping her head up and down my shaft. That shit just turned me on even more.

"I bet you want me to nut in your mouth right now, don't you?"

Again she moaned and my horny state heightened. My dick

hardened between her lips and I knew that if I didn't stop soon, I was about to do exactly what she wanted.

"And you'd swallow that shit right up, wouldn't you, you nasty little bitch?"

She moaned again and I smirked to myself before stopping my movements. I released my dick from her mouth, told her to get up and once she rose to her feet, I grabbed her waist and sent her over my shoulder.

I heard her giggle lightly and I led the way to my bedroom upstairs. Her gentle hands stroked my back, and my heart couldn't help but warm at her touch.

By the time we entered my bedroom, my motion sensor lights switched on and the room was illuminated for us.

"Alexa, dim the lights by 50-percent."

There was a brief pause before the female robotic voice announced, "Dimming the lights by 50-percent."

I crossed the room and once by my bed's side, I dropped Danaë down to it. I headed to my ottoman and grabbed the Magnum sitting on it. I tore the packet open with my teeth and guided the plastic shield over my shaft. Once done, I went for the other required tool sitting on my ottoman. I stood in front of my bed, watching her watch me and my hands as I unwound the rope.

There was a fire in her eyes. One of lust that seemed to grow stronger the more she observed me handling the rope.

"Is that for me?" she queried before sinking her teeth into her bottom lip. I saw her take a peek at my hanging member then she focused back on me.

"You know it is."

Now that the rope was free from its knot, I walked round to the bed's left side. I admired the sight of Danaë now stretched out on my bed, still looking as mouth-watering as ever in that lingerie of hers. Just as I crouched down to reach under the bed's mattress, she spoke up.

"So you tie up women often?"

I felt a smirk grow on my lips and I pulled out the steel ring anchor point that had been specially drilled into my bed's frame.

"Only the ones that intrigue me enough," I confessed, placing the rope through the ring. "Which isn't as often as you think."

I formed a tight knot, tugging on it to make sure it was secure before eyeing Danaë's hand that was by her.

"So I intrigue you?"

"You do," I confessed.

She dropped her focus once again to my dick. I knew she wanted him, but she wasn't about to get him again for a while. Not until I was ready for her to.

She looked over at the rope currently knotted to the silver ring in my bed's frame. I'd brought out my finest stash out tonight for her. Bamboo silk ropes that I didn't just use on anybody. I actually hadn't used these on a single soul. Not even Evoni got the chance to have these bad boys on her. They weren't cheap and I just didn't think to ever use them on Evoni. They seemed too special to be used on just anyone. They were red too, matching Danaë's lingerie. That damn lingerie that I was still so pleased by.

"Are you ready for me to tie you up or are you going to keep playing twenty-one questions?" I asked, ready to see this rope wrapped around her flesh.

She smirked and as she lifted her hand towards me, heat curled down my spine.

"I'm all yours, Capo."

I didn't bother wasting a single second after she spoke. I grabbed her hand, tying the rope around her wrist. Not super tight but tight enough to the point where it was secure. I made my way round to the bed's opposite side and did the same.

Once finished, I came to stand in front of my bed, admiring the new position I had her in. I'd only tied her wrists to the bed but kept her ankles free. I had a feeling this was her first time being placed in this position and I didn't want to overwhelm her completely with the feeling of being restricted. I'd told myself this was only one night between us but a part of me wanted to see her here again with her ankles tied to my bed too. Maybe see her again so I could do shibari on her and brush up on my technique.

Knock it off, Cass. This is only for one night.

She still had a lustful look on her face and from the way I was looking at her now, it wasn't about to go anywhere.

I climbed onto the bed, grabbed her ankles and spread her legs wider apart. She swiped her tongue across her bottom lip as our eyes stayed connected. I suddenly pulled on her ankles, sliding her down the bed as far as she could go while tied to my bed. Surprise settled on her pretty face.

"I hope you know I'm holding you to that, Danaë."

She blinked a couple times out of confusion, so I decided to remind her about her words from minutes ago.

"You just told me you're mine." I lifted her legs up, bending them back till they were by her sides. "This pussy's mine." I stared at her shielded pearl that had formed a wet patch on her thong. "Mine to touch..." I pressed a finger to the middle of the red fabric, and she shivered at my touch. "Mine to taste..." I crept down low to administer a gentle lick to her pussy. She was so wet that I could taste her juices through her panties. And my God did she taste good. "Mine to fuck..." My lick turned into a push of my tongue against her covered clit, resulting in her to whimper. I gazed up at her, unable to stop the smile appearing on my face.

"All fucking mine."

After speaking, I decided to shut up and quit with all the talking for now. I was starving and the only food I needed for the rest of the night was the heavenly center between Danaë West-brook's thighs.

I hadn't even given her a real punishment yet, but it was fast approaching. She'd agreed to be my slut for the night and there was no going back now. Tonight, she belonged to me and I was about to make sure she never forgot that shit.

CHAPTER 9

~ DANAË ~

"You just told me you're mine." He lifted my legs up, bending them back until they were by my sides. "This pussy's mine." The way he was looking at my pussy as he staked his claim on me turned me on in the worst way. "Mine to touch..." He pressed a finger to my middle and I shivered at his touch. "Mine to taste..." Watching him bend low to lick my warmth set my soul on fire. "Mine to fuck..." He pushed into my entrance through my thong, and I whimpered. His eyes found mine and an alluring smile appeared on his plump lips.

"All fucking mine."

His words confirmed what I already knew. What I knew from the moment I got into the Bentley that he'd sent to pick me up from my place. Tonight I was his for the taking and there was no turning back now.

He didn't waste a second getting my panties out the way. He snatched them down my thighs until he was able to pull them off my ankles and throw them over his head. That alluring smile of his remained and he flashed me one last sexy look before his tongue darted out his lips. He dove right in, keeping his hands in place around my thighs.

At first I felt nothing.

His muscle moving against my muscle felt like gentle yet soothing rubs. Something I thought I could handle especially since I was still tied up. I was the type to touch on the lucky man who got the privilege of tasting between my thighs but with my wrists bound to the sides of Cassian's bed, I was stuck in place. Unable to touch him as I saw fit and believe me, every part of that hot body of his I wanted to lay hands on. This man was attractive with clothes on but without clothes? His attractiveness had gone off the charts and laying eyes on those large muscles and rock-hard abs made me feel the urge to want to lick and kiss on every part of him.

Moments into his gentle laps on my lower lips was when I suddenly felt... *everything.*

"Cassian... uhhh..."

He worked his magic, using his tongue to stroke my folds before dipping into my hole and curving his flesh inside me. It was an action that he repeated over and over again that had me moaning louder and louder with each passing breath.

"Cassi...annnahh!"

The more he repeated it, the louder I moaned and the wetter I got. My eyes shut, unable to stay open because of the pleasure racing through me.

My legs started to tremble but that only seemed to encourage Cassian to keep going faster, fucking my pussy with his talented tongue. Faster and faster to the point that I could feel a high coming until he suddenly stopped.

His head popped up and I'm sure he could read the disappointment showing on my face. He didn't utter a word which was something he hadn't bothered to do ever since he first started eating me up like his most adored food. He was a silent beast, focused on driving me to the point of insanity.

He pressed his lips to my left inner thigh, gently kissing on it up and down. The tickling of his beard against my skin made a small smile grow on my lips.

This little tease.

He moved to my other thigh, kissing all up on it. His kisses turned to long, wet licks and I was anxious to feel those licks on my yoni once again. His licks continued for several moments until I couldn't take the teasing anymore. I needed him to give me what I needed.

"Cassian, please," I begged him in a low tone that made the corners of his mouth quirk up.

"Hmm?" he groaned in response, still licking on my skin, making goosebumps pepper my flesh.

"Please," I repeated, watching him closely as he watched me. "Taste me."

Finally, he granted me my wish, planting a kiss to my entrance and diving right back in the one place I needed him to be. His tongue seemed to dive deeper this time and my mouth parted wide to form an 'o' shape.

"God... Cassian!"

My cries filled his room and my back arched as Cassian ate me out in the best way. This was the fourth man that I'd had devour me like this and all the others before him were being put to shame. Compared to him they were all amateurs. None of them had my mind blown like this.

This man right here was a demon. He had to be because the way he knew how to use that tongue of his just didn't seem godly at all. How could it be when he had me cursing out to the gods above?

"Ahhhhhh, fuck!"

I attempted to touch on him, but my hands couldn't move, and I remembered the position I was placed in.

Damn it.

Again he stopped tasting me and I sighed, feeling my body sink deeper into the bed. His lips landed back on my thighs, kissing me softly and that's when I realized his game or should I say his punishment for me.

Oh, he definitely wasn't lying when he said I was getting punished tonight.

Cassian's constant removal of his lips from my pussy just when I could feel my orgasm approaching, was a reminder his truth. And it angered me.

"Cassian," I called out to him. "Enough with the teasing. You're driving me crazy."

He didn't say a word. Those piercing eyes of his held me hostage and the longer he refused to speak up, the more my frustrations heightened.

"Just give me what I want, Capo," I demanded.

The sudden thrust of two fingers into my tightness made me jolt right up but of course I was still held down by my tied wrists.

"You seem to have forgotten who's in charge here, Danaë."

"Cass—"

"I'm not done talking," he voiced, slowly sliding out my walls. "You can speak when I'm finished."

I was taken aback by his command but also turned on even more than I already was. This man had a way with words that was truly powerful. He could tell me to shut the fuck up right now and not speak for the rest of the night. Would I actually do it? Probably not because of my slick ass mouth but I knew I would love hearing him attempt to put me in my place.

"You've not only seem to have forgotten who's in charge here..."

A soft whimper fell from my lips when he rocked his warm fingers into me.

"You seem to have forgotten that you're on punishment."

Out they came. Then they slid right back in again.

"You don't get to cum until I want you to."

He was talking but a part of me had lost concentration because I was enjoying the feeling of his fingers constantly moving in and out of me.

"I say when you've been punished enough, not you."

After that statement, his fingers were replaced by his lips and he started to deliver my punishment all over again. He brought my thighs to his shoulders, keeping them hooked in place with his hands as his tongue dipped into my warmth. He would get me to the point of complete excitement, having me cussing and moaning his name then let go. Leaving me with nothing.

Denying me of the right to cum.

It was a true mind fuck if you ask me because I couldn't even reach down and make myself climax. My hands were literally tied. Sweat beads had broken out on my forehead and my entire body was on fire.

"You're so cute when you're mad."

A chuckle escaped him as he watched me. I badly wanted to flip him the bird but of course I couldn't. I knew my next words were about to be a risk but I didn't care. I needed to lash out because of the way he had me feeling.

"And you're a piece of shittttttttttttt!"

My eyes widened and my head lifted to the white ceiling above as Cassian's mouth devoured me. This time he didn't stop and his hands gripped my thighs tighter as his tongue brought me to euphoria. Stroke by stroke I felt myself melting into his embrace and before I knew it, my peak was reached.

"Ughhhhhh!"

My first, long anticipated orgasm of the night came through but I didn't have a chance to relish in it because Cassian's fingers started rubbing on my clit. Bringing me to another orgasm at the same time as my current one.

My entire body shook as I rode the incredible wave that Cassian had brought me to. I was no longer seeing the ceiling of his room. All I could see were white spots of different sizes as I lost control of my mind, body and soul.

Oh my God... this man is a demon.

It was the only explanation as to how he knew how to get my body to submit to him like this, this damn soon.

I eventually came down from my high and my head dropped, allowing our eyes to meet. He looked me up and down, carefully taking in my lingerie. When he looked at me, that same approval that had been present when I first gave him a presentation of what I'd worn just for him returned but right alongside that approval came desire.

His large hands moved up my body, giving birth to a swarm of butterflies in my stomach. He stroked on my stomach only sending that fluttery sensation into complete overdrive. His hands reached their destination, gripping my breasts to provide them with a tight, generous squeeze.

My thighs fell from his shoulders as he stretched over me. He lowered himself, still squeezing on my mounds and brought his face near to mine. The weight of his body settled on me, sending a surge of heat down below. He brought his lips closer to mine and just as I welcomed the moment of our lips joining, he remained frozen.

I tried to read him but all I saw was an emotionless expression. He was trying to hide his emotions from me which I didn't really get but my confusion vanished when he meshed his lips to mine.

He led and I followed, letting him take control of my mouth

and kiss me in a way that took my breath away. With deep sweeping strokes of his tongue, Cassian took possession of me, making it clear who was in charge here. He allowed me to taste my juices on his tongue.

He sadly broke our embrace seconds later and my heart felt like it was shrinking. I wasn't ready for our kiss to end at all but I guess Capo was.

Cassian suddenly yanked my left bra cup down, wrapping his mouth around my nipple and hungrily sucking on it. He released it only to spit eagerly on my hard bud using his warm saliva to coat it before sucking it all off again. Once satisfied with his work, he moved onto the next one, doing the same thing and I helplessly moaned, loving how nasty he was being.

The moment we'd both been dying for quickly followed and he raised my thighs, pushing forward to enter his new home. A part of me was fearful because of how big he was but I shook it off. I'd wanted the python that he carried between his thighs way before I'd laid eyes on it and since I'd already sucked on it, the only thing left was for me to have it within my walls.

Inch by inch he pressed into me and my muscles tensed with each inch. Pain followed his motions but as soon as he retreated and slowly nested back into me a couple times, the pain began to vanish. All that remained was...

Nirvana.

"Aghhhh..."

Each time he pulled out, I was hungry for more of him and he gave me what I needed. Diving in and out my portal in gentle, smooth motions. His hips slapped into mine and I did my best to meet his pounds, thrusting upwards.

His groans sounded and I was sure I could hear a couple moans too. He was dead right about me turning him into my bitch. This pussy had him going crazy and he couldn't deny it even if he tried. The noises coming out from him and the hardened expression he held proved it.

"Cazzo... non so se riuscirò mai a starti lontano adesso."

He muttered something in Italian and I wanted to ask what it meant but his thrusts got faster and I got caught up by his overpowering pounds. I was then reminded that this man didn't carry a python for no reason and I was beginning to feel him so deep inside that I was afraid I was about to burst a lung or something. His dick had a slight hook to it and I swear it was poking spots I didn't know could be poked.

"Oh my... Oh my Godahhhhhh!"

Why does it hurt so good?

"Who's a piece of shit?" he asked, reminding me of my words from before.

"Aghuaaaahhhhhhhh!"

Speaking coherent sentences was now a lost art to me. All that emitted from my mouth were sounds of ecstasy. He laughed at my inability to properly answer him, pulling out of me only to dive back in.

"Uh-huh, that's what I thought."

His hips started winding in circles in my cave and I swear I lost it one hundred times more.

I wanted to run. Take a break at least but it was a foolish thought. There was nowhere to run from the savage that this man was. I was no longer giving him the same energy as before. His strokes had become too overwhelming and I'd frozen in place with wide eyes and a wide mouth. Sensing my shift in energy, he gripped my thighs and lodged them in place around his torso.

"Keep that same energy and take what you wanted, Danaë." Deeper and deeper he worked my middle. "You wanted me to have my way with you the first night we met, now you're being a weak bitch?"

Wow. He was right. I'd wanted this from the start and here I was trying to run. Run from everything that I'd wanted when I first laid eyes on him. I just didn't know it was going to be this intense.

Why did I feel like I was going to cry?

"I'm no... I'm not weahhhh!"

I felt his hands cup my jaw and squeeze tight as his eyes bored into me.

"Say that shit like you fucking mean it."

"I'm not weak," I obeyed him.

"Yeah you ain't." He chuckled. "You ain't weak cause you're taking this dick just how you're supposed to, Danaë. You better make that pussy nut all over this mothafucka too. Make me repeat myself, I fucking dare you. Soak my shit all the way up as you take him all."

I nodded, water filling my lids.

So that's what I did. I took Cassian Acardi until I couldn't no more. I allowed him to voyage through the deepest part of me, connecting us as one. I allowed him to take me to the highest of peaks that I never wanted to come down from. I allowed him to whisper the nastiest shit to me while he dove into me nonstop. Reminding me of how much of a slut I was for him. His pretty little slut that he had bound to his bed and willing to take every inch of him. I allowed him to make me cum so many times that I lost count after six. All I knew was that they kept coming one after the other. Most of all, I allowed him to leave a mark on me. A mark so strong that I wasn't sure it could ever be removed. I now felt bound to him as if being with anyone different after him would be a mistake. A curse even.

Capo had me wrapped around his little finger and I didn't see a way out.

CHAPTER 10

~ CASSIAN ~

*O*ne night was what I'd convinced myself that I needed with Danaë Westbrook and now I wanted one hundred more.

I was hooked.

I didn't want to admit it but what was the point of denying the truth to myself? Seeing her right beside me this morning was an alluring sight that I didn't want to tear away from. Her curls from last night were still somewhat present, much looser and slightly tangled from all the hair pulling I'd been doing. But they still perfectly framed her face and made her look like the goddess I needed in my bed every single night. Even in the morning, she was a marvel, and I knew if I didn't get out of bed, I would spend the rest of the morning watching her like one creep.

Beyonce asking about a crowd going apeshit blasted in my ears as I did my daily run along the lakefront trail and the Chicago Riverwalk. I was religious when it came to working out and despite how much it had been a struggle getting up at six a.m., I wasn't about to let procrastination get one up on me.

As I ran, heat radiated through my chest not just due to my physical activity but also because of the woman currently tangled in my sheets.

Letting a woman stay the night in your bed? That never happens, Cass.

Okay me saying *never happens* was a big stretch but it wasn't something I'd done in over two years. Back when Imperia and I were together was the last time I let a woman stay the night in my bed because since she was carrying my child, Imperia lived with me.

No woman had ever stayed the night in my bed since my situation with Imperia. It just wasn't something I could be bothered to do with another woman. If we were fucking, I'd either:

1. Fuck her in my bed and sending her on her way once we were done.

OR

1. Secure an unoccupied hotel room for her and meet her down there when I was ready. When we were done, I'd leave.

Things with Danaë were a whole different ball game and I didn't know how to feel about it. This was only supposed to be one night, and I'd gone against the grain, allowing myself to indulge in the possibility of seeing her again. I'd been foolish to think one night would be enough now that I'd gotten my dose of her. She was carrying a very addictive treasure between her legs and I wanted more.

I slowed down once at the midpoint of the Riverwalk and rested my hands against my knees, quickly catching my breath.

I pulled at my armband that sat on my left bicep and slid it down to my forearm until I was able to see my iPhone through the band's plastic screen. I unlocked my device, went straight to my security camera app, entered in my password and clicked on the live feed of my bedroom.

She was still asleep which wasn't a surprise since it was six-thirty a.m. Her face was masked by her hair again, like it had been when I'd woken up. I'd moved it out the way, but it was back in place, telling me that she'd been fidgeting in her sleep.

I watched her carefully, feeling the urge to cut my run short and head home to join her.

Nah, leave her be.

Just as I stood upright and decided to stop my endless staring, Danaë's legs started shifting under the sheets. Once those hands started moving under the covers and tried to feel for me, I knew she was awake.

She continued to search for my body with her hands. Upon realizing she wasn't finding anything; she removed her hair out her face and those dark browns fluttered wide open. I quickly pressed the microphone button on my screen and spoke to ease her panic.

"Don't worry, I'll be back before you know it and you'll be able to use those hands the way you really want to."

She started looking around, trying to see where my voice had come from. She wasn't going to find what she was looking for though because I'd had this little bad boy installed into my bedroom so good that even I struggled to find it at times. When she realized she couldn't find it, silence was all I received from her until her raspy morning voice sounded through my beats.

"I'm not sure I want to use these hands anymore since I've been left here all alone."

The corners of my mouth curled upwards into a smirk.

That damn mouth of hers... that mouth I'm liking more and more of.

"Is that your way of telling me that you're missing me?"

My gaze drifted to my Apple watch which I tapped on, heading to my messages app to contact my hotel's manager.

Breakfast needed, I typed then pressed send.

"You wish," she said, and I could hear the smile in her tone before I looked back at the screen to see it. "How'd you know I was awake, Capo?"

Fuck.

Without being able to stop him, my third leg swelled in my pants. I'd been called that name plenty of times before by others but every time it now came out of her lips, I was turned the fuck on.

Ding!

On it sir, my hotel manager texted back.

"Security cam."

"I see," she responded, sighing softly. "So you can see me right now?"

I had automatic blinds in my bedroom that I operated whenever I woke up. Since Danaë was in my bed, I'd only opened them up halfway, allowing a small ray of light to filter through the windows.

"Yes."

I observed as she lifted the covers from her frame, revealing her naked state. She slowly placed a hand between her thick thighs, spreading them further apart as she touched herself.

Here I now stood. On the edge of Chicago's Riverwalk, staring down at my screen with a moist mouth, tense muscles and a hard dick. Luckily, it was quite early in the morning and hardly anyone around but me. So no one was about to notice me drooling over this temptress.

"I think... I think I've found a better use for my hands after all."

She dipped two fingers into her cave, and I took a deep breath to calm myself.

"I don't remember giving you permission to touch yourself without me, Danaë."

"I don't remember giving you permission to leave me here all alone, Cassian."

The laughter that fell out my mouth, I couldn't stop even if I tried.

"So you do miss me," I commented, my eyes sealed on her fingers that slid in and out of her. Those fingers that I wished were mine.

"Maybe."

"Admit it and I'll give you what you want."

"And... and what's thaaaat?" Her voice rose in pitch as she continued to rock her fingers back and forth. "Uhhh..."

The fact that she was playing with herself with the sound of my voice in the background almost made me want to buss in my pants, but I kept my control.

"For me to replace those fingers with something better."

"Mmmhh..." She threw her head back and cupped her left breast with her freehand. "Sounds tempting."

The more I watched her finger herself and play with her boob, the more I wanted this run to be officially over. I needed to go home and not just enter my actual home, I needed to enter my new home inside Danaë.

"But I think I'll pass," she voiced and that cocky tone of hers only made me ten times eager to get home.

She must want to get punished again.

"You think you'll pass?"

She nodded, bringing her fingers out her portal, raising them to her mouth and slipping them between her lips. Her freehand was still on her breast, flicking away at her nipple as she sucked her nectar off her fingers. I almost groaned at the sight.

Why the hell is she so goddamn sexy? I let out a strained, heavy breath. *That still doesn't change the fact that she's being stubborn as hell though.*

"A'ight bet," I agreed. "Make sure you shut my door on your way out my crib when you're done getting ready to go. Pierro will be waiting for you outside."

"Huh?" Her brows squished together, and she jolted up the bed.

"You heard me."

"You're kicking me out?"

Reading the annoyance wash upon her face made me smirk.

"I'm simply telling you to shut my door on your way out, Danaë."

"Which is your way of telling me to get the fuck gone, right?"

"You're the one that refuses to admit what you want," I reminded her.

"You know what I want."

"And you know I'm not giving you what you want until you say that shit."

She went quiet and I spotted the roll of her eyes which added to the list of reasons why she was getting punished as soon as I walked through the door. She began to smile, and I did too when she said the words I'd been dying to hear.

"I want you, Cassian... right now."

Bingo.

"I bet you do," I answered. "Breakfast is on its way to you in a few so get cleaned and get dressed so you can eat. I've left you a fresh towel and some clothes in the bathroom."

"Aren't you joining me?"

"No."

"Why not?" She pouted. "I just told you I want you right now. You know you want me too."

"I'm still in the middle of my run which I'm not cutting short for your stubborn ass that refused to tell me what I needed to hear when I first told you to. When I'm done, I'll be back."

I didn't bother waiting for her to reply. I turned off my mic, locked off my phone and slid my armband back into place on my bicep.

Continuing my run was now my only focus and despite how difficult it was to move with a swollen bulge, I made it work and concentrated on finishing my workout.

Thirty minutes later, I made it back to The Palazzo. I was greeted at the front desk by a few employees and once in the elevator, I leaned against the silver walls, watching the elevator head up to the top floor. Moments later the doors slid open. I stepped off the elevator with purpose and also desperation. I'd put on a good front so far, but the truth was, I'd wanted Danaë just as bad as she'd wanted me.

I arrived at my front door, pulled out my key card from my iPhone's armband and hovered it above the door's sensor. When I got the green light, I rushed in, kicking the door shut behind me and I made a bee line for my bedroom upstairs which turned out to be a big mistake once I got to the middle of the stairs and realized I'd sensed movement below me.

I backtracked, stepping down a few steps and turned my head to look over the stairs. That's when I spotted her through the glass windows. Sitting on the patio's outdoor sofa with her legs crossed underneath her and nothing but a champagne flute pressed to her lips.

I started walking down the stairs, keeping my attention anchored on her. I was able to see her wearing my white shirt and from where I was, it seemed my white shirt was all she wore but I wanted to get closer to make sure. The closer I got, the better I was able to see the rays of sunlight glowing on her melanin rich skin. She had no makeup on, a complete fresh face and she still looked prettier than anything I'd ever seen. Just like I'd guessed, she was wearing nothing but my shirt. Her cleavage was slightly exposed but still cloaked.

I stood in the middle of the open doors, crossing my arms against my chest. Danaë placed her now empty glass to the white coffee table and I noticed all the half empty plates scattered across it. A silver tray was nearby with barely any food left on it.

"Someone's been eating good."

"Free food always tastes so much better," she commented, dropping her gaze to my attire with a small smile. "How was your run?"

"Good."

"Good." She nodded to herself. "You get it all out your system?"

I felt heat rise within me at her query.

"Get out what?"

"You pretending not to want me when we both know that you do."

I let my arms drop from my chest and I sauntered over to her. She seemed unbothered by my movement until I was directly in front of her and able to grab her waist.

"Cassian!"

I said nothing in response and flipped her over until she was laying on her stomach. She started giggling and that's when I raised my shirt off her backside to deliver a loud, hard smack. She both whimpered and moaned at the sensation.

"Cassian..."

I delivered another slap and once again she cried out in pleasure and pain. I directed my hits directly on her sweet spot that sent vibrations to her pussy.

"Ahhh!"

I gave her a couple more spanks until I was satisfied. I bent low to caress her sore flesh with my lips. Her moans filled the atmosphere as my lips glided along her warm skin and just when I could sense her enjoying it too much, I bit into her softness. While biting into her, her scent consumed me. Everything about my Sauvage soap on her skin had me gassed and my desire for this woman skyrocketed to the point of no return.

How does my shit smell ten times better on her?

"Once I get out that shower I promise you you're about to pay for all that teasing shit you did on camera," I announced, gently scraping my teeth across her skin before using my hands to squeeze her butt cheeks into my face.

I only stopped squeezing so she could hear me clearly say, "You've forgotten who had you moaning and squirming like a little bitch last night, huh?"

"Cassi—"

"Uh-uh, don't moan my name. That shit ain't gonna save you now 'cause you knew exactly what you were doing, Danaë. Playing with your pussy without me. You're so fucking nasty."

I squeezed her cheeks tighter then spread them apart, bending low to spit into her slit a couple times. I marveled at the sight of my saliva dripping down her back passage for a few seconds before pushing forward to suck up all the mess I'd made.

"Shitttt and you call me the nasty one," she whispered after I was done sucking on her. "I don't wanna wait until you get out the shower. I want you now, Capo."

I released my grip from her butt and straightened up. She quickly turned her head over her shoulder to look at me. The hunger burning in her eyes was unmissable and I'm pretty sure she could see the exact same thing in mine.

"Please," she begged me with those innocent looking orbs of

hers. "I want you to teach your slut a lesson for all the teasing she was doing on your camera... punish me... please, Capo."

Shit, she didn't have to tell me twice.

"Get up," I ordered, stepping away from her. "I want you over the balcony. Hands behind your back."

She obeyed, flashing me her pearly whites as she made her way to the balcony.

"And lose the fucking shirt. Don't be hiding that body from me."

By the time twelve p.m. arrived, Danaë had been dropped home by Pierro and was on her way to work. She'd gone home in my Essentials hoodie and sweats and even though that shit looked big as hell on her, she rocked it well. She hadn't brought any clothes apart from the lingerie she'd turned up in last night. The lingerie that had been torn to shreds. It had definitely served its purpose but after a while I just wanted her naked.

Despite being late for work, Danaë was still keen on going in and I admired that about her. She was still prepared to go into work even though she'd been dicked down to the point that she could barely walk or stand properly.

I on the other hand, needed a breather before I started my day. I took an hour nap after eating a quick meal and by one p.m. I was getting dressed into my custom suit and heading downstairs with Imperia's voice talking through my AirPods.

"I'm glad you finally decided to call me back after five hundred years, Cass."

"Chill." I tittered at her dramatic remark, seeing that I was four floors away from the basement level. A level that you could only get to through my private elevator. "I've just been busy is all. You good?"

For the first time in ages, I didn't feel uncomfortable while talking to Imperia. Having a phone conversation with her right now felt natural. Like two friends that were just casually talking.

"Yeah," she replied. "I just wanted to check in on you and hear your voice, it's been a minute since we caught up."

"Yeah it has been but like I said I've been busy."

"I get it, you're a busy man. That ain't ever gonna change," she acknowledged.

"I'm sure you're been busy too, being on your boss woman shit," I said, a smirk creasing my face. "How's business going?"

"It's going good. I can't complain."

"That's what's up."

Imperia owned a luxury perfume brand that she'd started two years ago. A year after we lost the baby. She used it as a way to distract herself and it paid off pretty well because her perfume line had quickly become a household name amongst women worldwide. Since it was a women's perfume brand, it wasn't something that particularly interested me, but I made sure to give her a fat check to help kick off her company before she launched it. A check that she'd clearly used well since she was selling out after every restock in her first year. Now that she was more established, she had a bigger team and bigger stock, so her bestselling products were readily available.

"Did you need something, Imperia?" Now that I was one floor away, I was eager to end this call.

"Not really," she admitted. "Like I said I just wanted to check in and hear your voice... I miss you, Cass."

"I feel you." I ignored her comment about missing me, not wanting to delve into the topic of her feelings. The elevator doors granted me my exit and I stepped out, walking ahead down the narrow hardwood walkway. "Appreciate you checking in and I promise to do the same sometime soon."

"Okay, Cassian. I'll be holding you to that."

I knew she would because one thing about Imperia, she couldn't let go. Even after all these years of our child being dead and our relationship being no more, she was still bent on holding onto me. A part of me wished she would just find some other nigga to bother but I understood why she didn't want to let me go. I was the first and only man she'd carried a child for and in her mind that shit really meant something.

Once our call ended, I was at the end of the walkway and looking at the various bodies moving through the main space. I was greeted with head nods, waves and verbal hellos and I simply gave them all a respectful nod without saying a word. That was the number one thing I could count on with my guys, they knew exactly what to do and didn't have to be coddled.

The sight of my soldiers doing their jobs without having to be told what to do always made me feel at ease. Since I was in charge of moving guns through the city, the perfect spot for me to do so was underneath my baby, The Palazzo. By combining both my businesses together, I'd created an easy workflow for not just myself but my soldiers. They could come and go as they needed to through the discrete tunnels beneath the hotel.

While I watched my soldiers' package various gun models, my mind drifted to this morning and how elated I'd been to see Danaë in my bed. Other than the mind-blowing sex we'd just had during the last couple hours that had put a pep in my step, I was still sprung on waking up to her this morning before I went for my run. She seemed to fit right at home and brought a vibrance to my place that I'd failed to ever do. Her presence alone had comforted me and that pearl between her thighs... yeah, she'd done a motha-fucking spectacular job at sucking me in.

"*Cazzo ... non so se riuscirò mai a starti lontano adesso. (Fuck... I don't know if I'm ever going to be able to stay away from you now).*"

The Italian I had uttered to her yesterday while we had sex

had been a dangerous truth that I didn't want to face. It was only supposed to be a one-time thing and I'd gone and let myself comfortable with the thought of having her over here again.

Nah, it's not happening. One night was what you wanted, and you got that and more when you fucked her all over your apartment this morning. It's over with, Cass. It's strictly business between you and her from here on out.

CHAPTER 11

~ DANAË ~

*A*ll the men before me were now nobodies.
Nobodies.

Nobody worth talking about or thinking about because the only person worth my attention when it came to sex was Cassian. I'd met this man last Saturday and three days later he'd turned my entire world upside down. Four days had passed since we'd been intimate and the flashbacks that constantly flew into my head, particularly at the most inappropriate times, had me blushing.

He'd had his way with me just as I'd wanted when I first laid eyes on him. He'd brought out a side of me that I didn't bring out for any man. I would be lying if I said I didn't want the chance to be in his bed again.

Could you really blame me though?

That man not only exuded big dick energy, but he also carried one and he knew exactly what to do with it. I'd been won over by his savage, yet charming ways and I was entertaining the idea of us continuing whatever the hell it was that we'd started.

However, I had to ask myself several times if that was a good idea. I had never had a friend with benefits before and I'm not saying that I couldn't handle one, I just wasn't sure if I could be bothered to handle one.

What if I catch feelings?

I wasn't about to act like I was this emotionless being, willing to throw caution to the wind and fuck whoever with no feelings involved. All I'd ever done in my life was feel. I didn't know how to turn that shit off. So there was a strong possibility that if I continued to mess around with Cassian, I would catch feelings for him. Something I knew was a bad idea because Cassian would never feel the same way.

How did I know that?

Well, it didn't take an Einstein to recognize that Cassian's skills in the bedroom were due to his vast experience with other women. Other women who had most likely caught feelings before he ditched them. I didn't want that same predicament to be mine which is why I knew being in his bed again couldn't happen.

Knock! Knock!

I looked up from my Mac and saw Deyjah standing in the doorway of my office.

"Lady D." A smile clung to my lips as I heard the personal nickname Deyjah had coined for me. "Miss Brown here to see you."

I got up from seat, my smile growing as I laid eyes on the beauty that appeared as Deyjah stepped out the way.

Imperia Brown was an ebony skinned baddie that I'd felt privileged of sharing the company of. She was taller than my five eight stature, giving the aura of a super model only she wasn't skinny. Imperia was thick with curves gracing her tall frame. Thick thighs definitely saved lives because the short skirt Imperia wore today allowed her thighs to shine and I was certain I'd been saved laying eyes on them. Her inky black hair was in a half up, half down ponytail, emphasizing her sculpted face. A thin nose sat above her heart shaped lips and as a grin split her face in two, her gleaming white teeth revealed themselves.

We became connected over a year ago when Imperia found my financial consulting company and brought me on to help with her finances. She owned a luxury fragrance company that was doing extremely well and from all the profits she was bringing in monthly, Imperia wanted assistance knowing what to do with all her new money. As we worked together we began to get closer and today I could consider her a friend. We hadn't seen each other in almost a year though, which was why I was now rushing over to her with open arms.

"I see someone remembered that she has a life in Chicago," Imperia announced as she welcomed my tight embrace.

We squeezed each other and I giggled, glad to finally be back in her presence. Her jasmine aroma filled my nostrils as our hug continued. I looked over her shoulder to see Deyjah giving me one last smile before she stepped out the room, closing the door behind her. Our hug lasted for a few more seconds until we broke away from each other.

"I've missed you, girl. It's been too long," I said, holding onto her hands and gently rocking them from side to side.

"Too damn long," Imperia replied, smiling wide.

I led her over to the teal chair in front of my desk and took the identical seat next to her so we could be close.

"You're back in Chicago for good this time, right?"

I nodded.

"No more sneaking off and leaving me all alone with a bunch of amateurs who haven't got a damn clue what they're doing with my coins."

A chortle slipped out my lips at Imperia's disapproval of the other consultants she'd tried to hire after my abrupt departure.

She'd fired them all because she said they just didn't know their shit like I did. Rather than wasting time and energy trying to find my replacement, she decided to tackle the advice I'd given her and began managing her investments all by herself.

"I'm serious, Nae. No one knows what the hell they're talking about the way you do."

My cheeks flushed at her compliment.

"Promise to never leave me like that again?"

Her doe shaped eyes immediately pulled me in and had me shaking my head 'yes'.

"Scout's honor," I assured her with a mock salute gesture which made her laugh.

I decided to dive deeper into the topic of Imperia's company and finances to find out what exactly I'd missed. I reached across my desk for my notepad and pen, bringing it to my lap and finding a blank page as I listened to her mellow voice.

She told me all about how Imperia Perfections LLC was doing in terms of sales and marketing and I was glad that her fragrances were still popular till this day which wasn't a surprise to hear because her perfumes smelled divine. I'd run out of my last bottle and needed to re-up ASAP.

I took notes while Imperia talked about her baby and I swear seeing the fire in her as she talked was inspiring to say the least. I loved being around people who had suddenly woken up one day with a great idea and were now making money from the physical manifestation of their imagination.

Imperia told me all about the new investments she'd made over the last few months, the new bank accounts she'd opened, her retirement funds and all her future financial goals.

Hearing that Imperia had been handling her finances well without me was great to hear and it was even greater knowing that although she'd been doing quite well without my guidance, she still wanted me back in the fold.

After Imperia was done catching me up on her business and personal finances, I took over the conversation. As a financial consultant it was my job to make sure that my clients were in the best possible financial position that they wanted to be in, if not better and make sure that they were using their wealth in the best way possible. Imperia had a major goal to be a multi-millionaire before she turned thirty and right now, she was twenty-seven which gave her three years to reach her goal. With me back by her side, we wouldn't need all those three years to reach it.

Our business meeting lasted for about an hour before we left my office and made our way in an Uber to *Dynasty*, the hookah lounge we were meeting Adina at. I made sure to book Imperia in as my last meeting of the day at five p.m. so that once we were done, we would head straight to my bestie.

It took our Uber driver twenty minutes to arrive and once we entered the cozy venue, I scanned the smoke-filled space for Adina. There were a few bodies in the lounge, enjoying their time with their hookah, food and drinks. The melodic sounds of Ariana Grande's 34+35 played in the background. I eventually spotted my favorite person, sitting on a two-seater sofa in the far-right corner of the room and she noticed us too, waving her hand high with a cheerful grin.

"Took y'all long enough," she greeted us, jumping out her seat and allowing me to admire the tight-fitting purple dress printed to her shapely body. "Money Maker Imperia, is that you?"

"The one and only, honey."

Adina and Imperia embraced, and I smiled at their interaction before my eyes fell to the hookah and various drinks laid out on the black coffee table in the middle of our seating area.

"Hey, boo." Adina reached out her hand to me and I grabbed it, allowing her to pull me in so we could hug and kiss each other's cheeks.

"Hey, sexy," I greeted her back while we hugged.

Adina broke our hug so she could look me in the eyes to ask, "Have a good day at work?"

I nodded and her grin widened.

"Did you?"

She returned my nod then motioned for us to sit down and I took the sofa opposite Adina's whereas Imperia took the empty seat next to her.

Adina didn't waste a single second lifting tequila shots our way. Imperia and I took them back like champs, knowing we had no choice but to give into Adina's wild ways. She'd already gone ahead and ordered shots, cocktails and the hookah for us all so I knew she wasn't here to play games about our girls' night out. The hookah had been set up and Imperia and I reached for a pipe after receiving a fresh tip from Adina.

"It's been too long, girl," Adina told Imperia. "How have you been?"

"I've been good, just working nonstop."

"Aka making those coins!" Adina exclaimed, making me and Imperia giggle.

Someone's already started getting lit without us, I mused, noting the fact that Adina's eyes were low and her tone dripping with exhilaration.

"I love that for you."

"Thank you, love," Imperia replied.

While they caught up, I smoked on my hookah, taking it deeply into my lungs and exhaling to release a strong, thick cloud of strawberry smoke.

"How about you? The last time I saw you, you were looking for a new job right?" Imperia questioned her and Adina nodded.

"Yup and I got one..." Adina turned to look at me. "At Danaë's new baby Daddy's company."

I playfully rolled my eyes at her, lifting the hose from my mouth and trying my hardest to keep a straight face.

I just arrived and somehow, he's already the topic of this conversation.

Another tell of Adina being lit was the fact that she'd brought up Cassian. She was a motor mouth when she had liquor flowing through her veins, both a blessing and a curse because it meant that she would tell you whatever you wanted to know. Tonight, I had the feeling she was going to spill everything she knew about Cassian and I, making it a curse because I was now subjected to think and talk about the man I hadn't heard from in four days.

The morning I'd arrived home after being with Cassian, the first person I hit up to tell was of course Adina. We'd exchanged a few texts with mostly Adina sending shocked and delighted texts of what had happened so fast between Cassian and I.

Dina: *What. The. Fuck!!!!!!!!!!!!!!!*

Dina: *Are you fucking kidding me?*

Dina: *Tell me you're not playing with me right now, Danaë Louisa Westbrook.*

Me: *I'm not playing with you.*

Me: *I was with him last night.*

Me: *And this morning.*

Dina: *OMG.*

Dina: *You sneaky little hoe!!!!!!!!!!!!!!!*

Dina: *How? Where? Why?*

Dina: *Tell me everything. Right now.*

I sent her a few laughing emojis.

Dina: *Actually no. I'm coming over tonight. You can tell me everything then.*

That night Adina came round to mine and I'd spilled the

beans on everything that had happened with Cassian. From the drunk emails I'd sent him, to him coming to my office and us doing the deed at his breathtaking penthouse. She was my best friend so naturally I felt inclined to tell her everything that had happened, but I made sure to keep the intimate details to myself. She didn't need to know exactly how we'd had sex, just that we had it and I'd loved every second of it... a bit too much I think because I still couldn't stop thinking about him.

"Her baby Daddy?" Imperia's brow shot up into the air. "I didn't know you had a child, Danaë."

"I don't," I said while Adina chuckled at Imperia's comment. "Adina's just being crazy."

Imperia and I were good friends because of the business we had together but we weren't super close. Now that I really thought about it, we didn't actually know all there was to know about each other. I didn't know her past, and she didn't know mine. She didn't even know the real reason behind while I'd suddenly fled Chicago ten months ago. We were friendly but didn't share super personal secrets with each another. Our friendship was mostly based on the financial advice I gave her to help her grow. Adina was only friends with her through me because I'd invited her to party with us a few times and they too weren't the closest. However, now that I was back in the city, I could sense that things between the three of us were going to change in a good way because we'd genuinely missed each other's company. I could see us having our own little squad and I'm sure Adina wouldn't mind turning our duo into a trio from time to time.

"So who's her baby Daddy that she doesn't actually have a child for?" Imperia gave into Adina's running joke before smoking on her pipe.

"You comfortable with me sharing that saucy piece of information?" Adina queried, flashing me curious eyes.

She'd already brought it up and the interest flowing in Imperia's voice told me that she wanted to know. There was no point of shying away from the topic now. I shook my head 'yes', grabbing the dirty martini that Adina had ordered for me and pressing it to my mouth.

"Cassian Acardi," Adina announced as I sipped the crisp liquid. Hearing his name made every hair on my scalp stand to attention and my cheeks burned. "Owner of The Acardi Palazzo, my boss, a client at Danaë's father's accountancy firm and the new man dicking down our pretty friend right here."

Imperia suddenly started choking on her hookah and Adina moved nearer to quickly pat her back.

"Damn, girl, you okay?"

Imperia nodded but said nothing and her face was blank while she regained her breath. She lifted her pipe back to her lips while her focus stuck on me. I didn't have time to think anything of her silence because Adina kept talking after seeing that Imperia was fine, distracting me.

"That's her new baby Daddy."

"He is not." I shook my head at Imperia.

"Is toooo," Adina sang then stuck out her tongue at me.

"He isn't," I disagreed. Imperia broke her gaze away from me and reached for another shot on the center table. "We had a bit of fun but it's not going anywhere."

Adina and I were now focused on each other while Imperia flung back her shot and listened to us talk.

"This is coming from the woman who told me you were keeping things professional between you and him," Adina countered. "I'd say it is going somewhere."

"It isn't though. We haven't spoken since then. He hasn't hit me up and I don't intend to do the same."

We didn't exchange numbers before I left him four days ago

which wasn't necessary anyway because we had each other's emails. However, I didn't feel like emailing him and I guess he felt the same way because he hadn't emailed me either. I'd left Deyjah in charge of emailing him and Christian to remind them about our meeting next week, so Cassian and I had no real reason to hit each other up unless we really wanted to. I'd convinced myself that I didn't want to even though deep down I knew I was lying.

What would I even say?

Dear Mr. I've Got A Big Dick And I Know How To Use It,
Thank you so much for the amazing sex! Let me know when you're free so we can do it again? Oh, and please don't hesitate to tie me up again. I absolutely loved it!

Hell no! I wasn't sending him shit.

I didn't want to come across as needy and by emailing him first, that's what I felt was going to happen. If he wanted to contact me, he would've asked for my number or given me his, but he didn't so it was what it was.

"But you're seeing him next week for your meeting?"

"Yeah but that's with Christian," I reminded her. "A *professional* meeting... besides it's been four days since we last saw or spoke to one another. If he wanted to see me again, I'm pretty sure he would have said something. I don't think it's going anywhere and I'm okay with that. I'm not looking for anything serious and I'm sure he's not looking for anything serious either."

My attention fell back on Imperia who still hadn't said a word yet. She looked slightly uncomfortable for a split second before she spoke up ask, "So you're just tryna have some fun which means you've got plenty other options on your rosta, right?"

"Not really." I shrugged. "The last man I was with was secretly married and the men that tried to talk to me while I was abroad, I brushed off. I'm just doing me right now."

"I see." Imperia gave me tiny nods. "Well if you're interested in tryna have some fun with someone different, I could always hook you up with a few of my investor friends. I'm sure they'd be a much better distraction."

"I much prefer Cassian for her," Adina chimed in. "He looks like the type to rock your world in one night and have you coming to his door with a boombox playing *Let It Burn*, begging him to make you his forever."

"I can't stand you!" I laughed at her reference to one of Jazmine Sullivan's greatest hits. "There is no way I'd do tha—"

"*I wanna be good to you, baby!*" Adina suddenly sang, throwing her hands in the air.

My mouth hung open at her outburst.

"*Call me crazy but I think I found the love of my life, that's right!*" She leaped out her seat and clutched her chest.

"Dina!" I laughed at her as she loudly sang and started swaying side to side to the rhythm in her head.

"*Have you ever felt warm on a cold, cold night?*"

Imperia laughed too and I looked around to see eyes on us as Adina sang *Let It Burn.*

"Dina, people are staring! Stop." My laughter couldn't be contained at her antics.

Adina decided to stop singing, took a glance around the room and when she noticed the faces staring, she confidently waved and smiled at everyone before sitting back down. Cackling wildly to herself.

Yeah, she's definitely lit right now. That's that liquor coming through for real.

"You're stupid," I joked, shaking my head at her. "There will be no boombox outside anyone's door thank you very much. I'm good with doing me."

Adina frowned.

"Bu—"

"So enough with the baby Daddy talk, missy," I cut Adina off before she could talk again. "Imperia and I have each taken shots, but I haven't seen one go down your throat yet."

Adina was already lit but I had no problems getting her even more lit. She smirked, reaching forward for a shot glass and pressed it to her lips, quickly gulping it down.

Cassian became a distant memory as our girl's night commenced. We talked about our lives, work and even placed a spotlight on Adina's love life. She claimed she didn't have one and was living vicariously through me. The last relationship she'd been in was back in college and ever since then, Adina only had occasional hook ups with old flames and rare dates. She wasn't looking for love and quite frankly, I didn't blame her because like Amy Winehouse had sang, love is a losing game.

Our night continued and we ordered more drinks including food. I enjoyed spending time with Adina and Imperia, and it was great getting to know Imperia better. She didn't share much about her love life other than briefly mentioning her last relationship and how she'd fallen in love with her best friend. Her best friend who she'd experienced a great loss with. She didn't go into detail about who he was or what they'd lost. She spoke mostly about her plans for the future with Imperial Perfections, her interests and a bit about her family but that was really it. I understood she wasn't about to be complete open book and she'd open up more in her own time. I was cool with that as I was doing the same. I gave her doses of me without giving too much away.

Spending time with the girls was a real vibe that I didn't want to end. Sadly, I was in my bed by midnight, drunk and horny for one man. I let my tired state take me away from reality so that my thoughts about him wouldn't get the best of me.

The temptation to send him drunk emails ain't about to catch me slipping again!

I was up the next day at ten a.m. with a headache and a sore throat. After an Advil, a hot shower and a bacon omelet, I was back to being my normal self and the payback of all those tequila shots and cocktails had faded from my system.

Three hours later, I was sitting on my father's couch, watching proudness settle in his wrinkle free face.

"One week and you've already done more than my top two accountants have done in a month," he expressed. "Well done, Angel. You're fitting right at home just like I knew you would."

I smiled and thanked him for his kind words.

"You're getting to the bag," he said, surprising me at his use of a phrase mainly used by my age group. "Isn't that what y'all young folks say?"

"Yes, Daddy." I chuckled.

"That's what I thought." He chuckled too before reaching into the plain black gift bag beside his armchair. "So, since you're getting to the bag it's only right you get a brand-new bag to match, right?"

He slowly pulled out a white box and I instantly clocked the black Chanel logo.

"Daddy..." My lips curled upwards. "You shouldn't have."

"But I did. Anything for my Angel. You know that."

I swear the way my father spoiled me with Chanel bags and various other designer bags was a habit that I was sure he loved more than I did.

I left my seat and walked over to him, circling his neck with my arms and holding him tight while my chin rested on his shoulder. He held me tighter and provided me with affectionate rubs.

"I'm sure your mother would be proud of all your hard work, Danny."

The mention of my mother made both a heavy and warm feeling form on my heart. I didn't even remember the woman but the one thing I knew was that I missed her dearly.

"She would have loved seeing you in action, being a better accountant that the both of us combined," he said, his voice slightly breaking.

Talking about her was always a sensitive topic for him but he still talked about her with me. It was his way of keeping her memory alive.

"Thank you, Dadd—"

My words were cut off by a voice that came from behind me.

"Lunch is ready."

I silently sighed, knowing that my father and I's heart to heart had been cut short. I peeled away from him, turning to see Kamora standing by the living room's exit with a content smile.

The one thing my father truly wanted from me was to get along with Kamora so that's why I made sure to come over to his house today for Saturday lunch prepared by her. I offered my help in the kitchen which she took for about an hour until she suggested I go keep my father company.

Minutes later, the three of us were sitting around the dining table, enjoying the cuisine that Kamora had prepared. She'd made a barbeque brisket, mixed roasted potatoes, lobster mac and cheese, butter fried broccoli and fresh salad.

I couldn't even lie; she'd done her thing in the kitchen and I complimented her on the meal while we all ate. Seeing the smile on my father's face as Kamora and I interacted was all I needed to know about how well I was doing in being nice. We shared small talk and my father gassed me up in front of Kamora, telling her how well I was doing at the firm. She seemed elated hearing my success and I appreciated her positive reaction. Once we were finished eating, Kamora and I cleaned up. I scraped plates clean, and she put them away in the dishwasher.

"You're lucky to have a father who spoils you rotten with expensive gifts."

"I am," I agreed placing a dish on the side closest to Kamora's reach.

From my peripheral view, I was able to see her reach across for the dish and place it into the washer.

"Even though we both know you don't need them."

And there she is.

I bit my tongue, trying to deflect away from the quick comeback I wanted to send her way.

There's the Kamora that can't stand how much my father spoils me.

"It's a waste of his money," she continued talking. "You have so much already."

I turned to look at her. For someone so pretty, she knew how to get under my skin and made me see her in an ugly light. Kamora was a bronze skinned woman with maple brown irises, sleek auburn hair that fell past her shoulders and full, pouty lips.

"I do which I'm grateful for, but I can't stop my father from wanting to treat me right," I explained in a calm tone. "He grew up with nothing and made himself into something alongside my mother. He's allowed to spend his money on whoever he wants whenever he wants. I'm also allowed to appreciate and accept everything he gets me."

Instead of responding, Kamora's lips pursed together, and she held my gaze for a moment before looking away without another word. Satisfied that we were no longer speaking, I went back to scraping plates.

Like I mentioned before, Kamora had turned down many of my father's luxurious gifts. If it was an act, she'd done a phenomenal job at putting on a show and now that we were on cordial terms, she felt the need to try coax me into joining her performance. That wasn't happening though.

What Kamora didn't know was that Chanel was my mother's favorite brand when my father and her were in college. A brand she couldn't afford but she'd placed a Chanel bag on her vision board which my father had seen. When Morgan & Westbrook blew up and they started bringing in real money, the first thing my father ever gifted my mother with was that same Chanel bag.

The bags my father bought me were more than just materialistic items. They were the constant reminder of my late mother and how hard they'd worked together to bring their dreams into fruition. It was a sentiment that only him and I truly understood.

Kamora could feel some type of way all she liked. She couldn't come between the bond my father and I had and I believed that's what irritated her the most. Her irritation was her own problem to deal with because I didn't care for her opinions on the wealth of my father or what he chose to do with it. At the end of the day, I was his only child and if the man wanted to spoil me rotten then that's exactly what Trenton Westbrook was going to do. She could either get over it or leave our lives for good.

The choice was hers.

CHAPTER 12

~ CASSIAN ~

"You ou do know I'm getting old right, Cass? Are you going to wait until I'm on my death bed to introduce me to the woman who has your heart?"

"There is no woman who has my heart," I told her bluntly. "And you're not getting old, Zee. Quit saying that. Don't forget we had an agreement. You're gonna live forever, remember?"

Frankie laughed with the corners of her lips tugging up as she watched me.

"So you're telling me there's no one?"

My eyes fell to the gold metal watering can I held and I tilted it to provide the soil below me with water.

"Nope."

"I see," she replied.

I looked back over at her, seeing that she was sprinkling fertilizer onto her rose beds.

This was the only woman who could have me in a pink floral gardening apron on a Sunday afternoon while we tended to her magnificent rose garden. Zietta loved roses and for the past twenty years, she'd been growing them in the backyard of her Winnetka mansion.

Frankie had two residences. A twelve thousand square foot mansion in Chicago and a twenty-five thousand square foot one in Winnetka. Chicago to Winnetka was a thirty-minute drive and Zietta loved the connivence of being able to leave busy Chicago and enjoy the tranquil suburban feel of Winnetka. I didn't blame her because Chicago sure could get hectic sometimes.

"Are you going to wait for me to introduce you to my woman before you introduce me to yours?"

It was no secret in The Family that Frankie was attracted to both the opposite and same sex. Thankfully, when she came out to her father at the age of twenty-one, he was supportive and made sure that everyone else in The Family followed suit. Over the years, Frankie had her fair share of suitors but it wasn't until she reached the age of thirty that she realized women was who she preferred.

She had a long-term relationship with an unknown woman but ended it ten years ago, for reasons that Christian and I were still unaware of. We'd wanted to know why things had broken down but we didn't want to probe into Frankie's heartache because that break up definitely fucked her up in the worst way. She tried to hide it from us but we definitely noticed it. Ever since then, Frankie hadn't been with anyone and it somewhat bothered me that my auntie didn't have a life partner to keep her company.

"Touché," she remarked, sliding an amused expression my way. "You know... I might be mistaken. Maybe I've already met the woman who has your heart."

My forehead creased and I shook my head 'no'.

"You sure?"

I began to scan my mind, trying to figure out what she was getting at and when I realized what it was, I relaxed my face.

"Nah, that's over with. Been over with."

She was referring to Imperia. The only woman in my life she'd ever met.

"Death has a way of pulling people together," she said. "But in your case, it pulled you both apart unfortunately."

"Yeah," I muttered, focusing back on watering the pink roses below me.

"You would have made a great father, Cass." My heart skipped a beat at her words. "I hope you know that."

Deep down I did and that's what pained me the most. I would have been a great father but that chance was gone. I had no desire to think about becoming one ever again. At my current age of twenty-nine, all I cared about was getting money and making sure The Family was good. I was certain that's all I would care about for the rest of my days.

I nodded without saying a word and Zietta took this as her cue to keep shit light and change the subject. We spent the rest of the afternoon together, gardening, watching Zietta's new favorite Netflix show, The Crown, and enjoying a homecooked meal together.

I'd lost my mother at the age of four and sadly, I didn't remember her. Fortunately, Frankie was the best mother figure I could have ever asked for and I was blessed to have her.

Hours later, I was heading home and my baby brother's voice sounded through my car's speakers.

"She got your goofy ass gardening again, huh? And I bet you loved every single second of that shit."

I sucked my teeth at Christian's teasing remark. My eyes stayed glued on the lane ahead as I eased into the slip road to join the interstate 94.

"And your goofy ass missed out on all the bomb ass food," I taunted. "I definitely loved all that shit."

"Yeah, yeah whatever, nigga." He was trying to mask his jealous tone but I could hear it and I chuckled.

"You get Deyjah's email about tomorrow?"

"Yup."

"You excited to see your future wifey?"

"She's not my wifey, fool."

"That's not what those eyes were telling me when I told you I'd be tapping that ass if it wasn't for your interest in her."

Christian was unaware that Danaë and I had slept together and I had no plans on telling him about it right now. I never just came out and told him about the women I was with. If my decision changed then I'd tell him but for now Danaë and I's night and morning of pleasure was our little secret.

Christian and I talked for a few more minutes, catching each other up on mainly business and of course Christian filled me in on his latest escapades with the opposite sex. By the time our call ended I was pulling into my reserved parking spot at The Palazzo.

Once inside my home, I showered, got dressed into nothing but my Calvin's and got familiar with my sheets. I turned on my side, staring at the empty space that she'd been in five days ago.

I pictured that sienna brown skin that my hands had the chance to touch all up on, those irresistible eyes that I'd gotten lost in many times and those full lips that I'd not only kissed but also had wrapped around my member.

Five days later and I still couldn't get her out of my damn head.

I'd ignored all of Evoni's texts that she'd sent during the week because the thought of sliding into her after I'd slid between the thighs of a woman I was convinced was a goddess, just seemed laughable.

The temptation to email Danaë or rock up at her apartment

one night was something I struggled with a couple times. I'd been certain that one night was all I needed with Danaë and post nut clarity would snap me back to my senses but that was the very last thing that had happened. I wanted her again but my mulish ways were hell bent on keeping things between us professional.

Instead of fighting my thoughts for the rest of the night, I pulled my covers out the way and slid my boxers down my thighs. Allowing my aching erection to jump free. I grabbed it and massaged myself with slow, steady motions. The face of Danaë Westbrook was the only thing I had in mind. I stroked myself to that familiar, addictive wave of ecstasy that I'd been reaching every night since we'd parted.

Monday morning arrived and I stood suited in front of my closet's mirror, feeling light on my feet. Staring into my reflection and noticing the gleam in my eyes told me one thing.

You're excited to see her, aren't you?

I was and twenty minutes later as I pulled up in my Lambo outside the Morgan & Westbrook building, my excitement surged through me nonstop.

Christian and I made our way into the building, were let in by the firm's new blonde receptionist and told what floor to go to. Although I already knew exactly what floor to go to, I acted oblivious so Christian wouldn't suspect a thing. Upon our arrival on the third floor, Deyjah's radiant face appeared and she escorted us to our destination.

"Mr. and Mr. Acardi, it's great to have you back here again."

"Great to be here, Deyjah," Christian replied to her as she led us to Danaë's office. "Your pretty ass got a promotion, huh?"

A slight flush of Deyjah's cheeks appeared and she smiled as she nodded at him.

From the way she was looking at my brother, I could tell she was already falling for his entrancing ways. She focused on looking ahead again as we inched closer to the glass door. Once in front of it, she tried to make a move to push it open but was halted by the pull of her arm.

"Uh-uh, allow me," Christian said, making me shake my head with a small smirk.

Anything for the pussy, this nigga will do.

"Why thank you." Deyjah allowed him to push open the door for her.

"A beauty like you should never have to open your own doors."

He and Deyjah lustfully locked eyes one last time before she walked ahead into the room.

"Lady D, Mr. and Mr. Acardi here to see you."

There. She. Is.

"Thank you, Deyjah," she announced, standing in front of her white marble desk.

There's that voice I've missed moaning my name.

"Gentlemen, it's a pleasure to see you both again."

The sight of her in a navy belted bodycon dress made heat course through my veins and land in the one spot that had missed her all week.

"Please come on in and take a seat."

Christian and I stepped forward to the seats in front of her table and just before we sat down, Danaë reached out to shake our hands. Christian beat me to punch which he was clearly pleased by because of the toothy smile he held as they shook hands.

"Good to see you again, D. You don't mind if I call you that right?"

"Of course not." She smiled back at him. "You mind me calling you Chris?"

"You can call me whatever you want, beautiful."

This nigga.

Their hands parted and she turned to me, holding her hand

out with that same smile that had been for my brother. I grabbed her hand, allowing my gaze to linger over that gorgeous face I'd missed kissing all up on. I let my eyes trail down to her body then they lifted back to her face.

I hadn't said a word yet and I didn't plan to for a while. Today all I wanted to hear and see were those sexy lips of hers talking.

The meeting seemed to fly by way too fast for my liking. I never thought I could be turned on by hearing a woman recommend all the ways I could get richer until now. She'd come prepared with locations that she'd scouted out for where Christian and I could open our second hotel location. She informed us about the tourist appeal to each location, its distance away from the airport and the physical appeal of the areas. She also talked about the additional investments we could be making and all the ways she was here to help whenever we wanted her too.

When the meeting came to a close, we were all on our feet again and saying our goodbyes.

"Glad we have you on board, D," Christian told her while they shook hands.

"Glad to be on board, Chris."

During the meeting, Danaë and Christian had gotten real comfortable calling each other nicknames and it lowkey made me jealous.

She ain't even said my name once during this damn meeting.

"I'll be seeing you both soon," she said once our hands joined.

"Definitely," Chris agreed, causing Danaë to smile.

Feeling her hand leave mine so soon made heaviness settle on my chest and before I knew it I was walking out of her office with Christian right by my side.

"I'm with D on us opening up the new branch here rather than outside the city. Tourists mostly come here so it makes sense..."

Each step we took away from Danaë's office was a step I didn't want to take.

Where the hell are you going, nigga? You know fully well you're not done with her ass yet.

I stopped moving and observed Christian walking ahead while he yapped away about the things we needed to get done soon. Things I didn't care about right now.

"We need to hit up our builders and..." Noticing that I'd suddenly stopped, Chris turned around with knitted brows. "Cass, you coming?"

I remained silent but my silence was more than enough to clue Christian onto my plans.

"I should have known you wouldn't have left here without the chance to speak to your wifey alone." He chuckled as I extended my middle finger toward him. "Hurry up, nigga. You're my ride home, remember?"

I shot him a devious smile before turning around to head back in the direction of Danaë's office.

I didn't bother knocking. My only goal was to cut all the distance and professionalism that had formed between us for the past hour. Two things I'd never despised so much until now.

"Mr. Acardi?" Her confusion not only shined in her brown pools but was laced in her voice. "Did you forget something?"

I took bold strides into the space, watching her watch me. I didn't stop moving until I had made it to the other side of her desk and was able to twist her chair to my direction. She gazed up at me, parted her lips to speak but didn't have a chance to say a damn thing because I pulled her up from her seat and brought her to stand in front of her desk. I pressed my chest against her back, pushing her hair to the side so I could have easy access to her neck.

"Cassian," she moaned my name once my lips met her flesh

and I started kissing her. She smelled ten times better than I'd remembered.

"So you finally remember my name after all," I said in a low tone, brushing my lips up her warm skin and kissing her a couple more times.

"I never... I never forgot it," she whispered.

"Yet you failed to call it once during our meeting." I pecked her skin a few more times before adding, "But you had no problems calling my brother by his."

"...Someone jealous?"

"No," I replied, knowing fully well I was lying. "I'm just making an observation."

I slowly slid my hands up her dress, caressing her body through the delicate fabric.

"The same way I observed how good you looked sitting behind this desk, advising me on the money moves I should be making with my company."

My hands went up her thighs, landing on her stomach.

"I bet you'd look ten times better on it though."

"I'm working, Cassian. I can—"

"You can't what?" I cut her off. "You can't be my pretty little slut again, Danaë?"

She was silent but that didn't deter me from moving my hands up her frame until I was able to palm her juicy breasts. Before I could squeeze them, Danaë grabbed my hands.

"No, I don't think I can."

My face scrunched up at her words.

"Why not?"

"Because I hadn't heard from you since the last time we had sex, Cassian," she retorted, trying to move out my grasp but I remained firm in my stance behind her, keeping her trapped in front of me.

"So that's why you gave Chris most of your attention today." I tittered and the tightness eased from my face. "You're mad at me."

"No," she voiced. "I'm just making an observation."

Yeah, I definitely missed all that sass of hers.

"Did you want to hear from me?" I asked her, genuinely curious.

"Maybe."

I let one of my hands leave her breast and wrapped it around her throat while pulling her into me. Bending my head to hers, I curled my lips around her ear lope, sucking on it gently before I dropped down to her nape. My teeth sunk into her flesh, making her whimper.

"Whenever I ask you something, I want a straight answer, Nae," I whispered. "That's not up for debate either. Answer me. Right the fuck now."

I loosened my grip slightly, allowing her to speak.

"Yes, I wanted to hear from you."

I let my hands fall from her body before grabbing her waist, turning her around and branding my lips to hers. My tongue dipped between the seam of her pillow soft lips as I devoured her mouth.

It was the connection I'd been craving for what seemed like forever. All I'd wanted to taste was her lips and now I finally was. She met my tongue and gave it teasing laps with her own.

Our kiss lasted for a few more moments before I pulled away and said, "Be ready at eight. We've got plans."

Just before I could walk away, Danaë grabbed my face and pulled me back towards her lips. Again we connected, tongues colliding and the tension building stronger between us.

I knew that if I didn't end this, I was going to forget all about the fact that she was on the clock and I had somewhere to be. I would clear her desk, lay her on it and give us what we both needed. I quickly tore away from her and stepped back.

"Eight, Nae. Not a single minute later."

A devilish smile appeared on her face and she nodded as she said, "Yes, Capo."

I was then rushing out her room, without looking back to avoid giving into the mental whispers telling me to bend her over on that desk and dick her down for the rest of the morning, not caring about who could walk in and catch us.

"You missed me?"

She nodded, sinking her teeth into her bottom lip. A silk blind-fold shielded her eyes, keeping her from seeing me.

"Say it."

A smirk grew on her lips and she shook her head 'no'. Knowing exactly what trouble she'd started.

"Oh someone's feeling bold, huh?"

I turned to my right, picking up an ice cube from the silver tray by the edge of my bed and slipping it between my lips. I extended my body over hers, bringing my lips to the space between her breasts and trailing the cold cube down her skin. She shuddered at the contact and I saw her move her arms but it was a failed attempt. She wasn't going anywhere and she knew it.

I traced around her hard nipples, taking my time with each one. Her breaths came out in tiny pants as the coldness glazed her skin. I moved down her chest until I reached her bikini line. My eyes flashed up to hers and I watched her carefully, giving her a chance to redeem herself by telling me what I needed to hear. When she didn't say a word, I dropped below her bikini line, letting the cube sit on my tongue as I lapped against her warm folds.

"Ahhhh, Cassian!"

A high-pitched moan escaped her lips and she shook in place, trying to break free. She wasn't going anywhere though because her wrists and ankles were tied in place to my bed. I trailed my lips back up to her bikini line, drawing a triangle before I allowed my cold tongue to rub on her most sensitive bud once again.

"Okay, okay, okay!" she cried. "I missed you! You know I did."

Hearing her confirm what I already knew had me glowing inside. However, I wasn't about to let her off that easily. By now the ice had melted but I continued massaging her pussy with my tongue, causing her to squirm and shake in her spot.

I don't know what the hell it was that had me hooked on Danaë, but I was going to let it take me. I'd lied time and time again to myself about things being strictly business between us. How could it be when seeing her talk business today had only made me want her even more?

Her moans echoed through the space as I ate from her sacred spot, not holding back from making her go crazy. I'd missed tasting her and I wasn't going to hold off on showing her how much I'd missed her. My tongue went from diving into her tightness, rubbing on her moist folds and sucking on her clit.

"Uh-huh, that's right... nut on my face," I ordered between my licks.

"Cassahhhhh!"

"I said..." I pushed a thumb into her butt, causing her to arch her back as much as she could while being tied back. "Nut on my fucking face."

It didn't take long for her juices to spray my beard, lips and tongue and even when she'd came, I dove right back in, devouring up her haven nonstop.

I was hooked, lined up for her alone and I would sink into this woman's treasure for as long as I wanted to. This was only lust and I was sure that nothing was going to come out of this other than two beings enjoying each other. When we both no longer wanted this, it would be done and dusted.

CHAPTER 13

~ DANAË ~

I think I need some time away
I took a little time I prayed
We gon' be alright okay

I opened my handbag, pulling out my phone and smiling as I read the caller ID.

"Hey, boo."

"Don't '*hey boo*' me," she retorted. "Where the hell have you been?"

The elevator doors slid out my way and I stepped off, walking ahead to my desired destination.

"Busy, love."

"We're all busy in this life but you know damn well you're not too busy to let your bestie know you're okay," Adina voiced in a serious tone. A serious tone that only lasted for a few moments before she said in softer tone, "I miss you."

"I miss you too," I replied, feeling bad that I hadn't been hitting her up as frequent as I usually did. "I'm sorry for not hitting you up... I really have been busy."

I arrived outside the white door and wedged my phone between my ear and shoulder so I could bring out my key card.

"Daddy Warbucks working your ass too hard over there?" Adina queried, making me smile at the nickname she commonly referred to my father as. "I think I need to hit him up and convince him to let you take another vacation, this time with me. All expenses covered by yours truly of course."

"Good luck trying that." My key card was now in hand but I hadn't used it to get inside yet. "After the vacations I've taken these past couple months, I don't think he wants to see my ass on a plane for a very long time."

Adina chuckled.

"You're back home from work, right? I could come over in a few and we can catch up on all the time you've spent ghosting from your girl."

"Umm... how about tomorrow?"

"Okay," she replied, going silent for a few seconds before adding, "So you're not at home because that's the first time you've ever declined my offer to come over."

My heart palpitated at her realization.

"Where are you, Danaë?"

"I'm at home," I lied.

"No you're not," she insisted. "You know you can't lie to me, Nae. I'm your best friend. I know you better than you know yourself."

This was true. Adina knew me like she knew the back of her hand which is why I rarely lied to her. She could always figure it out.

"Besides, I heard your footsteps just a few minutes ago. You were walking somewhere... the question is where?"

I pursed my lips together and stared down at the silver key card that had the name 'Acardi' carved into it. Adina suddenly gasped and I winced, sensing the earful that was coming my way.

"Danaë Louisa Westbrook!" she yelled. "You haven't been too busy to hit up your best friend, you've been too *dickstracted* by Cassian Acardi!"

She'd figured it out, just like I knew she would. Deep down I knew that's why I hadn't been hitting her up as frequently.

"Dickstracted?" I snorted. "You really just made that word up right on the spot, Di. I am not distr—"

Her loud laughter almost burst my ear drums.

"You little heifer! You've been getting your back blown by him again and you didn't tell your one best friend. You're too cruel, girl."

"Dina, it's not like that and you know it."

"I don't think it's going anywhere," she suddenly mocked my voice, saying the same words I'd said on our night out over a week ago. *"I'm good with doing me."*

Her laughter continued.

"See this is why I didn't want to tell you yet," I admitted, sighing softly.

"Why?"

"Cause I..."

My words halted when I noticed twisting of the door's silver knob. The door was pulled open and I looked up into the mesmerizing eyes of the only man I wanted to see.

"Dina, I gotta go."

"Uh-uh, we're not done he—"

"Dina, I'll call you later. I promise," I concluded, hanging up on her and staring ahead at the man that held me captive with one look.

I stepped forward, closing the gap between us and standing up on my tippy toes to reach him. When I tried to press my lips to his, he leaned back with a look of disapproval.

"What's wrong?" I asked, sliding a concerned expression his way.

"I told you that Pierro would pick you up."

"And I told you that I was already on my way," I countered, reaching for the back of his head and pulling him into me.

Our lips joined and my soul was set on fire at the connection. I'd been missing those soft lips of his all day. I didn't get a chance to savor the moment though because Cassian pulled away, making me groan.

"Cass, let it go. I'm here now."

I knew why he wasn't happy. He hated me driving to him in the middle of the night. Having Pierro drive me to him made him feel much more comfortable but what Cassian was staring to realize was that I was a woman who walked to the beat of her own drum. I did whatever I wanted, whenever I felt like it.

His disapproval remained ingrained in his face for a few short moments until he softened up and wrapped his arms around my waist.

"You're still getting punished for disobeying me," he stated, leaning into my neck and kissing me.

I smiled, rubbing on his back as he coated my skin with his kisses.

"I'm looking forward to it," I replied.

For the past seven nights, I'd found myself in Cassian's bed. Every night was an experience like no other and I was introduced to more and more of this man's thrilling ways. Some nights he'd tie me up, some nights he'd let me free but keep me blindfolded and some nights even both. Some nights he'd practice shibari on me, an art of Japanese rope bondage, that proved to be a strongly satisfying experience for me and other nights he'd use nothing but those large hands and that incredible tool he'd been blessed with down below.

Who was I trying to fool when I said that I didn't see things with Cassian going anywhere further than the first night we'd had sex?

Yes I still had my doubts about being able to handle a friends with benefits and yes I was still cautious about catching feelings for him but for now I was pushing that all to the side. We were enjoying each other's company and I wasn't going to keep pretending like I didn't want him when I knew fully well that I did. All that extra shit I would deal with when I was ready but for now? All I wanted was him.

"Open up."

I did as he wanted, opening up for him and allowing him to place the wooden spoon into my mouth. The rich tasting sauce settled into my taste buds as I tasted from the spoon.

"Mmmh," I moaned, closing my eyes to savor the taste.

I heard him chuckle and I looked over at him as he stood back in front of the stove, stirring his sauce.

I reached for the glass of red wine sitting to the right of me and brought it to my lips. Letting my gaze fall on the shirtless figure a short distance away. I admired his majestic upper back tattoo of an eagle, flying high. His muscles flexed as he stirred and the sight caused desire to burn a hotspot in the pit of my stomach.

I sure could get used to this...

This hunk of a man, making me one of his favorite Italian meals with nothing but his boxers on. While I sit back on this island with a glass of his expensive Tuscan wine that I didn't know how to pronounce the name of and wait to be served.

I could definitely get used to this.

"I think I'm going to need to ban you from raiding my closet," he commented and my smile strengthened.

He slowly turned to face me. His eyes fell to my clothing which was his white shirt that I'd put on after our moments of pleasure together. It was not only a more comfortable choice than my own clothes but it had his scent, allowing me to feel that much closer to him.

"You look much better in my shirts than I do."

I stopped sipping and rested the foot of my glass to my knee, still holding it tight.

"That's why I wear them," I teased. "To show you how to actually rock them."

A grin appeared on his handsome face and he turned back around to complete his cooking.

It took about fifteen minutes for Cassian to finish cooking and by the time we were finished eating, I relaxed back into my seat and happily sighed. A smile crossed Cassian's lips as he watched my reaction to the fire ass meal I'd just devoured.

We eventually moved to his living room area and sat on a three-seater together. My legs laid across his lap and an episode of Snowfall played on his mounted tv screen but we weren't really paying attention.

Cassian was no longer shirtless but that didn't stop me from stroking across his chest and feeling on his solid frame. His hands would massage my legs that sat on top of him and he'd caress my neck with his lips, tickling me with his beard and making me lightly giggle.

"Please let your momma or father know that I am truly thankful for the cooking skills they passed down to you," I announced, grabbing my glass from the center coffee table and taking a sip of the wine it housed.

"Well I'm sure my aunt would be glad to hear that I'm not out here poisoning people," he replied, making me smile while I drank. "Those cooking skills all came from her."

This was the second time during our time together that Cassian had cooked for me. The first time he'd made lasagna and today he'd made pesto sauce with pasta and shrimp. Him cooking Italian meals told me that he was very much in touch with his Italian roots.

"She raised you?" I asked once I was done sipping from my glass, placing it back down to the white oak table.

This was the first time he'd brought up his family and now that the topic had appeared, I was intrigued to know more.

He nodded, placing his lips to my shoulder and kissing me through his shirt.

"I lost my mother at four," he explained, avoiding my eyes. "My aunt, Frankie, is the only mother I've ever known."

"I'm sorry to hear that," I told him, raising a hand to the back of his neck and stroking his warm skin. "I'm glad you had someone to raise you."

"So am I," he replied in a low tone, lifting his lips off my body and turning to the tv.

We were both quiet, our focus now on Snowfall. Actually it was more of Cassian focused on the show and me glancing at him occasionally.

I was curious to hear more about his family life but I didn't want to pry. We were still in the early stages of getting to know each other better so I knew he wouldn't feel comfortable revealing his entire life story in one night. If he ever decided to open up, I would be here willing to listen.

"See something you like?" Cassian spoke up moments later, making me realize I'd been caught red handed staring at him.

"...Maybe."

He turned to look at me and a sexy smile graced his lips.

"If you want something I'm going to need to hear you say it, Danaë." Those hands started stroking my calves again. "You know how I feel about you using your words."

I leaned in closer to his face, bringing my mouth to the same breathing space as his. I brushed my lips against his a couple times before capturing his bottom lip and biting it. His hands gripped my legs tighter and I smiled, kissing down his beard until I was able to drag my tongue across his neck.

"I... want... dessert," I whispered, licking on his smooth skin.

His breathing became ragged as I licked on him and moved my hands down his chest, onto his shorts and stroked the bulge growing in his pants.

"Stop being shy and bring him out," he ordered.

I bit into his flesh causing him to groan.

"No." I sucked on the pain I'd inflicted on him. "I'll bring him out when I'm ready. Not when you're ready."

Clearly I was feeling like I was the boss this time around but Cassian soon put me in place and reminded me of who ran this shit.

"Capo, please," I begged him. "Put him in."

Cassian had me laying across his couch, legs hiked up to my sides and his tip making slow circles across my entrance. He ignored me, continuing to trail his head along my folds, up to my clit and back down to my opening. The anticipation was surely going to kill me and I was tempted to just push him in myself since my hands were free but I knew he'd punish me even more.

"No." My frustrations mounted at his word. "You don't get him until I'm ready for you to have him."

He used my earlier words against me, continuing to tease me in the worst way before eventually giving me what I wanted.

"Cassiannnnn!"

His thrusts were so deep I'm sure I could feel him in my guts. The deeper he filled me, the deeper my nails dug into his back.

"You said you wanted dessert, right?" He whispered into my ear, pumping in and out my tightness. "You were talking all that shit earlier, huh? Move that fucking hand and take your dessert, Danaë. Don't make me fuck you up."

My moans increased in volume and pitch but they did nothing to deter Cassian from fucking my brains out. He eventually slowed down only to rotate his hips with his length still nested deep inside me and those attractive eyes glued to mine.

"Take. Your. Dessert."

Between each word, he slammed into me, causing my lips and eyes to widen. My entire body shook as his motions took over my soul, sending chills to every corner of my body.

Cassian leaned into my neck, pressing his lips to my flesh to kiss me and shortly into his kisses, he spat on my neck. Then he sucked up his saliva, causing me to be highly aroused by his unusual act.

"Cassian," I moaned his name.

"Hmm... you like that shit, don't you?" He did it again, spitting on my skin and vacuuming it all up, making me moan louder while his pumps between my legs quickened. "You like when I spit on you and lick up all the mess I've made."

"I do," I cried out as he fucked me harder and sucked my skin.

"I know you do, you nasty little girl... fuck... you feel so fucking good, Danaë."

As far as I was concerned, this man could be the boss of me any day, any time. There was no point denying it now, he had me dickmatized and there was no cure. Cassian Acardi was my new addiction.

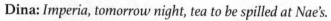

Dina: *Imperia, tomorrow night, tea to be spilled at Nae's.*

Dina: *Be there or be square.*

Imperia: *What tea?*

Dina: *Our good friend Nae, is back messing with her future baby Daddyyyyy!*

Imperia: *Cassian?*

Dina: *The one and only.*

Dina: *So tomorrow we find out all the juicy tea at Nae's.*

Dina: *You're coming, right?*

When I was reunited with my phone, hours after Cassian had finished breaking my back in the best ways possible, I was ambushed to texts in my group chat with Adina and Imperia.

After our night out, Adina created an iMessage group chat for the three of us to easily communicate and arrange our next meet up. We'd barely used it because for one we were all busy ladies and secondly, no one had taken charge in setting up our next girls date. Usually it would have been me but like Adina had said I was too busy getting *dickstracted* by one handsome fella. Seeing that Adina had taken the initiative to get her and Imperia in my house tomorrow night made a smile crease my face.

Ding!

Imperia: *Pretty backed up with work right now.*

Imperia: *I'll let you know though.*

Imperia's response to Adina's invitation wasn't surprising because Mrs. CEO didn't make all those coins by staying free twenty-four-seven. It would be nice to see her since the last time I'd seen her had been with Adina but I understood if she couldn't make it.

A new day arrived and by the time work was over for me, I was back home, awaiting the arrival of my favorite person who rushed through my door less than three hours later.

"Spill, spill, spill, spill!" Adina exclaimed, shaking me by my shoulders.

"Alright, alright." I laughed at her eagerness.

She hadn't even let me get a word in, asked how I was or asked what I had to eat in my fridge which was something she never failed to ask cause my bestie sure as hell loved her food. Clearly my situation with Cassian had her not thinking about anything else.

She now sat crossed legged on my couch, ready to hear everything about Cassian and I. I filled her in on what went down after our meeting last week, how I'd been picked up and driven to his that same night and been with him every night until today.

Just like I'd figured, Imperia wasn't able to make it tonight. I'd just have to catch her up on all things Cassian another time.

"Well, damn." Adina sipped on the glass of white wine I'd provided her with. "You've really been living it up haven't you?"

I'd just finished telling Adina everything she needed to know. I felt my cheeks warm at her words and I let my head fall back, staring up at the ceiling as I reminisced on the bliss I'd been experiencing for the past week.

"So he's basically your new boo?"

My head dropped, allowing me to gaze into her chestnut eyes.

"Not exactly. It's just sex. Really amazing sex," I admitted, knowing that I'd basically confirmed Cassian and I's status as friends with benefits. "We're just... going with the flow I guess."

"And you're okay with that?"

I nodded.

"Oh yeah you're definitely dickmatized, boo," she voiced, making my bottom lip drop.

"Cause I ain't ever heard you say the words 'we're just going with the flow'," she stated, putting up air quotes as she said my words in a mock like tone of mine. "You usually go into your situations letting the men know that you're not here for games."

"Well..." A calm breath dropped from my lips. "I guess I'm doing things different this time 'round."

No man had captivated me the way Cassian had and no man knew how to bring me to heights as great as the ones Cassian brought me to. Whatever this was, I was enjoying it for as long as it lasted and I didn't want to mess things up by bringing up the topic of a relationship. Shit, we barely knew each other still and I didn't mind taking things slow... for now.

"Whatever you say, mama." Adina raised her hands up in surrender. "Just let me know when you need that boombox. I'ma find you the best one on eBay."

I flipped her the bird, causing her to chuckle loudly and just before I could ask her how her day went, my phone started going off.

Ding! Ding! Ding!

I reached forward to swipe it from my coffee table.

Hey, Danaë. I was wondering if you were free sometime soon?

It was a text from Kamora who I'd decided to rename on my phone from 'The Witch' to her actual name. I guess my guilt started settling in about naming her a derogatory term and seeing as she was my father's girlfriend, it only seemed right to rename her to her actual name.

Our little spat at my father's house was something I wasn't going to dwell on. I guess you could also say after being dicked so good this past week, I was seeing everything with a positive lens. I was still slightly salty about her trying to get involved with my father's decision to spoil me but I understood that she didn't understand our bond properly. It was simply ignorance that had her feeling some type of way about my father's sentimental gift giving.

I wasn't dwelling on the tension that arose between us about the designer bags but I didn't want to see her ass that soon yet. After that dinner I'd spent in her presence, I needed my space away from her. Call me crazy but Kamora's energy was one of the main reasons why I just couldn't stand her sometimes. After being in her presence for a while, I'd come out feeling weird and uneasy. I really couldn't explain that shit at all. All I knew was that I didn't like being around her for too long.

Kamora: *I'd love to come over and cook you a home cooked meal.*

Kamora: *Just the two of us.*

"That bae texting you?" Adina queried, wiggling her brows at me.

"No, it's Kamora."

"The Witch?"

"The one and only," I confirmed.

"Ugh," she groaned. "What does she want?"

"She wants to come over and cook me a meal." I sighed. "Dad really wants us to get along even though I've told him five hundred times, it's not me that causes the issues between us, it's her."

"True but at least she's trying to be nice after that stupid shit she said about your father spoiling you." Adina knew about what had went down at my father's because I'd texted her about the whole ordeal that same night. "That must count for something, right?"

"I guess." I shrugged.

"I think you should let her come over. What's the worst that could happen? She can't poison you cause Trenton will kill her ass over trying to harm his little Angel."

That she was right about.

"Just give her a chance, Nae."

Adina always knew the right ways to cajole me to listen because before I knew it, I was texting Kamora back telling her that I'd love for her to come over and that this coming Sunday would be best.

I was giving her a real solid chance. I just prayed I didn't end up regretting it.

CHAPTER 14

~ CASSIAN ~

*D*ing!

Danaë: *Did you miss me?*

Me: *I asked first.*

Me: *Yes or no?*

I watched her read receipt come in before three grey dots appeared in our chat.

Danaë: *Maybe I did. Maybe I didn't.*

Me: *Not good enough.*

Me: *I want a real answer.*

Danaë: *Well you're not getting one.*

Danaë: *So what now?*

Me: *You're trying to get in trouble before I see you tonight.*

Me: *That's what.*

Danaë: *Trouble?*

Me: *Yes trouble.*

Me: *You forget the last time you got in trouble for not answering properly?*

Danaë: *I didn't forget.*

Danaë: *Besides I think I like being in trouble with you, Capo.*

"Sorry for keeping you all waiting, my sons."

The sound of Julius' voice filled the room and I quickly pocketed my phone, standing from my seat at the same time as everyone else.

Julius had called an impromptu meeting today and so here I was, with Christian and my cousins, ready to hear what was so important.

We were all standing around a narrow dining table, waiting for Julius to take his seat before we all took ours again. When he did, we sat down with our focus solely on him.

"Frankie is leaving town for a few weeks. Her jet is taking her out the country as we speak. She needs a break from Chicago and Winnekta, that's all. It's business as normal, I'm just giving you all a heads up as Frankie wants."

What I wanted to know was why Frankie hadn't told me herself that she was leaving the city? It was unlike her to let me and Christian find out about her personal plans through a business meeting. We were practically her sons and knew about most of her moves before she told the rest of The Family.

"Before you overreact, son, she didn't feel the need to tell you privately because she only decided on leaving a few days ago. She knows how busy you are and didn't want you coming all the way to see her just to hear her say she was leaving."

Shortly after the meeting, Julius pulled me to the side and addressed my thoughts without me having to speak. That was the thing about having family as tight as mine, we knew each other's tendencies well. He knew how fond and overprotective I was with Frankie so of course he was here to make sure I didn't lose my cool about my mother figure leaving the city without telling me.

"Got it," I simply said, staring deep into his tawny eyes.

Something about the whole ordeal felt off but I wasn't about to dwell on it. I'd speak to Frankie soon and hear from her own mouth why she'd decided to leave on vacation without saying goodbye.

Hours later, I was in my penthouse, getting dressed for my night out when my phone started sounding off from my bedroom. I walked out my dressing room and headed to my phone that sat on my bedroom's ottoman.

Coconut Head: *Lost my first game this month.*

Coconut Head: *No biggie though.*

Coconut Head: *Re-match next week.*

Caia and I hadn't caught up in a minute which was odd because I spoke to her via phone at least once a week. I guess time was getting the best of me these days because I found myself losing track of things.

Time ain't getting the best of you, nigga. Danaë's getting the best of you.

Shaking off my thoughts I unlocked my phone and started responding to my sister's texts.

Who's the fool that had the audacity to beat you? Give me a name and he won't be a problem anymore.

Send.

Ding! Ding! Ding!

Coconut Head: *Cassi!*

Coconut Head: *No threatening my competitors.*

Coconut Head: *I win all my games fair and square. You know that.*

Me: *Yeah I know.*

Me: *But ain't nothing wrong with me making sure my baby sister beats whoever she needs to beat.*

Me: *Now what's his name?*

She sent a few laughing emojis into our chat.

Coconut Head: *You're something else, Cassi.*

Coconut Head: *His name?*

Coconut Head: *Nunya.*

Me: Nunya?

Coconut Head: *Nunya damn business!*

Now it was my turn to send laughing emojis into the chat.

We texted for a couple more minutes. Caia caught me up on how things were going in LA and her plans to go back to school in a few months. She loved playing games so damn much that she was interested in learning how they were made. The thought of designing her own game had crossed her mind and now she wanted to explore it. Anything she put her mind to she could do so I was positive that her new venture would serve her well and like always, I was here to support her in any way that she needed me to.

After we caught up, I was back in my dressing room, putting the finishing touches on my outfit by placing my silver cuff links to my shirt and wearing my blazer.

All day I'd been looking forward to tonight and now it was finally here. I took one last look at my reflection in my mirror before leaving my room, ready to be next to the woman who'd been running through my mind since I'd woken up.

"Am I still in trouble?"

I couldn't take my damn eyes of her. The cross-neck dress she wore tonight hugged her gorgeous figure to a T and revealed those beauties that I'd had the honor of sucking on many times. It had an open back, was in a camel color and had a slit going up one of its sides, revealing more of her thigh. Fueling my thoughts that were tempting me to clear all this shit off our table and have her here right now in the middle of this restaurant.

"You know you are," I told her.

She beamed, lifting her fingers and running them through her hair. She'd straightened it tonight and it fell past her shoulders. Despite how much I loved her curls, I loved the straight look on her too. She was still breathtaking either way.

"But that can wait," I said, lifting my glass. "Tell me about your day."

It had been over a week since I'd been at Danaë's office, the day I'd made my intentions known on wanting to see her again. Almost every night since then she'd been in my bed and honestly, I'd loved it. The only night she hadn't been in my bed was yesterday when she'd told me about how Adina wanted to see her. I didn't complain but deep down I knew how much I'd loathed not having her in my arms.

If it wasn't for the fact that we both had to work and live our lives, I was sure that my bed would've easily become our permanent home. Only leaving to eat, clean and pee then hopping right back in to enjoy our mind-blowing sessions.

Tonight I'd decided to take Danaë out to one of my favorite steakhouses in the city, STK. I'd told myself that this wasn't a date, just two people going out for a nice meal but even I couldn't deny now how much of a date this felt like.

"You found what you want to eat yet?" I asked as I observed her staring hard at her menu.

"...Umm... I'm not really sure." She lowered her menu and looked over at me. "How about you order for me?"

"That's what you want?"

"Yes." She lifted her hand to her throat, stroking it gently as our eye contact intensified. "I want you... to order for me."

A smile appeared on her lips and I returned it before swiping my tongue across my lip. We hadn't even been at this restaurant for more than fifteen minutes and Danaë already had me feening for her like a damn crackhead.

I remembered exactly how I'd made it known to her that I was taking her out tonight.

Be ready for nine p.m. Dress & heels. Don't ask me no stupid ass questions either.

To which she replied: *Is that your way of asking me out on a date, Mr. Acardi?*

Me: *And there you go with the stupid ass questions, Danaë.*

Danaë: *So that's a yes then. Got it, meanie.*

Now as Danaë talked to me about her day at work, I enjoyed the sound of her soft voice and I enjoyed the fact that I had her here with me tonight.

Our starters came out first: crispy calamari, crab cake and tuna tarte. Then our main meal came out and we feasted. I'd ordered us both steaks with various sides. Our conversation flowed smoothly while we ate. I wanted to hear more of her talking so I mainly asked the questions.

I asked Danaë about her desires to become an accountant in the first place. She also told me more about her parents, their love for all things numbers that had been passed down to her. Her late mother was brought up too and I was surprised to hear that like me, Danaë had lost her mother at the age of four. We had a lot more in common than I thought.

"I mean... I don't remember her at all but when I see her face in pictures, I feel this longing for her to be right by my side, seeing the woman I've become, hoping that she's proud of me."

"What's there not to be proud of? You're a beautiful, intelligent, hardworking woman who is killing it right now at her father's firm. I'm sure she's proud of you, Danaë."

Her cheeks wouldn't stop hiking after my compliment and seeing her smile brought a warm, fuzzy sensation to my center.

You know you enjoy her company and clearly like having sex with her but that's all this is, right? Sex.

That's exactly all it was in my mind and I was sure that soon we'd both be bored of each other and end whatever this was. But the more I was learning about this woman, the more I wanted to be around her. She exuded an aura that I couldn't explain. When I was around her, I felt at peace and filled with a breath of fresh air that was unlike any I'd experienced before.

After dinner, we were both in the backseat of my Bentley while Pierro drove us home. Danaë's head rested on my shoulder while she looked out the window and I looked down at her.

She really is so damn beautiful.

Danaë was the brown skin stunner that I really couldn't get enough of. Just when I was sure that I'd both received and given her enough pleasure, something new would arrive and I was giving and wanting her more. The kink I had in the bedroom to occasionally tie up my partners, she'd been introduced to and seemed to love it as much as I did, if not more.

Pierro arrived at The Palazzo's parking lot and parked in the reserved spot beside my Lambo. Danaë lifted her head off my shoulder and moved nearer to the door. Before she could grab it, I reached for Danaë's hand and asked Pierro to give us a moment.

Pierro had left on the car's interior lights and blue ambient lighting surrounded us. Allowing me to admire that face that I hadn't been able to tear away from all damn night. The LED lighting reflected off her brown skin, defining her exquisite features. Those bold eyes that sat below gold shimmer eyeshadow, that button nose I wanted to rub mine on and those plump lips that I'd wanted to feel against mine all night. She'd gone with a natural beat of make up tonight, by far my favorite look on her. Even with the most minimal make up she still looked like a work of art.

"You okay?" she asked, her voice filled with concern.

"Yeah," I said, pulling on her hand and ultimately pulling her nearer to me.

I just couldn't wait till we got upstairs to get you alone, I said in my head rather than out loud.

There was now a small gap between our faces and I leaned forward to close it, meshing my lips to hers. I gave her strong doses of me, combining our tongues together and making my hunger for her evident. One of her hands stayed joined to mine while the other rubbed on my chest, reminding me of how this woman's touch always seemed to bring me weak to my knees.

I soon broke away, letting my lips trail down her face until I was coating her collar bone with smooches.

"Mmmh, Cass..."

What is she doing to me?

One minute I wanted to fuck her senseless, the next I wanted to bombard her with kisses and hold her tight.

I hadn't even fully opened up to her about my life or let her truly know who I was but here I was, feeling bound to her in ways I couldn't describe. My guard was lowering around this woman and I wasn't sure how to feel about it.

The last woman I'd lowered my guard around was Imperia and no other woman had come close until now. Losing a child was one of the worst heartbreaks ever and I was sure that the experience had made my heart turn cold for good. After losing Zeroni, I was certain that being in a relationship and trying to start a family was not for me. But I'd been lying if the thought of being with Danaë in the long run and potentially starting a family hadn't crossed my mind during our time together.

It couldn't happen though. I was not about to get my hopes up when I'd had it crushed many years ago.

"I missed you," she whispered, cutting into my thoughts and

making me realize that she'd admitted what I wanted her to text me earlier.

Without responding, I let my lips crash into hers and I began to show her just how much I'd missed her with my dominating yet sweet kisses.

You need to end this soon. You're getting too comfortable having her around.

It was what I knew I needed to do but as my lips stayed joined to hers, I knew it wasn't what I wanted to do. It was the last thing I wanted to do.

CHAPTER 15

~ DANAË ~

"If this is what you and Cassian call going with the flow then count me in, baybeeeeee."

The smile that fell on my lips was one I couldn't hide even if I tried.

"Mmmh, right there, sugar... I think mama's gonna need to take you home with me, Jared."

Luckily for me, Adina couldn't see my smile nor could she hear the silent laughs I was making. Both of us were laying on our stomachs on separate massage beds. Our heads were slotted into the bed's face hole while our backs were soothed in the best ways known to mankind.

Cassian had done the unexpected and treated me to a free spa day at The Acardi Palazzo. A spa day that he allowed me to have with anyone of my choosing. My initial choice was him but he shut down my want to ask him when he told me that he couldn't join me because he had business to tend to. Business on a Saturday wasn't stereotypical but Cassian Acardi wasn't a stereo-typical man and I recognized his duty to business calling. That man didn't have a multi-million-dollar hotel empire by not staying busy.

My next obvious choice for the spa day was Adina. When we arrived at The Palazzo and were escorted to the spa section of the hotel, I saw that our names had been placed on the doors of our treatment room in gold elegant font.

Today I'd learned the true meaning of a luxury hotel. The Acardi Palazzo had a spa that embodied every part of luxury. From its fitness center, sauna and steam rooms, monsoon shower, spa pool, exercise pool and facial and massage rooms, this place was the oasis of luxury.

Adina and I were currently getting the best massages of our lives by two talented souls who I was certain had hands of gold. Jared was the masseur that Adina had been personally assigned to and I on the other hand had a masseuse called Natalie.

Of course I teased Cassian the first chance I got about the fact that my massage therapist was a woman. I grabbed my phone while Adina and I stripped down for our massages to hit him up. His response had me blushing nonstop.

Me: *I see someone couldn't handle another man's hands on me.*

Cassian: *That was for your sake, not mine.*

Me: *???*

Cassian: *You'd make such a mess, Danaë.*

Danaë: *A mess?*

Cassian: *Yes a mess.*

Cassian: *Cause you know damn well you won't be able to handle another man's touch when all you'll be thinking about is my touch on your body and all the ways you like being fucked like a slut.*

Cassian: *All that thinking will have you making a big, wet mess that I won't be able to clean up until I see you tonight.*

Cassian: *Now go enjoy your massage, Danaë.*

Cassian: *Try not to think about me too much.*

Sometimes I hated how he knew all the right things to say to get me wet and after his reference to the big, wet mess I'd make, a mess was already beginning to form between my legs as I felt my arousal for him drip out of me.

Adina and I enjoyed our massages and facials and by the time we were done, we were enjoying our spa suite's hot tub with a bucket of champagne and fruit salad posted on the tub's edge.

"You're lying."

My face scrunched up as I stared at Adina.

"Huh?"

"You're lying," she repeated, lifting her finger out the water and wagging it at me. "You lied to me about where you were that day I called you and I have a feeling you're lying about you and Cassian."

The confusion flowing through me got stronger and it showed because Adina continued talking to clarify her point.

"You said you and Cassian are just having sex. Going with the flow?"

I nodded.

"Nae, this isn't just sex... this..." She circled her finger around the room. "This is much more than just sex."

"It is?"

"Girl, you know damn well that a man who's just having sex wouldn't go out his way to do all of this for you and your bestie."

I relaxed against the tub's edge, letting out a gentle breath as I reflected on Adina's words.

"I mean... he does own the hotel."

"Exactly," she agreed. "He owns the most expensive hotel in the city and he let you and I use the entire spa that costs over five hundred dollars per customer with our own private suites."

I placed my champagne flute to my lips to take a sip as I contemplated about the fact that Adina and I hadn't paid a dime for this spa day. It'd all been on Cassian's dime. I'd tried not to read too deeply into Cassian's gesture but now that Adina had pointed it out, it got me thinking.

This does look like a lot more than just sex...

"He likes you," she said matter-of-factly. "Just like I knew he would."

"That's why you wanted me to go up to him all those weeks ago," I said, referring to our night at Evoni's. "You just couldn't help yourself, Miss Matchmaker."

She grinned, lifting her flute towards me before drinking from it.

"But I'm not lying, we really are just having a good time together," I admitted.

"And what happens when this good time turns into something more?" she asked curiously. "Will you tell him how you feel?"

"...I don't know. It's too early to say. We're still getting to know each other."

"Hmm... I guess you're right," she replied. "As much as I wanted you to get your back blown, I also wanted you to find someone who could treat you right especially after that bullshit that other nigga put you through. Yes, Cassian's my boss but I've only been graced with his presence a few times during board meetings and the times that I have met him, I'm drawn to him the same way I'm drawn to you. You're alike in the sense that you're both on your shit and carry yourselves as the bosses you are. You deserve a boss by your side, Nae and I'm certain that's him."

Silence was the only answer I returned back to her but it didn't stop her from speaking.

"And believe me when I say that this looks like a lot more than just sex."

I sipped more on my champagne, remaining quiet as a ghost.

Hours later, Adina's words still danced in my head. After we'd enjoyed a three-course meal in our suite together, Adina and I parted ways. She headed home while I went up to Cassian's penthouse.

She said this was more than sex and yes, I realized that Cassian going out of his way to treat me made it seem like this was more than sex but what if she was wrong? Yes, he'd given me a personal key card into his hotel, cooked me delicious meals, taken me out for dinner and treated me and my best friend to a spa day at his expensive ass hotel. But what if these were just Cassian's little ways of keeping me bound to him for as long as he wanted and then he'd ditch me? What if the feelings I had for him grew and I admitted them and he threw me away like nothing we'd done together even mattered to him? What if he had other women on the side who were at his beck and call?

This is why I told myself four days after first sleeping with him that being in his bed couldn't happen again. But did I listen? No.

Now it was coming back to bite me in the butt because deep down I knew Adina was dead right. This was becoming more than sex each day. When I was with him, I felt like I was floating on the highest cloud. When I was away from him all I wanted to do was run to him. She said that I needed a boss by my side but how could she even be sure that that boss was him? How could she be sure that Cassian and I were meant to be when I didn't even know if he was feeling the same way?

I didn't even know much about him. He still hadn't opened up the way I wanted him too. He kept things short and sweet, telling me small details but not going all the way in. I knew he was a sex god that knew how to pleasure my body in ways I didn't know existed. I knew he had a brother, a half-sister, an aunt that had raised him from the age of four and a successful hotel but I knew he was holding back. There were more layers to him that a part of me wanted to know but the other part was lowkey afraid.

The smart thing for you to do would be to leave before things get too deep, Danaë. Leave before you let this mysterious man steal your heart.

It was what I told myself I needed to do and I tried to convince myself to leave his bed and flee his penthouse, promising to never come back but it was all a big fat fail. I ended up falling asleep, waking up hours later to kisses on my face.

My eyes fluttered open and his head blocked my view. Our eyes found one another and he pressed one last kiss to my lips, pulled on my bottom lip and sucked it before backing away from me.

I looked up, taking him all in. He was dressed in casual clothes. A gray t-shirt and matching gray sweats. One of my favorite colors on him because it made him look even more like the sex god that he was. It made me want to call him Daddy with a z. Those large arms of his were out, sending me to flashbacks of when I'd last had those arms wrapped around my waist.

"You enjoy your day?"

That deep baritone of his vibrated along my nerves, reminding me of how much I'd missed hearing him talk. I nodded, lifting my head and sitting up on the plush mattress.

"Thank you for the spa day, Cassian, but you shouldn't..."

The serious look that crossed his face, made my words trail off and I realized that trying to do more than thank him would be a mistake. It was clear that when he wanted to do something he was doing it, so there was no point of telling him that he shouldn't have done it. I decided to change the subject.

"Did you enjoy your day?"

"It was decent," he replied, reaching for my hand. "I know I'm about to enjoy it ten times better now though."

There he goes, saying things that make me think that this could be something more...

I let him grab my hand and pull me up from the bed. I came

to stand on my feet and he led the way out his bedroom. I assumed he was going to lead me to the kitchen where he would ask me if I was hungry and cook me something new. Instead of turning in the direction of the kitchen when we arrived downstairs, Cassian pulled me over to the glass doors that led out to his balcony.

Without saying a word, Cassian led the way out his home and once outside he stepped out the way to let me get a clear view. My eyes widened at the white clothed table separated by two chairs. The table that had a candle lit in its center and the balcony's handrail was layered with mini candles. A soft, warm glow illuminated the space around us.

I suddenly felt weightless and when he turned around to face me, I opened my mouth to speak but found myself tongue tied.

"Cass... I... this..."

His eyes gleamed at the same time that his smirk formed. We were still holding hands so he was able to pull me closer to him, pressing my body into his. I instantly sank into his mighty frame and inhaled his spicy scent that never failed to make me want him even more than I already did.

"Figured we could eat out here for a change," he said, planting a peck to my lips. "How you spent almost every night here and we haven't eaten outside together in front of this view?"

He turned to look at the breathtaking night view of Chicago and while he looked, I looked at him. Feeling myself melt more and more for this man. He then took me over to the table, pulled out my chair and waited 'til I was seated until he took his seat.

Like a true gentleman.

"You hungry?" he asked, his tone heavy with sarcasm because he knew damn well from seeing this dinner layout, hunger was the only thing on my mind.

I nodded with a smile.

I was hungry but hungry for so much more than food right now. But that could wait.

"So what did you cook for me tonig..." I stopped talking when a man dressed in a chef uniform appeared from Cassian's penthouse.

"Good evening, Miss Westbrook," the toffee skinned man greeted me. "I'm Charles, your personal chef for your dinner tonight with Mr. Acardi..."

Wow.

This man really hired a private chef for little old me?

"Mr. Acardi tells me that seafood is one of your favorite cuisines so I've prepared a seafood platter consisting of..."

As Charles rattled off all the dishes he'd prepared, I was still trying to wrap my hand around the fact that there was a personal chef here for us tonight. I'd been too busy trying to find the right words on how to say thank you to Cassian for the candle lit dinner set up and here he went adding more things to make me tongue tied. Here he went adding more things to make me go crazy.

Was this man trying to turn me into a feen for him? Was he trying to turn me into a crackhead that wanted a sniff of only him every single day for the rest of my life?

Our food came out to us no later than ten minutes and the dinner was everything I needed it to be. We not only had a personal chef, but we also had a personal waiter and a personal wine server who topped up our glasses whenever we needed it. We ate seafood that had me moaning between each bite – much to Cassian's approval – drank a new bottle of Tuscan wine that I still didn't know how to pronounce and you know what made it ten times better? Cassian confirmed to me that I was the only one he was doing all of this for.

"You sure know how to charm a girl..." I watched him stroke

his beard and my insides stirred with heat as I thought to myself, *'Look at him... stroking my future seat.'*

While we'd been eating my desire for this man had shot up through the roof and I wanted to ride his face until the sun came up.

"Your aunt teach you that too?" His thick brow shot up so I elaborated. "How to charm the ladies?"

"Nah." He chuckled. "That's all me."

"So you charm all the women you sleep with?"

It was definitely the wine that made me feel courageous enough to ask him that question but fortunately for me, he answered it without skipping a beat.

"I'm only charming you right now, Danaë," he revealed. "You don't see anyone else around here do you? You're the only one up in my bed every night and the only one taking this dick."

I felt my cheeks burn and I reached for my glass, hoping that my wine would provide relief to the fire flowing through me.

It didn't.

Once finished with our food, I thanked Cassian's chef and food servers for all their great work tonight. After all my thank yous, Cassian grabbed my hand to lead us upstairs but I led the way closer to the edge of the balcony and he obediently followed. Candles still sat on the balcony's rail, burning around us and adding to the romantic vibe. I stopped a short distance away from the balcony's edge and Cassian's arms enveloped my waist from behind, bringing me to stand in front of him as we both admired the magnificent city.

"Thank you so much for tonight, Cass... you're so sweet."

His way of saying, "You're welcome," was by kissing my neck and sending his kisses all along my collar bone while his hands rubbed on my stomach.

I released a quiet moan once his kisses turned to licks, sucks and bites. Cassian really was my own personal vampire, minus the blood sucking part of course. I was lucky that I was of a darker hue than him because I knew for a fact if I shared the same light complexion he did, I would be turning up to work with extremely visible love bites.

His seduction continued and when his hands started moving up my body, apprehension filled me because of the bodies moving in and out of Cassian's penthouse, clearing up our table.

"Cass... your employees are still he—"

"They're not your concern," he said in a low tone, squeezing on my breasts through my t-shirt. "Your only concern right now is how you're going to show me just how thankful you are for tonight."

The fire I'd done a shit job at trying to keep low, burned stronger inside me ten times more. It didn't help that I could feel his erection poking my back, telling me that he wanted me just as bad as I wanted his fine ass.

"You gonna show me, Danaë?"

I nodded, a smile creeping on my lips because I knew exactly what was coming next. A firm hand circled my neck and I couldn't stop the devilish grin that appeared.

"You tryna make me fuck you up right here, right now on this balcony? You know I don't give a fuck about who sees us, Danaë." My left nipple was suddenly pinched. "What I tell you about that nodding shit?"

"I'm... I'm sorry, Capo," I whispered. "I'm... I'm gonna..."

"You're gonna what?" He turned my neck so that I could look back at him.

"I'm gonna show you how thankful I am," I confidently told him. "You know much I like to be fucked like a slut so that's exactly what I want you to do to me tonight, Capo." He groaned in my ear, making my grin widen. "But when we get upstairs, I want you to make me get on my knees, let me suck you all the way to the back of my throat and don't stop 'til I've swallowed up every last drop of your nut."

The next few minutes happened so fast, causing my entire soul to go into a frenzy of pure excitement. Cassian flung me over his shoulders, rushing inside while I shut my eyes not wanting to make eye contact with the clean-up crew who I'm sure knew what was about to happen between us.

By the time we were in his bedroom, he chucked me onto the king-sized mattress and began stripping each article of clothing off my body. I tried to reach for his clothes to undress him too but he pushed my hands above my head, firmly pressing them down to the bed.

"Keep those there," he ordered. "Don't make me go get some rope."

I bit my bottom lip at his words, knowing deep down I wouldn't mind being tied up as it'd been a while since he'd last done it.

Once I was naked, Cassian stood up on his bed and let his eyes linger over my body while he undressed himself. Watching him strip was one of the best views of my life and I was certain that I could die a lucky lady from all the times I'd gotten to see his heavenly physique. His well-defined body exposed itself and moments later I was left with a moist mouth and wet middle as my eyes dropped to the extension of him that never failed to bring me joy.

"On your knees."

I obeyed, sitting upright onto my knees and scooting over to where he stood a short distance away. As soon as I was close enough, my hair was yanked up into a ponytail and my mouth positioned at the tip of his erection.

"You said you wanted me to let you suck me up, right?"

He grazed his tip against my lips, not letting it go all the way in just yet.

"Do your shit."

That was all the confirmation I needed to bring Nasty Nae all the way out. My lips wrapped around his swollen head, sliding all the way down as much as I could go before sliding back and doing my shit just as he'd requested.

"Ughhhh, Nae..."

From the moans that left him minutes later, I knew he knew I wasn't here to play games. I went from swirling my tongue around his tip, pushing him to the back of my throat till he touched the flesh that hung there, twisting both hands around his base, spitting on him before slurping up all the nasty mess I'd made and sucking each of his balls like they were my own personal lollipops.

"Shit... Suck on those balls... just like that... fuck... you nasty fucking girl."

When I did my shit, I played to win and from the sounds emitting from him, he knew that. Thanks to that little thumb trick Cassian had told me the first time I'd given him head; I was able to keep my gag reflex at bay a couple times. Allowing me to swallow more of his thickness. The more I deep throated him, the more his rod expanded between my lips and the louder his moans got.

A few minutes later, he suddenly eased out my mouth and slapped my hands off him. I looked up, reading nothing but hunger in his eyes.

"Hold those breasts together."

I listened, pressing my hands to my breasts and holding them close together. Cassian leaned forward, crouching slightly to slide his long length between my boobs. He began to thrust back and forth and I was turned on all over again. His thrusts quickened and I smiled at the pleasure settling into his handsome face. I started spitting on his tip every time it popped up closer to my face, occasionally grazing my chin. I would let my spit slowly drip down to coat his dick while he pumped up and down.

"God damn it, Nae Nae... you are so damn nasty... my nasty Nae.... Fuuuuuck!"

Seconds later, his load came splurging out, hitting my face and dropping to my breasts. I kept my mouth open, causing a few drops to fall into my mouth.

Cassian then pushed me back and I fell to the mattress. He climbed on top of me grabbed my mounds, squeezing tight and rubbing the traces of his cum into me. Then he lowered his head and sucked it all off my breasts. He went from sucking them, flicking his tongue over my nipples, biting them and kissing all up my chest until our lips branded together.

"See what you do to me?" He spoke up after our tongues collided.

He didn't give me a chance to reply though because I felt my thighs being pushed apart and he pushed past my wet seal causing me to cry out his name.

"I don't wanna fucking hear it," he snapped. "You wanted to be fucked like a slut, huh? You like being slutted out, huh?"

The ride began. In and out he dived within my walls that tightened around his shaft with each thrust. There was no condom sheathing his rod which made things one hundred times more intense. This was the second time he'd been inside me without one. I'd been on birth control prior to us having sex because they helped with my periods and he knew that but he hadn't slipped up in not using a condom until one time on his couch and of course now. Whenever Cassian got lost in the moment I realized that a condom was the last thing he was thinking about. All he wanted was to feel every last part of me.

"Uh-huh... squeeze it... squeeze this dick with your pretty pussy just like that."

Each pound almost broke me I swear. The deeper he pumped, the more I felt like I was about to pass out.

"Make me nut all up in this fucking pussy the same way you made me nut all over your titties. And the same way I sucked my nut off you is the same way I'ma suck it out your pussy too."

This man right here! He was the only man who could be nasty, rough and sweet all at the same time.

How was I supposed to ever get enough of him?

"So tell me... is there a special man in your life that you've been hiding from your father?"

I opened my mouth and bit into my egg roll while shaking my head 'no'.

"I see," she replied before looking down at the fork she was twirling into her noodle box.

Now that it was Sunday, Kamora was in my home, spending the afternoon with me. Initially in her offer to come over, she'd stated her plans to make me a meal but I didn't want her to hassle herself trying to figure out what I wanted to eat and how to use my appliances which is why I'd ordered us some Thai takeout.

So far her visit seemed okay. We'd made natural conversation here and there and hadn't clashed yet. It felt slightly awkward having her in my space but I suppressed any ill feelings trying to form inside me. I was going to make a real effort with Kamora and prove to my father that we really could get along not just because he was in the room. Most of all, I was going to make him proud.

Neither Kamora nor I had told my father about our day together. We made the mutual decision to keep this from him so we could work on getting to know one another without his influence.

"I guess you're quite busy to be worrying about men right now," Kamora said and I simply nodded in agreement knowing fully well that I was lying.

Yeah we were getting to know each other but it was still early days. There was no way that I was going to spill my guts to Kamora about my situation with Cassian. Firstly, we were nowhere near being super close and secondly, telling Kamora would be me ulti-mately telling my dad because I knew in a heartbeat she would tell him that his precious Angel was sleeping with a top client at his firm. I could keep the identity of Cassian a secret but I didn't feel comfortable sharing my personal details with Kamora just yet.

I wasn't sure if I was ever going to tell Trenton about Cassian and I. I guess a part of me was scared to tell him because I didn't know how he would react and another part of me thought: *There's no point, you and Cassian aren't in an actual relationship.*

Then why did last night feel like one?

"Do you know how your father and I met?" Kamora asked me, breaking me away from my private thoughts.

"He mentioned it," I replied, lifting my last egg roll from the silver tray on the center table. "You hit his car."

She laughed as I ate my roll.

"Is that what he told you?" She playfully rolled her eyes. "No, sweetie, he hit *my* car but according to him, it was all me. Calling him out on it would mean that Trey would have to admit that he's a really bad driver."

Now it was my turn to laugh because she was one hundred percent right about that. My father's driving was terrible. He drove too damn fast, cut other drivers off, used his horn far too much, occasionally cut red lights and couldn't park to save his life. It was honestly a miracle on how he had secured his license in the first place. He didn't want to admit his bad driving skills but we all knew he knew because he'd hired a personal driver to take him around the city whenever he needed, claiming that he was getting too old to drive on the roads of Chicago.

Kamora and I began to bond over the fact that my father was a terrible driver and before I knew it we were laughing my entire apartment down.

"That man really cracks me up," Kamora commented between lighter laughs. "But I know that's why I love him so much."

"Awww look at you," I teased her. "Getting all soppy over my Daddy... the bad driver."

We burst out into laughter before sighing calmly.

"Danaë?"

"Yeah." I looked over at Kamora who was sprawled out on the other end of my sofa. During our bonding over my father, we'd each gotten comfortable on my four-seater. She laid on one side and I did the same on the other end of the corner sofa.

"I really love him."

"I know." I sent a warm smile her way which she returned.

She loved my father and I knew that. They had a big age gap and I still found it slightly strange but I was opening up to their relationship bit by bit.

"And I know you know that he has no plans to remarry but I'd really like to marry him someday soon."

"...Right."

My smile slowly faded as I felt a quiver in my stomach.

"As his daughter, you're the number one priority in his life and his Angel so I'm sure he'd listen to you if you were to convince him to change his mind."

"Well I can talk to him and hear his thoughts on wanting to get married again," I told her in a supportive tone.

I was only feeling open to talk to my father about marriage because I understood that his relationship with Kamora was important to him and because Kamora and I had been bonding well, I felt nice enough to help her get my father's thoughts on remarrying someday. However, my open feelings quickly changed when Kamora and I's conversation took a whole new direction.

And who was to blame for this new direction?

The one and only witch I knew, Kamora.

"Yeah but I'm gonna need you to do more than that, Danaë, I'm going to need you to give him your blessing to marry me."

"My blessing?"

Kamora sat up on my couch and it was at that exact moment I felt her entire mood switch on me. That friendly look she'd donned earlier had vanished and all that remained was seriousness and a hint of annoyance.

"You said it yourself you know I love him and he loves me just as much. I know he made a promise when your mother died but promises break all the time, Danaë. He's finally found happiness with me and it would be selfish for you to let him lose out on more happiness that he could experience being married to me."

There. It. Was.

There was the reason as to why Kamora had decided to visit me. There was the reason why Kamora was suddenly being so nice. She wasn't here to get to know me. She was here for her own personal agenda. She wanted to marry my father who had vowed to never get married again and she needed my help to do it.

"Kamora, why do you need to get married to my Dad so bad?" I asked her. "If you love him like you say you do then you'd respect his wishes and be his life partne—"

"It's not enough," she cut me off. "I want us to live a long-married life together. We deserve that."

I sighed at the fact that this conversation had taken a very wrong turn. I sat up on my couch, no longer feeling comfortable in my own space.

"We deserve that, Danaë, and you owe it your mother to let

your father experience love with someone else. Don't let your selfish intentions get in the way of what you know is right."

I frowned, getting irritated by the fact that she was constantly bringing up my mom, like she'd personally known her.

"I'm not letting my selfish intentions get in the way of anything. The only one being selfish here is you, trying to get me to convince my father to do something he doesn't want to do. You knew about his past with my mother when you first started dating him and you accepted it then. Now you're trying to change his wishes because you believe you deserve it?" I scoffed. "Please spare me the bullshit, Kamora. I can't and won't make my father change his decision to remarry. The sooner you get that into your head the better."

"The sooner you stop holding onto your mother like she's going to come back from the dead and steal your father away from me the better. She's dead and he's mine. You need to get over it."

This was the third time Kamora had brought up my mother and this was her final time. I'd had enough of talking and I most definitely had enough of her.

"Get out."

Kamora's eyes grew large but she didn't move an inch.

"Get the hell out of my apartment!" I yelled, my blood boiling.

"You're kicking me out because you can't face the truth?" A look of dismay flashed over her face.

I rose from my seat, pinning her with my eyes.

"Get the fuck out, Kamora!" I shouted again, pointing at my door.

There were so many insults I wanted to hurl at her but out of the respect I had for my father I held my tongue. She slowly got up, her face contorting with anger.

"You're so selfish," she said, reaching for her handbag on the coffee table. "At least I know you didn't get that from your father."

She stood up straight with a smug look. "That all must be from your dead mo—"

Slap!

Kamora never got the chance to finish her sentence because I lunged at her, sending a hard slap her way. She turned at the impact, grabbing the cheek I'd hit and gasping.

"Don't you ever speak on my mother again," I spat. "Now get the fuck out before I drag you out."

She looked at me, still holding her face. Anger burned in her brown pools but she stayed silent and walked to my door. She opened it and just before stepping out, Kamora turned to me with a vicious stare.

"Wait 'til your father hears about what you just did to me. Let's see how long you'll still remain his little angel after hitting the love of his life."

She rushed out before I could respond and slammed the door behind her. My heartbeat pounded away and I began to tremble as my fury crashed through me.

That bitch!

I'd let her get under my skin and attacked her. What she'd said wouldn't matter to my dad because he'd be too pissed once Kamora told him that I'd hit her.

There was no point of calling him before she got to him because the reality remained. I'd hit her and I felt no remorse about it. She'd brought out a side of me I hadn't shown since my high school days when bullies attempted to mess with me, but it was what it was at this point. The damage had been done and I was certain about my new stance.

I wanted nothing more to do with Kamora. She was dead to me and I would never accept her as my father's girlfriend.

Never.

CHAPTER 16

~ CASSIAN ~

"You hit that didn't you?"

I extended my arms up, lifting the silver bar above my head and exhaling deeply.

"You ain't even gotta say it 'cause I know you hit that. Walking around like you won the damn lottery, nigga, I know you hit that!"

I inhaled, lowering the bar towards my chest and remaining as stable as I could with the heavy weights racked on the bar. My view was the slated ceiling above until russet brown irises identical to mine appeared just as I lifted the bar back up. Blocking my above view.

"You hit that," he affirmed as he looked down at me.

I ignored him, continuing to bench press but was stopped when a hand gripped the middle of the bar, keeping it in place.

"Tell me you hit that."

The corners of my mouth lifted and I raised my arms, pushing Christian's hand up along with the bar. He sucked his teeth at my strength and let go of the bar.

"Man you gotta lay off those damn steroids. You tryna end up like the Hulk?"

I tittered at his stupid joke and turned to see him sauntering back over to the dumbbell rack a short distance away where his face towel hung.

"Yeah," I confirmed, lifting the rack one last time. "I hit that."

Just as I'd placed the bar back on its stand, Christian turned around and flashed me a bright grin.

"I fucking knew it."

I sat up on the bench and swiped my water bottle from the floor.

"And you're still hitting that aren't you?" he queried, walking back over to me while I gulped down my water. "That's why I've barely seen your ass, you've been too busy getting lost inside your future wifey."

Christian and I hadn't caught up in a minute. The last time I had seen him had been at The Family meeting over a week ago and despite the fact that we were basically neighbors, Christian and I didn't bump into each other as much as you would think. He had his life and I had mine but it wasn't like us to go completely ghost on one another.

We owned a hotel together but we'd employed some of the best people ever to run our shit while we focused on our other ventures. The Acardi was our baby yes but our family business always came first. I had guns to move and Chris had counterfeit bills to shift. Our roles in The Family would always remain top priority.

"How many times do I need to tell you that she's not my future wife?" I announced after clenching my thirst.

"As many times as you like, nigga." He smirked. "That's what she is."

I ignored his comment, got up from my seat and turned to the mirrored wall behind us. Sweat beads had formed on my forehead and my entire vest was drenched in sweat due to from all the workouts I'd done today. My face towel was hanging off the side of a nearby treadmill which I grabbed and used to dry my face.

One of the best things I loved about owning my own hotel was that I could build whatever the fuck I wanted in it. Christian and I had decided from day one that we wanted to build our own private gym that was exclusively for us to use. So while our guests had their own private gym downstairs we had our personal one down the corridor from our penthouses.

"You clearly like her and she likes you too."

My vision shifted to my brother's reflection, allowing me to read the certainty cradled in his face.

"That doesn't make her my future wife," I stated. "We're just having fun."

"Fun?"

"Yeah fun."

Christian's smirk grew before he nodded with understanding.

"Besides you know I have no intentions of getting married."

Christian frowned at my statement before asking, "You're still on that anti-marriage shit?"

I turned to him so I could look him dead in the eyes as I said, "Yes."

"So you have no intentions to settle down with anyone? Raise a family?"

"I tried that already," I muttered, unscrewing the cap from my bottle to take another sip.

"You didn't marry her though, Cass..." He paused and I could sense he was trying to find the right words to say next. "What happened was fucked up but that doesn't mean you can't try again."

"Nah," I replied after my last sip. "That's definitely not for me."

Christian pressed a hand to his neck, looking uneasy all of a sudden which wasn't a surprise because every time the topic of that godforsaken day came up, shit became awkward between us. I didn't like talking about it so I didn't say much whenever he or Zietta brought it up. I became cold and my family felt it because they would either change the subject or stop talking all together. Christian chose the first option.

"You spoke to Frankie?"

I nodded, my mind flashing back to the phone call I'd had with my aunt.

"I'm fine, bambino (baby)."

"Are you sure, Zee?

"Yes."

"Do you need me to get on a flight? Just say the word and I'm ther—"

"Don't be silly, Cass. I promise you I'm fine. I know me leaving without saying goodbye wasn't nice but I just needed a break away from the city. I'll be back before you know it. Just keep being good like you always are for me."

She claimed she was fine and a quick getaway out the city was what she needed. I just didn't like the fact that she'd taken off without saying goodbye but it was cool. I'd see her when she returned.

Now that our gym session was over, Christian I headed up to our floor, parting ways once we stepped off the elevator.

"Say hello to the wife for me," he said as we dapped.

I rolled my eyes, watching the amusement spread across his face.

"Or I'll just tell D myself when we see her next together." He chuckled, knowing he was getting on my last nerve especially since he'd called her by the nickname he'd coined for her during our last meeting.

Once back in my bedroom, my first instinct wasn't to get into the shower but to find my phone to hit up the only woman currently on my mind.

She'd left my side early this morning because she had to rush home to get prepared for her day with her father's girlfriend, Kamora. From what Danaë had told me about their interactions, the woman sounded like a total nightmare but she was now trying to make the effort to get to know Danaë. For her father's sake, Danaë was willing to put the effort in too so the pair were spending the afternoon together.

It was almost midday so I had a feeling Danaë was still getting ready for Kamora to come over or she might have decided to come over earlier. There was only one way to find out.

The witch there yet? I typed once I had my phone in hand. After pressing send, I took my seat on my ottoman, staring down at my phone.

Ding!

Her response came shooting in seconds later.

Danaë: *Nope.*

Danaë: *She'll be here in an hour.*

Danaë: *Wish me luck.*

Me: *You don't need luck.*

Me: *You'll be fine.*

Me: *Just get to know her.*

Me: *Like you said you would.*

Danaë: *Okay.*

Danaë: *Have a good day.*

Me: *You too, beautiful.*

Danaë. Danaë. Danaë.

I was supposed to end things between us ages ago but instead I found myself going out of my way for her. Letting her use expensive services at my hotel for free with her girlfriend, hiring private chefs to cook for us and doing the freakiest shit with her that I didn't do with anyone else. Oh and how could I forget about me giving her a key card to get into my penthouse whenever she wanted.

"We're just having fun."

The words I'd told Christian echoed in my head.

Fun.

This was only supposed to be us having fun. Fun that was lasting more and more each moment we spent together.

Are you really going to keep lying to yourself, Cass? You know damn well this isn't just you having fun. This isn't just sex.

Deep down I knew that but again, being stubborn was my Achilles heel and because of it, lying to myself about my situation with Danaë, was second nature. We weren't in a relationship. I was certain of that but at the same time I wasn't messing around with anyone but her.

I'd basically cut Evoni off. She'd tried to see me the week before last but from my blunt replies telling her that I was busy and there was no room for us to meet up, she knew what was up. Then last week she'd tried to get me to come over to hers but again I hit her with the 'I'm busy' text. She never responded after that. I knew deep down that she understood that our time together had come to an end which is why she hadn't stressed me with texts, begging to see me.

After showering, I got dressed into a casual fit, headed downstairs to my kitchen to eat some leftovers in my fridge and dived into an episode of Snowfall.

Danaë's gonna be pissed you're watching this without her.

I smiled at the thought, knowing that Danaë and I had been watching crime drama series together over the past couple of weeks. I'd put her onto the show and ever since episode one she'd become hooked.

Ding!

I pulled out my phone from my hoodie, not taking my eyes off the screen ahead until I'd lifted my device in front of my face.

Cass, are you free today? I really need to see you.

A deep sigh seeped out of me at the newest text from Imperia.

From some strange reason, Imperia had been texting me all week, asking me when I was free. The same treatment I given to Evoni; I'd given to Imperia by texting her that I was busy. Unlike Evoni, Imperia wasn't compliant with understanding that I wasn't trying to see her.

The last time I'd been in a room with Imperia had been three months ago and we hadn't exactly been doing any damn talking unless you counted all the moans she made. The only way she was able to get close to me these days was through text messages that I would take hours to reply to and a rare phone call I'd only set up a month ago because she'd gone out of her way to pester my brother about not hearing from me. She'd used the excuse of being hurt about our loss of three years ago and of course me having a soft spot for her made me reach out. During our phone call I'd told her I would reach out again to her sometime soon but with all the time I'd been spending working and being with Danaë, I never found the time to hit Imperia up.

Me: *Busy.*

Imperia: *On a Sunday?*

Imperia: *Stop lying, Cass.*

Imperia: *I know you're free.*

Imperia: *Just come over.*

Imperia: *Please. It's urgent.*

Me: *If it's so urgent then say what it is now.*

Imperia: *I can't say in person.*

Imperia: *Stop acting like I'm some stranger to you, Cass.*

Imperia: *I carried your baby for goodness sake.*

My heart skipped a couple beats as I read her words.

Imperia: *Just please come over.*

As frustrated as I was by her persistence and triggered by her mention of our baby, I knew that if I didn't give into her ways, she was going to keep hounding me down with texts until I eventually gave in.

Me: *On my way.*

I got up from my couch and headed to my bedroom to grab my Yeezy's. I was out my penthouse ten minutes later with my lambo keys in hand and heading down my private elevator to the parking lot.

I arrived at Imperia's crib less than half an hour later and to my surprise, the front door of her apartment had been left ajar for me to enter without knocking.

"Imperia, where you at?" I called out to her as I stepped through her foyer, staring at her open space living room that was coated in the colors gray, brown and lilac. A vanilla scent greeted me as I walked deeper, trying to see where she was. Her kitchen was on the other end of the space and unoccupied which made me frown.

"Imperia."

Seeing that she wasn't in her living room, I made my way through the corridor leading to her bedroom. I hadn't been here in three months but I still knew the place like the back of my hand. My footsteps sounded as I walked across the gray oak floors, soon arriving in the middle of her bedroom's doorway since her door had been left wide open.

I stepped in, my eyes travelling around the room as I searched for her once again. My jaw clenched when she was nowhere in sight.

"Imperia, where the hell are yo..."

The bathroom door to the left of me slowly opened, revealing Imperia.

"Hey, you."

She stood in the doorway's middle, a towel wrapped around her womanly frame and her hair wet and curly from the shower she'd just stepped out of.

"What's so urgent that you needed to see me in person?" I queried, trying to ignore the fact that she was in nothing but a towel right now.

She ran her fingers through her wet tresses, sighing softly.

"Talk, Imperia," I snapped, getting irritated by her reserved manner. "What is it?"

Imperia stepped forward, bringing her hands to the top of her towel and unraveled it. By the time she let it drop to the floor, there was a short gap between us. My eyes dropped to her figure, feeling my bulge grow below at her curves, perky breasts and that slit between her thighs that I hadn't slid up inside in a hot minute.

It was at that moment that I realized what was so damn urgent. It was at that moment that I realized that Imperia had used my soft spot for her due to our past to get me into her home so she could show me what was so urgent.

"Imperia, I don't hear you talkin—"

"Shhh," she hushed me, dropping to her knees and grabbing my sweats, slowly pulling them down to my ankles. "This is urgent."

I looked down at the lust sparkling within her eyes as she kept a sealed gaze on me. Then her view went to my dick that was lengthening above her. I licked my lips at the sight of her grabbing him tight and shivers went up my spine at her touch.

"You've been playing around, Cass..." She stroked my tip, causing me to bite my lip. "Acting like you don't miss me... acting like you don't know where home is."

I was now finding it hard to concentrate because her lips enveloped me, sliding down my mushroom head as far as she could go before popping her lips off and smiling up at me.

"Did you miss me?"

I didn't answer. Instead I was reaching for the back of her wet head, trying to get her back in the position she needed to be. But she shifted her head out of my reach, shaking her head at me.

"Did you miss me, Cass?"

"You know I did," I told her what she wanted to hear, knowing fully well missing her was the last thing I'd felt for the past couple weeks. But she knew what she'd started when she pulled my pants down and started playing with my dick.

Her smile strengthened and she secured her dainty hands around my base, opening wide and pushing my shaft down her throat.

Why I'd even listened to Imperia's texts about needing to see me was still a mystery to me but I wasn't going to dwell about it now. She wanted me and quite frankly, I was going to let her have me.

Maybe this was what I needed to no longer be hooked on Danaë. Maybe fucking Imperia could be my way of proving to myself that what I had with Danaë was nothing but sex. Nothing that couldn't be forgotten about in an instant.

CHAPTER 17

~ DANAË ~

"*L*ady D... Your father wants to see you."

It was the one statement I'd been dreading to hear all day because I knew it was coming. I didn't know what time it was coming; all I knew was that it was coming and lo and behold it had finally came.

The minute Kamora left my apartment yesterday, I focused on cleaning up my living room, switching off my phone, having a soothing bath and getting ready for bed. I didn't want to have to deal with the trouble that was coming my way until tomorrow morning.

Tomorrow morning was here and the second I stepped into my office; I was on edge. My phone had been switched back on and to my surprise, there were no missed calls from my father, no missed text messages, no voicemails, nothing. Complete radio silence. Telling me that the trouble coming my way was still en route and this trouble was going to be dreadful.

My father wasn't a silent man so his uncommunicative nature after I'd slapped the love of his life was a red flag. A big one.

Now at 1:45 p.m. as I stared into the chocolate eyes of Deyjah, a sour taste formed in my mouth because I knew that trouble was here.

"Thank you for letting me know, Deyjah."

She nodded, giving me one last affectionate smile before she left my office.

You've got this, Nae. Just tell him what happened. No biggie.

No biggie? Girl you slapped his girlfriend, this is most definitely not no biggie.

I got up from my seat and left my office. Each step towards the elevator was a step that I didn't want to take. Each step I took made my heart race, making me think I was on the verge of a damn heart attack. Eventually I was on the elevator and heading up to the top floor. Once the doors slid out the way for me to walk down the corridor leading to the glass doors of my father's office, I got the urge to turn around and pretend like this wasn't happening.

Get a hold of yourself, Danaë. You're not scared of your father.

I wasn't scared of the man but I was most definitely scared of his anger. It was an emotion that I'd only been acquainted with a few times in my life on this planet and it wasn't a sight that I liked to see.

I took a deep breath, let it out and walked bravely to his office. The glass doors slid out the way once I'd arrived and I pressed forward, immediately laying eyes on my father sitting behind his desk.

"Have a seat, Danaë."

His tone was firm yet still gentle at the same time. Surprisingly, I couldn't hear or see anger within him which made my muscles ease up slightly and I obeyed his order.

I took my seat, crossing my legs and placing my hands to my lap as I waited for him to speak. The seconds began to pass as our eyes remained anchored on each other and both our mouths remained shut.

I expected him to start the conversation off but he just continued to stare at me with an emotionless look that was starting to make me nervous.

Fuck it.

"She starte—"

"Danaë Louisa Westbrook," he called out my entire government, making me swallow hard. "Do not even think about trying to pin this on her. Don't even think about it."

"But she di—"

"When have I ever raised you to put your hands on people?" He interrupted me again, his eyes now cold. "When?"

"Daddy, she spoke on mo—"

"Answer me."

I sighed deeply, knowing I wasn't about to get a word in unless I answered his questions.

"You haven't."

"I haven't and you do the one thing you know not to do," he snapped. "Have you lost your actual mind, Danaë? What the hell were you thinking?"

"Are you going to let me speak or are you just going to keep painting me as the one to blame here?"

His lips pursed together and he placed his hands in front of him, linking his fingers together. He motioned for me to speak with a nod.

"She was the one that brought up mom, not once, not twice but three times. She called me selfish when she's the selfish one trying to use the excuse of mom being gone as a reason for you to move on and get married. Did she even tell you all the crap she said?"

His face remained unmoved by my words, much to my dismay.

"She told me to stop holding onto my mother like she's coming back from the dead to steal you away. That mom was dead and I needed to get over it. How you can even be with someone who disrespects your late wife is beyond me! She has the audacity to speak on my mother as if she knows her and you're blaming this shit on me! She has the audacity to call me selfish and claim I got it from my mom and you expect me not to get angry! I'm the one that gets disrespected time and time again but I'm the bad guy here!"

"Do not raise your voice at me again, Danaë. Did I raise my voice at you?"

My chest heaved up and down as I now glared at my father.

"Did I raise my voice at you?"

"No," I muttered through gritted teeth.

"I know what she said because she told me everything." My eyes widened. "And because of what she said, Kamora and I have broken up."

Just like that, every part of my body that had been filled with rage started filling with joy.

"But that doesn't excuse your behavior, Danaë. You hit the woman that I have feelings for. We may have broken up and what she said was out of order but that doesn't change the way I feel about her."

I looked at him, unreactive to his feelings for Kamora. It didn't change the way I felt about her. She'd disrespected me by not only insulting me but by also bringing up my mother and there was no coming back from that.

"You need to apologize, Danaë."

The rage quickly began to overpower me once again as I watched my father.

"You need to apologize so that we can all move on from this. You, me and Kamora."

"I will do no such thing."

"Danaë."

"No."

"Danaë, stop being stubbo—"

"I said no," I cut him off, shaking my head. "No, no, no, no, no!"

"Danaë, are you fucking serious? You're really behaving like a five-year-old right now because you refuse to apologize for putting your hands on my girlfriend."

"*Ex*-girlfriend," I corrected him with a sly smile.

He gave me an unimpressed look.

"I'm not apologizing."

"Yes you are."

"No." I lifted my head high and didn't take my eyes off him. "I'm not."

"Danaë, do not make me have to choose between you and the woman I'm trying to spend the rest of my life with."

My mouth went dry.

"What?"

"You heard me."

"No, I don't think I did," I said. "I think I heard you say something completely stupid, Dad."

He went quiet, unclasping his hands and running his hand down his face.

"Danaë."

"You would rather choose a woman you've known for five fucking minutes than your own daughter who you brought into the world?"

"Watch your mouth," he coolly warned me. "Kamora and I have been together for two years, Danaë and you know that. You know we've been committed to one another."

"I don't give a fuck!" I jumped up from my seat and slammed his table. He didn't flinch though. "She's evil. Evil, evil, evil!"

"Dana—"

"And I hate that bitch," I spat, glaring down at him. "If you choose her over me, go ahead but just know choosing her over me means that I don't want anything to do with you anymore."

"You don't mean that, Danaë."

I didn't but I was going to keep pretending like I did.

"I'm not apologizing and I don't want her in my life."

"Now look who's being the selfish one after all," he commented, cradling his chin in his hand as he eyed me closely.

He was using Kamora's words, ultimately telling me that he agreed with her about me being selfish and because of that, I was done with this conversation. I lifted my hands from his desk and turned to leave.

"Danaë, we're not done."

"Well I am." I strode to the exit.

"I said we are not don... Danaë Louisa Westbrook, do not walk away from me when I'm speaking to you!"

His yell caused me to halt and I clenched my fists, breathing deeply.

"I'm not one of your little boyfriends that you can run away from when shit hits the fan." His reference to my situation with Houston made my pulse slam in my neck. "You're not fleeing from this, Danaë. You will apologize and you will make amends with Kamora."

"I'd rather drink bleach," I said, not turning to face him. "She's dead to me."

I began walking once again, ready to get the hell out of his office. This conversation was over whether he liked it or not.

"Danaë, get back here right now!"

I ignored him, no longer wanting to hear a word from him. He continued to shout my name even when I'd walked through his glass doors. I knew that walking away from him when he was still talking – more like shouting – was rude but I had no care to be kind right now. Our heated discussion had confirmed to me what I already knew from the moment I woke up this morning. My father had taken Kamora's side even though she'd spoken on his late wife. His late wife who was the *real* love of his life.

Tears pricked my eyes with each step I took away from his office. Disagreeing with my father was something I rarely did and the disagreement we'd just had was the worst one we'd ever had.

The second I got on the third floor, I rushed to my office, ready to do what I knew best.

Run.

I didn't care about the two meetings I had to attend today with co-workers and a new client. I wanted to be anywhere but here. I wanted to be in my bed, far away from here and I wanted Cassian right beside me. More than ever I needed to feel his strong embrace around me and hear him tell me that everything was going to be okay because right now it felt like my life was falling apart. It felt like I was losing the most important man in my life to a woman that didn't care about anyone but herself.

Running became a failure when I arrived a short distance away from my door and spotted Deyjah standing outside.

"Lady D," she greeted me, looking quite flustered.

"Deyjah, is everything okay?" I blinked back the tears trying to fall from my lids.

"Imperia's here to see you," she announced. "She didn't listen to me when I told her you had a meeting in five minutes."

I looked down at my watch's gold face to see the time was 1:55 p.m. My meeting with my co-workers who I'd been working on a large company's accounts with was in five minutes. The meeting I'd already decided I was going to miss because I was ready to get the fuck out of here. ASAP.

"Thank you, Deyjah. It's okay. Could you let the guys down-stairs know I won't be able to make it?"

"Sure," she said, surprise filling her eyes. "Is everything okay, Lady D?"

I nodded, walking past her to enter my office and putting on a fake happy smile as I slipped in. Much to my surprise, I found Imperia sitting behind my desk with her legs and arms crossed.

"Hey, girl," I greeted her, the door shutting behind me. "You never told me you were coming over. You okay?"

"I'm fine," she said and it was only now I noticed how irritated she looked. "But you won't be unless you stay away from Cassian."

I blinked rapidly.

"Sorry?"

"You heard what the hell I just said, Danaë," she snapped. "You need to stay away from my man."

Huh? Her man? What the hell is she talking about?

"Adina filled me in on everything," she voiced. "The private dinners, the spa and apparently you have a key card into his penthouse?"

Hearing her rattle off what Cassian had done for me wasn't a surprise because I knew Adina had told her everything. They texted each other from time to time and I was glad to know that they were bonding without me.

"Cassian and I were in a relationship," she continued to speak. "A serious relationship. The best friend I had a great loss with? Yeah that was him."

My heart almost stopped at her words and I parted my lips to talk but she didn't let me get a word out.

"I had his baby. A baby girl..." She started shaking her head at her own personal memory. "A baby girl who suddenly died seven months into my pregnancy. She'd died in my stomach and I had to deliver her. I had to deliver *our* dead baby."

The more I heard her speak, the more I wanted to be told that this was some sort of sick joke. This had to be a joke right?

"Of course Cassian and I's relationship hasn't been the greatest ever since that day but it doesn't change the fact that we love each other very much. Now I had no idea about your father's firm when I first met you or about Cassian's relationship to this company but now that you two have met, I know everything. And I bet you're wondering, why would I sit there at the hookah lounge and listen to you keekee with Adina about my man? Well, I truly believed that you were just another one of his jump offs who he likes to keep in rotation, because believe me he's had many of those over the years. I still believe that you're nothing but a jump off, something for him to do until he gets bored of you. You're not the first and you won't be the last. I allow him to do what he likes but he's very much mine, Danaë, and if you know what's best for you, you'd stay far away from mine. Because I can tell you right now, I don't play about mine."

This had to be a twisted joke. One sick, twisted joke that wasn't funny at all. I was left speechless, unable to respond to all that Imperia had just said. I was still trying to register the fact that Imperia and Cassian had had a baby together.

What the hell!

"And before you go ahead and tell me our business relationship is done, let me be the one to say it first. Your services are no longer required both in my business and with my man. Stay away from Cassian."

"You must be joking," I blurted out.

"I'm not," she said.

"No but you must be." I couldn't believe this shit. "There's no way that you would be dumb enough to sit back and listen to me talk about my interactions with your man if he really was your man."

"Like I said before, ever since we lost the baby, things have been rocky between us but it doesn't change the way we feel about each other," she stated. "We were together yesterday."

My heart skipped a beat and my stomach hardened.

"I've texted you the proof so you can see for yourself that we definitely were." A smug grin grew on her lips. "Whatever you think you've been doing with Cassian, believe me it's nothing but sex. All the wining and dining is just a part of his charm. Don't think you're special because you're not. You're just another itch for him to scratch, just another woman for him to fuck. You have no idea who he really is and what type of world he comes from. You only know what he wants you to know and I promise you, that ain't much at all. If you know what's best for you, you'll stay away from him. Not just because I'm telling you to but because it's what you need to do."

Imperia then rose to her feet. Her grin still plastered on her lips as she walked around my desk.

"It's a shame we couldn't be friends after all," she said. "I quite liked having you around before you started messing with my man."

She came to stand in front of me, looked me up and down like I was dirt on the back of her shoe then left my office. I remained frozen as a statue in the middle of my office. Unable to talk and unable to think straight.

Cassian... Imperia... a baby... she loves him... he loves her... with her yesterday.

Remembering Imperia's mention of sending me proof made me move. I raced to my desk where my phone sat on the other end and snatched it, wanting to see for myself this so-called proof.

"Imperia, I don't hear you talkin—"

"Shhh... This is urgent."

My eyes misted with tears as I watched the video playing on my screen.

"You've been playing around, Cass... Acting like you don't miss me... acting like you don't know where home is."

Imperia was naked on her knees, stroking on Cassian's member. They were in her home. I knew that because it didn't look like Cassian's bedroom so the only other option had to be her home.

"Did you miss me?"

He was silent, more focused on reaching for the back of her head and trying to push her back down in place to suck him off. Imperia moved out of the way so he couldn't grab her just yet.

"Did you miss me, Cass?"

"You know I did."

I stopped the video, my bottom lip trembling and my hands shaking as I clicked out of it.

It was all true.

Here I thought he was single and only messing with me. He'd told me that I was the only woman he was with.

"I'm only charming you right now, Danaë. You don't see anyone else around here do you? You're the only one up in my bed every night and the only one taking this dick."

That fucking liar!

The same emotions I remembered feeling when I'd found out my ex were married was resurfacing. My whole body was on fire and I couldn't stop shaking.

I've been played for a fool. Again. I let myself fall for a man that I was never supposed to fall for. A man I didn't really know. A man that I'd allowed to seduce me with his charming ways... all those irresistible ways that made me weak at the sight of him.

The tears wouldn't stop falling now. I backed into my desk to gain balance as my legs suddenly felt too weak to stand.

Why the hell are you crying for? You knew this wasn't a relationship. You knew from the start this was nothing more than sex, Danaë.

Just because I knew it was just sex didn't mean that I didn't wish it was more. That didn't mean that I hadn't fallen for him. Each day we spent together, each night I was in his arms, I'd fallen more and more for Cassian Acardi. There was no point denying it now.

Ding!

My phone chimed, making me lift a hand to wipe my tears away from both cheeks. I then looked down at my phone to read the new message.

You're getting tied up tonight, Nae.

Ding!

Pierro's coming to get you from work when you're done.

Ding!

I'm not waiting 'til eight for you to come over.

Ding!

We've got a lot of catching up to do since you weren't in my bed last night.

Ding!

Don't even think about complaining because it's not up for discussion.

Heat coursed through my body as I read each incoming text. Heat that wasn't from desire. Oh no, desire was the last thing I felt towards this man.

How dare he?

He had the nerve to text me after he was laid up with his on and off girlfriend/ex-baby mama yesterday. He had the nerve to text me like we were in a relationship.

I slid up my screen, heading to our chat and my fingers typing away as rage swept through me.

I won't be seeing you tonight. Tell Pierro not to bother.

Send.

I locked my phone, placed it down to my desk and went to take my seat. After the numerous bombs that had just been dropped by Imperia, driving home was the last thing I could do. I was too angry to drive anywhere. What I wanted to do was smash something. Smash his stupid little fac—

Ding!

My eyes dropped to his text: *You're complaining, Danaë. Just like I told you not to.*

Cassian: *You must want me to come get you now myself.*

I unlocked my phone and typed, *No, I don't. I don't want you to do anything to me.*

Cassian: *What the hell is that supposed to mean?*

Me: *It means that whatever the hell we've been doing is done.*

Me: *I'm not going to be one of your little jump offs anymore.*

Cassian: *Are you drunk?*

Cassian: *What the fuck are you talking about, Nae?*

Me: *Ask the woman who had your child what the fuck I'm talking about.*

Me: *The woman you were with last night.*

His read receipt came in but he didn't respond right away so I kept typing.

Me: *Yeah I know.*

Me: *Imperia told me all about it.*

Again his read receipt came in and like before he didn't respond. I waited for three gray dots to appear but they didn't.

I think I need some time away
I took a little time I prayed
We gon' be alright okay

The seductive vocals of Jorja Smith filled the space and I was now looking down at the caller ID on my phone's bright screen.

Cassian

The phone continued to ring as I watched it. I had no desires to hear his voice right now and quite frankly, I wasn't about to give him the satisfaction of hearing how hurt I was because I knew the moment I picked up and answered the call, my voice would break.

> *I think I need some time away*
> *I took a little time I prayed*
> *We gon' be alright okay*

I let it ring out and eventually it stopped and I sighed, relieved that he was no longer calling me. Sadly, my relief only lasted for a few short moments before I was back to feeling tense.

> *I think I need some time away*
> *I took a little time I pra—*

I hit decline and before I knew it, my phone started going off.
Ding! Ding!
Cassian: *Pick up the phone.*
Cassian: *Right now.*
Me: *Leave me the fuck alone.*
Cassian: *Pick up the phone, Danaë.*
Cassian: *Now.*
Cassian: *Clearly you've lost your damn mind.*

Cassian: *Don't make me have to help you find it.*

Once again my phone started ringing and just before I could press decline, my office door was opened and I looked up to stare into the brown eyes of my father.

"Danaë, we weren't finished."

I quickly declined the call and put my phone on do not disturb.

"Dad, I can't talk abo—"

"No we're definitely talking about it," he affirmed, striding into my office and taking his seat on the teal chair on the other side of my desk.

His arms crossed over his chest and he rested back against his seat. His serious eyes fixed upon mine.

"I don't want us keeping this tension between us because that's not us, Danaë. You know it's not us. It's never been us and I don't want us starting now. This situation is getting rectified one way or another. I don't care how long it takes."

I said nothing, feeling myself crumble inside as I remembered Imperia's words.

Don't think you're special because you're not. You're just another itch for him to scratch, just another woman for him to fuck.

"Tell me everything you don't like about Kamora."

"Dad…" I stole a glance at my locked phone, sensing the endless amounts of texts and calls Cassian was sending my way. The do not disturb feature was truly my saving grace right now.

"Just tell me. I can take it."

"I really can't do this right now. Please."

I made a move to get up, pushing my chair back but the second I did my father shook his head 'no'.

"Well we're doing it." I rose to my feet. "Sit down, Danaë."

"Dad, I c-can't!" Tears pricked my eyes.

Not only was I not in the mood to have any more conversations about Kamora, the witch, I wasn't in the mood to talk. I just needed to leave.

"Danaë... what's going on?" My father's face softened and he leaned forward, trying to read me carefully.

"I... I just need to go home."

"Why, Angel? What's wrong?"

My first tear dropped and that was enough to make my father rise to his feet, zoom around my desk and bring his hands to my shoulders. His touch brought an instant warmth to my heart and when he pulled me close, I melted into his loving arms and the tears were endless.

"Danny, baby, talk to me... is this about earlier? I'm sorry, Angel. I didn't mean what I said about choosing you over her. You're my daughter, I would never..."

I kept silent, continuing to cry and sink into his loving embrace.

"Danaë, talk to me please." He moved back, lifting my chin and making me look up at him. "What's going on?"

He was one of my best friends and he knew all there was to know about me... except what was going on now. I wanted to tell him everything. Tell him all about my situation with Cassian, how I'd fallen for him and how it had all been one terrible mistake. How I never should have allowed myself to get entangled with that man. Tears continued to stream down my cheeks and I looked up at him, feeling hopeless.

"Talk to me, Angel," he pleaded, rubbing my back.

"I... I..." My sobs weren't allowing me to speak properly.

"Take your time, baby... just breathe."

I followed his instruction, inhaling deeply and exhaling.

"Tell me what's wrong," he requested, still massaging my back gently.

I was now torn on what to do. I didn't like keeping things from my father but this secret felt too terrible to share. But now that I'd broken down in my father's arms, he wouldn't let me leave his sight until I at least told him something.

It took me a few minutes to finally speak up and when I did I decided to keep things as vague as possible.

"...I fell for someone."

"Who?"

"Someone I wasn't supposed to fall for," I said, sighing deeply.

"Okay..." He was silent for a few seconds, staring into me as if my eyes told him all the answers to my current misery. "And this someone... do they know how you feel?"

"No... well, I don't think so... maybe... but it doesn't matter. Him and I are done. He made me feel something that wasn't real. He was just using me for sex."

"Did he admit that to you?"

"...He didn't have to," I revealed. "Someone else did."

"His wife?"

I shook my head 'no'.

"He's not married to her but they have history. History I didn't even know of until she told me. They're still seeing each other and he lied to me that he was only seeing me."

"Have you spoken to him?" he queried.

I shook my head 'no'.

Cassian and I had only exchanged a few texts but I hadn't seen him in person and I had no plans to. I just wanted to be left alone.

"I don't want to speak to him, Daddy. We're done."

"Okay then don't speak to him. Send him a text and keep it moving. You don't need that type of man in your life. No one uses my daughter for sex."

He lifted his fingers to my cheeks, wiping them dry.

"And no one makes my daughter cry."

I gave him a weak smile, closing my eyes as he pressed his lips to my forehead.

"I know it hurts but you will get through this." I fell back into his warm embrace. "You're a fighter, Danaë." He hugged me tighter. "That's how I raised you and you always come out on top. You know that."

He was right. I was a fighter but something about this situation felt different. The feelings I had for Houston were nothing in comparison to what I felt for Cassian. How was I supposed to just keep it moving when Cassian was a part of my work life?

It wasn't a question I wanted to try and figure out the answers to. I no longer wanted to think about my feelings for Cassian Acardi because every time I thought about them, I broke down.

"Are you going to tell me who this fool is, Danaë? You might not want to speak to him but I do."

"No, Daddy... he's nobody important anymore. Trust me. You don't need to get involved."

There was no way that I could let my father find out that the man I was talking about was Cassian. They had a very good business relationship and I wasn't about to ruin that because that would mean messing up some of my father's coins. That was the last thing I wanted happening.

Imperia's words had cut deep and not only had her words cut deep, but I was also reminded of the video she'd sent me of her and Cassian. Her vindictive little way of confirming to me that she had a hold on him that I would never be able to have.

"Did you miss me, Cass?"

"You know I did."

They still had a thing for each other and in no shape or form did I want to compete with it. I would need to figure out a way to get myself removed off the Acardi's accounts without my father suspecting a thing because being in the same room as Cassian after all I'd learned today was the last thing I wanted. All I wanted was my bed.

Trenton and I had been hugging silently for a while now with his hands stroking my back and rocking me gently. Providing me with a remedy that only a father could.

"Dad... I still really wanna go home," I quietly spoke up, breaking our comforting silence.

"Alright," he agreed, patting my back. "Let's both head home early, Angel. It's been a long day."

I nodded in agreement with him.

"Let's stuff ourselves full with pizza, coke and your favorite show... what's it called again? The vampire books?"

"Vampire *diaries*," I corrected him with a chuckle.

"Vampire diaries it is," he confirmed. "And you know how much I hate junk food but I'll do it tonight for you. It'll be my little cheat night."

My spirits soared at the mention of my father and I having our own Netflix party but then I remembered his connection to a woman I wasn't trying to see and panic rolled through me.

"But Kam—"

"She's not there," he said, easing my wary thoughts. "She's staying at her place for now... we need the space."

Once again I nodded and smiled, glad that my father and I were going to spend time together tonight. Lord knows I needed it.

"Grab your stuff and I'll meet you downstairs in five."

He pecked my forehead one last time before backing away from me and heading towards my door. I turned to the coat rack behind me, doing as he said. I heard my door open just as I placed my trench coat behind me to put it on.

"Cassian?"

A coldness hit my core, almost stopping my heart and I became paralyzed, unable to move from my stance.

"Trenton," his deep voice made the hairs on the back of my neck stand up.

"What are you doing here, son?" he questioned him. "I didn't realize you had a meeting today with my daughter."

"I do," he confirmed which made me slowly turn around to see him standing in the doorway of my office, shaking the hand of my father.

Our eyes locked and I became breathless at the sight of him dressed in a navy suit. The color never looked better and it burned me at how I couldn't deny how fine this man still looked. Even after all the negative emotions I felt towards him in this current moment, Cassian Acardi was still a sight too alluring to break away from.

He held me prisoner with his stare as he announced, "Danaë and I have a lot to discuss right now."

CHAPTER 18

~ CASSIAN ~

"I've heard great things about the way you do business, Acardi. That's why I know this partnership is meant to be." He lifted his tatted hand towards me. "I'd be a fool to buy ammo from anyone else in town but you."

I raised my hand to join his and we shook hands while sharing a look of understanding and respect.

"The bitcoins are being transferred as we speak," he told me. "Full payment, just as we discussed."

I nodded before saying, "You'll have your supply before the end of the day."

I'd just stepped out of a business meeting with Donovan Hill, an affluent member of Chicago. He owned a few strip clubs and night clubs but they were nothing compared to the amount of narcotics he pushed through the city. Narcotics that were provided by my cousin, Santiago. It was through Santiago that Donovan had sought out my services and we'd just had a meeting at Donovan's club located downtown, finalizing our deal.

Now I was in the backseat of my Bentley, being driven back to

The Palazzo. I whipped out my phone from my blazer pocket, seeing that the time was 2:05 p.m. as I headed to my messages.

"Pierro, I need you to go get Danaë as soon as she's done at work," I announced, entering the chat I had with her.

"No problem, Capo."

You're getting tied up tonight, Nae, I typed before hitting the send button.

I sent three more texts her way.

Pierro's coming to get you from work when you're done.

I'm not waiting 'til eight for you to come over.

We've got a lot of catching up to do since you weren't in my bed last night.

Then finally: *Don't even think about complaining because it's not up for discussion.*

I stared down hard at my screen, waiting patiently for her response. Only God knew how much I'd missed her. We'd seen each other on Saturday but last night away from her had been hell. I'd made a mistake going over to Imperia's. A big one.

"Imperia... Imperia... stop."

"...What's wrong, Cass?"

"This."

"What?"

"This is wrong. I don't want this. I don't want you."

"Wha—"

Ding!

My thoughts were suddenly interrupted by the sound of my phone going off and my eyes focused in on the newest text from Danaë.

I won't be seeing you tonight. Tell Pierro not to bother.

My chest tightened at her response.

Me: *You're complaining, Danaë. Just like I told you not to.*

Me: *You must want me to come get you now myself.*

Danaë: *No, I don't. I don't want you to do anything to me.*

The tightness got worse and I felt my jaw twitch. *What the fuck is she on right now?*

Cassian: *What the hell is that supposed to mean?*

Danaë: *It means that whatever the hell we've been doing is done.*

Danaë: *I'm not going to be one of your little jump offs anymore.*

Me: *Are you drunk?*

Me: *What the fuck are you talking about, Nae?*

Danaë: *Ask the woman who had your child what the fuck I'm talking about.*

Danaë: *The woman you were with last night.*

What the...

My face squeezed as I realized that she'd just made reference to my whereabouts yesterday with Imperia.

How the hell did she know about Imperia and I?

Ding!

Her newest response only brought more tenseness to my body.

Danaë: *Yeah I know.*

Danaë: *Imperia told me all about it.*

How the hell does she know Imperia? What the actual fuck is going on?

Instead of wasting time texting back and forth, I decided that my questions needed to be answered with a phone call. I clicked on Danaë's name and hit the audio button to make the call. My eyes went to the tinted window next to me, looking outside at the moving city with my phone glued to my ear.

The line rang but it wasn't answered right away, making me clench my fist.

"Hey, its Danaë, sorry I can't get to the phone rig—"

I cut off her voicemail and quickly called her line once again. The line was cut off just seconds as it began ringing and I became blinded with anger.

Pick up the phone.

Send.

Right now.

Send.

"Pierro," I called to my soldier without taking my eyes off my screen.

"Yes, Capo?"

"Take me to Morgan & Westbrook," I ordered, seeing gray dots appear in our chat. "And step on it."

"Sure thing, boss."

Danaë: *Leave me the fuck alone.*

Me: *Pick up the phone, Danaë.*

Me: *Now.*

Me: *Clearly you've lost your damn mind.*

Me: *Don't make me have to help you find it.*

I called her once again. Only this time, the call wasn't declined. It went straight to voicemail before it could even ring.

"Hey, it's Danaë, sorry I can't get to the phone right now but please leave a message and I'll..."

As I listened to her voicemail, my only motive right now was to get to her. She wanted to keep declining my calls and sending stupid text messages my way? No problem. Clearly this was a conversation that needed to be had face to face and clearly Danaë needed to be reminded what type of nigga I was.

Since we were nearby, it took Pierro five minutes to pull up outside Morgan & Westbrook. I thanked him for his efficiency, rushed out the car and entered the building. I was greeted by the security guards and let in by the receptionist.

Before I knew it, I was on the third floor, walking straight to my desired destination and arriving outside her office door, about to open it only to be beaten to the punch.

"Cassian?"

My eyes fixed on Trenton Westbrook, standing in my way.

"Trenton," I greeted him and watched as he brought out his hand for me to shake.

"What are you doing here, son?" he asked as we shook hands. "I didn't realize you had a meeting today with my daughter."

"I do," I confirmed and she slowly turned around, allowing me to lock eyes on her. "Danaë and I have a lot to discuss right now."

"I'm afraid that won't be possible," Trenton voiced with a light shake of his head. "Danaë is heading home earl—"

"Dad, it's okay," she spoke up in a low tone. "I'll meet you downstairs in a few."

Trenton turned to face her.

"Danaë, are you sure?"

She nodded.

"I've just got a few things to tell him and we'll be done," she said. The words 'done' coming out of her lips sounded final.

Like I'm letting that shit happen, I mused, knowing fully well *done* was the last thing happening between Danaë and I.

"Okay then." Trenton turned to me again. "See you later, son."

I gave him a simple nod and we shook hands one last time. I moved out the way for him to get to the door and held it open while he passed through. Before leaving, Trenton looked over his shoulder to give Danaë one last look. A look of love and concern but no words followed that look. Instead he went on his way out her office. I let the door shut behind him and once it did, I quickly strode over to Danaë's desk.

"Don't."

I ignored her, keeping my mouth sealed and taking hasty strides to where she stood on the other side.

"Cassian, I said don't!"

Her yell caused me to stop.

"Don't come anywhere near me!"

Not only did I despise the fact that she was yelling at me, but I also despised how much she didn't want to be around me. I could see it in her eyes. That mixture of fear and hate. Two emotions I'd never seen within her before and I hated that I was seeing them now.

"Explain to me how you know Imperia," I demanded, standing firm in my stance.

I badly wanted to close the gap between us but I would respect her wishes.

For now.

She took a deep breath before saying, "She's my client."

What the fuck?

"Well *was* my client," she corrected herself, shaking her head and avoiding my eyes. "She was also someone who I considered a friend until she walked in here less than an hour ago, telling me to stay away from you. The man she carried a child for."

A coldness filled my heart at the mention of Zeroni.

"I was her financial consultant prior to me even working for my father and we..."

I listened as Danaë explained her relationship to Imperia. The more she talked, the more I thought about how fucking coincidental it was that Imperia and I both happened to be in Danaë's life without even knowing. Once Danaë mentioned all about Imperia finding out at a girls night out that we'd slept together and not saying a word about knowing me, I knew that this was no longer coincidental. Imperia had known about Danaë and I for a while and waited for the right moment to strike.

"She told me and showed me the truth about you and I," Danaë said, her voice breaking slightly but she continued to talk like nothing was up. Like she wasn't affected by Imperia's lies.

"She made me realize that I don't know much about you and that I never will because I'm nothing but sex to yo—"

"You know damn well that's not true, Danaë," I cut her off, stepping forward but stopping when Danaë stepped back. "You're not just sex to me."

"Yes I am," she countered. "You don't need to say things just to make me feel better. I know you don't car—"

"Stop trying to make it seem like I don't care about you because I do."

"The same way you care about Imperia, right? The woman you were with last night." Her eyes briefly found mine again before they drifted away, making me pissed off at the fact that she wasn't looking at me properly. During the entire time she'd explained her connection to Imperia she failed to give me eye contact for more than five seconds and it stung me to the core.

I went silent, trying to search my brain for the right words to say about the dumb mistake I'd made yesterday by going over to Imperia's. It was at that moment I remembered Danaë's words about Imperia showing her the truth.

"You said she showed you the truth about you and I."

"She sent me a video of you two... together." She shot me a tense look.

My brow raised.

"She was on her knees, giving you exactly what you wanted."

That. Little. Bitch.

It was now that I was able to connect all the dots as to why Imperia wanted me to come see her so bad. I'd never wanted to wrap my hands around her throat until this very moment in time.

"Did you watch the whole video?"

Danaë's face twisted with rage.

"What kinda stupid ass question is that? Of course I didn't watch the full video."

"Well you should've," I stated, no longer prepared to keep this bullshit ass distance between us. As soon as she realized I was coming nearer, Danaë stepped back until she hit the accent wall behind her.

"Cassian, I told you to stay aw—"

"Because if you had watched the whole thing you would've realized that it wasn't that long."

"Oh and that's supposed to make it all better?" I'd now made it round her desk. "Cassian, stay aw—"

"Yes I went over to her house but only because she hit me up, pretending to need to see me about something urgent. As you now know, we have a past together, a serious one which is what Imperia used to her advantage."

By now I was two steps away from closing the gap between us.

"But what Imperia quickly realized yesterday is that our past doesn't matter to me anymore."

I stepped forward and Danaë's eyes dropped to the floor.

"I don't want her and I made that clear when I made her stop and left her apartment without turning back."

I pressed forward again, closing the space between us and lifting a hand to Danaë's chin. Her glossy eyes found mine.

"I don't have feelings for her anymore, Danaë. She caught me in a moment of weakness but that's all it was. A moment of weakness. She sent you that video out of spite because she knows deep down that I have feelings for you."

And after speaking, I joined my lips to hers, trying to push out all the negative feelings that Danaë was feeling for me.

"No." She pulled away seconds later, pushing against my chest in the hopes that it would move me away but I stood my ground in front of her.

"Nae Nae..."

"No, you still went over there. You still let her get on her knees and have you. If she hadn't recorded you and shown me or even revealed your connection today, you wouldn't have told me about you two. You wouldn't have opened up to me about your past with her the same way you haven't really opened up to me at all. All this time we've been spending together and I still don't know who you really are."

I remained silent, feeling torn on what to do or say. One part of me wanted to tell her everything. About Zeroni, about my family and all the power we had throughout the city. But the other part of me couldn't bring myself to do it. Once I opened that box there would be no going back and the number one question I had to ask myself was could I really let her in? Could I really let Danaë in to see all the ugly and bad in my life?

You know you can't.

"...Nae. It's complicated."

"What's so complicated about opening up?" she asked, hurt staining her pretty features. "What's so complicated about opening up to the woman you said you have feelings for?"

I don't know if you'd still want to be around me once you find out all I'm capable of. What role I play in a system too powerful to destruct.

"That's what I thou—"

I branded my lips to hers, pushing my tongue through the seams of her lips and dominating her mouth. She tried to protest – well fake protest – by pushing against my flesh with hers, trying to get me out but it only led to our tongues colliding in the best way and her moans seeping through. Eventually I let her go, allowing us to both catch a breath and pressing my forehead to hers.

"Just give me some time, Nae," I whispered to her. "Give me some time to open up to you... Please."

I couldn't believe that I of all people was begging for a woman's time. It was always the other way round but with Danaë shit was different and I knew that clear as day right now. I had feelings for this woman. Strong feelings that were growing more and more every day. I was done pretending like this was just sex.

She hadn't responded to my request but her face had relaxed and her eyes much softer than before. Now that I was much closer to her, I could tell that she'd been crying by her puffy eyes that only made me want to inflict pain upon Imperia ten times more than I already wanted to. I lifted my hands to Danaë's cheeks and gazed into her dark browns that always knew how to make me weak for her.

"I'm sorry..." I pressed my lips to her cheeks. "Just give me time, Nae... I promise..."

Silence filled her office once again and I waited for her response.

"I'll think about it," she replied. "Right now I just need some space."

A sharp pain formed in my chest. Space was the last thing I wanted from her but I understood that she was hurt by my actions so whether I liked it or not, space was exactly what I needed to give her. I nodded before planting a kiss to her forehead and stepping back.

"Imperia will never be in contact with you ever again. You have my word. And I promise you, she'll never have access to me ever again. We're done."

But you and I are not, Danaë.

I gave her a final look then took my leave.

She could have her space as she wanted but it wasn't going to be a forever thing. Now that I was sure I had feelings for her, letting her go wouldn't be an easy thing at all. It was the last thing I intended on doing but the main thing I knew that had to be done was making sure one woman understood that our connection to each other was officially dead.

～

"I always knew the day that you'd stop taking your medication would come."

Her eyes grew large and she parted her lips to speak but I injected before she got the chance to pipe up.

"That sick shit you pulled by recording me yesterday, consider it one of the last ever memories you have of you and I. Including this one."

"Cass—"

"I had love for you due to the fact that you carried my child and were one of my good friends but that's all dead now. This..." I pointed from me to her. "This is dead. Any connection you had to me is no more."

Imperia blinked a couple times, clearly in disbelief that I was cutting her off. But what exactly did she expect to happen? That sneak shit she'd pulled with Danaë wasn't something I was going to let slide. Why she'd even done it in the first place I had no idea. But it was her own misdemeanor and she would deal with the consequences by never having access to me again.

"You're cutting me off because of a random that you've been fucking from time to time?" I remained stoic, knowing deep down I was burning at her mention of Danaë being a random. She was far from it but that wasn't something I felt the need to clarify because I knew Imperia already knew the truth. I wouldn't be cutting her out of my world if Danaë was just a random. "A random that doesn't even know who the hell you are and what you really do?"

I watched her as she stood on the other side of the room we were in. One of the Palazzo's conference rooms to be exact. After my run in with Danaë, I was quick to want to see Imperia but rather than being the one to hit her up, I made one of my soldiers go to her home and bring her to me. Whether she was home or not, I didn't care. I would wait. She didn't arrive home 'til two hours after my soldier was posted up outside her house. Now here she was, standing by the seamless window wall that showcased Chicago's breathtaking view.

"What goes on between Danaë and I is really none of your business, Imperia. It never fucking was," I snapped. "Not only will you no longer have anything to do with me, but you will also never step to Danaë again."

Again her lips parted but I pushed past the words that dared to seep from her lips.

"And if you ever have the audacity to step to her, I promise you, love, you'll be answering to nobody but me."

Silence.

Nothing but silence followed and the annoyance that flashed in her eyes did nothing to move me. I didn't care how Imperia felt and I was sure that after today, I never would ever again. Our history was exactly that, history and any positive feelings I'd had for her, any affection I had for this woman was gone. She'd gotten in the middle of something she had no right stepping in the middle of and for me that was all I needed to give her the boot out of my life for good.

"All this for a woman that doesn't know your past, present or future. She doesn't know about our dead child, your power in the streets oh and how could I forget..." Imperia sported a fake surprised look. "She has no idea that you're next in line to be head capo."

Sometimes I really hated how much Imperia knew about my world. How could she not know it though? When she was the daughter of one of my father's best friends who happened to be an old associate of the Acardis.

It was how we'd gotten close in the first place. Imperia and I were practically raised together. I'd known her all my life because she'd always been around, not constantly in my face around but around enough to be remembered and for me to grow fond of her. It was when my father passed that her father retired as an Acardi associate and decided to enjoy the fruits of his labor overseas with his many concubines. Her mother on the other hand was living it up in Las Vegas, enjoying the revenue she'd gained after their divorce. You would think Imperia would have followed suit and no longer indulge in anything to do with the Acardis but she just couldn't stop lying to herself thinking that her and I were always meant to be. That shit was dead and I was here to make sure it became permanently ingrained into her head.

"You haven't let her in, Cassian, because you and I both know that what you're doing with her is nothing real. Nothing like what we had. You don't let people in, shit, I was barely let in even when I was carrying your daughter and I still know more about you than Danaë ever will."

Now it was my turn to be silent as I contemplated her words.

"You know deep down that she could never handle a man like you because you're not the type to open up fully, the way a woman needs you to. The way I needed you to."

There it was. There was Imperia's way of making this entire situation about her.

"The only time I got you was when Zeroni was here, growing inside me." She pointed to her stomach. "And when she was gone, so were you."

Again I remained silent, letting her say her piece. This was clearly something she'd had on her chest so I wanted her to empty her clip before I put the final blow to our situation.

"So were you, Cassian!" she yelled, on the verge of tears. "Our child died and you treated me like nothing. Like our love meant nothing to you. Like we weren't going to spend the rest of our lives together."

"Now we both know that's not true," I chimed in. "Our child

died and you became adamant on making another one because you knew that without a child in the picture, you and I were never going to be. Even when I was still mourning our loss, you were steady trying to plot on how you were going to replace her."

"That's not true. You wanted another baby with me."

"Stop lying to yourself, Imperia. You know that night between us was a mistake. A drunken mistake that I let get too far. I wanted Zeroni and I was willing to be one big happy family for her sake and you knew that."

She shook her head from side to side, her eyes still watery but no tears had fallen yet. Her crocodile tears did nothing to me though. They didn't change the way I felt about her one bit.

"You loved me."

"As a friend, Imperia," I finished her sentence off. "A friend. You knew my love for you but you took advantage of that shit, the same way you took advantage when you recorded us and sent it to Danaë. The woman I have feelings for."

Her face went pale at my revelation.

"Not some random. Not some jump off. A woman I fucking care about."

My cursing was a result of the weakness I felt at revealing my feelings. Something I never did. But today was turning out to be full of surprises. Firstly, by me telling Danaë how I felt about her and secondly by me now telling Imperia. I didn't have to tell Imperia I had feelings for Danaë though because we both knew she knew that shit. That's why she'd gone out of her way to find out more information through Danaë's girl about us, gotten me to come over to her crib to record us and sent a stupid ass video of her sucking me off to Danaë. She knew from the start what was up and the lies she'd spurred out to Danaë today had caught up to her.

"She won't ever understand or accept you the way I did. She

won't ever love you, Cassian... all the fucked-up parts of you. She doesn't understand your world and she never will. That's why you haven't let her in because you know she won't be able to handle who you really are. Who you're destined to be one day. You'd be a fool to think she'd accept the true Cassian after she realizes what a monster he can be."

A tightness formed in my jaw but I tried to keep it together by not folding. I didn't need Imperia seeing how much her last few words had affected me and quite frankly, I didn't need to be having this conversation with her anymore.

"Stay away from Danaë. You know how much of a monster I can be so don't tease him, Imperia. This is your final warning."

The tears that had formed in her ducts, she'd managed to blink away and now all that remained was a frosty stare sitting on her face.

Our situation had officially run its course and I was cutting ties with all things Imperia. There was nothing left to be said because she no longer existed to me. Without another word, I turned away from her and stepped out the room. Despite leaving her, the tension that had formed within me didn't ease up. Her words had scarred me but I was going to try my hardest to push them out.

Danaë didn't need to accept the fucked-up parts of me because they weren't important. They didn't affect her. In her mind, I was just a typical businessman with the means to get whatever I wanted whenever I wanted it. I wasn't in charge of the Acardis yet and I didn't see that happening in the next decade or so. My auntie still had at least a year in charge and even when she did step down, it would be my cousin, Julius, that would be taking charge. Not me. I wasn't head capo so I didn't need to worry about Danaë needing to accept who I really was. She didn't need to know the monster that I could be and I had no plans to tell her. Acardi women knew everything there was about The Family but with

Danaë I just wanted to keep things pure between us. I didn't want anything getting in the way of what we were building because I knew that I was falling for that woman more and more every single day.

I wasn't keen on letting Danaë know about my family or our power but I would try to make an honest effort to let her into my past with Imperia. I would open up to her just like I told her I would but in my own way. I could give her enough of me while still keeping her out of harm's way. It was the least I could do after the bullshit Imperia had pulled today. I just prayed that this whole space shit that Danaë was asking for didn't last long because I didn't have the time nor patience for it. If I wanted her back in my bed next week, tied up and ready for me to dick her down in the best ways possible then that's exactly what was happening.

CHAPTER 19

~ DANAË ~

*R*etail therapy proved to be one of my greatest habits in the past and something that never failed to put a smile on my face but as I now sat in a discrete corner in one of my favorite stores, a smile was the last thing that spread across my lips. Rather my lips were tucked in and my expression hard as I gazed down at the newest text from my father.

I really can't believe you two right now, the first one read.

What is so hard about putting your differences aside and coming together for one night? The second one read.

"So... what do you think?"

My eyes darted up from my phone to lay eyes on a true beauty. She'd just stepped out of a dressing room and now stood in front of me. Slowly swirling around for me to get a good view of the garment hugging her curvy frame. She turned around to face the mirror behind her, closely examining her appearance until my voice interrupted her.

"I think my best friend is one bad bitch."

Adina laughed, smoothing her hands down the gown.

"Are you sure? I mean I know I look good but do I really need this dress?"

We both knew that she didn't need it but that wasn't about to stop her from convincing herself that she did. The same way she'd convinced herself that she'd needed a brand-new Louis Vuitton bag, a brand-new Gucci purse and a belt to match. This Jacquemus dress that cost over a thousand dollars wasn't about to stop my bestie. I didn't blame her because she worked hard for her coin and deserved to splurge. Besides I quite enjoyed watching Adina spoil herself. It was far better than me trying to do the same. I'd brought myself a Louis Vuitton tote bag but that surge of satisfaction that came whenever I treated myself, failed to show up.

As Adina debated with herself about a dress she knew she would purchase the second she laid eyes on it, my focus went back on my phone. My father's text were still displayed on my screen and I rolled my eyes at his attempt to reunite two beings that didn't need to be together.

Five nights ago, I'd spent time with my father without having to worry about bumping to The Witch. It'd been comforting being in his presence, watching my favorite show and chomping down some pizza. It'd even been a great way of taking my mind off the fuckery that had gone down with Imperia and of course what happened with... *him*. Thinking back to those dreadful moments back in my office had me feeling glum.

I'd told my father that I'd only spend a few minutes telling Cassian a few things and then we would be done. I'd only been right about one of those things and it wasn't the second one. The only reason why I'd decided to let Cassian have a "meeting" with me was because I didn't want my father getting suspicious about the identity of the man I was talking about being Cassian. And I also saw that unwavering look in Cassian's eyes as he stared at me.

Telling me that he didn't intend on going anywhere until we talked. Even after I told him that I needed space, I could see it was the last thing he wanted.

Now back to the issue with my father. Our night together had been a great time to bond and take my mind off everything going on with Cassian but two days after our quality time, my father was back to pestering me about Kamora. He wanted me to sit down with her and apologize for slapping her which I said I would do if she apologized for being disrespectful. Of course she disagreed, wanting me to be the only one to apologize. Now my father was going back and forth with the both of us – mostly me I was sure – trying to get one of us to be the bigger person. Well, it most definitely wasn't about to be me and because of that, my father and I's bonding time seemed non-existent. Our relationship was now strained and I was constantly frustrated at him trying to pin Kamora on me.

What part of I didn't want anything to do with her did he not understand?

"It's a shame I don't know where that trick lives because boy oh boy does she deserve a beat down."

A grin tugged at my lips but I suppressed it as best as I could and opened my mouth to eat from my fork.

"At least I cussed her ass out good via text before she blocked me. Dumb ass hoe."

After our retail therapy session at Saks Avenue, Adina and I were now enjoying a meal at Tanta, a Peruvian restaurant.

Adina had been filled in on all the bombs that had been dropped into my life. From Kamora to Imperia and Cassian, she knew it all. And she was much more enraged by everything than I was and she wasn't even the one dealing with everything. But that was my Dina. Ready to go to war for me whenever and wherever.

"I know you don't really wanna talk about him but I'm curious, how long do you intend to keep this space between you two?"

I shrugged with a mouth full of food. Adina was also fully aware of my feelings for Cassian. Her words about things being more than sex had been confirmed. This was way past just being sex.

"Has he tried to call or text?"

I shook my head 'no', knowing a part of me was relieved he hadn't hit me up but the other badly missing him. Even with the turmoil I felt about his situation with Imperia, that man still had me sprung on him.

"Now I feel like shit for even connecting you two in the first place. I know I said that I was certain that the boss you needed by your side was him but that was before I knew about his past with Imperia. Him and Imperi—"

"Had nothing to do with you," I assured her, reaching across our table for her free hand.

The corners of her mouth lifted into a small smile that didn't quite reach her eyes.

"You never could have known about their history. The same way I never knew when I first met her. This is not your fault, Di. Don't even think about trying to pin this on you."

I squeezed her palm in mine and that was enough to boost her smile, enabling it to reach her eyes.

What I didn't want was Adina blaming herself for a situation that wasn't her fault. How was she to have known about my ex-client being connected to her boss? It was a fucked-up situation but one that neither of us could have predicted.

Hours later, I was driving home in my Benz after spending a long-needed girls day with Adina. Being around her was always a great pick me up and despite how conflicted I'd been this week; Adina was the number one person I wanted to be around.

I arrived at my apartment's parking lot in less than ten minutes and was too preoccupied parking in an empty spot to notice a familiar Bentley parked in the far-right hand corner of the space. Not far from where I'd now parked my GLA.

I reached for my handbag and the black Saks shopping bag sitting in the backseat before exiting my car. I placed my bags over my right shoulder and just as I set the locks in place and began walking in the direction of the exit was when I heard the call of my name.

"Miss Westbrook."

I knew that voice well. A bit too well which is why my body stiffened and my mind went blank. My head slowly turned and that's when I spotted *it* and *him*.

It being the Bentley I'd been picked up in many times and him being the tall tawny skinned man that drove me to his capo. His face mirrored my mind, blank and unreadable. That was something I had grown accustomed to being around him but a few times he would crack and present me with a smile.

Not today though.

He strode over to the passenger side of the vehicle and opened the door. His way of signaling for me to get in.

It was only now that I took a closer look at the car and spotted a figure positioned behind the driver's seat and my heart began to race.

No.

Instead of gracing Pierro with words, I faced my front and focused on getting the hell out of this parking lot.

"Miss Westbro—"

"Danaë, take one more step away from me and you and I are going to have a serious problem."

I halted. Not actually wanting to but feeling like I had to all of a sudden. His deep baritone sent chills all over my body and five days away from him and I could still feel the hold he had on me.

I heard his footsteps and that was the signal I needed to begin moving but I refused to listen. Instead I remained stuck in place, listening to his footsteps draw nearer to me.

It was at the exact moment that his footsteps stopped that I decided to turn around only to wish I hadn't.

Those browns were sealed on me, daring me to look away, knowing fully well I couldn't. Not now that he had me trapped under his spell. He had a fresh line up with his hair cut low and a taper fade. That beard never looked better – well groomed, trimmed and looking like the only seat I wanted to ride. A silver stud was locked in each ear and my eyes fell to his attire. A gray short sleeved t-shirt that had a loose fit but did nothing to disguise that muscular physique and matching basketball shorts, revealing those toned legs of his. White air force ones covered his feet. He was looking like a snack – scratch that – he was looking like a whole damn meal and I hated it because all I wanted to do was eat him up.

"Danaë."

He was looking at me the same way that I knew I was looking at him. Like I missed him and wanted to badly remove the short distance between us.

"What are you doing here, Cassian?"

"You know exactly what I'm doing here, Danaë," he voiced, seriousness laced in his tone.

"I told you space."

"Which you've had for five days," he reminded me.

Five days of complete agony.

"And I'll take five days more or however days I see fit."

I turned away from him in an attempt to walk free but an attempt was all it turned to be when my hand was grabbed before

I could make another move. His touch sent electric pulses across my skin and his scent... that manly scent of his that I had missed, that always made me ache with need for him to be inside me.

"Cassian, please."

I refused to look at him once again because I wasn't trying to be seduced by those eyes of his. Or that face. That face that was convincing me more and more that my idea to take space had been nothing but stupid. A stupid, stupid, stupid mistake.

"Look at me."

My vision was the row of parked cars ahead and I was determined to keep my vision the same.

"Nae Nae... look at me."

Until he called me by the nickname that only he had the right to call me.

His hand that had grabbed mine, pulled me closer into him and before I knew it my sights were nothing but him.

"You've had your space," he said, his lips so close to mine that all he had to do was pucker up and we'd be connected. "Enough."

I wanted to speak up and protest but the pained look I now read within him made me stay mute.

"I'm sorry. You know I am. Imperia was a mistake and you also know that. A mistake I'm never going back to."

I remained quiet, not bothering to confirm what I already knew. I wasn't mad about Imperia anymore and now that I really thought about the situation, I don't think I was ever mad at Imperia. I was mad at him and only him. By going to Imperia, he'd made me feel like what we were doing – something we'd never put a title on – was nothing to him. Obviously I knew that was far from the truth because he'd told me about how he felt five days ago but my feelings had still been valid. I still had a right to be mad.

"Five days was more than enough," he added sternly. "Too fucking much."

"Says who?" My left brow arched.

"I do," he concluded before meshing his lips to mine.

It was the one thing I'd been longing for and now as our lips moved in a perfect sync, I was again reminded of how 'space' had been the dumbest idea.

You couldn't blame a girl for being hurt though and you couldn't blame me for distancing myself from the man that had brought me that hurt.

Our kiss deepened, tongues dancing, exploring and devouring each other. One of my hands was still joined with his while the other now held the back of his neck. His other hand circled my waist, keeping me as close as possible. We didn't stop even when we both had to come up for air. It wasn't until my eyes shot open moments later and I spotted Pierro with his back turned that I remembered we weren't alone.

"Mmmh... Ca... Cass..." I eventually managed to break away from Cassian but as soon as I parted from him, he pushed forward still planting pecks on my flesh.

"Cass..." I tilted my head back, feeling a smirk form on my face at the disapproval setting on his face. "Pierro."

"Not your problem," he told me, leaning into my chest and kissing up my neck.

My head remained tilted back so he couldn't get access to my lips.

"Not here, Cass."

He refused to listen, peppering my collar bone and throat with his enticing kisses.

"Five days away from me clearly had someone losing their mind," I teased which earned a sharp bite into my skin. My whimper was instant.

"Cass..."

"You're absolutely right," he agreed. "Which is why you're going to pay for every single one of those days."

Five minutes was all it took for Cassian and I to get through my front door. Clothes went flying everywhere before my door was fully shut and I went flying over Cassian's shoulder once my nude body was exposed.

"Five days."

My lips parted wide but I found myself speechless. Speechless because of the powerful thrusts now entering my being.

"Five days."

His finger pressed against my clit and that was all it took to make my moans burst through.

"Five fucking days."

Our eyes were fixed on each other, my legs locked in place around his torso and my hands anchored in place above my head by his hand. His way of making clear: *You can't run from this.*

The determined look his handsome face housed as he dived into my haven and teased my clit nonstop told me further about not being able to run from his drilling. He wanted me to feel his wraith and realize that those five days away from him had been an error. An error that couldn't happen again.

"I don't want to hear the word space come out of your mouth ever... again," he ordered, slamming into my tightness one last time.

He didn't have to tell me twice. Five days away from him had been horrible and not having the chance for us to be this connected had been ten times worse. I nodded with breaths so fast that I felt like I was about to pass out.

"Tell me you won't ever say it again, Danaë." He remained frozen inside me, giving me a chance to focus and say what he needed to hear.

"You... you won't ever hear me say it again," I promised, staring up into his piercing eyes as he towered over me.

"Good girl."

Before I knew it, he was back to sliding in and out of me, reminding me of all the pleasure I'd missed from having him inside me.

"Cass!"

"This is my shit," he proclaimed. "My. Shit."

My head bopped up and down at the same time his hips moved in and out my middle.

"Yes."

"Ain't no one else allowed up in my shit but me."

"Yes," I agreed. "No one."

"Louder," he ordered, slamming into me.

"No one else but you, Casssss! I promise!"

His million-dollar smile flashed down at me. Then he leaned into me, catching my nipple into his mouth while he worked my cave in the best ways that only he could.

Five days away from him was never happening ever again. I knew that for sure.

It was too early into the next day for us to still be up but here we were. My body enclosed by his mighty frame, his soft breaths tickling my skin and both our hands joined as we laid up against my headboard.

"It's a name..."

Cassian had an Arabic tattoo on the upper left-hand side of his abdominal muscles, just under his left pec. I'd started tracing my fingers on it and found myself wanting to ask what it meant but then I remembered his words about giving him time to open up. I didn't want to force him to have to say anything he wasn't ready to bring up yet but it's like Cassian knew my thoughts because he was one step ahead, filling in the blanks in my mental.

"A name?"

"Zeroni," he clarified, his tone heavy all of a sudden.

Without even needing to hear him say it, I knew who Zeroni was.

"My daughter."

Imperia had briefly mentioned the child that they'd had together and it'd hurt me knowing that Cassian had gone through such a loss. I couldn't even really be mad about the fact that he hadn't brought up his late daughter because losing a child was a terrible thing that I wouldn't wish on anyone. Not even my worst enemy.

"She died in the womb due to complications of the placenta."

"Cassian, I'm so sorry."

"Don't be. There's nothing to be sorry about something you didn't cause... It was just a fucked-up situation that I couldn't do anything about."

Silence followed. I wasn't sure what to say because what could I say other than sorry?

"Don't go all ghost on me," Cassian whispered to me, pecking my cheek. "What's on your mind?"

"I'm... I'm just in shock," I replied. "And I really am sorry that happened to you. I can't even begin to imagine how heart breaking that was for you."

I turned to look at him, instantly reading the sadness in his orbs. This was a touchy subject for him. The wounds from Zeroni's death hadn't healed and I didn't expect them to. How could one ever get over losing a child?

The one thing I wanted him to be certain about was that I was here for him. In any way that he needed me to be. I was here.

"You can talk to me about anything to do with Zeroni, Cass... don't be afraid to open up to me. I'm here for you. I'm here for us."

I leaned closer to him, planting a loving kiss to his plump lips before leaning back to look at him once again.

"Us," he repeated my last word. "You really mean that?"

"Yes."

"No more five days away from me?"

"No more," I promised and that was all the confirmation he needed to lock our lips together as one.

I was serious about being here for Cassian and everything that he came with.

You have no idea who he really is and what type of world he comes from.

Imperia's words had been dancing in my head for a few days now. It didn't take a rocket scientist to realize that Cassian Acardi came with a lot more secrets. Imperia had only been a small part of the large pile of secrets. I wasn't born yesterday and I recognized that Cassian had to be part of something bigger. Something powerful.

The way Pierro, his driver, respected him was the first inkling I got about this man being much more than just a successful hotel owner. But I tried to shake it off as Pierro just being a devoted employee. However, Imperia had confirmed to me what I'd been trying to fight off all along. Cassian Acardi came from a world far different from mine.

Was I afraid?

No.

My feelings for this man ran too deep for me to be afraid of what world this man was part of. All I wanted to be was by his side and that's where I planned to be. Anything else was unimportant.

CHAPTER 20

~ CASSIAN ~

"The new Palazzo's exterior will be identical to the original..."

I couldn't divert my attention away from her even if I tried. She had me hooked on her alone, not just from her words but from her ability to look so damn good while she talked business. It was one of the things I knew undeniably that I loved about her. She was the only lady in the room yet still managed to be the biggest boss in here. I finally could understand what Beyoncé had been talking about on *Top Off* because my Nae Nae was most definitely the realest nigga in the room.

"...Its interior will have many upgrades such as..." She turned to the projector screen behind her and clicked the button on her remote. "A state-of-the-art gym, both indoor and outdoor, combined swimming and jacuzzi pools, a rooftop lounge and restaurant, keyless room entry accessed via smartphone..."

Each feature she listed appeared on each slide she clicked through. Since I was standing at the back of the room, I was able to see the reactions of all my investors and directors. Their eyes lit up as they watched each slide and they would occasionally look at each other, shooting pleased nods around the room.

Ten minutes later and Danaë was saying her final words, thanking the men for listening and now finished with her presentation. The twelve men that sat around the rectangular conference table each got up and left their seats to individually shake her hand and thank her for her presentation. She gave them each warm smiles and thanked them for their time. Once each suited man was done greeting her, they would come to me, offer me a hand shake, their verbal agreement with the deal and be on their way out the conference room.

It's not like they had a real choice on the expansion of The Palazzo but their support was appreciated. Christian and I didn't actually need investors for our hotel but it was Zietta that had convinced us that it would be a good look with the hospitality industry. And of course her being right about everything meant that she was right about this. Having investors got our hotel in the radar of some of the most important people in the hotel industry and essentially put a whole lot of extra paper in our pockets.

The doors shut behind the last man and I watched as Danaë turned off the projector before she turned to face the back of the room. Where I stood with my hands nested in the pockets of my pants. Her mesmerizing eyes glued to mine.

No one said a word. Not that words were needed at this current moment. My steps did all the talking as I took quick strides across the room. Passing the black leather seats bordering the conference table and stopping once I was a short distance away from her.

She pressed her hands down to the desk, leaning forward which allowed me to get a view of her cleavage peeking through her V-neck blouse. A smile slowly took possession of my lips as I observed her and her new antics.

My little tease.

"Did you like the presentation, Mr. Acardi?"

I nodded without speaking up, letting my gaze slip to her breasts, then to her long legs cloaked by her high waisted slacks before I found her face once again.

"What did you like about it?" she asked, leaning forward even more.

"Everything."

I pressed ahead, coming to stand next to her and grabbing her waist. With one swift motion I placed her on top of the table and positioned myself in the center of her open legs. My lips found their place on her neck and she extended to the right, giving me more skin to kiss.

"Mmm, Cass..."

While I planted kisses all over her flesh and squeezed her mounds through her shirt, her hands went to the back of my head, stroking gently. Then my kisses went up her throat, landing on her chin and dropping to her lips.

I still couldn't believe that one month had passed between us. We hadn't put a title on our relationship but we both knew what was up. One month later and I still wasn't sick of being around and inside Danaë Westbrook. If we weren't spending some part of the day together, whether having lunch, dinner, going on dates around the city or her being in my bed or me being in hers, I felt incomplete. She'd become a fixture in my life and I didn't see her leaving.

Minutes into our tongue battle, I began unbuckling my belt and decided to cut our heated kiss short. Ignoring the look of displeasure that crossed her pretty face, I grabbed her waist and brought her to her feet. I turned her around and rested my chin on her shoulder while bringing her wrists out in front of her. We both looked down as I brought my Tom Ford belt to her wrists, wrapping the smooth leather around her skin and securing it tight with a knot.

"Cass... the door."

"Ain't got shit to do with you."

I pushed her onto her stomach, making her lay on the table. She stretched her arms up, placing her tied hands above her head.

"You knew exactly how hard you were making me when you were leading that meeting, didn't you?"

She didn't respond but I could already sense the smirk forming on her mouth despite not seeing it since her face was down.

Spank!

"Cass!"

"Answer." *Spank!* "Me."

"Yes," she answered. "I knew."

I soothed my hard hits by caressing her skin through her satin pants.

"So you must know how hard I'm about to fuck you."

"Yes," she repeated, her voice barely above a whisper. "I want it, Capo. You know I do."

My hands wasted no time in unclasping her top button and pulling down her pants. Mine quickly followed.

"Ahhhh, Cass!"

"Uh-uh, you wanted it," I reminded her as I thrusted in and out of her tight slit. "Take this dick, Danaë."

"Cassaaahhh!"

"I'm not going to tell you again. Take this mothafucking dick."

"Yes, baby... I'm... I'm gonna take it."

"Such a... fuck... such a good fucking girl. Take your dick."

"Mmh... Make sure... make sure you put it in my butt, Capo. I wanna take it there too."

Her nasty words made me pull a stank face. Only she could

match my nasty and that was one of the reasons why I adored her. She was just as nasty as me and I was convinced that she was becoming more and more each day that enjoyed each other's bodies.

"Oh best believe you're about to get it there too... You better not run, D."

One month later and we still couldn't get enough of bringing each other to the greatest heights of pleasure. One month later and I still had her right where I wanted her to be. With me.

"I can't feel my damn legs."

I chuckled and before I knew it I felt a playful hit on my arm.

"It's not funny, Cassian."

I grabbed her hand just as she drew it away, gripping it tight in mine. I pulled on it so that her back was pulled off her seat, bringing her close to me.

"Hmm... You managed to get into your seat with no problems," I said. "Maybe we need to clear this table and go another round to make sure you really can't feel your legs."

"Uh-uh," she protested, shaking her head from side to side. "You've worn me out, Capo."

More chuckles fell from my lips and I lifted her hand to my lips, planting a kiss to the top of it which made her smile. I then let her go so she could resume the meal we were eating.

We were seated in a center table at Oriole, one of the best high-end restaurants in the city and a restaurant that Danaë had grown to love, thanks to me. I'd made sure that we were the only ones in the restaurant and the service solely focused on us. After a successful meeting at The Palazzo, the least I could do was treat Danaë to a private meal.

"You really were great today," I told her, watching as she placed her salmon into her mouth. My sights went to the two yellow-gold Cartier bracelets dangling on her right wrist. The bracelets I'd gifted her weeks ago that she seemed to never take off because every time we were out, they were on. She had a gold Rolex on her other wrist, another one of the gifts I'd slid her way. Danaë was a baddie so it was only right she got a rollie to match.

This afternoon, Danaë had led a meeting at The Palazzo in front of my investors and directors to show them the upcoming plans and expenses for the new sister hotel. She was the only one who knew how to explain my newest baby best which is why I'd requested she be the only accountant from Morgan & Westbrook to lead the meeting. Despite having numerous accountants handling The Palazzo's accounts, Danaë was of course my favorite and honestly, she was the best. She knew her job well and I was rest assured knowing she was taking care of the hotel's finances.

Christian had been invited to the meeting but said he couldn't attend because he had somewhere to be. I figured it was family business he had to take care of so I didn't think anything of his absence.

"I might need to steal you from your father and bring you on permanently as one of my employees."

She smirked, chewing on her salmon before swallowing.

"No need to steal what's already yours, Cassi bear."

Now it was my turn to smirk at her use of a nickname that she'd coined recently.

Cassi bear.

It was cute and slightly annoying but coming from her lips I could tolerate it. She got the idea to call me it because she'd heard me on the phone to Caia one time and Caia calling me Cassi had Danaë smiling nonstop while she listened silently in the background. Adding bear to my nickname Cassi had been Danaë's way of reminding me that I was one big bear that appeared scary because of my strict, no nonsense nature but deep down I was a softie. Her exact words too which were one hundred percent right. I was a softie. A softie all for her pretty ass.

"He still giving you the silent treatment?"

Danaë nodded, sighing softly.

"Things just really aren't the same between us and I hate it," she replied, slouching in her seat.

"Yeah but you know what you can do to fix things, Nae."

"I'm not apologizing first."

Things with Danaë's father had gotten more strained during the last month. Between Kamora not wanting to apologize for bringing up Danaë's mother and Danaë not wanting to apologize first for hitting her, Trenton had been torn between the two women. Eventually he had enough of trying to make his daughter be the bigger person and that included talking to her all together. The only discussions they had these days was business but anything outside of that, Trenton had no input.

I'd tried my best to get Danaë to budge on doing what her father wanted especially since I knew how close they were but Danaë refused to give in. She was set on being stubborn and standing her ground. Despite how much it was killing her each day not talking to her father in the way she would like, Danaë was running in full force with her stubborn streak.

"But Dana—"

"I'm not, Cassian. You know I'm not," she cut me off with a stern look. "She disrespected me and my dead mother which is why I hit her. There's no way I'm apologizing first."

"I know what she said and that shit was foul but it's been a whole month now. You've had time to clear your head about the situation and you've had time to be away from her. Surely there must be a part of you that's had enough of this tension with your father. You miss him, don't you?"

She gave me a blank look as she shrugged.

"Not really."

"Nae Nae... don't lie to me."

"Okay." She finally cracked, her brown pools filling with misery at the fact that her and father weren't on the best terms. "I miss him."

"So what's wrong with putting your issues to the side for him?"

"But I have been putting my issues to the side for him," she countered. "I've been doing that shit. He knew from the start that she and I didn't get along. He said it himself that he doesn't want to get re-married so she played herself by pushing the issue in the first place. I just don't see why he can't accept us not being in each other's lives."

"Because even though he doesn't plan to marry her, he loves Kamora and still sees a future with her," I reminded her. "You know that."

She was silent.

"You're his life, Danaë. Always have been and you always will be. That's why he wants this to work. That's why he wants the two women he cares about the most to get along. He can't accept you two not being in each other's lives when you're the two people that make up his life. It won't work."

More silence followed and her eyes fell to her half empty plate of food. I leaned back in my seat, eyeing her closely as I tried to think of the best way to get Danaë to be more open to fixing things with her father.

"If I was by your side when you sit down with Kamora, how would you feel?"

Her eyes lifted to mine.

"By my side?"

"Yes," I confirmed. "You, me, your father and The Witch."

A smile was on the edge of her lips.

"I'll be by your side and support you every step of the way. We can even have the sit down at my penthouse."

She was silent but because her focus was on me, I could tell she was thinking about my proposition.

"Besides, it's about time your father knew about us," I added. "Don't you think?"

She nodded before speaking, "Y-Yes."

Her nervous tone had me grinning.

"So you're in?"

"This sit down is only happening if I agree to apologize," she announced skeptically.

"Which is exactly what you're agreeing to do, Nae," I ordered. "I know what she said hurt but you're better than this. My Nae is a boss and handles her shit. No one said you need to love the woman but fix this childish ass beef and be civil with her for the sake of your father. Please, Nae Nae."

She was quiet for a few seconds then her next words made me brick hard.

"I love it when you beg me, Capo."

"You do, huh?" I reached for my glass of Henny.

"Yes."

"Do what I say and you'll have me begging you all night to ride my face until you cum all up in my mouth."

Her eyes widened with lust and I lifted my glass to my lips, sipping while keeping a sealed gaze on her.

"Yes."

After my sip, I placed my glass back down.

"Yes what?"

"Yes, I'll have the sit down with you, my father and The Witch."

I leaned back in my chair, gently tapping my fingers against our table. My mouth became moist and my blood now rushing down below.

"I think I want you riding my face right now, Nae."

She took a quick glance around the empty establishment and the apprehension in her eyes made me speak up.

"Don't worry about them. They know to give us privacy for the rest of our meal," I said, pushing my empty plate back to make a space on the table so it was suitable to be sat on.

I knew she was worried about us getting caught but she didn't need to be. I had it handled.

"Please, Nae... right now. I need you."

Those words were enough to get her out of her seat and onto my lap. We'd been sitting right next to each other so there was no need for her to walk over to me. I was about to have my favorite dessert right in the center of one of my favorite restaurants and no one was about to stop me.

Or so I thought.

Zing! Zing! Zing!

Moments later, the vibrations of my phone in my blazer pocket sounded and I sighed just as I began pulling down Danaë's panties. She now sat on the table in front of me, legs hiked to my shoulders and mine for the taking.

We shared a look of annoyance and I lifted my hands off her body, reaching in my blazer's pocket without taking my eyes off her. It was hanging off the back of my chair. I only took my eyes off her once the phone was out and below me.

On the screen appeared a text from Zietta that made my body go numb.

I'm back in the city and I need to see you tonight, bambino. Please come over around eight.

"Everything okay, baby?"

My head shot up and I was staring into the concerned eyes of Danaë.

"Yeah," I lied, locking my phone's screen and pushing my phone back into my blazer. "Now where were we?"

She revealed her pearly whites and I drew closer to her, reaching for her panties. As I buried myself in the treasure between Danaë's thighs, I knew deep down that everything was far from fine but right now all I wanted was her. Everything else could wait until later.

Hours later and evening had come. I was now driving out of Chicago to my auntie's Winnetka mansion.

When I'd seen Frankie's texts earlier, numbness filled my core for two reasons. Firstly, I didn't even know that she was returning home today from the long ass vacation that I hadn't been a fan of in the first place and secondly, she wasn't one to text me. If she needed to see me then she was calling me and telling me that shit straight out of her own mouth. Nonetheless, I was on my way to see her now and all of my queries would be answered one way or another.

I'd hit up Christian a couple times after dropping Danaë back at work after our meal but he hadn't hit me back. I guess whatever the hell he was doing was taking up all his time right now and I would hear from him later. If not, I would have to go looking for his ass because it wasn't like him to go missing on me.

"You know I can't, Cass."

Danaë's voice sounded through my car's speakers as I drove on the highway.

"Since when was I can't an option?"

"I can't, baby... I've got a meeting at nine a.m. A meeting that I can't miss."

"You won't miss it."

"That's what you said before I missed the last one."

I chuckled, remembering how she left my penthouse in such a rush two weeks ago with her t-shirt on backwards.

"See?" She laughed too. "I can't but... you could always come over? Nala hasn't seen you in a while."

I tittered at her reference to her goldfish.

"And I'm guessing she told you this herself?"

"As a matter of fact she did."

"Oh so you can talk to fish?"

"Yup and she told me to tell you she misses you."

I grinned before replying, "Tell Nala I'll see what I can do."

She groaned.

"So that's a no."

"No..." My grin widened. "That's not a no. I'm just not sure how late I'll be working tonight and I don't want to wake you up when I slide through. How about lunch again tomorrow? My treat."

"Adina's been dying for a lunch date so I'm out with her tomorrow but I'm free Thursday and Friday afternoon for lunch."

"Good. Lock me in for both days."

"I like the sound of that," she said and I could hear the smile in her tone. "Sounds like a plan, Capo."

"So I'll be seeing your sexy ass on Thursday for lunch, Nae."

"For lunch," she agreed. "Don't stay up working too late, okay?"

"I'll try my best, sweetheart."

Our call eventually ended and while one hand worked the steering wheel, my other hand cupped the back of my neck.

Danaë was under the impression that I was working late

tonight when I wasn't. I didn't want to tell her about Zietta's text because it wasn't anything she needed to worry her pretty head about. One month had passed between us and I'd been doing a decent job at keeping my relationship with Danaë separate from my life as an Acardi. I opened up to her about Zeroni's death, my childhood with Christian, being raised by my Zietta, my sister Caia and even shared details about my father but nothing about being part of a powerful organization. That was a detail I was keen on keeping away from her.

I was let in by Zietta's uniformed security guards once I arrived outside her front gate minutes later. They each sent a respectful nod my way as I drove through her driveway, heading forward to park in my regular spot. Imagine my surprise when I noticed not one but five cars already parked ahead.

What the hell?

That eerie feeling I'd gotten after receiving Frankie's text earlier but tried to brush off was back. I parked my car behind a car I quickly recognized as Christian's Ferrari.

So this is where this nigga's at.

Without wasting any more time, I cut off my engine, left my car and rushed towards Zietta's front door.

The door was already open so all I had to do was push and enter. I took quick steps through the foyer, passing the entryway table and aiming to head upstairs only to suddenly stop when I was called.

"Bambino *(Baby)*."

I turned to the left and spotted five faces looking at me like someone had died. They were each scattered around the room. My brother stood, Julius sat, my two cousins stood and my sister sa—

Wait a damn minute!

"Caia?"

I walked into the space, staring deeply into the hazel eyes of my sister.

"Hey, Cassi."

Her tone was downhearted and so were her eyes which didn't make any real sense to me because I hadn't seen her ass in over a year. Why the hell was she looking sad to see me of all people? Her favorite brother in the whole wide world.

"Bambino *(Baby)*," I heard Frankie call out to me again.

It was only now that I realized that Frankie hadn't turned around because she was on the sofa backing me. I rounded the chair and made my way over to her but as soon as I laid eyes on her, I stopped as fear gripped my heart, paralyzing me.

God, no.

This couldn't be my Frankie... *Hell no.*

There was no way that *my* Frankie was sitting on this couch, looking frail as ever with pale skin, a shaven head and an IV drip injected into her arm.

"There's my capo," she announced, reaching out for me to come into her embrace. "My handsome bambino *(baby)*."

I was unable to move, rooted in my spot because of the fright still paralyzing me.

"Cassian... come," she requested with her thin hands still out towards me. "Please, my love."

Giving in, I moved forward and immediately dropped down to my knees as I fell into her arms. My bottom lip started trembling and I shut my eyes, trying my hardest to keep the tears at bay. But of course Zietta knowing me better than I knew myself at times, started rubbing on my back with her hands and whispering to me.

"It's okay, Cassian. Everything's going to be okay."

But that was the far from the truth. Everything wasn't going to be okay and everyone in this room knew that before I did. I tore away from her, got back up and backed away, shaking my head with disbelief.

"This can't be happening."

"Cass—"

"This can't be fucking happening!" I yelled, cutting off my Zietta before she could call out to me again with that mellow voice of hers that always warmed my heart. "Why the fuck am I the last person in this room, Zee?" I took a glance around the room to see everyone still looking as depressed as ever. "Why the fuck am I last person to find out that you're sick?"

"Cassian, watch your mou—"

"No," I cut Julius off. "Don't even try to talk to me right now because you've known for fucking weeks what's been up with her and you didn't even tell me!"

He'd known from the second she'd decided to take that bull-shit ass getaway without telling me first. He'd known my Zietta was sick and not told me!

"I didn't want any of you to know until I was ready, Cassian. Please understa—"

"No!" I punched the air, actually wanting to punch the wall but I wasn't about to fuck up my aunt's crib because sick or not, she'd beat my ass. Well at least try to. "Fuck that. I should've been the first person you call. The first fucking person!"

"Cass, calm down," my brother intervened, trying to step closer to me but I lifted a hand, warning him to stay away.

"Cassi, just listen," Caia spoke up.

"All of you shut the fuck up!" My breaths quickened. "Not one of you are allowed to tell me how to feel right now. My mother is dying and you want me to fucking calm down!"

I let my eyes fall on her petite frame once again and my chest caved in at the sight of her sitting there, looking like a shadow of my once youthful, lively auntie.

"Cassian, please... I just need my son by my side right now. Please."

I took deep breaths, trying my hardest to remain calm but it was such a fucking struggle. How was I supposed to stay calm seeing my aunt like this? How was I supposed to stay calm knowing that a woman I loved more than anything in this world was leaving me?

I didn't even need to hear her say that it was bad. I knew from everyone's reactions that it was bad. Whatever she had was bad and there was no cure.

"Please, Cassiano."

Hearing her call me by my actual name made me stop pussy footing around and just relax. I released my final breath and sauntered over to her, taking the empty seat to the right of her. She then took my hand in hers and squeezed tight.

I watched her slide a smile my way but I couldn't bring myself to return it. I simply squeezed her hand back, my way of silently telling her that I was here for her the way she needed me to be.

Who would have thought that hell would be coming for my ass this soon? I knew I'd done a lot of terrible things in my lifetime so far but if this was karma's way of making me pay for my sins, I wanted out. I'd already been karma's victim when I'd lost Zeroni. Now I was losing Frankie?

Fuck no.

I didn't want to lose Frankie. The one woman who had raised me as her own. The one woman I would trade my life for in an instant. The one woman I would do anything for.

Frankie was dying and there was nothing I could do about it. I was losing my mother and I knew that from this day onwards, life would never be the same. I would never be the same man. That ice box that had formed when I'd lost Zeroni was cementing its place around my heart again.

Julius pulled me to the side hours later, telling me a fact that I already suspected from the second I sat by Frankie's side.

"Frankie's stepping down and she wants you in charge, son. She says you're ready for this and I have to agree with her. That's why you were the last one in the room, son. Frankie wanted to let everyone know her decision so they could know her undivided faith in you. She already had plans to retire in the next year or so but with this situation, her plans have been sped up. But that doesn't change the fact that you're ready. It's time for you to take your rightful place, Cassian."

A time I thought was far away had been thrust into my lap and I had no choice but to step in place to do my rightful job. Frankie was stepping down and I was taking her place. Nothing else mattered but doing what I needed to do as head capo and that meant no one else mattered but The Family.

No one.

CHAPTER 21

~ DANAË ~

*M*y *focus was on the spectacular view of Chicago but only for a few seconds before my chin was pulled to the left and several pecks were placed on my mouth, warming my insides. I suddenly leaned back to stop him from having the chance to keep kissing me.*

"You little tease," he whispered, circling a hand around my neck that brought an instant grin to my mouth. "I want my kisses."

Cassian pulled me forward, bringing my face closer to his.

"You know you want my kisses too."

I nodded, grinning wider. Cassian branded our lips together and his tongue met mine, providing me with a pleasure I could never get sick of.

"Still can't believe you did this for me, Cass," I announced after our lips parted.

He'd surprised me with a picnic on the rooftop of his hotel. A picnic I wasn't expecting at all.

He'd led me out of his penthouse while a silk blindfold covered my eyes. It was when I felt cool air hit me, causing goosebumps to rise up from my skin, that I realized we'd left the building.

"*Well believe it, beautiful,*" *he replied, reaching for my hand and interlocking our fingers.* "*I just wanna make you happy, the same way you make me happy.*"

He always knew just the right words to say.

"Danaë."

He always knew just the right ways to make me fall deeper in lov—

"Danaë."

I blinked rapidly and my attention focused on the unimpressed face of my father.

"Yes Da... sir?" I quickly corrected myself, remembering that my father and I were in a professional setting with his other employees.

"Anything to add?"

I shook my head 'no' before fixing my gaze on my father's employee, Jasmine, who sat on the couch opposite me.

"Everything Jasmine said was right about Wrice Enterprises. Their accounts are up to date and all queries settled."

My father nodded.

"Alright, that's it for today everyone. Thank you for your time."

Everyone got up from their seats except for me. I stayed seated with my legs crossed, watching my father who had crossed the room to head over to his desk.

The meeting he had just led had been in the seating area of his office which gave me the advantage I needed today. By the time my father took his seat, everyone had left the room and I was quick on my heels to head closer to him.

"Dad."

He sighed at the call of his name but didn't look up from his MacBook that he was now seated in front of.

"Yes, Danaë?"

I took the vacant seat in front of his desk.

"I'm willing to apologize to Kamora."

There. I said it.

Cassian had convinced me to do the unthinkable and I couldn't lie, him taking over the whole sit down was a huge turn on. He was right about my Dad needing to know about us and even though I'd had my fears in the past, those were far gone. My father deserved to know about Cassian and I. I knew that once my father knew about Cassian and I he would connect the dots and realize the man I'd brought up last month had been Cassian. That's why I would explain things to him privately and tell him how it was one huge misunderstanding.

Now that I'd just told him I would apologize to Kamora, I expected him to look up and start smiling at me – he could even start clapping or cheering if he liked. But that didn't happen.

"I'm afraid it's a little too late for that, Danaë."

My forehead creased.

"Sorry?"

He looked up from his Mac and his brown orbs settled on mine.

"It's too late," he repeated. "Kamora doesn't want your apology."

"Okay..." Relief flowed through my core at the fact that I no longer needed to apologize. "So what does she want?"

"Nothing," he voiced. "She wants nothing to do with you."

Fine with me.

"Okay."

"She doesn't want me to have anything to do with you either, Danaë."

I frowned.

"She told me that it was either you or her. And that she wasn't sticking around if you remained in my life."

Wow. Kamora had really given my father an ultimatum between her and I. She really was as crazy as I thought.

"Well goodbye to her then," I said, my face relaxing as I realized that Kamora was out of our lives for good.

A realization I was sure of until I peeped how quiet my father had gotten. His eyes fell from mine but he couldn't hide that conflicted look even if he tried.

"It's not goodbye to her, is it?" I questioned him, feeling my blood boil. "It's not goodbye because you chose her didn't you?"

"No." He stared back at me with a sincere expression. "I didn't."

If he hadn't chosen her over me, why the hell was he looking so damn torn? And why had our relationship become so distant over the past couple weeks?

Because he hasn't chosen you either, Danaë.

"And you didn't choose me," I said matter-of-factly.

I didn't need to hear him say a word to know that it was true. His silence told me everything.

"Wow." I nodded to myself. "I guess that's all I need to know about our relationsh—"

"That's not true and you know it, Danny," he interrupted me.

"I don't know what to know anymore." I leaned forward, giving him a hard stare. "When my own father would rather choose a woman who has disrespected his daughter and late wife than his own flesh and blood."

I was speaking in a peaceful tone when peace was the last thing I felt.

"I didn't have to choose because she knew from the second she asked me what my choice was going to be. I didn't have to say it but I did."

"So why the hell have you been giving me the silent treatment for the past few weeks? Why have you been treating me like an outsider?"

"I admit I shut you out but that was because I'm hurt and drained by this whole situation," he revealed. "How do you think it made me feel being stuck in the middle of this shit, Danaë? I'm tired and honestly, I just needed space away from you. You're my daughter and I love you beyond anything in the world but you drove me crazy these last few months. You and her."

Hearing how hurt and tired my father was of the Kamora situation made heaviness fall on my heart.

"Kamora and I are done. For good. I can't keep trying to force something that isn't working. She knew about my wishes to never get married but she still went behind my back to get you to help her change my mind. When that didn't work she disrespected your mother which was the reason I broke up with her. I thought we could make it work after some long-needed space but clearly it's not working. She refuses to have you in her life and I refuse to be without my daughter. Kamora and I haven't been the same ever since she brought up your mother. She disrespected me too when she did that and I'd be a fool to ignore the signs."

Trenton got up from his seat and walked over to me.

"It's time for us to move on and focus on repairing our relationship, Angel."

He held his hand out for me to grab once in front of me. I grabbed it and rose up from my seat.

"I'm missed you, baby," he said, opening up his arms.

"Missed you more," I responded, falling into his warm embrace.

He stroked on my back while I hugged him tight.

A moment I'd finally been longing for had arrived and was here to stay for good. Kamora was out of our lives and I no longer had to worry about her meddling in my relationship with my father. Deep down a part of me was feeling some type of way about my father's happiness because by ending things with Kamora, he was now a single man. But there were plenty other fish in the sea and my Daddy was a great catch. He'd find a new woman, a better woman, much closer to his age, in no time.

Since Kamora was out of our lives for good there would be no need for Cassian to plan the sit-down at his penthouse. However, he could set up his home for a different occasion, right? A special occasion where him and I could tell Trenton about us.

The thought had me feeling giddy inside and after leaving my father's side to head to my office, that giddiness heightened. Once inside my office, I was reunited with my phone and quickly headed to my messages.

My father ended things with Kamora for good, Cass.

Send.

There's no need for the sit down but I'm thinking we could still have it so that we can tell Trenton about us like we talked about?

Send.

After sending my texts to Cassian, I locked my phone and got buried in the remaining work I needed to get done for the day. While working, I would occasionally glance at my phone with the hopes of seeing a new text come in from Cassian.

Hours went by and nothing new came in. Home time came along at five p.m. and I was still stuck on the fact that Cassian hadn't replied to any of my texts.

He must be really busy today.

Three hours later and I'd driven home, parted from my work attire, checked on Nala, eaten some left overs and still hadn't heard a word from Cassian.

I'd be lying if I said that this lack of communication didn't make me feel some type of way because Cassian wasn't the unresponsive type. But rather than worrying about him like one lost puppy, I convinced myself that he'd hit me up later when he was less busy. Besides we had a lunch date tomorrow that I was very much looking forward to.

I continued to watch TV until late into the night before leaving my living room to get reacquainted with one of the best things in my life – my bed. After changing into my silk nightdress, I got under my sheets and said my prayers to the Lord above. My eyes shut and before I knew it, my slumber took me away from the land of the living.

Cass, where are you? We had a lunch date remember?

Send.

A new day had arrived and the lunch date I'd been looking forward to very much seemed to now be cancelled. I glanced up at the mounted clock on the white wall ahead, pouting as I read the time.

1:45 p.m.

The time for lunch was quickly passing but it wasn't the time that had me mad. It was the fact that Cassian hadn't bothered to hit me up all day. All my texts from yesterday hadn't been replied to including the ones I'd sent today. I'd also called him twice and my calls got sent straight to voicemail.

Something must be wrong. This isn't like him.

Rather than working up a fuss, I decided to head to the canteen downstairs to grab a quick bite before they closed up shop at two p.m. I grabbed a chicken wrap and a bottle of Fiji water before heading back up to my office.

While I ate, the only person on my mind was him. I was filled with worried thoughts about my boyfriend.

My boyfriend.

I instantly smiled, knowing that that was exactly what he was.

My boyfriend I hadn't heard from or seen in over twenty-four hours.

My smile faded.

Okay... he must be really, really, really busy to not be answering my texts or calls. No biggie. I'll just go over to his place after work and wait for him to get home or hopefully he's already there when I slide through.

So that's what I decided to do. After work, I first went home to change into more comfortable clothes then made my way to The Palazzo. I'd be lying if I said I wasn't concerned about Cassian. More concerned than I'd been yesterday. How could I not be? I hadn't received a single text or call from him and him standing me up for lunch didn't ease my worries.

The only way I knew I could be rest assured was by waiting for him to get home from whatever the hell it was that had him so preoccupied that he couldn't hit his girlfriend back to let her know that he was okay.

"Cassian?" I called out to him as I stepped through his penthouse.

I shut the front door behind me and walked deeper into the space, listening carefully for movement.

"Cass?" I stepped into his living room, hoping to see him but sadly it was empty.

The minute I'd stepped through the front door, I'd caught a whiff of his manly scent and now that I was in the living room, I could smell it ten times more, making me miss him more than I already did.

I pulled my coat off my frame, walking back to his coat rack and kicked off my Nike sneakers. Once I'd hung my coat, I decided that I needed a glass of one of his finest Tuscan wines. I found my desired bottle in one of his cupboards, grabbed it and a clean glass before making my way back to the living room. I got comfortable on his three-seater, put on an episode of Vampire Diaries and sipped away.

It must have been the wine that got to me or the incredibly

long work day I'd had that made me fall asleep because before I knew it I was out like a light. When I woke up, I had no idea how long I'd been out for but what I did know was that the flat screen TV was no longer on like it had been before I'd fallen asleep.

I stretched my arms up, yawning as I did so and lifting my back off the sofa. I looked over my shoulder and that's when I spotted him, standing by the kitchen's island with a glass in hand. His emotionless eyes stuck on me.

"Cassian, you're home."

I bolted from my seat, desperate to close the space that formed between us. Within seconds, I was standing in front of him, wrapping my arms around him and pulling him close to me.

"Where have you been, baby? I've been texting you..." I was too caught up on the fact that I'd missed him to truly noticed that Cassian wasn't hugging me back. "...All day. Is everything okay?" I pulled back, looking up at him.

That emotionless look remained and instead of speaking up, Cassian pulled away from me and stepped back so that I was no longer holding him. He chugged down the remaining brown liquor that his glass housed before placing his glass down to the island then finally spoke up.

"You shouldn't be here, Danaë."

I looked at him like he'd suddenly grown two heads.

"What?"

"I said you shouldn't be here," he repeated, like I hadn't heard him the first time. "You need to leave."

"Why? Is something wrong?"

I hadn't done anything to him so I had no idea as to why he was telling me to leave.

"I don't want you here."

Those words made a chill go down my spine.

"What?" My face hardened. "What do you me—"

"You heard what I said, Danaë," he retorted. "I don't want you here."

I opened my mouth to talk but found myself at a loss for words.

Is he really trying to kick me out right now? But why? What the hell have I done?

"Cass, what's wron—"

"Nothing's wrong!" He yelled, turning away from me so I could no longer see his face. "Just go, Danaë. Leave."

I took a breath, stepping forward and reaching for his back but the second I put my hand on him, he moved further away.

"Cass..."

"I said leave."

"Well I'm not going anywhere," I placed my hands on my hips, standing my ground. "I'm your girl and I have a right to know what's wrong, Cassian. Tell me what's wrong... please, babe."

Cassian looked over his shoulder, glaring at me like I was suddenly his worst enemy.

"You're not my girl."

My heart suddenly felt like it was shrinking and I was speechless again by him. In my mind I was his girl but him coming out and saying that I wasn't, definitely stung. Cassian turned around to face me completely and continued to glare at me.

"Imperia was right. This was nothing but sex," he said, his tone cool and calm like he hadn't just sent an invisible bullet right through my heart. "I let myself get caught up with you, Danaë, but it's over. We're done."

The tears that pricked my eyes I couldn't stop even if I wanted to.

"H-How... How can you say that to me, Cassian?"

"Because it's the truth," he simply replied, crossing his arms across his chest. "This was nothing. You were never my girl; I did all those things to get what I wanted from you which was pussy. I've had plenty of that now and I don't need it anymore. I don't need you, which is why you shouldn't be here, Danaë. So get the fuck out and don't bother coming back."

I had to be dreaming. I just had to be. Because there was no way that this was real. This had to be a dream, a nightmare in fact. One terrible nightmare that I was going to wake up from right this second.

Wake up, Danaë. Wake the hell u—

"Are you deaf? I said get out."

My blinks were rapid now as I was trying to hold back the tears daring to fall from my lids. The tears that were coming out not just because of his callous words but because of the way Cassian now stared at me. Like I meant nothing to him. Absolutely nothing.

All my blinks ended up being pointless because my first tear dropped seconds later.

"C-Cassian, y-you don't mean that," I croaked out, brushing my hand against my wet cheek.

"I do," he affirmed, turning to the side and lifting his finger to the door. "Get out before I make you get out."

I was certain that Cassian had to be lying. This wasn't real! He didn't mean all the shit he was saying right now. He couldn't mean it...

But he did.

He meant every last word and he wasn't fazed by my tears. He wasn't fazed by the fact that he was breaking my heart.

The tears wouldn't stop falling and I knew that there was nothing left to be said. What could I say to the man that had just crushed my heart into tiny pieces?

I rushed past him and headed to his foyer, grabbing my coat from the rack. My vision blurry as I reached for my coat but I refused to stop. I just needed to get out of here. Now!

Once I had my coat in hand, I swiped my sneakers from the floor and didn't bother staying around to put them all on. I needed to get away from this monster. This monster that had been playing me like a violin for weeks!

I turned to the door, racing to it and reached for the door's handle but seemed to have forgotten how to fucking open the door because it wasn't opening.

"W-Why the fuck..." I pushed against the door, trying to get it to open while water streamed down my cheeks. "Won't this door... open!" I shouted to myself, pushing hard on the handle.

I could barely see but I could feel my shaky grip on the door. I was too distracted by my failure to open it to focus on the footsteps now sounding behind me.

"Nae."

But I definitely heard him call my name and I froze, sighing deeply.

"I-I'm trying to go," I whispered between my sobs, looking down. "The door won't fucking open!"

His hand appeared from behind and he grabbed my hand that held the door's handle. He pulled and both my hand and the handle moved. Suddenly, I felt like the dumbest woman on earth for pushing on a door that needed to be pulled. A door I'd pulled open many times but all the words Cassian had thrown at me made me lose all common sense. I wasn't even sure if I remembered my right from left at this point but what I did know was that I still had to get the hell out of here.

"Dana—"

"I'm leaving, just like you want," I spat, snatching my hand from under his.

I pulled open the door and rushed out his home, slamming the door shut behind me. The tears started falling harder but I ignored them as best as I could as I ran to the elevator to get out this hell hole.

He'd said all he needed to say and there was nothing else that had to be said. I'd been wrong all along and I'd been a fool to think this was something more. I'd been a fool to fall for his charming ways. I'd been a fool to fall in love with him.

We were done.

CHAPTER 22

~ CASSIAN ~

"I'm leaving, just like you want," she concluded, snatching her hand from under mine and opening the door wider.

She rushed out and slammed the door shut behind her.

Every part of my body had stiffened once she was gone. My legs, my muscles and the worse of them all... my heart.

"Fuck!" My knuckles crashed against the wooden door and pain sliced through my fingers.

Everything I'd just told Danaë had been a lie. One big fat lie that I'd never in a million years thought I would be telling Danaë. Never in a million years did I think I would tell Danaë to get out of my home and not come back.

It was what I knew had to be done though. Danaë couldn't be with a man like me. I didn't deserve to have her in my life with all the sins I'd committed. I'd been playing myself from the jump thinking that we could be together long term. She was too good for me. Way too good for me.

Everything good in my life I seemed to lose. First Zeroni and now Frankie. Clearly I wasn't meant to have good things. Clearly I didn't deserve love. And now that I was boss, I would need to remain focused on nothing but The Family.

"She won't be able to handle who you really are. Who you're destined to be one day."

Imperia's words had been playing in my head over and over again like a damn broken record that wouldn't stop playing the same old song. I'd thought I could keep Danaë and my world separate but now with Frankie stepping down for me to take her place, that wouldn't be possible. I didn't want to have to explain my world to Danaë because I was scared. Scared that Imperia was right.

How could Danaë want to be with a killer? A killer who didn't care about those he took from the world?

I didn't want to stick around and hear Danaë tell me that she didn't want to be with me so I did it for her. Although it had been harsh, it's what needed to be done. And I admit seeing her breakdown and struggle to leave made me want to take it all back. She hadn't even put her damn shoes on.

That voice in my head told me to just tell her. *Tell her you're hurting about Zietta. Tell her you're slightly stressed about becoming king this soon. Tell her you love her.*

But I refused to listen. Instead I let the other voice in my head convince me that I was undeserving of love.

She won't ever accept you. She won't want to be with a man like you. A killer. A monster. You'll lose her like you lose everything good in your life. First Zeroni, now Frankie. What makes you think Danaë will stick around? Get rid of her before she decides to get rid of you.

That was the voice I was set on listening to so I gave in and did what it told me. Pushing Danaë away for good was what I had to do and it was done. Three hours later and I was by the side of the only woman I wanted to see.

"Stop worrying about me, bambino... I told you I'm going to be here for as long as you need me to be."

I said nothing, gripping her skinny hand tighter with both my hands. Every time I looked at her I was almost brought to tears.

Stage four breast cancer.

It had spread to her bones and lymph nodes, making it incurable. The only thing that could be done was making sure that she received the best treatment to control the disease and her symptoms.

Anything that could keep her longer with us was being done. Hormone therapy, chemotherapy and radiotherapy were the treatments so far that Frankie's doctor had listed as the possible treatments. Frankie was on board with trying chemotherapy first so that was her current treatment plan and had been for the past two weeks which explained her hair loss.

How had the cancer spread this quickly without Zietta realizing? We didn't know. What we did know was that she'd barely had any symptoms so that bitch cancer had come like a thief in the night to take over my Frankie's immune system. Her lump had been quite deep in her breast which was rare but possible so she hadn't noticed it until a month ago. She'd gone to her private doctor who had done the necessary tests and came back with the horrible news. Frankie was stuck with cancer for the rest of her remaining life.

"And we're going to be here for you always," a soft voice sounded from the corner of the room and I looked over at Caia standing with a friendly smile.

The impromptu vacation that Zietta had taken had turned out to be her way of secretly visiting Caia in LA, telling her the news of her diagnosis. She also wanted Caia by her side as they jetted off around the country, searching for the best doctor who could treat her and prolong her life for as long as possible. And they'd found her. Dr. Monica Adedeji was one of the top African American oncologists in the country, specializing in metastatic breast cancer. They'd found her in New York and told her that they wanted her onboard in helping with Frankie's treatment. Monica had been generously funded and set up with a brand-new lab in a private hospital ten minutes away from Zietta's Chicago residence. Her accommodation and monthly expenses were all taken care of too. I'd even slid in a damn G-Wagon for her to drive around in. Just as long as she knew to do her job and keep my Frankie here as long as possible.

I understood why Zietta had gone to her niece for counsel rather than me. Caia was a woman like her and women could relate far better to each other. I appreciated Caia dropping everything to be by Frankie's side. She'd moved into Frankie's home and was now her official caregiver. Despite their differences in the past about Frankie wanting to train Caia as next in line for the throne to continue the matriarchal rule and Caia running away from our family to pursue her own dreams, Caia had dropped her gaming career and her dreams to take care of the woman who'd raised us and I respected that more than anything. It was a reminder of how I had to stay focused on The Family.

It sucked that Danaë and I were over but I could no longer think about her. I had to stay focused on my new role and make Frankie proud. I didn't know how much time she had with us left but I was going to try my hardest to make her proud while she was still here to see it.

"You ready for this, Cass?"

I turned to the left to see the curious eyes of my baby brother. I nodded without saying a word before pushing the two mahogany doors ahead, allowing us to enter.

The second I stepped in with my brother right by my side, everyone stood up and gave us their undivided attention. I walked deeper into the large space, my eyes darting across the room at the faces. I knew them all but for some this was their first time ever laying eyes on my brother and I. So I wasn't shocked by the hard, inspecting stares.

I went to take my place at the head seat of the table and Christian took the empty one to the right of me. My head remained held high as I looked down each side of the long table, gracing each member with eye contact. From capos to associates, they were all present.

When I took my seat, everyone followed suit and sat down, patiently waiting for me to speak.

I decided to hold off on speaking right away though. The silence was quite comforting and there was something about having everyone on their edge of their seats that brought me great gratification. All this power felt fucking fantastic and I hadn't even really started throwing my weight around yet.

"Appreciate you all for coming on time tonight," I announced. "Keep that shit up and you won't have no problems with me. As you know, Francesca is stepping down as boss. I'll be taking her place and Christian will be my second in command. If for some reason you're unable to reach me then Christian is your best next source."

Nods appeared around the table and I kept a firm glance on everyone as I looked down the table.

Francesca's illness was something she wanted to keep amongst intermediate family members only. That included me, my siblings, Julius and his kids and her cousins. As far as everyone else was concerned, she was retiring early.

"First on the agenda... Matthew," I called to the olive-skinned man sitting next to Chris.

"Yes, boss?"

"Give me a run down on the movement on the ports. Did you secure our fourth ship?"

"Yes, I did. We..."

Adriano was in charge of overseeing our shipments that we received and shipments we sent out the city. He was responsible for paying off important officials to make sure that we had no issues receiving our valuable merchandise for our various businesses and I wanted to hear the updates on us securing our newest ship.

I intended to hear updates of everyone's role in the empire which I was fully acquainted with. I knew everyone's names, their role in the family and their importance to Frankie. Now that I was in charge things would be stepping up a whole new level. I wanted all our businesses to expand and we were taking this shit out the states. There was more money to be made across the pond and I had a couple connects in Asia & Europe that wanted the Acardis expertise. I would happily provide and there would be no room for procrastination as we expanded and no room for mistakes. The only thing I wanted was efficiency.

Christian and I being half Italian didn't mean anything to The Family. The Acardis had brought on many associates and soldiers of all different races to help run their empire so other cultures were embraced in my world.

"Still can't believe this is all happening," Christian said, reaching for his glass and bringing it to mine.

"Believe it, bro'."

We clinked our glasses together before throwing our shots back. Christian's face went funny, mirroring mine as the liquor burned down our throats.

Two hours after our family meeting and we were the only ones left in the meeting room. Now we were each taking tequila shots after our productive meeting.

I dropped my glass to the table below and stared at Christian who'd just recovered from his shot.

"Seriously though, I'm proud of you, Cass. First meeting and you handled it like a pro."

A smile tugged at my lips and I lifted my fist towards him. He reached out his, connecting our fists as we dapped.

"I wonder how wifey's gonna feel knowing she's with the head of the Acardis."

My chest tightened and that same tightness formed in my jaw. I cut my eyes away from Christian and reached for the Azul bottle. Quickly unscrewing it.

"You are going to tell her, right? There's no way you'll be able to not explain the soldiers around you twenty-four-seven, the late nights..."

I began to tune him out, pouring myself another shot.

"Cass."

Once my glass was filled to the brim, I lifted it and gulped down the clear liquor. Fire burned through my core, not just due to the tequila but because of the anger crashing through me.

"Cass."

Christian was aware of how things had grown between Danaë and I over the past month. He'd not only seen her come in and out of my penthouse many times, but he'd also seen us together in meetings at Morgan & Westbrook and seen our flirty interactions, teasing us every chance he got. He knew what was up – well what had been up.

"Cass, you didn't."

And because he was my brother, he knew exactly why I was refusing to look him in the eye right now.

"Cassian."

I reluctantly allowed my gaze to fall on him.

"What did you do?"

I was silent but I'm sure my eyes revealed all.

"Don't tell me you... you end—"

"It's over with," I cut him off.

"But why? You lov—"

"I said it's over with and that's all you need to worry about," I interrupted him once more. I decided to change the subject. "I want you taking full control of The Palazzo. Both the original and new one. I won't be attending meetings with the builders, directors, investors or meetings at Morgan & Westbrook with the accountants."

"But Cas—"

I reached for his shoulder, holding it firmly.

"You're in charge, baby bro'. Run it as you see fit and feel free to turn my penthouse into your little bachelor pad. That's all you now."

I patted his shoulder, letting him know that this conversation was officially over. As his older brother I'd always had the final say but now that I was boss, that point was ten times clearer.

Christian slowly nodded and that was all the confirmation I needed from him. I dropped my glass to the table and walked away to the exit, leaving Christian alone in the meeting room.

Nothing else needed to be said.

~ One Week Later ~

Zietta had allowed Christian to turn her Winnetka mansion into a palace of fun to celebrate my newly appointed status. I insisted that I was cool on having any celebrations. All I wanted to do was work and be right by Zietta's side as she underwent her treatments. But she insisted that I celebrate my role and said she didn't want me near her until I did so. Having no choice but to respect her wishes I decided to give into Christian's plans to get me to turn up. It turned out to be his palace of fun rather than mine because of all the bottle girls he had prancing around the crib in nothing but a crop top and thong. Bottle girls I hadn't even asked for. He'd also invited our cousins, capos and associates to all hone in on the fun too but I wasn't interested in any of the festivities.

Christian tried to get me lit by forcing shots of rum, tequila, and whatever else he could get his hands on, into my hands but it didn't perk up my mood at all.

All week I'd been grouchy. Anyone that I thought was looking at me in the wrong way, I'd snap on them. Anytime I felt my new driver was driving too slow, I would snap on him too. Even my soldiers who moved my stuff into my new seven-bedroom home, I berated for moving too damn slow.

I'd been a real terror to be around but I didn't care. I was too angry with my own thoughts to care about what anyone thought about me.

I missed her.

"Thank you so much for tonight, Cass... you're so sweet."

It'd only been eight days since I'd ended things but I missed her beyond anything in the world. Not even burying myself with work could fight off the visions I had of her. Sleeping was even worse because all I dreamt about was her.

"No need to steal what's already yours, Cassi bear."

I missed holding her, hearing her voice, talking to her and of course I missed sliding between those gorgeous thighs of hers.

"I want you, Cassian... right now."

Now as I sat idly in the study of my home, I stared off into space, thinking about nobody else but her. I pulled out my phone moments later, heading to the last messages I'd received from Pierro.

Work. Home.

Work. Home.

Work. Home.

Work. Home.

I didn't care that she was doing the same shit every single day. I still made sure that my head soldier gave me updates every day on her locations. Now that I was away from her, I was more pressed about knowing what she was doing.

I'd told Pierro to give me as few details as possible. One word would suffice but if more were needed then he could use more but keep it short. I didn't need a story about the shit she was doing, I just needed quick and snappy texts informing me of her day. I'd ended things with her but that didn't mean I couldn't keep an eye on her.

No, you just want to make sure she's not entertaining any other nigga after you.

Luckily for her she hadn't because if I'd discovered that she'd moved on that quickly, I knew for a fact I wouldn't be able to control myself when I made the call to get rid of him.

Call it selfish all you like. I'd decided I couldn't have her but that didn't mean I wanted her with anyone else.

Was it fucked up? Yeah but I didn't care.

"I didn't know the party had been moved upstairs?"

The voice of a man I respected very much was heard and I turned to see him standing in the doorway of my study.

"I needed some peace and quiet," I revealed in a low tone.

Julius nodded with understanding, moving into the room and shutting the door behind him.

He came over to the mahogany desk I was sitting behind and took his seat on the chair on the other side.

"Some peace and quiet to do what?" he queried, resting his elbow on the arm of his chair while cradling his chin with his palm.

I sighed, running my hand down my face and leaning back.

"Just think some shit over," I muttered, not willing to give too much detail.

It didn't matter about me not wanting to give because his next sentence told me that I had a tattle teller as a brother.

"About Danaë?"

My eyes widened at his query and I sighed once again. In the past I'd been keen on keeping the women I dealt with away from my family. Especially after the whole Imperia situation. In my mind, they didn't need to know about who I was sleeping with because those women weren't anything serious. But Danaë...

"Yeah."

Danaë was different. Christian knew it and now Julius knew it.

"Remind me to fuck Christian up for being such a snitch."

Julius chuckled.

"I'm afraid I won't be able to do that," Julius voiced. "Because the only reason why he snitched was because I made him so I guess you'd have to fuck me up too, boss."

I tilted my head to the side, inspecting Julius closely.

"It was your first full week and you've been biting off everyone's heads, son. Did you think I wouldn't notice?"

Since Frankie had stepped down, Julius was no longer second in command because I'd given that role to my brother. Frankie's absence meant that Julius was free to retire or stay on as an advisor. He'd decided to stay on as an advisor and promised to be here whenever I needed him. I hadn't asked him to come to my very first meeting with The Family because I didn't want everyone thinking I couldn't handle things without my uncle/cousin right by my side. I was a boss and bosses handled things on their own. I could do meetings without Julius overseeing things.

I shrugged in response to his question.

"He called her your future wife," Julius said. "Now after the way you've been acting, I have reason to believe that's true."

"It's not," I replied, bitterness laced in my tone. "She and I are no more."

"Why?"

"I don't want her."

Julius lifted his head from his hand and his eyes narrowed.

"You sure about that? Because just me mentioning her made your eyes grow large."

I went quiet.

"What happened, Cass?" he asked gently. "Why have you pushed her away?"

How did he know that shit?

I hadn't told Christian any of the details that had led to me ending things with Danaë but somehow Julius knew what I'd done.

"Nothing happened. We can't be together. End of story."

"You can't be together? What's that supposed to mea—"

"Unc, just drop it."

He silently stared at me, doing as I said or so I thought.

"Zietta never told you or Chris the story of what happened with her lover, did she?"

I didn't bother shaking my head because we both knew he already knew the answer to that shit.

"She ended a relationship with the love of her life because she thought that being in love was off the table once she became boss.

She didn't want her lover getting caught up in this lifestyle – her exact words – so she pushed her away, made her think that she'd cheated on her with someone else. Someone else that she was more in love with. Of course that was a lie."

The story I'd always wanted to know had finally been revealed to me and who would have known it would end up being extremely similar to the current tale of my life.

"Frankie thought she was doing what was best but I can promise you till this day she regrets that decision. She made a decision without once stopping to think about what her lover would think. She thought she was doing what was best for The Family but in the end, it made her miserable. She sacrificed her happiness because she thought it was for the best but I can tell you right now, Cass, seeing her breakdown when she found out her lover was engaged to someone else wasn't for the best. Seeing her pretend to be okay wasn't for the best."

A pain filled my center at the thought of Danaë being engaged to another man.

Over my dead body.

"But what if her lover didn't want to be part of her life after finding out who she really was? What if Frankie let her in and it was all for nothing?" I questioned him, still on the fence about Danaë knowing the true extent of who I was and what I did.

"Those are questions that we'll never know the answer to because Frankie never gave her the chance to choose," Julius responded. "You don't even know if Danaë will run and you're already making her run."

"I just... I just thought it'd be best pushing her away. She doesn't know this side of me because I've kept it hidden and now that I'm boss, this is a side I can't just hide. It's who I am. And if she decided that she didn't want no parts, that's a loss I won't be able to deal with. I can't deal with another loss, Unc. First Zeroni, soon Frankie... pushing her away was for the best."

"So this is about you being scared of what she might think of you?"

I nodded and added, "That and I've done too much bad shit in this life to think I could ever deserve a love as good as hers. I don't deserve her. The same way I didn't deserve Zeroni. That's why I lost her before I could meet her."

"But that's not true," Julius countered, compassion spreading over his face. "You've allowed yourself to think that because you somehow convinced yourself that Zeroni dying was your fault. When it wasn't."

Wasn't it though?

Zeroni hadn't even had the chance to experience this world and all its many wonders. How could I not think my sins had a part to play in that? She died before I'd even had the chance to see her cute little face. Before I'd even had the chance to kiss her and tell her how much I'd loved her.

"When someone loves you, really loves you, they love you flaws and all, Cassian. I would know because I've been married for twenty-five years to a woman that loves all the good, bad and ugly parts of me."

His wife, Natalie aka my aunt, definitely loved every part of him and it was always a great sight to see the two of them together. But me being on my anti-marriage shit in the past, didn't entertain the idea of me one day being like them. That was until I'd fallen for Danaë Westbrook.

"You haven't even given Danaë a chance to love the bad and ugly because you've pushed her away."

I sighed, knowing that he was right. But I couldn't help my stubborn ways. I couldn't stop my inner demons from telling me that Danaë and I weren't meant to be.

"We're done, unc," I said one last time. "It's for the best."

Now it was his turn to sigh, disappointment filling his eyes.

"Okay, son. If that's what you really want then who am I to stop you."

I gave him a respectful nod and that was the end of the discussion on Danaë.

I was done talking about her.

CHAPTER 23

~ DANAË ~

"*Girl. I not only feel like I haven't seen you in ages, but I also know I haven't seen you in ages. Let me know when we can go get drunk. I miss you. Call me back, bitch. Love you.*"

For the past week, all I'd been doing was work, work and work again. It was the only suitable distraction that took my mind off the terrible predicament I'd found myself in just last week.

Adina had hit me up during the week, wanting to meet up but I'd dodged all of her calls. I hit her with the following text a few days ago:

Hey, love. Sorry I missed your calls. Been super busy at work. You know me, never taking a damn break. I'll let you know as soon as my schedule frees up. Love you always.

The truth was I had no plans to see Adina right now because seeing Adina would mean that I would have to tell her what had happened. What *he* had done to me. And I couldn't bring myself to do it. Not yet. As much as I loved my best friend dearly this heartbreak was too raw and too embarrassing for me to have to explain right now. I was embarrassed by what had happened and I was embarrassed that I'd allowed myself to get tricked by Cassian's charms.

"Imperia was right. This was nothing but sex. I let myself get caught up with you, Danaë, but it's over. We're done."

The night I'd arrived home after Cassian ended things, I remember walking in and dropping to the floor. Then the cries came harder and I was reminded of the fact that Cassian had broken my heart. Imperia had been right all along and I'd been a fool to think any differently. I'd been a fool to let Cassian convince me with his lies that we were something more. I made sure to block Cassian's number, delete all our texts, emails and even our call logs.

All gone! The same way he was. Gone for good out of my life.

Next to go were all the things he'd given me. From the Rolex to the cartier bracelets he'd gifted me, his Essentials Fear Of God hoodie and tracksuit he'd given me after our first night together, his t-shirts I'd stolen after our various nights together, I stuffed them all into a trash bag and attempted to throw them out... but it was a huge fail. Throwing away the expensive items he'd gifted me wasn't the smartest idea in the first place so I knew I would either need to sell or donate them. However, the same way I hadn't had the strength to throw out his stuff was the same way I didn't have the strength to sell or donate them. So currently, they were sitting in the furthest corner of my wardrobe until I had the courage to get rid of them for good.

"You're a fighter, Danaë. That's how I raised you and you always come out on top. You know that."

I cried for a few more minutes that day before I was reminded of my father's words. I was a fighter and although this shit sucked – really *fucking* sucked – I couldn't allow it to get to me. I couldn't allow the pain to win. The only way I could cope was by getting lost in work to somehow mask the pain that I was feeling.

The only thing I was dreading when it came to work was having to see Cassian's face in meetings for The Palazzo. Their new building was already being constructed and was projected to be finished in the next two years and seeing as I was their lead accountant, I was in charge of tracking all the building's expenses and investments. Over a month ago when Imperia told me the truth in my office about Cassian and I, the first thing I wanted to do was get removed off The Palazzo's accounts. But I couldn't lie, that was now the last thing I wanted. I loved working on The Palazzo's accounts and it was my favorite account to work on.

Luckily for me, I got an email yesterday from Christian's assistant explaining that he was the only CEO onboard for The Palazzo from now on. Cassian would be stepping down and no longer be in meetings. Learning that Cassian wasn't co-CEO anymore was a relief but also a surprise. But I shook off my surprise and the want to know why Cassian had stepped down and focused on the relief I felt about not having to be in the same room as Cassian Acardi. The Lord had answered my silent prayers and I was glad that meetings regarding The Palazzo would be with Chris alone. I could deal with that Acardi, but not the other.

The weekend had arrived and I was sitting in the middle of my living room floor. My MacBook sat ahead on my center table and a glass of red wine was posted up right next to it. Of course I was doing work on a Saturday. It was not only a great distraction but a great way to kill time.

Hours into me staring at the profit and loss data of one of my clients at my consulting company, my eyes wandered away from my bright screen and found the glass tank sitting on the cabinet below my mounted TV. I squinted at the aquarium and noticed Nala floating on her side.

"What the..."

I rose to my feet and walked towards my gold fish's tank. Once in front of the glass, I bent low and my chest caved in as I stared into the cloudy, sunken pupils of my goldfish. Flakes of her food were sitting in the tank uneaten. I continued to stare at her upside-down body and the longer I stared, the more my eyes welled up. I eventually straightened up, sighing deeply as the tears slowly dropped.

There was no reason for my grown ass to start crying over a damn goldfish but I was. She'd died, so I had every right to be heartbroken over her death. She'd died and she wasn't coming back. I rushed to my bathroom to get tissue as the tears kept on falling.

I knew deep down I wasn't really crying over Nala's death and as I now stood in front of my reflection, wiping away my tears, I knew I was crying over Cassian.

It still fucking hurt.

I'd done a pretty decent job at keeping up a front, pretending to be strong but Nala's death had triggered me. Reminding me of the fact that what Cassian and I had was dead. Our relationship... or whatever the hell we'd been doing was dead because of him. All because of him and his lies.

I didn't want to be in Chicago anymore. All this burying myself in work and pretending to be okay when I really wasn't, was officially over. I was about to do what I did best.

Run.

~ *Twenty-Four Hours Later* ~

"What do you mean you're taking a vacation? Why, Angel? You had plenty of vacations months ago. Remember that? When you were jetting off from country to country without a care in the world."

"I know, Dad, but I... I need this. I really need some time away from the city. I've worked my ass off since I started working for your company and you know that. Just let me have this. Please, Daddy."

"...And what about your meetings? Your clients?" I could hear the dissatisfaction in his baritone.

"They've all been taken care of by Deyjah," I explained. "I haven't left any tasks unfinished and by the time I'm back it'll be like I never left. Deyjah's got it handled. I trust her."

"I still don't feel comfortable not seeing you before you go, Danny. Come over tonight and you can tell me all about where you plan to go."

I went silent, knowing fully well that coming over to Dad's tonight would be impossible.

"Miss Westbrook, here's that sex on the beach for you."

My eyes fluttered open and I looked ahead to see a handsome ebony skinned man, uniformed in a white shirt, royal blue waistcoat and matching blue bowtie. He lowered the silver tray in his right palm so I could reach for the cocktail sitting above it. I reached ahead, my spirits soaring at the presence of alcohol.

Just what I truly need.

"Danaë, who the hell is that? Sex on what beach?"

"Thank you so much," I mouthed to the kind gentleman who was smiling wide at me.

"Don't tell me... Danaë, don't tell me... you're already on vacation aren't you?"

"Yes, Dad," I replied, lifting my cocktail to my lips and sucking on my silver straw.

"Danaë Louisa Westbrook..." He sighed. "You really are going to be the death of me one day."

I chuckled.

"Now you're just being dramatic, Dad. Look, I'm sorry for not telling you before I left... *again* but this is just something I needed. Please understand."

"Well I guess I have no choice but to understand since you're already there," he responded before softening up his tense tone to ask, "So where has my daughter decided to get lost in today?"

"St. Lucia," I revealed, holding my cocktail close while I stared off into the breathtaking sea that surrounded my private resort.

"Sounds great... and you're alone?"

"Yes."

"Taking all the precautions? Not telling strangers where you're staying, not staying out too lat—"

"Yes, yes, yes," I cut him off. "I'm safe, Dad. You know I am. I've travelled solo plenty of times before."

"And I'm still worried about you every time you go, Angel," he stated in a gentle tone. "...Did something happen, Danaë? Is that the reason for this random vacation?"

"No," I lied.

"Are you sure, baby? You know you can talk to me about anythin—"

"I'm fine, Dad. Everything's fine. I just needed a break. I'll be back soon."

"How soon is soon?"

I took out my left AirPod, preparing myself for what was to come.

"Two weeks."

"Two weeks!"

I winced as his yell sounded into my right ear drum.

"Danaë."

"Daddy."

"Two weeks is too long."

"It'll fly by and I'll be back before you know it. I promise."

He groaned.

"Daddy."

He groaned once again before saying, "Two weeks and you'll be back. No detours, young lady."

"Yes, sir," I promised, smiling to myself. "No detours."

And that was the honest truth. All I needed was two weeks away and I would be fine. I would be okay. St. Lucia would be my solace and I would be back in Chicago better than ever, no longer scarred by my heartbreak.

~ Two Weeks Later ~

St. Lucia had been everything I needed it to be and more. Since I was staying in a luxury resort with my own over the water bunga-low, there was really no need for me to even leave my resort. It came with an outdoor hammock for me to relax over the water, an outdoor and indoor shower and bath, see through glass floors inside, a king-sized bed that I was sure had to be crafted by God himself and a personal butler who came calling to my every desire.

Of course I'd be a fool to not visit the gorgeous sights that St. Lucia had to offer. My resort was in Gros Isle, allowing me to visit a water park, go on an ATV tour through the village, attend a fun street party, go on a private cruise, zip line, hike and don't even get me started on the food! Overall, St. Lucia had been an experience like no other and I didn't want to leave. But I remembered my promise to my father.

Two weeks.

So sadly, here I now was. Collecting my suitcases from baggage claim.

"Ethan and I are five minutes away, Angel. Sorry about the wait."

"No worries," I said as I dragged my luggage behind me. "Terminal two, don't forget, Daddy."

"I've got it. I'm not that old you know."

I giggled before sighing at the fact that I'd missed him very much. After our phone call two weeks ago, he'd made me e-mail him all the details of my vacation including my flight home details. I didn't bother protesting because I knew how protective my father was over me. It didn't matter that I'd been on solo vacations more than I could count on one finger and had been safe every single time. He still wanted to know exactly where Danaë Westbrook was and the minute she returned home.

"See you soon, Danny."

"See you soon, Dad."

The call ended and I continued walking towards my terminal's exit. I'd left baggage claim and was now heading out the airport. Various bodies moved through the airport around me and I pressed ahead to the glass doors leading outside.

I need a break to get over you
I need the space, it's been overdue

Chicago's warm breeze stroked my cheeks as I stepped out the airport and walked up to the car pickup zone. The stunning vocals of Joyce Wrice sounded through my AirPods as I came to a stop and made my luggage stand up right next to me while I waited for Ethan and my father to arrive. Pulling out my phone, I headed to my messages and clicked on the unopened texts from Adina.

You better be prepared to give Mr. Warbucks a heart attack next month because you and I are going on a vacation even if I have to kidnap your ass and stuff you in my suitcase myself.

A smile creased my face at her first text.

Dina: *Still can't believe you went to St. Lucia without me, hoe.*

Dina: *At least you're back and you can finally tell me what the hell happened with you and Cassian.*

My heart almost stopped and my smile quickly faded.

Dina: *And before you try to lie – Don't.*

Dina: *I've already spoken to Chris who confirmed that something happened between you two but won't say what.*

Dina: *You would think after being his favorite employee that he would tell me the tea that my best friend failed to tell me.*

I didn't even know how to respond to her. She still didn't know what had happened between Cassian and I but she knew that something had happened. That was all the info she needed in order to bug me for all eternity until I told her the truth. A truth I was hoping to hold off for a little while longer because I wasn't ready to say.

Two weeks in St. Lucia and I still couldn't pluck up the confidence to tell my best friend how my heart had been broken. Two weeks in St. Lucia and I still hadn't been able to stop thinking about him.

I hated him for dashing me away like I'd been nothing to him. I hated him because I couldn't stop thinking about all the moments we'd shared together and all the conversations we'd had together. But most of all I hated him for making me fall in love with him.

Less than ten seconds later, my father's Aston Martin pulled into the airport's pick-up zone and the tension that had been filling my core instantly released. I pulled my AirPods out my ears, pocketed them and rushed towards the SUV's doors.

"Daddyyyyy!"

"There's my Angel."

I hadn't even let my father get out the car before I'd raced into his arms while he still sat in the backseat. His embrace was the one thing I'd needed after St. Lucia and now I finally had it and I had no plans on letting it go for a while.

"Hmm, someone missed me after all, huh?" my father hummed lightly then chuckled, squeezing me just as tight as I squeezed him. Our hug finally ended and my father ushered me in by reaching for my hand.

"Come in, baby. Ethan will get your bags to the trunk."

My father shuffled down the car's seats so I could sit next to him and he took my hand in his, stroking the top with his thumb.

"So how was St. Lucia?"

I suddenly became an open book, regurgitating out all the exciting activities and adventures I'd experienced while in St. Lucia.

"St. Lucia was out of this world amazing! I..."

The entire car ride to my apartment, I talked and my father listened. He would constantly nod, his eyes filling with joy and a smile constantly gracing his lips. He was of course glad that I'd had a good time on my impromptu vacation but I also knew he was glad to have his daughter back where she belonged.

Home.

Less than fifteen minutes later, Ethan pulled up outside my building.

"Are you sure you don't need help with your bags?"

I shook my head 'no' at my father and leaned in closer to wrap my arms around him.

"I'll see you bright and early on Monday, Daddy," I told him while we hugged.

"Get some rest and I'll see you on Tuesday."

"Dad." I broke our hug to give him a smug grin. "No special treatment, remember?"

"Says the woman who took two weeks off without telling her boss? I think we're way past you not receiving special treatment, kid."

I laughed and he laughed too before pressing his lips to my forehead.

"Have a longer weekend just this once so you're prepared for all the work I'm sending your way next week. You have a lot of work to do, missy. We've got new clients and I want my best accountant taking charge on them all."

"Yes, sir."

Ethan helped me get my suitcases from the trunk and before I knew it, I was waving goodbye to my father and walking into my apartment building. While I headed up to my floor in the elevator, a sudden thought struck me.

Shit, I haven't texted Adina back.

I knew as soon as I stepped through my door and placed my luggage to the side, I would need to text my bestie before she hounded me down with texts and calls. We had read receipts on for our messages so I knew she would see it and flip out about me ignoring her. Even once I explained that it was an accident, Adina wouldn't care. She wanted to know the truth about Cassian and I and I was going to have to stop being scared and tell her what had happened.

Once outside my door, I pulled my key out from my handbag and keyed it through my door.

Home sweet home.

I stepped in, pulling my bags in behind me. I caught an instant whiff of my reed diffuser's red roses scent and smiled at my neat living room. But then my smile vanished once my eyes wandered to my apartment's floor to ceiling window on the far right and I saw the one person who had brought me misery like no other. Standing in my apartment as if he had any right to be here. With a bouquet of red roses in his hand.

"Get. Out."

"Dana—"

"I didn't ask for you to speak, I'm telling you to get out." I avoided his eyes by looking over at my sofa and I felt my hands shaking. "Get out right now."

This. Can't. Be. Happening.

But it was. I had no idea nor did I want to know how the hell this lunatic of a man had broken into my apartment. All I knew was that I wanted him out.

"Get the fuck out before I call the cops, Cassian!"

My gaze refused to fall back on him. I couldn't do it. I couldn't look into the eyes of the person who had used me. I didn't want to look at him. I'd never wanted to see him again but here he was.

And he's still here after I just told him to leave!

"Get ou—"

"I'm not leaving," he cut me off. "Not until you hear me out."

Enough of this. I need him gone.

I ignored him and removed my handbag off my shoulder. Completely focused on getting my phone out to dial 911.

Just as I grabbed my phone, a figure appeared from the other side of my door and I looked up to see Pierro now standing in front of me.

"Miss Westbrook."

Where the hell had he come from?

He looked the same as always. Unemotional, professional yet still attractive with his black suit cloaking his tall and mighty frame. Pierro lifted his hand out towards me to hand over my phone and I shook my head 'no'.

"Both of you need to get out of my apartment and leave me the hell alone!"

"Danaë, I'm going to need your phone please," Pierro ordered in a calm voice and I just realized it was the first time he'd ever called me by my first name.

"No." I shook my head from side to side, stepping back.

"If you promise to just hear him out then I won't need it."

"I'm not promising anything to a man that has broken into my home with his crazy ass boss."

"I can assure you no force was used to enter your home, Danaë. Cassian made a request for your key to be copied and it was done."

My face twisted with rage.

"What? Why the hell would you do th—"

"So I could be here once you stepped through that door, Nae," Cassian intervened and I heard him step away from my window and that was enough to make me back away even more despite the fact that we were nowhere near close.

"So you could see me face to face once I told you that I love you."

What did he just say?

I'd been glaring at Pierro while Cassian spoke but the last three words I'd heard him utter made me look over Pierro's shoulder to see Cassian a short distance away. He had placed the roses down to my coffee table. It was only now that I took a better look at him and saw that he was clad in a black Nike tracksuit. Another one of my favorite colors on him after gray.

"I know I fucked up; D. Believe me I know I fucked up in the worst way possible but if you just let me expla—"

"You're lying." I chortled. "You don't love me."

"Nae, I do."

"No you don't!" I yelled, dropping my handbag to the floor and pushing past Pierro. Walking up to Cassian till I was directly in front of him. "Because if you loved me you wouldn't have said the shit you said to me two weeks ago, making me feel like nothing!"

My eyes bored into his guilty ones.

"You are a fucking liar and I don't want you here! I want you to leave and don't bother coming back! The same way you told me not to bother coming back, remember? You told me to get out so you need to do the same!" I pushed against his hard chest. "Leave me alone!"

"Danaë, please," he begged, his tone low and sorrowful and he reached for my hands, clutching them against his chest. "I didn't mean any of the shit I said. I only said it because I thought I was doing what was best. I thought pushing you away would be better than you finding out the truth about who I am and then pushing me away when you no longer want me."

I heard the door shut behind me and I turned around, water filling my lids. I realized that Pierro had left my home. I guess since I was hearing his boss out, he no longer needed to attempt to confiscate my phone. I slowly turned back around and Cassian let go of my hands and reached for my cheeks.

"I'm sorry, Nae Nae... please," he pleaded, stroking my skin. "I made a mistake. A huge mistake."

The first tear dropped and I was done for.

"These three weeks away from you have been hell. I considered getting on a flight to St. Lucia to come get you myself but I knew that the only reason why you'd left the city was because of me. Because of what I'd done to you."

The tears wouldn't stop falling and I was reminded of all the pain that I'd experienced when I'd last laid eyes on this man.

"I'm so sorry, my love... please forgive me."

He started kissing on my wet cheeks, his way of wiping my tears away but the more he kissed, the more they fell. The pain had come rushing in again and I couldn't get any of it out. Everything still hurt so damn bad. Then his kisses trailed over to my lips and he joined our flesh as one, giving me the one thing I'd missed badly these past couple days.

Him.

The more our lips meshed together and his tongue collided with mine, I was reminded of everything I loved about him. From the way he talked, the way he smelt, the way he kissed me, the way he would make love to me whether it was in those nasty little ways of his by tying me up or just with smooth, steady strokes. I loved this man. Every part of him. Even the parts I didn't truly know. Even the parts I was sure I was supposed to hate. But he'd hurt me bad. He'd hurt me real bad. I wasn't about to just let him back in and think that shit was sweet when it wasn't.

"No," I whispered moments later, pulling away from him but I didn't get far because he kept me nearby reaching for my waist, circling his arm around me.

"Y-You hurt me," I croaked out. "Why?"

He sighed before replying, "I was scared of you knowing who I am, Danaë. Scared of you not accepting the real me and who I am now."

Confusion filled me as I stared at him.

"My aunt is sick and I've had to take her place. I'm now the head of one of the biggest crime families in the state. I have an entire organization at my beck and call that answers to me whenever and wherever I need them. I protect those I that love. I kill those who try to harm those that I love and whoever stands in the way of what I want."

So this is what Imperia had been referring to all along. What I'd suspected prior to her hinting at the world that Cassian came from. By now my confusion had left me but I hadn't responded to what Cassian had said. I just continued to look at him with a blank stare.

"Did you hear what I said, Danaë?"

"Yes," I replied.

"You're not surprised by what I've just told you?"

"No." I lifted his arm from my body and surprisingly, he let me do so and I stepped back. "I already suspected you were part of something powerful. Imperia confirmed my suspicions when she told me that I have no idea who you really are and what world you come from."

His eyes widened but I pressed ahead with my words.

"You made a mistake when you decided to assume that I would push you away because of who you are and the world you come from," I revealed. "And because of that mistake, you've lost me."

"What?" He stepped forward, trying to reach for me once again but I pushed his hands away. "No, Nae Nae."

"I'm pushing you away because you crushed me, Cassian, three weeks ago when you treated me like a nobody."

"But I've told you I'm sorry, Danaë. I love you."

"You wouldn't hurt someone you love, the way you hurt me." I shook my head at him. "That's not love, Cassian."

"I messed up but I'm trying to make things right. I'm trying to fix us."

"Why? You seemed pretty certain on us not being together two weeks ago. You were so keen on pushing me away. So why the hell can't you just stick to your fucked up plans and leave me alone?"

"Because I'm fucking crazy about you!" He yelled, watching me like I was the one that had suddenly lost my mind. "I can't sleep properly; I can't even eat properly without thinking about you!"

He strode over to me and reached for my waist, pulling me into him so that my body was pushed against his. The only thing separating us was the small distance between our faces and I was slightly intimated by his intense stare as he held me close.

"When you left for St. Lucia, I started losing my mind at the fact that I couldn't come and see you even if I wanted to because you were on a seven-hour flight leaving the city. Leaving me for good."

He closed his eyes, taking a breath and releasing it, fanning my skin. Then he opened up and his intense stare had disappeared. All that remained was a look of love.

"I love you; Danaë Louisa Westbrook and I know you love me too," he whispered, holding me prisoner with his gaze.

I lowkey hated that he was right.

"I know I hurt you. I know I messed up but I'm trying to make things right. Please let me make this right. I have never in my entire life begged anyone the way I'm begging you. I made a mistake that I will forever regret but I want you... No, I need you more than ever right now."

I remembered his words about his aunt being sick and my heart felt heavy at what he'd been going through. If he'd just let me in then this wouldn't be happening. I wouldn't feel so much anguish towards him and I could have been there for him. The way he needed me to.

"You're right. I do love you." Joy began to settle on his attractive appearance. "But that's not enough right now." Then the joy began to fade.

"You should go, Cassian."

A flicker of anger flashed in his eyes.

"Please don't make this any harder than it has to be," I added, hoping those words would be enough for him to release me.

He remained quiet, watching me with a dulled expression for a few more seconds before he reluctantly nodded. He let go of my body and walked away from me. I didn't turn around to watch him leave but I heard the door shut seconds later, confirming his departure.

Once the door shut behind him, I was left alone and left reeling at all that had gone down.

"Oh. My. God."

I buried my head into Adina's pillow, feeling like the entire world was on my shoulders.

"Bitch you're in love with a real-life Mafia boss."

I groaned into the pillow before bringing my head up and staring into the dark browns belonging to Adina Lewis.

"Jesus Christ, why didn't I see this coming?" She asked herself. "I mean I said it from the jump, he's a boss but I didn't realize he's the actual head honcho of his entire family. Wow. Wow. Wow."

She was looking at me but she was no longer focused on me because her eyes were wide and unblinking. A cue of her being lost in her thoughts.

"Di."

"I've always felt like there's something more with those two. I could never put my finger on i—"

"Dina."

She blinked a couple times before offering me an apologetic smile.

"Sorry, sorry, I got lost in my conspiracy brain," she said, shifting over to me and wrapping her arms around me. "I'll still beat him up if you want me to. Just say the word and his ass is toast."

I suddenly laughed at the thought of Adina attempting to beat up Cassian. It wouldn't even work. He was ten times bigger and stronger whereas Adina was a pony in comparison to him.

I'd come over to Adina's today to spend the entire Saturday catching her up on all the fiascos of my life. I also planned to sleepover because Lord knew I'd missed being in the company of my bestie.

Adina had gotten the entire rundown on everything she'd missed in my crazy whirlwind of a life. She knew about Cassian breaking up with me, me running to St Lucia, she even knew about my goldfish, Nala, dying, the thing that had triggered me to leave in the first place. And of course she knew about Cassian's intrusion into my home yesterday with his soldier, Pierro. It felt great to reveal everything to her without fear of being judged. And despite how embarrassed I'd been feeling about the breakup with Cassian, now that I knew he loved me, I no longer felt mortified. Still hurt nonetheless by what he'd done but the embarrassment had gone.

"And to think all of this started from a dare I made you do," she reminded me of what had happened months ago at the bar we'd gone to. "Crazy."

I sighed, snuggling up closer to her and my head falling on her shoulder.

"I love him, Adina."

"I know, honey." She sighed. "I know."

"But I hate him too. I hate him for treating me like shit."

"But you won't hate him forever. This will pass and soon you're going to realize that you still love him."

Another sigh left me.

"How do you feel about him being who he is now? Being leader and all."

"Honestly... I don't know what to feel. I'm not shocked, I'm not happy, I'm not anything. I've never seen that side to him because he hid it from me but I know that if I decide to be with him, eventually I'll see it all. I'll have no choice but to be in his world if I want him in mine."

"And do you want him in yours?"

"I... I don't know, Di." I closed my eyes. "When he ended things, I was broken but after St. Lucia I told myself that moving on was going to be key and although it would be difficult, I would try my hardest to do it. Then he shows up yesterday and tells me the three words I've always wanted to hear from him. That he loves me but how can he love me after all the shit he said to me?"

I opened my eyes and lifted my head off her shoulder so I could stare at her.

"Hurt people hurt people," she said. "I'm not defending him but you told me that he pushed you away before you could push him away. Sounds to me like Cassian Acardi has a defense mechanism set it stone. As silly as it is, he wanted you to go before he could lose you. He's lost a baby, now he's losing his aunt... losing you probably would have been too much. He wanted to control things this time round since he couldn't control losing his baby and now losing his aunt. Control freak 101."

Adina really was a pro at reading people. I would forever be grateful for her expertise.

"Well he's dumb because he lost me when he told me that all he wanted from me was sex," I retorted. "He never should have pushed me away."

"He says he's trying to make things right though... will you let him eventually?"

"I gotta think about it. It's too early to say."

"Ahh but I remember when you said those exact words when I asked about you telling him how you feel, when we were getting a massage." Her words sparked the memory. "You knew that things between you and him were something more even though you tried to play your bestie and act like it wasn't."

A smile creeped on my lips at her knowing nature.

"Take all the time you need, girl, but we both know that despite everything, you love him and he loves you. And he most certainly isn't playing about you! Still can't believe he had a copy of your key made without even having the damn key! With his crazy ass."

I still couldn't believe he'd done that too.

"At least we know the crazy gene is definitely in the family because Christian is definitely just as crazy."

My brow raised and I watched her closely.

"Uh-uh, girl, no. Don't look at me like that. You're the only one in love with an Acardi," she assured me. "Chris and I are just good friends especially since I'm so good at my job. We have playful conversation from time to time, he tells me all about the women he has sex with and I tell him that his dick's soon going to fall off."

"Hmm... are you sure?"

"Positive." She nodded. "That's my dawg. Even though I can't stand his ass most of the time and he's a damn hoe if I might say so myself."

I laughed before resting my head back on her shoulder.

"I missed you, Dina."

"Missed you one hundred times more, pooh. You ready for another round of Sancocho?"

"Ooooo, yes!" I exclaimed, ready to eat more of the Dominican dish Adina had cooked earlier.

Having a Dominican bestie sure came in handy because she was always introducing me to some of the best dishes her culture had to offer. We continued to spend the rest of the day together, eating, drinking and watching reality TV together, one of our guilty pleasures.

Moments like these could never get old because Adina was one of my favorite people to be around. We always had the best times together and she never failed to make me happy. She was the epitome of good ass vibes. Our time together continued into the next day and the hours passed once again as Adina and I made up for lost time.

Eight p.m. arrived and I decided it was time for me to head home. I was now hugging Adina tight as we said our goodbyes.

"Hit me up the second you get home, okay?"

"I will," I promised, squeezing her tight as we rocked side to side. "Love you. Thank you so much for this weekend. I needed it."

"Love you more, baby girl. Don't forget that I'm here for you whenever you need me. Don't ever feel embarrassed or scared to talk to me about anything ever again. Okay?"

"Okay."

After our goodbyes, I'd headed to my car parked downstairs in a space outside Adina's apartment building. Ten minutes later, I was heading through the city back home with thoughts of nothing but Cassian Acardi.

How could I love and hate someone at the same time?

Hate was a strong word but it was just how I felt at this current moment in time. I wanted to run to him, let him hold me and tell me how much he loved me but another part of me wanted to be far away from him. Not forever... but until this hate subsided.

I arrived in my apartment's parking lot less than fifteen minutes later and parked in an empty space. I grabbed my Christian Dior tote bag that had proved to be a great sleepover bag, left my car and locked it.

I started walking towards the exit, thinking I was alone in the lot until I heard the opening of a car door and turned around briefly to see an unknown man getting out his car. My sights focused back ahead to the exit on the other side.

"Excuse me, Miss," his deep voice sounded but I didn't stop walking.

I simply looked over my shoulder to see the light skinned man now slowly following me.

He was dressed in a black bomber jacket, denim jeans and black combat boots.

"Excuse me, Miss! Can I ask you a question? It's about your car."

I turned around to face him but kept walking backwards towards the exit, my way of indicating to him that I didn't have time to spare.

"Yes?"

"Your Benz, do you enjoy driving it? I'm thinking of upgrading mine soon and yours is a real beauty."

I looked over at his car. A BMW Coupé. It was then it dawned on me that the stranger was simply trying to make conversation about my GLA. I decided to stop walking backwards, allowing the stranger to shorten the gap between us as he walked closer to me with his hands stuffed into the pockets of his pants.

"It's a great car, smooth drive and hasn't caused me any problems since I got it."

"Good to know," he replied, shooting me a friendly smile as he got closer. "How long have you had it?"

Now that he was much closer, I could see that he was quite an attractive brotha. With 360 waves swirling his scalp, smooth beige skin coating his exterior, thick bushy brows, plump pink lips, pearly whites, a gold Cuban link chain hanging off his neck and a gold hoop earring locked in each ear.

"Since last summer. It's been doing me well and I'm sure it'll do you well if you decide to get it."

"It has to because seeing you drive it made me want it," he voiced. "It's a real beauty."

I smiled, nodding and deciding that this conversation needed to come to an end. I was ready to be in my bed.

"You have a good night and good luck with your car."

Just as I turned away from him, the next sentence he said made my entire body go cold.

"I'm already having a good night because I'm about to get exactly what I need," he announced, stepping closer to me and grabbing my arm. "Which is you, Danaë."

I quickly tried to shake him off until I felt a hard object press against my side. Alarm hit me like icy water and I froze.

"Run and I'll shoot. Scream and I'll shoot," he warned me, his friendly tone no longer heard. All of a sudden he sounded rough and aggressive.

"Finally got your ass. You went M.I.A. for two weeks and I'd thought I'd lost you but you're back now."

His words made me realize he'd been watching me and that was enough for several shivers to go down my spine.

"Kamora hadn't been playing when she said you were a beauty. You'll be perfect for Clyde."

What. The. Hell?

"Let's go."

He started dragging me along towards his car and that's when every part of me started going numb.

This can't be really happening. This can't be.

I wanted to run and scream for help but I didn't want to be shot. This stranger had a gun pressed into my back and he'd just brought up the name of a woman I hadn't seen in weeks. A woman I was sure was gone out of my life for good. It didn't help that we were the only ones in this parking lot. No one was coming to save me.

"P-Please," I managed to make out once I saw us inch nearer to his BMW. "Don't do this."

"Sorry, lady but no can do. Kamora paid serious money for this job and I'm just here to deliver. No hard feelings." He continued to drag me ahead towards his car. He was behind me with the gun pushed into my lower back.

Do something, Danaë. Fight him. Kick him. Punch him. Do something, girl!

Once outside his car, he opened up the passenger door and pushed me inside. Before closing the door, he kept the silver gun pointed at me and bent low to say, "Like I said, you run, I shoot and take your dead body over to Clyde anyways. He won't mind. A lot of sick mothafuckas out there who would love having a dead, pretty corpse laid out, ready for them."

The taste of vomit formed inside my mouth and my eyes refused to leave the gun. I spotted the stranger's hand that had a skull inked into his skin.

"The choice is yours."

He shut the door behind him and began walking over to the driver's side. This was the only small window I had to run but all I kept thinking about was that gun in his hand.

If I run, I'm doomed. If I don't run, I'm doomed anyways. God, why is this happening to m—

Pow! Pow! Pow!

I flinched at the deafening sounds of gunshots and a loud thud against the car's hood and my eyes squeezed shut as I shielded my face with my tote bag. My heart was now in my throat and I was barely able to breathe.

Shit. Shit. Shit.

My heart was beating so fast, I was sure it would take a life of its own and pop out of my chest. The gun shots had stopped but I remained still with my eyes shut and my tote lifted over my face.

You need to see what's going on, Danaë. Stop being afraid. You don't have time for that right now.

I slowly moved my bag out my face and my eyes popped open so I could see what the hell was going on. The stranger had dropped to the floor in front of his BMW and a short distance away, I could see a suited mahogany skinned man, walking forward while holding his gun out in front of him as he stared down at the man he'd just shot. The man who had just tried to take me.

My car door suddenly opened and I jumped and screamed at the unexpected movement.

"Miss Westbrook, my apologies for scaring you."

I focused on the new suited man who had tanned skin, now reaching out for my hand.

"Miss Westbrook, you're safe now. Please come with me."

"W-What?" I turned to look back over at the first suited man who was no longer pointing his gun. Instead he was now on the phone. His lips moving as he spoke to whoever was on the other line. "He shot... He shot... him."

"Miss Westbrook, breathe."

It was only now I realized I'd been holding my breath and quickly released it before looking back over at the man to the left of me.

"Who... who... who are you?"

I was sure I had to be dreaming. All that had happened in the past five minutes wasn't making any sense. I'd just heard a man get shot after almost being kidnapped by that same man. Now he was bleeding out in front of his car. The car I'd been forced into.

This wasn't real! This wasn't really happening. No way.

"Miss Westbrook, I can assure you I'm here for your protection. I need you to come with me now."

This man seemed genuine and from his accommodating demeanor and formal clothing, he reminded me of Pierro. But I still had my suspicions about going anywhere with anyone after what I'd just been subjected to by a cruel stranger.

"To where?"

"To Mr. Acardi. He wants you with him right now."

And just like that, Cassian's presence in my life was ten times stronger than it already was. These were Cassian's men that had come and saved me. Cassian's men had shot down the man trying to take me away.

"I..."

The suited man pulled out his phone from his pocket and handed it over to me. I looked at its screen to see the name 'Boss' and the call's time at two minutes and five seconds. And still currently running. I slowly lifted the phone to my ear.

"Cassian."

"Are you okay, my love?" The concern in his tone was unmissable. "Are you hurt? Did he... did he hurt you?"

"I'm fine," I whispered. "Cassian, what's going on? Why are your men with me right now? How did they... how did they know I was in trouble?"

"You have my heart in your hands, Danaë. I was never going to let you roam around the city without eyes on you, regardless of our situation."

I exhaled deeply.

"My men are bringing you to me right now. Sit tight and I'll see you soon, sweetheart."

"But Cassian, the man that tried to take me... your men shot him, he's... he's blee—"

"You don't need to worry about that mothafucka. He signed his death wish when he touched the love of my life. All I need you to worry about is getting into the car that will bring you straight to me. I need you in my arms tonight. So get in that car, sit tight and I'll see you soon."

And just like that the conversation was over and I realized I'd just been introduced to the side of Cassian that he'd tried so hard to keep away from me. The side that protected those he loved by any means necessary. The side that killed with no regrets. The coldhearted side that refused to let anyone stand in his way and that included me. Cassian Acardi wanted me right by his side and there was nothing I could do to stop him even if I wanted to. But I didn't want to stop him. All I wanted right now was to be in his arms.

CHAPTER 24

~ CASSIAN ~

"*Cass, there's a situation.*"

"*What kinda situation?*"

Silence.

"*Speak up, P. You know better than to keep things from me.*"

"*An unknown man is attempting to take Danaë as we speak from her apartment's parking lot with a gun pressed to her back. But I assure you Wilson and Dante have it handle—*"

"*What the fuck do you mean an unknown man is attempting to take Danaë as we speak? Who the fuck is he? Who the fuck would be stupid enough to touch my woman!*"

"*Cassian, please stay calm. The soldiers have this under control.*"

"*If this was under control, she never would have been touched in the first place with a gun!*"

"*Wilson and Dante were discreetly positioned at her apartment's lot, just like you requested. They watched her arrive from Adina's, park her car and leave. A stranger then appeared and he seemed innocent as he approached Danaë, making friendly conversation with her so him*" *trying to take her caught them completely off guard. Wilson's waiting for the perfect moment to strike once Danaë's out of shooting range."*

"Get me on the phone to those niggas. Right. Fucking. Now."

It was the worst news I'd heard all week after hearing Danaë tell me numerous times to get out of her apartment.

Man... these past few weeks had been hell on earth. Nothing seemed to be going right in my life. Even with all this new found power, all this extra protection in my life, I was like a lost soul with no real direction in my life. Everything just felt bleak.

I'd tried to convince myself many times that I could do this. I could live a life without Danaë. I could tell Pierro to remove the eyes we had on her and I would move on without worrying about Danaë Westbrook ever again.

What a fool I'd been to think I could ever do that dumb shit.

Once Pierro let me know that Danaë had hopped on a flight to St. Lucia two weeks ago, I was crushed at her departure. I don't know what crushed me more. Knowing that she'd left the city because of me or knowing that I had no easy access to her like I usually did unless I hopped on a flight to St. Lucia myself. And of course I'd been tempted many times to do so.

My sleeping pattern took a turn for the worst. I'd sleep for about two hours, wake up in the middle of my slumber and no longer be able to sleep. She consumed my mind when I was awake but when I slept, her hold remained. Dominating my dreams and making me regret everything I'd said one hundred times more than I already did. Food didn't even appeal to me in the same way because everything tasted bland. The main things that kept me sane was working and being by Zietta's side whenever I could as she underwent chemo and on the days she remained rested in bed. And the most important thing of all that kept me sane, was knowing that as soon as Danaë landed back in the city, I would be waiting for her in her apartment to tell her how sorry I was and how much I loved her.

Enough was enough.

I'd kept up this ruse long enough. I'd let my inner demons do all the talking they had to do about me being a killer, not deserving her and losing her the same way I'd lost Zeroni. Now I was no longer listening.

I was in love with Danaë and I wanted to be with her. I wanted to make things right between us and I just prayed she'd give me the chance to do that. I prayed she'd let me back in but if she didn't… I wouldn't force her to be with me. I couldn't force her to do something she didn't want. No matter how bad I wanted to.

It had been a real struggle to walk out of her apartment, not knowing what was to become of us. She'd admitted that she loved me but in the same breath told me that it wasn't enough. I was certain to prove her wrong and now as I stood on the front patio of my home, I was sure that I was on the right path of proving to her that love was enough. Our love would always be enough.

My sights were glued on the GLS SUV pulling into my driveway and it came to a stop seconds later a short distance ahead. I raced to the car's backseat door, pulling its handle and laying eyes on the beauty who melted my heart in ways I used to think were undoable.

I didn't hesitate to reach in, cradling her face that had turned towards me. I crashed my mouth to hers, needing to get a taste of her. Needing to feel that incredible high I felt whenever we connected with our lips and tongues alone. Needing her to feel just how bad I'd missed her and how I never wanted her to leave me again.

After giving her a hungry kiss, I pulled away and gazed into her brown eyes.

"Are you okay, my love?"

She released a deep breath and slowly nodded.

"I'm okay."

"I never wanted you to have to see the dark side of my world but anything to protect you will always be done."

Danaë silently surveyed me and I noticed an expression of understanding cross her face.

I took her hand and held it in mine as I said, "I'm going to find out exactly who was behind this shit. I promise."

"No need." I frowned but she kept talking. "It was Kamora."

"What?"

"The guy who tried to take me mentioned her name and how she paid for me to be taken away to some guy called Clyde," she explained with a haunted look. "It was all Kamora. She wanted me gone... She's always wanted me gone."

Kamora plotting against my Nae Nae? Now this was something I hadn't seen coming at all.

That evil, little witch.

There was nothing that needed to convince me about Kamora's days being numbered. It's like everyone had suddenly decided that they had a death wish and I was more than willing to give them what they wanted.

"I don't even want to think about what could have happened if your men hadn't come to my rescue."

"Don't think like that, Nae Nae." I shook my head at her. "You'll only torture yourself with fake scenarios about what could have happened. Scenarios that don't matter because you're safe now. You're with me."

I gave her one last kiss before leading her out of the car and to the door of my home where two guards stood posted by each side of the large wrought iron door.

"Where are we, Cassian?"

We were outside the twenty-five thousand square foot property that I'd chosen to be my new fortress. It had seven bedrooms, ten bathrooms and all the luxurious amenities that were fit for a king. I hadn't really cared too much for the home because it seemed lifeless with just me living in the space. Despite all the expensive furniture and décor, my home just wasn't a home yet. My old penthouse back at The Palazzo was more of a home than this place and I knew that was because of all the memories I shared with Danaë there.

"My house."

"You moved?"

I nodded, glancing at her and spotting the surprise filling her eyes.

"Why?"

"I promise to explain everything to you if you'll let me."

She didn't respond until we arrived outside my door.

"Okay."

Five minutes later, we were inside my living room. She sat on a four-seater whereas I decided it was best I just stood. It was best I stood for all the things I had to say. I braced myself, taking a deep breath before speaking up.

"The name Acardi isn't just a name, Danaë. It's my legacy."

I started from the beginning. Telling her all about my grandfather, how he made a name for himself in Chicago and created The Acardi Empire that I'd been born into. I told her about my father and how he'd ruled after my grandfather. Then about Frankie and how she'd been raised from the jump to be the fiercest woman in our family. How she'd taken my father's place once he'd passed away. Then I finished with Frankie stepping down, me now taking her place and all the duties I now had as king.

By the time I was finished Danaë wore a tranquil look despite all the chaos I'd just inflicted into her life by telling her all about the world I came from. But she hadn't responded and now as the minutes went past, my nerves began bubbling up stronger inside me as I realized that she still hadn't said one word.

"Danaë," I called out to her, stepping closer to her. "Say something please."

"I... I don't know what to say," she admitted, sighing softly. "I'm just trying to take it all in."

I dropped down to my knees in front of her, reaching for her delicate hands.

"As much as I don't want to let you go, I won't force you to stay where you don't want to be, Danaë." I couldn't believe the words leaving my lips but this is what love had done to me. This is what the love I had for Danaë had done to my icy heart. "I love you but I won't make you be with me. I won't force you to be in my world."

I knew I didn't want to lose her but at the same time I wasn't going to force her to be with me. It was up to her if our relationship was to progress in the way I wanted it to. Although it would kill me to have to let her go, if that's what she wanted then I would have to toughen up and let her go.

I lifted both of her hands, planting a kiss on each one before releasing them. But the second I did, she grabbed my hands, connecting us once again. I gazed at her, seeing affection glowing in her brown pools.

"I don't want you to let me go, Cassian," she said. "I never wanted you to let me go... I never wanted you to push me away."

"And I'm sorry for doing that dumb shit, Nae... I never should have pushed you away. It was one stupid mistake. A mistake I won't ever make again. I won't ever shut you out like that again, I won't ever make you feel like a nobody when that's the last thing you are to me. You're my weakness and happiness mixed in one. You're the woman who made me fall in love after I was sure that love was never for me. You're my everything and I'll be damned if I ever push you away again."

I leaned in closer to peck her lips.

"I promise it won't happen again, my love," I whispered.

It was a promise I intended to keep.

"I promise... I promise... I promise," I whispered once again and gave her a light kiss after each sentence.

I felt her wrap her arms around my neck, pulling me in closer and before I knew it, we were kissing away like two lovers who had been deprived from one another for too long.

Too fucking long.

Within minutes, I was able to whisk Danaë into my arms and take her upstairs to the one place I'd wanted her to be in for weeks.

"Cassian, baby."

I'd missed this. God knew how much I'd missed this. I'd missed being able to undress her, admire her beautiful figure, kiss all up on her body, caress her soft skin and most all I'd missed diving into the heaven between her thighs.

"Mmmh, Cass..."

And how could I forget how much I'd missed hearing her moan my name? I was convinced it was one of the greatest sounds on earth.

"I missed you," I told her as I delivered steady strokes within her tight slit. "So much."

Her pretty eyes widened and her mouth took an 'o' shape as our connection intensified each time our hips collided.

"And... and I'm sorry... I'm so sorry, baby."

I stared down at her, loving the faces she made while I moved in and out her wet middle and loving how her walls fit perfectly around my length.

"Forgive me."

She nodded but that wasn't enough for me.

"Say you forgive me, Danaë."

"I... I forgive you," she answered breathlessly.

I then joined my lips to hers, matching our hands that were joined above her head. I continued to submerge myself deeper and deeper inside her. Trying to prove to her just how sorry I was and how I would never do it again.

Never.

12:45 a.m.

Danaë and I had been making up for all the time we'd lost together. Five hours later and she was knocked out. And I'd almost been knocked out too but I was reminded that I couldn't rest until I collected something that belonged to me.

Ding!

My phone sounded off on my night stand and I carefully turned away from Danaë as she slept in my arms. She was too deep in her sleep to hear my phone chime so I didn't have to worry about her suddenly waking up, wondering what was going on. She'd learned enough about my world today. More than enough.

Dr. Miller done. Ready when you are.

Leaving Danaë was a struggle but I'd received the text I needed from Pierro. That was enough to tear me away from her side, get up, get dressed and head downstairs where my car and driver awaited me.

I was leaving Danaë all alone inside my home with no worries. She was protected by the various guards surrounding my home, a protocol that I lowkey hated for myself but for Danaë I was all for it. The previous Acardi bosses had all had the same top-notch protection that I now had. Guards around their homes, trackers on their cars and an extra car or two following them around when they roamed the streets. So I had no choice but to accept it. It's just that sometimes I hated having so many niggas around me. It made me miss the days of being just a typical capo, not having that many eyes on me twenty-four-seven and bodies around me. I guess you could say I liked my privacy and being alone but as leader, I had to be guarded at all possible times. Those days of having no one around me were long gone.

I arrived at my desired destination about fifteen minutes later and exited the car. Up ahead was one of the many warehouses I now owned as leader and the location of the man who owed me his life.

"Boss."

I gave the soldier standing outside the metal doors a respectful nod and he pressed the button behind him, causing the large door to roll up.

The large space revealed itself to me and I spotted Pierro standing at the far end of the space watching Dr. Miller as he administered an injection into the arm of his unconscious patient. Three of my soldiers were inside too, observing Dr. Miller from a distance.

I walked onto the concrete flooring, keeping my eyes on the man who lay on a hospital bed in a blue medical gown.

"Bullets removed and he's all patched up," Pierro told me and I nodded.

I came to stand next to Dr. Miller, placing a hand on his shoulder as he packed up his things.

"Appreciate you, Doc. As always you never fail to come through for me."

The short Caucasian man turned to me with a proud smile.

"He'll be up any minute now."

We looked over at him, seeing his fingers start to move and his face slowly shifted in place.

"You've received your payment in full, Dr. Miller. Your car is ready for you outside."

"Thank you," Dr Miller replied to Pierro, closing his duffle bag then carrying it by his side. "Cassian."

"Doc."

We shook hands and Dr. Miller was then escorted to the exit by a soldier.

"Boss, your gown and equipment are ready," another soldier said to me and I turned to my right to see a cart being pushed towards me with my coveralls, goggles, gloves, mask and all the tools I needed for tonight.

"He's up."

Pierro's voice made me look back over at our main attraction and my lips curved into a small smile as I watched him, watching me.

"Gregory, glad you finally decided to join us."

"Where... where am I?" he asked with a dazed look.

"Exactly where you need to be," I said, walking over to my cart for my coverall.

"I-I was shot."

"Indeed you were." I stepped into each leg of the coverall and pulled it up my body, clothing myself in it. "Feel rest assured that the bullets have all been removed."

I'd made it clear to Wilson, the soldier in charge of shooting. Gregory down, that I wanted Gregory alive. Wilson shot him down three times. Once in his shoulder and once in each leg.

"This isn't... this isn't a hospital."

No, Gregory it's not, I responded to him inside my head, more focused on getting dressed then granting him with an answer.

"Where am I?"

Your own personal hell.

While on the journey here, I'd been sent an email with all the details on the man dumb enough to touch my love. The man dumb enough to think he could take her from me.

Gregory Hicks. Twenty-six. Henchman of Roland Clyde "Big C" Jenkins. Owner of an underground brothel on the outskirts of Chicago. Another one of the three people that owed me their lives.

Now that I was suited, I turned to face Gregory and he used my attention being on him again as a chance to question me.

"I said where am I?"

The audacity of this man to think I even owed him an answer to his question. To any of his questions. Even the entitled look he now housed on his stupid little face pissed me the fuck off.

"I'm out of he..." It was now Gregory had decided to lift up his hands and try to move but then he realized, he was handcuffed to the bed. His feet were cuffed too.

"Uh-uh." I shook my head 'no'. "You're not going anywhere."

Gregory started inspecting me closely, his eyes roaming up and down my outfit and worry marred his face.

"You tried to take away a woman that has a very special place in my heart," I informed him. "A woman that I will kill for in a heartbeat."

It was then it registered to him what exactly was going on and how he'd messed up because his eyes grew large and he started pleading for mercy.

"I was only doing a job for Clyde and his sister, Kamora! Please, don't kill me! I don't wanna die."

"Shut it, scemo (fool)," Pierro snapped and I chuckled, remembering how much he hated men begging like bitches when they already knew what trouble they were in. When they already knew what fate had in store for them.

"Oh don't worry, you're not dying." I paused, noticing how relief spread across Gregory's face. "Yet."

His relief instantly dissipated.

I couldn't lie, Gregory had done a good job at discreetly watching Danaë, trying to find the right moment to strike. He'd been sticking to hiding out at her parking lot and of course when she'd gone to St. Lucia, he couldn't get her but her return to the city had given him all the incentive he needed. Night time was the perfect time to get her because barely anyone was around which is why after she'd returned home from Adina's, Gregory made his move. My guys hadn't noticed him before because they'd only started watching Danaë again once she'd returned back from St Lucia two days ago. Gregory had been coming to her apartment's lot for weeks, something that Pierro had figured out from the lot's security cameras which now had tonight's events erased from them.

"You've had your first surgery of the night but now's the time for your second one." I cocked my head to the side and grinned at him. "You thought shit was sweet trying to take my girl?" My grin widened and that only scared him more because his eyes bulged. "Well guess what? It's about to get even sweeter for me once you lose those eyes that you had the audacity to use to watch my girl, plotting on how you were going to make your move on her."

The color drained from Gregory's beige face after my words, turning him pale.

"No! P-Plea—"

"And boy oh boy is it about to get even better when I cut off each of your hands. The same filthy hands that you used to touch her."

"No, please! Don't! I'll do anything, anything for you! Whatever you want!"

"All I want from you is your life which I'll be taking after you've gotten what you deserve."

My soldier went closer to him, putting masking tape over his mouth to shut his ass up. His protests and screams became muffled and I sighed with satisfaction before turning back over to the cart of tools. I reached for goggles first, placing them over my eyes then put my mask on before reaching for the drill. I turned it on before turning around to face Gregory. Ready to make him pay for what he'd tried to do to my love. No one tried to take Danaë away from me and got away with it.

Absolutely no one.

CHAPTER 25

~ DANAË ~

*S*leep had been good to me. It had provided me with a peace that I'd longed for and knowing that I'd fallen asleep right beside the man I loved was an extra bonus for me. There was a moment in the early morning when that peace was almost disrupted but when I felt him return to my side and his strong arms pulled me in close, my peace was restored.

My eyes fluttered open and I instantly laid eyes on Cassian. He was sleeping but had an arm draped across my body while he lay on his front. Even asleep, the man still looked so damn good.

As I focused in on him, I was reminded of all the love I felt for him. Despite the heartbreak, the love still remained and now with all that had gone down I was positive that I loved him more than I could ever describe.

He'd protected me even when I'd told him to leave me alone. He'd been firm on making sure I was okay and because of him, I'd been saved from something I didn't even realize I would need saving from. I'd always believed that I could protect myself. However, that was the one thing I'd failed to do last night. I hadn't been able to protect myself from a man determined to take me away.

A man that Kamora had hired.

I was still in disbelief about what Kamora had set out to do and Lord knew that now more than ever I wanted to hurt her.

How could she pay someone to take me?

I knew from the way the man trying to take me away kept talking about how I'd be perfect for his boss that wherever I was going, I was going to be forced into doing acts that I really didn't want to do.

How fucking could she?

All this time I'd been calling her a witch and that's exactly what she'd proved herself to be. The biggest witch of them all.

My biggest fear was telling my dad. He would need to know that there was an attempt to kidnap me and I already knew he would be furious. What loving father wouldn't be?

But telling him about the kidnapping would mean that he would want to know exactly how Kamora's plans had failed and that would mean telling him about Cassian's men. That would mean him finding out about Cassian's world and I wasn't sure if I was ready for all that. I'd just found out the true extent of Cassian's family and power and I still didn't know what to think about all of it.

What would my father think?

Trenton still wasn't aware of Cassian and I and for me to now have to lay this all on him... it all just seemed a bit too much. What if he didn't approv—

"Tell me what you're thinking about."

Cassian's baritone not only broke my thoughts but it made my entire body flood with warmth. His arm tightened its hold on my body and he slowly opened his eyes to gaze into mine.

I shook my head from side to side as I said, "Nothi..."

But his firm look made me remember that lying to him was never a good idea because he always knew the real answer.

"Last night... Kamora... my father," I revealed to him my scattered thoughts with a light sigh. "I need to tell him what happened and telling him what happened means I need to tell him about us... including your world."

Cassian's firm look softened up and he propped himself up while still holding onto me. Then he pulled me into him so my back was pressed against his chest and both his arms circled around my waist. I melted into his body, sighing softly as the hard planes of his muscles enfolded me.

"Before I went on my stupid shit and pushed you away, we agreed he needed to know about us."

"Yeah but that was before you became head capo, Cass... I just don't know how he's going to react to all of that. He'll want to know how Kamora's plans were stopped and I won't be able to hide it from him... I can't hide that from him."

"What if I told you that you have nothing to worry about?"

I looked over my shoulder, narrowing my eyes at him.

"What do you mean?"

"What if I told you that you have nothing to worry about?" He repeated, looking down at me with a calmness in his eyes.

"I'd say that I do."

How could I not be worried about what my father would think?

This was my Dad. Trenton Samuel Westbrook. The one man that didn't play about me. What would he say about me being in the love with the head of the biggest crime family in the state?

"And if I told you to just trust me," he requested. "Would you?"

Without hesitating, I nodded.

"Yes."

"So trust me, my love." He pressed a kiss to the top of my head. "Trust me."

I still had my doubts about my father knowing about Cassian's world but I trusted him. We'd had our downs but we were steady on the way to having our ups and trusting him would be one of the ways to help us get to those ups. Besides, by protecting me last night, Cassian had shown me that trusting him was exactly what I needed to do.

We eventually got out of bed, cleaned up and got dressed. I had my overnight bag that I'd packed to Adina's with my clothes from yesterday and some clean panties. I decided to borrow Cassian's clothes, putting a hoodie and shorts over my underwear. I checked my phone after getting dressed and seeing that it was almost three p.m. told me we'd indeed overslept. I then made my way downstairs where Cassian was waiting for me.

The new house that Cassian owned was truly magnificent. It seemed more like a palace than just a typical house. I hadn't finished exploring the house yet but everything I'd seen so far screamed opulence.

I knew Cassian had money but damn... this man had money!

From his master bathroom alone I was reminded of that fact. It had a jacuzzi tub and bath, a steam shower, floor heating, halo lighting, decorative wall mirrors and don't even get me started on the waterproof TV installed into the gray marble walls.

I arrived in the dining room to find Cassian on one end of a rectangular table that had various trays, bowls and plates of food laid on it. He got up from his seat and walked towards me with an inviting smile.

"Figured you'd be hungry."

He'd figured right because after all the catching up we'd been doing yesterday; I'd worked myself quite an appetite during my slumber.

He reached for my hand which I gave him so he could lead us down the row of seats to the seat to the right of his. Well, that's where I thought he was leading me to sit until he let go of my hand and pulled out the head seat for me. I grinned and thanked him as I took his previous seat, glad that he found it appropriate for me to sit at the head of the table.

Just before we started to dig into the food prepared just for us, Cassian explained how his new kitchen crew had prepared brunch for us and I wanted to thank them but Cassian told me how he'd made them go for a break so that he could have me all to himself while we ate. He knew I'd be thanking them all day if I could.

I attempted to serve myself but Cassian was quick to want to serve me, asking me how much of each food I wanted and when I didn't say a large enough quantity, he would add an extra piece of food.

"Someone's tryna make me fat I see."

He smirked.

"No but you need all the energy you can get because after last night, I'm nowhere near done with you, Danaë."

Heat stained my cheeks at his comment and went straight down my center to my most intimate spot. Memories of him buried between my thighs flew into my head but I pushed them out, focused on eating our meal.

"You never did tell me what's wrong with your aunt, Cass," I spoke up moments into us eating.

Cassian's gaze fell from mine and his face went blank while he chewed the remaining food in his mouth.

I knew she was a touchy subject because he hadn't explained what exactly was going on with her. I had my suspicions about what her illness was but I wanted him to feel comfortable enough to tell me what was happening. I wanted him to trust me in the same way that I trusted him.

"Stage four breast cancer."

My heart dropped at his words.

"It's spread to her lymph nodes and bones... right now we're just trying to find the best possible treatment to keep her symptoms suppressed as much as possible. We're not sure how much time she has left with us but we're... we're praying for the best."

God no.

"Cass... Cass... I'm so sorry."

I knew how much his Aunt meant to him. She was basically his mother so I knew he had to be hurting. I could see the hurt all over his face as he talked about her. He'd tried to remain stoic but the pain had pierced through his handsome visage.

I reached across the table for his hand that sat by his half empty plate and secured it in mine.

"I'm so sorry, Cass."

He looked up from his plate and those sorrow filled orbs fixed on me. I lifted his hand to my mouth and kissed on it repeatedly before sliding back my seat and getting up to wrap my arms around him. He embraced me back, pulling me closer into him until I fell onto his lap.

"I'm here for you," I whispered to him while we hugged. "I promise."

His large arms held my frame tighter and I leaned back so we could look at each other. I was sure that the look I held on my face right now was more than enough to convince him of my promise. Even with all I knew about his family and his new role, I wasn't going anywhere. I couldn't. The way I felt about him wouldn't allow me to.

Just before Cassian could press his lips to mine, I leaned back and his left brow shot up in the air.

"Do you trust me, Cass?"

"With all my heart," he confirmed without a shadow of doubt in his eyes. "Yes, I do."

"So trust me enough to tell me where you went early this morning?"

I'd been in too much of a deep sleep to hear when he'd left but I remember hearing the bathroom's shower and feeling the bed dip once he'd come back to me.

"Do you really want to know?" He questioned me with serious-ness lace in his tone.

I nodded.

"I was taking care of the idiot who tried to take you."

I didn't need him to elaborate. I knew exactly what *taking of care* meant and from the deadly look that flickered in his eyes, I knew that Cassian had no regrets about what he'd done and I didn't want him to have any.

"You'll never have to worry about him again, D. Believe that."

"But what about Kamora?" I asked. "She wanted me gone for a reas—"

"What did I tell you earlier?" He gently interrupted me, sliding his hands up my back. "Just trust me."

He leaned forward to steal a quick kiss from my lips.

"Trust." Another kiss. "Me." Then another one.

I knew that I trusted him but I really needed to relax and prove that I trusted him by actually doing it.

Trust him, girl.

After we were finished eating, Cassian's kitchen staff came to take our empty plates away and I thanked them all for the mouth-watering food before Cassian took me to his home theater. The room was pitch black until we walked in and the room's sensor lights came on. Cassian led me to the front row and let me take my seat before he took his.

"So what do you wanna watch?"

His left hand gripped my thigh while he reached for the remote on the seat next to him with his right.

"And no, we're not watching that damn vampire show."

I pouted and that was enough to make him smirk as held the remote out in front of him. He first switched on the cinema screen before pressing a button that dimmed the lights until only the ceiling's star lights and stair lighting remained. Providing the room with ambient lighting.

While Cassian started browsing for a film, I was too busy browsing him. The room was dimly lit but I could still see those sexy russet brown eyes, those juicy, pink lips, that smooth light beige skin, that neat, low cut beard, those large muscular arms...

Cassian turned to me, flicking his tongue across his lip and that was enough to have me gushing ten times more than I already was down below.

After all the back breaking he'd done last night and the soreness between my thighs that I'd woken up to this morning, I still wanted more.

Much more.

And Cassian knew that because he ditched the remote in his hand, chucking it to the side and reaching over for my waist. I yelped as Cassian pushed me onto his lap before one of his hands left my waist to go over his side. Within seconds the seat's recliner came out, allowing him to stretch out his legs with me sitting on top of him. Allowing me to feel his growing arousal for me under his sweats.

He said nothing but the desire sparkling within him as he watched me told me everything I needed to know. Without wasting time, I lifted myself off him slightly to start pulling at his pants but he pushed my hands away, making me frown.

"Take all that shit off."

His eyes roamed down my clothed body.

I quickly obeyed, lifting his hoodie off my frame. My body now warming up despite the fact that I was now undressing. I didn't have a bra on, so my breasts quickly revealed themselves to him and he couldn't stop staring at them.

I got off his lap so I could take off his shorts and my womanly center appeared. Once again he couldn't stop staring and I found my libido rising rapidly at the fact that he was looking at me like he wanted to eat me up.

"Come ride my face like you fucking own this shit."

Like a good girl, I was here to obey his every last wish and desire. I walked back over to him, climbed on top and stood above him.

He was quick to press both his hands onto the back of my thighs, hiking them up so he could raise me slightly before lowering me onto his face.

He wasted no time in devouring me. His tongue dipped in, thrusting into my tightness and staking its claim over my haven, making it clear exactly who belonged between these walls.

Him and only him.

"God... Cass!"

His thrusts, sucks, licks and laps were sweet assaults on my middle, reminding me of how much of a beast this man was. Especially with that skilled tongue of his.

A beast all for me.

My hands clutched the back of his head as he dived deeper and deeper between my passage, refusing to slow down and give me a chance to catch a breath. I couldn't keep my eyes open, my legs shaking as his assaults quickened. He pressed a finger into my butt while working his tongue in and out of me, making me lose all common sense.

"Cassssss!"

I was the one supposed to be riding his face which I was but he had me undone.

Completely undone.

By the time he made me cum multiple times and pulled his pants down only to then guide me down his thick shaft, I was on a whole new level of high.

"Cassiaghhhhhhh!"

Each time he pounded into me, wind was knocked right out of me and my eyes rolled back so far I was afraid they would get stuck.

"Cass... too muuuuuuch."

"Shut the fuck up," he ordered, keeping my hands locked behind my back with one hand while his other hand stayed tight on my waist. "When you left for two weeks, taking this wet ass pussy far away from me that was too fucking much. You had the audacity to take my pussy away, huh?"

"Cass!"

"You ain't give my pussy to no other nigga did you?"

I shook my head 'no' before yelling, "No!" as his hard pumps continued.

"Yeah I know you didn't," he voiced with a groan. "You could never do that shit when you belong to me."

He lifted his hands off my waist to grab my throat and squeezed tight.

"You belong to me, Danaë."

I nodded.

"Say it."

"I belong to you," I replied. "Only... you."

It was a truth I could never deny.

∽

"Cassian, where are we going?"

He looked over at me with a smile that did nothing to ease my concern.

"Just be patient, my love. We're almost there."

I huffed, not liking the fact that he wasn't telling me where we were going. After I'd had a nap from the hours of sex we'd been having around his palace, Cassian told me that we had some place to be. I'd tried to get it out of him just before we left the house but to no avail. Cassian was keen on not letting me know a thing until we arrived.

About fifteen minutes later, our car pulled up outside a restaurant building that had the sign, 'Oriole' and my spirits soared.

"Cass, why didn't you say we were having dinner here?" I turned to him with a bright smile. "I could've gone home to get some better clothes."

He knew about how I loved coming here since he'd put me onto the restaurant a few months ago.

"I wanted it to be a surprise," he replied.

Well, a surprise indeed it was and now I felt like I'd been a big baby for pestering him on where we were going.

"Besides, you know how much I love seeing you in my shit."

I smiled, knowing that that was true. Right now I wore Cassian's Trapstar London hoodie and sweats pants. His clothing was always so damn big on me but I could still pull it off.

Cassian's new driver, Damien, came to open my door and I thanked him before Cassian approached me seconds later with his arm out.

I took this moment to admire his attire. A khaki long sleeve fitted t-shirt, black jeans and black Balenciaga sneakers on his feet. A Cuban link chain graced his neck, a diamond stud in each ear and a gold AP locked around his wrist.

My baby looking fine as ever.

Taking his arm, I allowed him to lead the way to the front entrance of the restaurant and once outside, the door was quickly opened for us by a suited man who I knew had to be one of his soldiers because he donned the same expensive looking suit all the others had. I was becoming well familiar with the suited men that were constantly around Cassian and seeing that I was around him, they were around me too. I owed them my life after yesterday so I wasn't tripping by their presence.

We entered the large modern space and I wasn't surprised to find it empty. Cassian loved it when we could dine here alone and I loved it too. Especially due to the fact that Cassian loved having dessert... aka me on the table once we were finished. It wasn't until we walked past a table and I focused on the other end of the room that I realized we weren't dining alone.

"Daddy?"

Sitting around a round table was my father with a menu in hand.

"Angel."

I rushed over to him, leaving Cassian's side because all I could think about in that moment was the memory of me being taken and almost never seeing him again. By the time I was in his arms, I felt water prick my eyes.

"D-Daddy, I..."

"Shhh," he hushed me gently as he rubbed on my back. "Everything's okay, baby girl. Everything's just fine. Daddy's here."

Me being the cry baby that I was, meant that the first tear dropped and the rest quickly followed. We remained hugging for a few more seconds until I heard Cassian's voice.

"Trey."

"Hello, son."

I pulled away from my father and saw his hand out which Cassian took and shook.

I looked from my father to Cassian and it was only now that I was able to focus properly on the situation at hand.

My father is here... because Cassian told him to be here... which means... he knows.

As if he could read my thoughts, Cassian reached for my arm and pulled me closer to him.

"Let's sit down, Nae."

He pulled out the seat opposite my father's and I sat down, watching my father intently. From what I could read on his wrinkle free face he seemed relaxed and that worried me more than anything. If he knew about what Kamora had planned and Cassian's hand to play in foiling her plans and was looking this relaxed? Yeah I definitely had a reason to be worried.

"Nae, relax. You have no reason to be looking so afraid," my father announced but his words did nothing to ease my worry.

"Dad... this isn't how I wanted you to find out about Cassian and I."

"Baby, I've known about you and Cassian from the very beginning."

My heart skipped several beats and I glanced at Cassian to see him leaning back with the same relaxed look my father housed.

"What?"

"Did you think I didn't notice the way you two looked at each other that first day in my office?" He asked me with a teasing smile. "And why do you think I was so eager for you to take his company's accounts?"

I stared at my father, speechless to all he was saying.

"Of course I wasn't pleased to find out that Cassian had upset you that day in your office and trust me I had plans to step to him myself which is why I tried to get you to tell me who it was, Danaë. That way when I went to him, I would know that I had your blessing to get involved. But when he showed up, I had a feeling that it was one big misunderstanding which is why I acted oblivious and stepped out the room to give you two some privacy."

Oh God.

Trenton had known all along and me being boo boo the fool by being so hellbent on keeping Cassian and I's situation away from him, only made him more privy to us. By telling him about the man that had used me for sex, Trenton knew exactly who I was talking about. I'd basically just filled in the blanks for him.

"Now after you went to St. Lucia, Cassian finally plucked up the courage to tell me what I already knew. That he's in love with you and wants to spend the rest of his life with you."

My eyes went back on Cassian who looked at me with a loving look before he reached for my hand.

"Of course I had my reservations... I knew that you two were going through a rough patch because of your impromptu vacation and now with Cassian being head capo, I wasn't sur—"

"You know?"

"Danaë, you must think I don't do my research on the people I do business with, huh?" He chuckled. "I've been a private associate of the Acardis for many years now. Cassian's father, God bless his soul, was one of the first clients your mother and I ever had. He started investing in a few night clubs around the city and wanted me to help him keep track of them all. Night clubs I still keep track of till this day. Of course I know, honey."

Oh wow. Information was just flying out the box with each passing moment and I still couldn't believe that my father had known all along about Cassian and I.

"I also know about that ingrate of a woman that tried to take me from you," he stated, a flash of temper lighting his eyes. "But thank God for Cassian because I don't know what I would've done if I'd lost you, my Angel." My father locked eyes with Cassian. "Thank you once again, son. You truly do love my daughter."

"I truly do," Cassian replied, holding my hand tighter.

"I wasn't sure about how your relationship with work when you'd stepped in place as head capo but I now know that I have nothing to worry about. I know you'll protect her no matter what."

"No matter what," Cassian repeated after him.

Again I was speechless. Looking from my father to Cassian and realizing that these two men had already had various conversations about me. Cassian hadn't been lying when he told me to trust him because I could trust and believe that he'd assured my father on our relationship and by protecting me, my father's faith in him had risen immensely.

"Is she here?" My father asked Cassian and Cassian nodded before turning to his solider standing on the other side of the room.

She?

He gave the suited African American man a nod and that was all it took for the man to step out the room. Within seconds, the man arrived back in the room, holding on to the arm of a masked figure with hands that were zip tied.

She was led to us and made to sit down on the vacant seat ahead. Then the black fabric over her head came off.

Kamora.

Her hair was knotty and thick from the lack of straightening and brushing, her mascara had smudged down her face, her maple brown eyes blood shot red from all the crying and her mouth sealed by black tape which Cassian's soldier stripped off her lips, revealing her dry cracked lips.

"T-T-Trenton!" she shouted at my father. "P-Please, help me! I didn't do it! I swear I didn't do it!"

"And what is it that you didn't do, Kamora?" My father queried.

Looking into the eyes of Kamora felt strange to me. Not only had I not laid eyes on this woman in months but as I now stared at her, I felt nothing. No hate. No love. Just nothing. I guess you could say, I knew what fate had in store for her so I didn't care to feel anything towards her. Her punishment was coming right her way whether she wanted it to or not. And she deserved it.

"Plan her kidnapping," she announced, not giving me any eye contact as she mentioned me.

"She has a name," Cassian retorted, shooting daggers her way. "Use it."

"Plan Danaë's kidnapping," she corrected herself. "I didn't do it."

"That's not what your brother Clyde told Cassian's men," Trenton informed her. "So which one of you is lying?"

"It's him! It's him!" she yelled, shifting in her seat. "He's a liar! I don't even talk to him anymore. I told you I never speak to him anymore, Trey... please, believe me!"

"Hmm... hear that, son?" my father turned to Cassian. "She says her brother's a liar and she doesn't speak to him anymore."

"Oh yeah I hear it all," Cassian responded, refusing to break his gaze on Kamora. "It's quite funny she would say all that when I have a screenshot of the bank transaction that she made to the so-called brother that she doesn't speak to anymore."

It was then Kamora's light skinned face went white.

"And thanks to the so-called brother she doesn't speak to anymore, I have the text messages that she sent of Danaë's address and her photograph," Cassian continued before leaning forward and letting go of my hand. He rested his elbow on the table and sat his chin on top of it as he surveyed Kamora. "You really thought in that sick little head of yours that you would get away with this wouldn't you? You really thought you could take the love of my life away."

"And to think I ever had any feelings for you," my father intervened. "You're pathetic, Kamora. A pathetic wom—"

"She's a stupid little girl that had to be taught a lesson!" Kamora blurted out, sending a dirty look my way. "All she's ever done is come between us, Trey! You were supposed to be mine! We were supposed to get married and have children of our own together but she just had to get in the way! Stupid Danaë getting in the damn way!"

My expression hardened at her words.

"You chose her over me and I just couldn't sit there and let that happen... I had to do something. I just wanted her gone."

"You wanted my own flesh and blood gone. My daughter!" My father banged against the table and from the way he was now looking at Kamora it was as if he wanted to flip this table over and fuck her up. "I swear to God if you weren't already going to get what was coming to you, I would get my gun and pull the trigger myself."

Never in my twenty-five years of life had I heard my father talk like this but truthfully, I wasn't surprised. Kamora had tried to take me away from him and that was enough for my father to want to raise hell.

Kamora's bottom lip began to tremble and her eyes welled up as she watched my father.

"She stole you away from me, Trenton... You and I were good together! We were going to get married."

"I told you I didn't have any plans to remarry but you refused to listen. You just couldn't let shit lie and you know what? I'm glad you didn't because I can finally see what type of woman you really are. You wanted to sell my daughter to your brother, the pimp! The pimp you claimed that you'd cut all ties with after finding out what type of business he did. You're nothing but a liar, Kamora, and I thank God I dodged a bullet by ending things with you."

By now Kamora's tears ran down her cheeks and she avoided my father's gaze.

Now that there was silence, I saw this as my opening to say my final words to Kamora.

"Kamora, I always used to call you a witch behind your back and there were times when I felt guilty calling you that. Seeing how much my father liked you made me soften up and try to look over our differences. I changed your contact name in my phone back from the witch to your name. I tried to make an effort with you, invited you into my home and bonded with you as best as I could. Even when you disrespected my late mother, I eventually gave in and agreed to apologize for hitting you. Now I see that all along my gut feeling had been right. You're a terrible person, Kamora. You were willing to sell me off into your brother's sex trafficking organization just to prove a point? How truly fucked up in the head you are and I really hope you enjoy hell."

Her teary eyes turned into slits and she sat up on her seat as she focused in on me.

"Don't even sit there and act like you're innocent! You put your hands on me and you just couldn't stand the fact that I made him happier than your stupid mother ever coul—"

"How dare you disrespect my wife!" My father hollered, rising up from his seat but as soon as he stood so did I, pressing my hand to his chest to calm him down. He'd had enough of not being able to get his hands on Kamora and from that rage burning in his eyes, he was ready to pounce on her.

"Daddy, don't. She's not worth it." I reached for the side of his face, stroking into his thick beard. "Dad, look at me. Please."

He listened, tearing his eyes away from Kamora and looking down at me. Instantly, the anger had receded from his face and he placed his hand on top of mine, caressing it gently.

"Take her away," my father said in a low tone, keeping a fixed gaze on me. "I can't stand the sight of her."

"Trey, please! Don't do this! You love me! You know you do!"

Kamora's protests sounded in the background but we all tuned her out.

"Take her away," Cassian ordered while I remained concentrated on keeping my father calm.

By the time Kamora and her shouts had left the room, my father's face lit up and it was like his outburst hadn't even happened. We then took our seats once again and my father spoke up.

"I promise you that if I ever bring another woman into your life she will be nothing like her." He let out a harsh breath. "But at this point, I think I'm done with women. Maybe your Dad just isn't built for the whole relationship thing, kid."

"Don't say that, Dad... you'll find someone. Someone who respects your wishes to not remarry."

"And someone who respects your beautiful daughter," Cassian added and I smiled at his statement.

My father nodded in agreement before reaching for my hand from under the table.

"So that rough patch between you two is over?" my father queried. "I don't need to beat Cassian's foolish ass up after all, huh?"

"You wish, old man," Cassian said which made me giggle and I looked between them both to see the smirks gracing their lips.

Their playful nature was cute to watch and I was glad that they were comfortable enough to tease one another.

"It's over," I confirmed. "I love him."

Cassian leaned in towards me and placed a kiss to my cheek, causing my body to sizzle. Even the little sweet gestures this man did to me had every inch of my body craving him.

"And I love her," he said, his breath tickling my ear before he pressed one last kiss to my face.

As he backed away, I looked over at him and the smile that now clung to my lips was one I couldn't force away even if I tried.

Cassian Acardi.

The man that had turned me into his little nympho and the man that undeniably held my heart. He'd been such a meanie when I'd first met him but now he was my softie. With all the pain he'd experienced in the past and the pain he was experiencing now, I had managed to melt his heart and make him fall in love. Even with all the responsibility on his shoulders and the new world I would be thrusted deeper into the more I stayed by his side, it didn't change anything about my feelings for him. I was in love with Cassian Acardi and I had no desire to ever stop.

CHAPTER 26

~ CASSIAN ~

"*Oh my... she's a real beauty. Where the hell have you been hiding her, bambino?*"

"*Yeah where the hell have you been hiding her, Cassi? She's gorgeous.*"

"*Thank you, Miss Acardi and Caia.*"

"*Call me, Frankie, bellissima (beautiful) or Zietta will do just fine.*"

"*And you can feel free to call me Cai or future sister-in-law will do just fine.*"

"*Okay.*" *Danaë shyly giggled.* "*Got it.*"

"*How about we go outside to check on my new roses? They should have bloomed by now.*"

"*Zietta has an entire rose garden that you just have to see, Danaë. Trust me you'll love it.*"

"*I'm sure she'll love it, Cai, since Cassian loves it just as much. It's been a minute since I've had him in his pink gardening apron.*"

"*Cassian has a gardening apron?*"

"*Yup and its pink too! I'm sure it's around here somewhere right, Zietta?*"

"Yes, it sure is. I even have pictures of him in it!"

"Aye, y'all need to chill. Danaë don't need to see all that."

"Oh I think I do, baby. I wanna see how cute you look in your little pink apron."

"Let's go find them before he tries to stop us, girls. Come on!"

Seeing my three favorite girls bond was one of the best things I'd seen in my life so far. And I was praying to God that He allow me to see many more days of them bonding together.

Two weeks after Danaë's attempted kidnapping and a lot had happened.

Gregory, Kamora and Clyde had all been dealt with and they were out of this world for good, making me one very happy man.

Zietta's chemo treatments were going well. Chemo was known to make patients weak and although Zietta had those days when she felt poorly, the chemo was helping relieve a lot of her other symptoms, giving her the strength she needed to do some of the activities she loved such as gardening and cooking. It was also giving her the strength to be with us for as long as possible.

I'd started going to therapy after Danaë suggested I should. Zeroni's death had happened over three years ago and I still hadn't dealt with the trauma of what had happened. I had been blaming myself for her death over these past few years and I needed to heal from all that. Therapy was a challenge but I was opening up more session by session about my emotions.

Finally, I was fitting in well as Capo. The Family was running as smooth as ever and even Julius complimented me on how well I was doing. And it wasn't easy getting a compliment from him so that's how I knew I was killing it.

"I'm glad you finally came to your senses," a voice sounded from behind and I tore my eyes away from the window that gave me a great view of my favorite girls talking while watering Zietta's rose garden.

My eyes meet the chocolate eyes of my cousin, Julius. He extended his hand out and I spotted the glass of brown he held for me. His other hand had an identical glass.

"Glad I did too," I replied, reaching for the glass and pressing it to my lips just as he came to stand by my side.

We both now looked out the window at the women enjoying each other's companies.

"She's breathtaking."

His compliment about my future wife made me smile as I sipped on some Louis XIII. The strong liquid burned my throat, turning my blood hot.

"I can see exactly why you were acting out."

I tittered, lifting my glass off my lips to agree.

"Yeah."

"She's accepted you just like I knew she would," Julius commented. "But know that it doesn't get any easier from here, Cass. She's accepted you but she will have her doubts and reservations. That's natural, she's a woman. Your woman. It'll be second nature for her to worry. There will be times when she worries so much that you'll be tempted to leave it all behind for her. Times you'll want to run away with her to your private island and never come back."

It's like he'd read my mind because I'd already been tempted to do that a few times during these past couple weeks.

"But I can't," I said, turning to him. "Not with all this responsibility."

Julius nodded, a firmness gracing his eyes.

"I know she knows that though," I informed him. "She knows how serious my role is and she's still here."

I looked out the window, shifting my sights to her once again. Admiring everything there was about her. That melanin rich complexion that seemed to glow more and more each time I stared at her, those big, dark brown eyes I could never get tired of, those perfectly shaped lips I loved kissing and that gorgeous body – I could die a happy man knowing I'd explored that body.

"You've found yourself a keeper, Cass." I felt his hand squeeze my shoulder. "Cerca di non respingerla di nuovo come una stupida *(Try not to push her away again like a fool)*."

I smirked before nodding, not taking my eyes off her as she laughed at something Caia had said.

"Mai più *(Never again)*."

I put my life on that promise. Pushing Danaë away was never happening ever again.

Hours after spending time at Zietta's, Danaë and I were in the backseat of my Rolls Royce, being driven to a destination that Danaë hadn't been disclosed to yet. She was too busy rattling off the good experience she'd had today meeting my family to think about where we were truly going. I was sure that in her head she thought we were heading back to mine.

These past few weeks, Danaë had stayed every night at my mansion. Something I love greatly. Since she had work Monday to Friday, she'd brought a few of her things over so she could have easy access to her work attire without having to worry about rushing back home before work. With her around twenty-four-seven, my mansion felt more like a home.

"Your aunt is the sweetest lady I've ever met in my life, I'm so glad she likes me. And your sister? So damn cute and funny!"

I simpered at the excitement dripping in her tone as she talked. It was clear she'd enjoying meeting my family today and I was pleased to know that they'd all gotten along.

"Your cousin was really nice too, I had fun today with your family, Cassi bear... thank you for bringing me to meet them."

"You're welcome, my love."

We were holding hands while we sat in the backseat, giving me easy access to lift her hand and press it to my lips. When I dropped our hands back down to the armrest between us, Danaë was quick to move closer to me, closing the small gap between us.

"I want those kisses up here, Capo." She pointed to her lips with her free hand and just the mention of her calling me boss made me hard as concrete.

"Oh you do, huh?"

She nodded, sinking her white teeth into her bottom lip.

"Come and get them." I leaned back in my seat so she would have to put more effort in reaching me and before I knew it, Danaë unfastened her seatbelt and was quickly climbing over her seat to mine.

I chuckled at her eagerness, cradling her up in my arms as she came to sit on my lap and came to get her kisses.

We spent the remaining journey, combining our lips as one and when I noticed from the corner of my eye that we'd arrived at our new destination, I pulled away from her. Causing her to groan loudly.

"Cassi bear... I want my kisses."

"And you'll get plenty of those later," I whispered to her, rubbing my nose against her soft one. "We've arrived."

"We're home already?" Danaë looked to her right so she could see through the tinted windows our surroundings.

"Cass... this isn't your house... we're at my parking lot."

"Yes, baby. We are."

"Why?"

"You'll see."

Our door was opened by one of my soldiers, allowing us to get out. We made our way hand in hand to Danaë's apartment floor. A soldier escorted us up to her floor but I made him wait by the elevator for us.

"What are we doing here, Cassian?"

I remained silent, leading the way to her apartment with our hands connected. We arrived outside her white front door and I pulled out my copy of her apartment key from my coat's pocket, pushing it into its lock and opening the door for her to enter in first.

She stepped in, taking a brief look at her place before turning to face me with her hands now on her hips.

"Are you going to put me out of my misery or are you going to leave me in suspense?"

I stepped forward, closing the gap between us and placing my hands on her waist. I slowly turned her around so that she was facing her living room area where her TV was mounted.

"Cass, what am I supposed to b..." She gasped once she laid eyes on what I needed her to see. "Cass, you didn't."

Her hands dropped from her hips and her body relaxed as she examined what was now sitting on the white oak cabinet below her TV.

I pushed her hair to the left so I could rest my chin on her right shoulder, pressing my lips into her warm skin so I could peck her.

"But I did."

I remembered not seeing Nala swimming in her tank when I'd visited Danaë's apartment when she was in St. Lucia. It was then I put two and two together and realized that she must have died. I knew how much Danaë had enjoyed having a goldfish so I made it my priority to get her a new one once the dust had settled between us.

"You are so damn sweet," she whispered. "But you shouldn't have brought it here... You made a mistake."

"How did I make a mistake?" I asked curiously. "You loved Nala, baby. It was only right you got a second chance with a new fish."

"I did love her, but you really shouldn't have brought it here, Cass."

Her tone started getting critical and I was baffled by her change of behavior towards my gesture. She moved away from me by stepping forward before slowly turning to face me. Her face now emotionless as she watched me.

"Why not?" My brow's knitted as I frowned. "I just wanted to make you happy, Nae. That's my job, baby."

"You shouldn't have brought it here because this isn't my home anymore."

My confusion heightened because this was the only apartment I knew for sure that she owned.

"It should be at my true home... which is with you, Cassian."

Then my confusion withdrew from my system and an electric feeling surged through me.

"That's where you should put it, baby. In *our* home."

I rushed towards her, wrapping my arms around her small frame and pulling her in close as I looked down at her.

"Our home. You really mean that Nae Nae?"

"Yes," she confirmed, sinking into me. "I'm with you every day, my stuff is everywhere, I might as well move into our home."

"We could always move into some place bigger, some place better, whatever you wan—"

"No, silly." She shook her head at me with a light giggle. "That house is perfect. It's beautiful and I love everything about it. You chose our first home well." She lifted her head to peck my lips. "That's our home and I want to be there with you properly. You, me and our new fish."

I smiled, stealing a kiss from her soft lips again. This time I made it last by probing my tongue into her mouth and gently lashed it against hers.

"Hmm... Cass, we gotta get home," Danaë said after pulling

away from me but I was quick to press my mouth back on hers, wanting a longer taste of her. "Ca... Cass, uh-uh." She pressed a finger to my lips and firmly shook her head 'no' at me.

"You can have plenty of all of this..." She gyrated her hips towards me beneath her Burberry trench coat. "When we get home, Capo."

"Hell no." I reached for her throat and circled my hand around it. "I want you now."

"But, baby, your men—"

"*Our* men," I corrected her.

"Our men," she said, lust growing in her eyes as my hold tightened around her neck. "Are waiting for us downstairs."

"I don't give a fuck. They're gonna have to wait a little while longer because I'm about to have you creaming all over this dick in a few minutes."

I moved nearer to her, placing my lips beside her left ear so I could whisper, "You forget how much of a nasty little slut you get for me, Danaë?"

"No, Cassian... I haven't forgotten," she whispered back. "How could I ever forget how good you beat this pussy up?"

Her query made me flash a grin her way and before I knew it, I'd let go of her throat, unbuttoned her trench coat off her body and chucked it to the side. Then I lifted her thighs and chucked her over my shoulder, making her wildly laugh.

"Cass!"

"You're lucky I ain't got no damn rope right now, D," I told her as I headed to her bedroom. "Because you deserve to be tied up right now."

"You're wearing your belt aren't you?" Her question reminded me of the leather garment currently around my waist.

I lifted my hand to her butt, causing her to whimper at the hard smack.

"You little freak. You want to be fucked like a slut right now, don't you?"

"Yes," she agreed. "Please, baby... fuck me."

She didn't have to tell me twice and I raced to the other end of her corridor, ready to give her exactly what we both needed.

You know the one thing that would never get old? Being in the company of those that I loved while we shared a delicious home cooked meal.

"No but I was the one that dared her to go up to him in the first place. It was all me!"

"Yeah but I knew from our very first meeting that they were destined to be which is why I let Cass meet with her alone for our next meeting at Morgan & Westbrook. Your dare flopped when Cassian brushed her off so really it was all me, darling. I knew from the jump that they were meant to be. I'm the reason they got together."

"No you are not, quit lying to yourself, homie."

"Homie? What are you? A Crip?"

We all burst out laughing at Christian's stupid remark.

"I can't stand him! Nae, please give me permission to kick his ass out."

"Nah, she can't give you permission to kick her future brother-in-law out of her house. Nice try though. I know you're still mad cause you know that I'm right about me being the reason that Cass and Nae got together."

It was quite entertaining watching Christian and Adina battle back on forth on their reasons for why they were the ones that got me and Danaë together. Christian had no parts to play in the situation because Adina's dare had really set things in motion for

Danaë and I. I would forever be indebted to her for being such a great matchmaker and thinking to pair Danaë and I together.

Danaë thought it would be a good idea for us to host a dinner for Adina and Christian in our home.

Our home.

God did I love the way that shit sounded. I was still over the moon that Danaë had decided to move in with me permanently. Our relationship was only getting stronger each and every day.

That was my baby.

I looked over at her and saw that she was staring right at me as Adina and Christian continued to fake argue. She sent an amused expression my way and I sent one back. We had our suspicions about these two being more than friends especially since Adina had been promoted to Chief Marketing Officer at The Palazzo by Christian himself less than two weeks ago. And since becoming sole CEO, Christian had taken a more active role in the company and made it more stable than it had been with two CEOs. Having one CEO showed a strong powerhouse and a company that was led by a single strong-minded leader. I was proud of my baby bro stepping up to the plate and doing what needed to be done for his company. I missed The Palazzo but I was rest assured knowing that it was in the great hands of my brother. Adina's promotion as CMO meant that she and Chris would be spending more time together.

A lot more time together.

Whenever they were ready to get their act together and stop playing around with the feelings that they clearly had for one another, Danaë and I would be here to assist their crazy asses tackle their new relationship. I wasn't one hundred percent sure if Christian was ready to hang up his player jersey just yet but the way he would constantly look at Adina, reminded me of the way I used to look at Danaë before we got together.

Like she was mine and no one else's.

She was mine and now as I stared into those seductive eyes of hers, I was reminded of how I couldn't wait to spend the rest of my life with her. I couldn't wait to see her walk down the aisle in her wedding dress made for me in mind. And I most certainly couldn't wait to put a whole bunch of babies in her.

We'd been through so much shit together and still come out on top. I'd been on my anti-marriage bullshit in the past but that was long dead. I had plans to give Danaë my last name and make sure that the whole world knew it. Whatever the cost of our wedding, I didn't care and whatever she wanted she could have. There was no budget on our love as far as I was concerned.

"I love you," she mouthed to me and that was all it took for a smile to form on my face.

"I love you more," I mouthed back, knowing that it was nothing but the truth.

This was the woman who had made me whole again. The woman that had melted my cold heart and shown me that I too deserved love. I couldn't wait to spend the rest of my life by her side forever.

EPILOGUE

"*T*he usual, Mr. Acardi?"

Cassian nodded, staring down at the silver band on his left ring finger.

It was a hot summer night. A cascade of souls moved around him, each in their own little worlds, some dancing to the smooth beats of Kaytranda and some sipping on their desired liquor while chopping it up with their little circle of friends around their round bar tables.

Everyone seemed to be having a good time but him. Everyone seemed to be living their best lives on vacation whereas he seemed downhearted as if he was lost without someone by his side.

Once his glass was placed down in front of him, Cassian looked up from his ring and gave the blue-eyed bartender a thankful nod. He reached for his cup, lifting it to his lips. As the cognac eased down his throat, Cassian felt the presence of a body approach him from behind. He turned to the side and spotted a woman too beautiful beyond description. He paid her no mind, looking ahead at the shelves of various liquors as he drank.

"Hi," her mellow voice greeted him.

Cassian placed his glass down to the bar's counter and decided to give her his full undivided attention.

She had glossy lips that looked as soft as silk, irresistible brown eyes, an intoxicating amber floral scent and he'd be a fool to not notice how good those short curls looked on her.

This encounter reminded him of a similar one that had happened over five years ago with a woman he believed was his everything.

"Are you lost?"

She blinked repeatedly, caught off guard by his dismissive nature.

"No, I'm not."

"You must be since you decided to come up to a married man."

"I'm not lost," she said, lifting her chin high. "But you must be since you're all alone with your wife nowhere in sight."

Cassian went silent, raising his glass and chugging down the remaining alcohol it housed.

"Does she do this often?"

Her question made Cassian look back over her while his mouth was still pressed to his glass. His brow arching above his left eye made her elaborate.

"Leave her fine ass husband all alone..." The beauty placed her hand on his forearm, caressing his soft skin upwards. "Allowing any woman to come up to him..." Heat stirred in the center of his body as her hand reached his bicep. "And give him the chance to make her cum."

He became hard as concrete, feeling wetness leave his tip down below.

The attractive woman then released her hold on him and her glossy lips curved into a smile. Making him imagine all the ways he could have her choking on his dic—

"I'm staying in the presidential suit, room two-twelve." He looked down and saw the gold key card in her palm with the name 'Acardi' engraved into it and the numbers she'd said below it.

"Feel free to take me up on my offer." She leaned in closer to whisper, "And I really hope you do..." Her warm breath fanned his skin. "Because I want you to have your way with me all night."

She didn't care that he was married. He knew that from the salacious look in her eyes, the look that was tempting him more and more with each passing second.

Cassian observed as she walked away, loving everything about the way her ass moved in her yellow sun dress as she disappeared through the crowded bar. The yellow sun dress that complimented her brown skin well. The yellow sun dress that Cassian now wanted to see removed from her body.

Cassian rose to his feet, leaving the bar and following after the brown skinned beauty that had the boldness to step to him. Knowing that he was a taken man.

He slowly trailed after her, watching as she moved through the hotel with such grace and such poise that he'd knew he would be a fool to not to take her up on her offer.

When she arrived outside the elevator, Cassian quickened his pace and came to stand behind her.

The elevator's doors slid open and she entered first with Cassian right behind. Once they were both inside, he turned to the side, pressing the button for the top floor. She remained facing the silver walls but just as the elevator's door shut, she turned around to face him. Looking up as his six five frame towered over her, turning her on in the worst way.

"You've got some real nerve coming up to me," he announced, staring down at her with a serious look. "Especially since you're married too."

Her left hand was lifted, enabling the both of them to gaze at the fat silver rock sitting pretty on her ring finger.

"Your husband know you're all alone right now?" He asked, moving her hand back down to the space between them. "Walking up to a stranger and requesting him to make you cum."

He placed her hand to his crotch and watched as a lovely scarlet flush colored her chocolate complexion.

"Making him want to do that and..."

"And?"

She pressed into his hardness, loving how the warmth felt underneath her hand.

"And punish you for being so damn sexy."

A grin split her face into two.

"My husband knows I'm never alone, the same way your wife knows you're never alone."

"Does your husband know you're such a tease?"

She nodded, bringing her lips closer to his and leaving a small space between them.

"I believe that's one of the many reasons why he loves me," she replied. "Because I'm a tease only for him."

She pecked his full lips, pulling back to gaze into his brown pools.

"Isn't that right, hubby?"

Cassian grinned, staring deep into the eyes of his beloved, knowing that she told no lies. He immediately turned to the elevator's buttons, pressing the emergency stop button.

He then grabbed her waist, lifting her up to his torso and pushing her hard against the silver walls.

"You have fun teasing your husband, Danaë Acardi?" He whispered, peppering her neck with delicate kisses.

"Maybe... Cass!" She suddenly cried out when she felt a sharp bite enter her skin. "Yes, I did. Did you have fun teasing your wife, Cassian Acardi? Pretending not to be mine?"

Cassian's hand disappeared under her dress, yanking down her thong while Danaë's hand went to his beach shirt, quickly unbuttoning it.

"I could never not be yours," he reminded her, allowing her to pull his shirt off his large arms.

Then his shorts were pushed down and his erection sprang forth.

"But hell yeah I had fun."

Their lustful eyes locked and Danaë secured her arms around his neck.

"And I'm about to have even more fun reminding my wife..." Danaë's eyes widened at his hardness pushing into her tight opening. "Exactly who she belongs to."

He pushed all the way in, causing pain to rush between her thighs. But as quickly as that pain formed, it began to subside once he started moving and that familiar wave of pleasure that Danaë was addicted to came rushing through.

"Baby..."

"That's my good girl... fuck... take that dick."

Cassian released deep guttural groans as their ride began. In and out his shaft went, making them both lose their minds at how good it all felt.

"You feel that shit?" His hands gripped her thighs tighter, keeping them locked in place as he rocked her up and down his dick. "You feel how good we are together? How good your tight ass pussy takes this dick?"

Danaë nodded, her breaths coming out in quick pants as their connection intensified with each time he stroked inside her.

"Answer." He slammed into her walls, her back crashing harder against the elevator's walls, making her whimper. "Me."

"I feel it, Cass... you know I do. I love you being inside me, Capo."

Cassian smiled at her, enjoying the love faces she made as he dived in and out of her nonstop.

"And I love being inside you, Danaë." Once again he pounded into her, causing her legs to shake. "Don't you fucking forget it."

"I won't, baby," she promised. "I won't."

Five years later and Danaë Westbrook was still the perfect woman for him. The only woman who loved the good, bad and ugly in him. The only woman who understood him and had stood by his side like the true queen that she was. And the only woman he wanted as his wife for all eternity.

~ *The Next Morning* ~

Their luggage had already been placed onto their private jet. Their pilot already in place ready to take them home. All that was left for them to do was leave the spectacular city that had provided them with so much joy over the last ten days.

"Thank you so much for your assistance on my trip with my wife, Ismail. Your men have been efficient taking us wherever we need to go and of course keeping us secure around the city."

"The pleasure is all ours, Mr. Acardi. You've done so much for us, there was no way we wouldn't return the favor."

Cassian shook hands with the Middle Eastern man standing in front of him, clad in a long white rob and a traditional white head-dress that had a black rope band sitting above it.

"Fazza is glad you and your wife enjoyed your stay and sends his regards." Cassian nodded in response. "He hopes you take him up next time on his offer to stay at his personal villa rather than The Palazzo."

"Tell his highness that I hope to take him up on that offer on our next visit. Staying at The Palazzo was my wife's request you see. She loves the fact that my brother was able to open a fourth location in Dubai so staying here was a no brainer for her. I can never say no to her. She's the real boss around here."

Ismail smiled and nodded.

After their goodbyes, Cassian left Ismail's side. He headed onto the private jet a short distance away and his forehead creased when he found his wife nowhere in sight in the main seating area. He then made his way through the jet, going through a narrow corridor leading to the master bedroom.

"Danaë?"

He pushed open the door to see Danaë sitting on the center of a double bed, staring down at her device with teary eyes.

"Baby, what's wrong?"

She turned her phone's screen around just as Cassian made his way over to her. He focused in on her screen, seeing the video playing on it. The video of their four-year-old swimming in the pool of their back yard with no help from her instructor.

"She's becoming a pro already." Danaë happily sighed, blinking back her tears. "My baby girl. I can't wait to see her. I've missed her so damn much."

The couple had been on a ten-day vacation in Dubai, living their best life. Whatever you could think of to do in Dubai, believe me they'd done it. They'd visited the Burj Khalifa, the Jumeirah Mosque, rode Camels, rode quad bikes, skydived, been to an opera house, shopped till they dropped and did many more exciting activities. Thanks to Fazza aka Sheikh Hamdan, The Crown Prince of Dubai's security detail, they'd enjoyed all that Dubai had to offer safely.

"And I'm sure she's missed you more, sweetheart."

The bed dipped as Cassian climbed above it, making his way over to his wife. Once near her, he swept her into his arms, pulling her close to him and she wrapped her arms around his torso.

She lifted her head, allowing him to plant numerous kisses on her mouth. His head bopping up and down as he pecked her repeatedly, making her smile brighter and brighter after each one.

"And I'm about to miss you when we get home because your attention is going to be far away from me," he voiced moments later after his kisses.

"You liar." Danaë scoffed. "You're the one that's going to have no time for me. Frankie's about to have her Daddy wrapped around her little finger just like she always does."

Cassian released a light chuckle at Danaë's truth. Their four-year-old daughter, Francesca Tanaya Acardi - named after Cassian's late auntie and Danaë's late mother - truly had her father at her beck and call. That was undeniable. Whatever she wanted in this life so far, she'd gotten.

"Still can't believe my own daughter has managed to steal my husband away from me."

"That's not true." Cassian pecked her lips once again. "You have me wrapped around your finger just as much as she does... if not more after last night when you convinced me to pretend not to know you... my own wife."

Danaë flashed him a coy smile.

"And you loved every second of it, Mr. Acardi," she reminded him. "Especially the elevator."

"Especially the elevator," he repeated after her and she nodded, giggling before puckering up her lips. He lowered his lips to hers, giving her a brief yet heartwarming embrace.

After their kiss, Danaë had a deep, thoughtful look on her face that made Cassian tell her to tell him what was on her mind.

"I know I said I wanted us to wait a little while longer until we tried for a second baby but Cass... I'm ready."

His eyes grew large. He hadn't expected her to mention them trying again for a second kid because their last conversation about it had been under a year ago when Danaë told him that she wanted to still be able to balance her career as COO of her father's accountancy company, CEO of her successful financial consulting firm and being a mother.

"But what about the firm, my love? You said you wanted to wait until after you'd inherited it from your father next year."

"I know, I know but I don't wanna wait anymore," she pouted. "I want a mini-Cassi bear running around who has me wrapped around his little finger. I want the big family I never had."

Cassian's heart warmed at her words. He knew how much having a big family of her own meant to her because she'd never had one. It had always just been her and her father after her mother passed.

Even with all the family she'd inherited by marrying Cassian Acardi, Danaë still wanted to have lots of children. Originally, she'd wanted to take things slow but taking things slow was the last thing she wanted to do now. Frankie deserved a sibling, many siblings in fact and Danaë would be willing to give her them including giving her husband all the babies he wanted.

"I stopped taking my birth control before we came to Dubai, Cassian," she told him. "So if I'm not already pregnant the—"

"Then I've not been doing my job right," Cassian cut her off, pushing her down to the mattress and quickly mounting her. Danaë laughed as he nuzzled his head between her breasts, groaning as he did so.

"Oh I'm sure you've been doing your job just right, Capo," she announced and his head popped up from her chest. "But ain't no harm in making sure."

Cassian said nothing but suddenly reached for her arms and pulled them over her head. Telling Danaë more than enough about how he felt towards her proposition. He started pulling down her shorts, making her heart race with exhilaration for what was to come.

"Cassian Acardi, are you about to have your way with me?" She innocently asked like she didn't know the answer.

Cassian remained silent and simply pulled her shorts down all the way to her ankles until he could pull them over her body and chuck them to the side. He watched as she pushed the straps of her tank top down her shoulders before raising the top over her head. Exposing those beauties that he always loved getting a taste of. Cassian lifted up her thighs, bending them to her sides.

"You know better than to ask your husband questions you already know the answers to, Danaë Acardi." He lowered his body towards her soft middle, seeing the wetness that had already caused a wet patch in the center of her panties. "From the second I laid eyes on you I knew I was going to have you. I was just being foolish thinking otherwise."

"In effetti lo eri, Capo. *(Indeed you were, Capo)*," she announced, making Cassian's mouth curl upwards.

Over the years, she'd been picking up more and more Italian words and phrases that Cassian spoke around his family, soldiers and associates and even to her from time to time. And since Frankie had been born, Cassian had been teaching his daughter his native tongue. Lessons that Danaë had listened and learned from too.

Two fingers thrusted into her, making her jolt up the bed and moan at the action.

"Cass..."

He'd slid her panties to the side and plunged into her wetness with no warning.

"Who do you belong to?" He asked, sliding his thick fingers out of her before bringing them to his lips and sucking her arousal off them.

Danaë watched him with a moist mouth and wide eyes, wanting that same mouth he was using to suck his fingers to suck her pussy.

"I belong to you, Cassian."

"Mmhh," he groaned while tasting her from his flesh. "That's right."

Once done sucking, Cassian held her captive with his eyes while moving his hands between her thighs.

"And I belong to you, my love," he replied, reaching for her blue panties and pulling them over her legs. Throwing them over his head. "Only you."

Danaë nodded but that wasn't enough for Cassian. It was never enough for him.

"Tell me who I belong to, Danaë," he ordered.

"Me," she said. "You belong to me."

And after her words, Cassian placed his mouth to her sex, reminding her of the pleasures that only he could provide to her. Reminding her of all ways he knew how to drive her crazy, turning her into his little crackhead. She was a feen for him and would die a happy woman being one.

Their love had started out unconventional. She'd been the one to shoot her shot at him first and five years later, it had been the best shot she'd ever thrown. She'd been the one to melt his cold heart and she had no regrets melting the heart of a capo because she knew that with him by her side, she would always be loved, always be protected and most of all, always be pleasured in the best ways possible. She had no regrets melting the heart of a capo. Her capo. And she couldn't wait to see what else the future had in store for them.

~ The End ~

A NOTE FROM JEN:

Thank you so much for reading my novel! It truly means the world to me. I hope you enjoyed reading about Danaë & Cassian's love. They drove me crazy at times, but they got it right in the end.

Please head over to my official website, where you'll be able to find out about me and find more of my novels:
www.missjenesequa.com

You can also join my mailing list via: www.missjenesequa.com/sign-up

Make sure you join my private readers group on Facebook to stay in touch with me and my upcoming releases: www.facebook.com/groups/missjensreaders

Follow me on Instagram: www.instagram.com/miss.jenesequa

I've also created Apple Music and Spotify playlists for the book which you can check out here: www.missjenesequa.com/playlists

Once again, thank you very much for reading! Please let me know what you thought by leaving a review/rating on Amazon. I'd love to know what you thought about my novel.

Love From,
Jen xo

MISS JENESEQUA'S NOVELS

Sex Ain't Better Than Love: A Complete Novel
Down For My Baller: A Complete Novel
Bad For My Thug 1 & 2 & 3
The Thug & The Kingpin's Daughter 1 & 2
Loving My Miami Boss 1 & 2 & 3
Giving All My Love To A Brooklyn Street King 1 & 2
He's A Savage But He Loves Me Like No Other 1 & 2 & 3
Bad For My Gangsta: A Complete Novel
The Purest Love for The Coldest Thug 1 & 2 & 3
The Purest Love for The Coldest Thug: A Christmas Novella
My Hood King Gave Me A Love Like No Other 1 & 2 & 3
My Bad Boy Gave Me A Love Like No Other: A Complete Novella
The Thug That Secured Her Heart 1 & 2 & 3
She Softened Up The Hood In Him 1 & 2 & 3 & 4
You're Mine: Chosen By A Miami King: A Complete Novel
A Love That Melted A Capo's Cold Heart: A Complete Novel

Made in the USA
Monee, IL
15 July 2021